Mod Superhero: Initialize

Origin, Part 1

Samuel Fleming

Ebook ISBN: 978-1-954679-70-2

Print ISBN: 978-1-954679-71-9

Cover Design by James, *GoOnWrite.com*

Contents

CHAPTER 1

Coasting

A superhero leapt across the rooftops, and Emmett watched from the seven o' clock bus.

He turned in his seat to follow them, but they were gone as quickly as they appeared. It could've been Lux or Graynight. They were both active on this side of Adelphi, but Emmett couldn't see well enough from the street.

Emmett turned back around in his seat, smiling—no one else on the bus had noticed, but he had seen them.

Then again, he'd also been lucky enough to look up at the right time. He'd been reading an article on his phone about the Summit of Heroes and their recent battle with the Antichampions. Their battle had started in Fallworth, but the Summit forced them into the surrounding desert where the most powerful teams of supers and villains had fought for two days, turning miles of sand dunes into craters and glass.

Reliable eyewitness accounts of such battles were scarce, but Emmett read all he could find, anyway.

Instead of going back to his phone, Emmett savored the moment and watched the streets of Eastside pass. When he was younger and riding the school bus, Emmett used to imagine himself leaping across rooftops and running faster than a car. Few days went by that he didn't daydream about it.

But the older Emmett got, the fewer options he had: He wasn't the son of an old god, didn't fall into a vat of radioactive acid, know magic, or have any telekinetic powers... The closer he got to graduating college, the more absurd he felt even reading about superheroes.

He was almost an adult—a real adult. Now he only daydreamed about spontaneously getting powers every *other* day.

Still, no amount of growing up could wipe the smile off his face. This was the first super he'd seen in weeks, and he took it as a sign that it was going to be a good day.

Maybe even a good week.

The Eastside of Belport was made up of technology companies and their research buildings, as well as the satellite campus of Belport University.

It was also where Emmett spent most of his time.

He hopped off the bus on 34th Street, pushed back his dark, shaggy hair, and put in his earbuds and music. Then he pulled up his hood and started walking. He'd been on a synthwave kick the last few months, listening to artists like Starquake, Lime Profond, and Endure. It just *fit*—he was a tech major listening to new age music.

Pieces were falling into place for Emmett. He'd finally found a major he loved, was almost at the end of his degree, finally got an internship, and got out of the house. The music was a bonus.

Emmett walked down the street, ignoring the screens and advertisements that lined the buildings, while glancing to the rooftops in hopes of catching another glance of a super. Beauty cream from Gnosis, the latest phones from Aquarius, fusion powered cars by Masuel... Emmett ignored them all.

No more supers—not this morning, anyway.

Emmett sighed and followed the sidewalk onto campus.

Then again, it was a wonder why any supers were patrolling right now; what serious criminals got started this early in the morning?

The Eastside satellite campus consisted of half a dozen buildings, all devoted to engineering and health sciences. It was a self-contained mirror of the surrounding sector—its own little ecosystem. It even shared the love of glass that all tech companies seemed to have. Most graduates and promising students would get jobs and internships just a few blocks away, snatched up by the research and development wings of those companies.

Emmett still had to finish out the semester—it was the end of February with three months left to go—but he was lucky to have already landed an internship. It might not have been with one of the usual *big name* companies but his work with Dr. Venture was much more engaging than being just another proverbial cog in the machine.

In fact, it had been harder to focus these last six months since getting his internship at the professor's small lab. Classes felt like a grind compared to his work in the afternoon.

Emmett climbed the stairs of the A Building to his Product and Process engineering class, nodded to the two people he was cool with, and took his seat in the back of the room.

He toggled his phone to his police scanner app. It had been a relatively quiet week as far as supers went—some scuffles between long-time rivals like Shatterspike and Death's Hand, and Isocauldron and Loverboy at the park on the West End. Honestly, those were the best kinds of super fights because they resulted in minimal collateral damage. Bystanders and taxpayers stayed happy, and capes and villains got to test each other and work out their creative differences.

Emmett listened intently, but after a few minutes of boring police calls he toggled back to music. Then he opened his notebook to last week's notes and continued doodling in the margins. Sometimes it was wiring diagrams or schematics for inventions, other times it was tiny superhero battles. Today, Emmett continued his breakdown of the pieces of Arsenal's armor. The former mask turned villain had specialized in battlesuits, and his current doodle was a mix of Arsenal's third gen design with a few of Emmett's own modifications—forearm lasers swapped out for sonic repeaters, afterburners changed to stabilizers.

Emmett kept doodling, even as the rest of the class filed in and as Professor Quinn started teaching.

He took his hood down and earbuds out, of course, and tried to listen as best he could.

But Emmett didn't hear the professor pause and walk over behind him.

"Ahem."

Emmett's pencil froze, and he turned to see his professor standing beside him. Even with her tiny and composed demeanor, it felt like she towered over him.

"See me after class, Mr. Laraway."

Emmett swallowed dryly. "Okay."

Emmett had gotten by his entire life by staying away from the spotlight.

In grade school, he did just enough to keep A's and just quiet enough that he didn't stand out. But the further along he got in school, the more his teachers took notice.

At the end of class, Professor Quinn dismissed them, and Emmett made a point of slowly gathering his things so that everyone else would be gone before he talked to her. He slung his pack over his shoulder and walked up to her desk, which was almost comically oversized for her.

"What are we going to do with you, Mr. Laraway," she said, adding a *tsk, tsk, tsk* at the end. "You're a smart lad, but you can't coast your way through life... even if you've managed to so far."

Emmett shrugged an apology. "It's just easier to apply things instead of sitting and listening."

She nodded. "I understand. You might not think so, but I do. I was once a student here at Belport... But I want you to understand that not all applications are created equal.

"I know about your work with that *Venture* and his lab. His *work* isn't science, and you would do well to remember that. Get what you can from him and move on to something stable."

Emmett held his tongue and nodded, but he didn't promise anything.

Professor Quinn must have seen through his facade because she waved him away without waiting for a response. "You have potential. Don't waste it. Go on... and Mr. Laraway, I'm looking forward to seeing your final project."

Emmett was already at the doorway when his step faltered. He hurried and continued down the hall.

Of course. *That* project—the one he'd totally forgotten about.

Emmett hiked down the stairs and out to the C building and his second class of the day, Machine Design.

Instead of listening to music and doodling, he spent the following hour half-listening and working on his project for engineering class.

Maybe Dr. Venture or Clara would have some ideas—not that the old man ever let him take any projects home to work on. The doctor was adamant that everything they worked on in his laboratory stayed there. He had a penchant for secrecy that bordered on paranoia.

Granted, Emmett wasn't about to call Dr. Venture out on it. He wasn't going to risk his internship.

At first, Emmett almost hadn't accepted the internship. He'd never heard of Dr. Venture, and neither had any other student. He claimed to have ties to several big companies, but it wasn't until he toured the doctor's lab that Emmett believed it. The doctor and his lab were on another level.

As far as Emmett knew, he was the doctor's only intern—Clara didn't count. She was his daughter.

Emmett sighed and Professor Quinn's words came back to him: *"You can't coast your way through life."*

For most of his life, that's exactly what Emmett was doing, just coasting in the background, but Professor Quinn was wrong—coasting wasn't what he wanted to do now.

It just felt like he'd outgrown his classes. Even his capstone classes were too easy.

So Emmett bided his time and paid attention as best as he could. He just had another couple hours to kill until going to work with Dr. Venture.

Only another few hours...

Chapter 2

The Lab

After class, Emmett walked quickly out of the C Building and across campus to catch the two o'clock bus to the edge of Eastside.

The far East side of the city was barren compared to the rest of the research district. Where earlier it was impossible to walk the block without being bombarded by billboards of electronic ads, here they were almost non-existent. The only two billboards were for Gnosis. Each one hung from a parking garage and covered the entire front of it. They changed throughout the day, but always showed some combination of their health and beauty products.

In contrast, the Gnosis headquarters across the street looked more like a military compound than a billion-dollar corporation. The buildings were pristine white and barren of anything except the Gnosis logo—a white square with a simple, blurry face staring back. And the entire place was ringed with razor wire and guards armed with military hardware.

Emmett walked past the first parking garage and the giant tub of facial cream on display

The entrance to Dr. Venture's lab was sandwiched between two parking garages for Gnosis. It was a nondescript metal door that looked more like a custodian's closet.

Emmett stepped up to the door, pulled back his hood, and waited.

A second later, the eye scan registered and a robotic female voice crackled with static. *"Thank you for verification. Please step through, Emmett Laraway."* Even after these months of working for the doctor, Emmett wasn't sure where the scan or the voice came from—there was no camera or speaker visible.

He shivered as the door creaked open, but for another reason: There was something about an inhuman intelligence watching him that Emmett still hadn't gotten used to.

If Gnosis across the street resembled a military compound, Dr. Venture's laboratory resembled a nuclear bunker.

Emmett descended the long stairwell, with only tiny lights on each of the steps to push away the darkness. Even from all the way up here, eerie clangs and hisses echoed from the lab. He ignored them and descended over a hundred steps to reach the bottom.

He followed the concrete hallway, passing half a dozen doors of reinforced steel and access hatches for the pipes and wiring that ran alongside the hallway like bundles of nerves. None of the doors were labeled—only numbered—and Emmett had only ever been in one of them. Each of them had a small camera and display next to it, no bigger than his palm, and each looked to be several decades old.

It puzzled Emmett why there was such a mix of old and new technology in the lab, but the doctor had never given him a straight answer. Emmett couldn't say why, but it felt like it wasn't an issue of funding... There were other things Venture pinched pennies on, but those were things like frozen meals instead of takeout or a clunky car instead of something new. Instead, it felt like some parts of the underground had been purposefully kept the same.

Emmett stopped at the door painted 003, and waited for the lab's artificial assistant, TINA, to scan him. After a moment, the door split along the seams and parted for him.

"Dr. Venture is expecting you," TINA said, appearing on the old display as a voice waveform.

Emmett stepped through into a small locker room. At some point, the number plates had been removed from all the lockers except those on the left wall and the rest of them had been welded shut. He stuffed his phone, wallet, and backpack into the first available one.

A short hallway and another set of reinforced doors separated the locker room from lab three's main room.

The walls of the testing hub were covered in display screens and readouts, and the center of the room was taken up by a metal platform that both served as a table and as a holographic display. Most of them were powered down, save for a small cluster of screens in the back of the room. That was where Dr. Venture stood. It would've given the impression of someone huddling around a campfire at night, except that his hands clasped behind his back, watching the screens intently.

Rugged was probably the best word to describe him; Venture was tall and broad, always wearing his titular greased-stained lab coat. He was always fiddling with his wide glasses, his hands calloused from working as much with wrenches as he did with programming. His face was always covered in stubble and his graying hair looked like he had just brushed it back a moment before someone entered the lab.

Venture glanced over his shoulder as Emmett entered, muttered a greeting, then said to the monitors, "That's enough for now, Clara. Come back up so we can resume work on the heat sinks."

Then he pushed up his glasses and turned to Emmett. As he did, the ambient light in the room gradually increased.

Emmett nodded in greeting, but Venture ignored it, instead bringing up a hologram in the center of the room.

"Tell me what you think about this design."

Emmett examined the diagram while ignoring the doctor staring at him. It was a test—something Emmett had gotten used to over the past months.

The hologram showed a thermoelectric system: Plates of carbon composites meshed together around a heat source. As heat emanated from the source and passed through the plates, the energy was converted to electricity.

Right away, Emmett noticed several things. He gestured to the hologram as he answered.

"Hydrothermal power is preferred in most instances, but this type of system is for small-scale applications where space is an issue. It doesn't scale well—the heat source can only be so powerful or the plates will melt. Stacking plates isn't a solution because the heat source will scale logarithmically, but power conversion is linear—"

"If I wanted a textbook answer, I would read a textbook. How would you improve it?" Venture's voice was firm as a math problem.

"If the scale can't change, then efficiency or materials are the only answers."

"Go on."

"The plates could be rearranged for greater efficiency, or another composite could be used..."

"You're missing something."

Emmett grit his teeth and looked over the hologram again. "Additional systems could be used to recycle or remove excess heat..." Then another answer came to him. "Power sources! Using multiple power sources instead of one large one would allow the system to scale."

Emmett turned, excited and waiting for confirmation. Dr. Venture merely nodded, his face stoic and unchanged.

"Not bad. When Clara gets up here, we'll work on integrating our heat sinks into the design."

Venture turned back to the other monitors, leaving Emmett standing in silence.

So he turned back to the hologram still hanging in the middle of the room. There was something familiar about it, but Emmett wasn't sure exactly what that was.

Before he could get too invested, Clara came through one of the adjoining doors. Her eyes met Emmett's as it slammed shut behind her.

In many ways, Clara was a reflection of her father: She had the same dark hair, though Clara kept it buzzed short. She was a head shorter than him, but she had his strong build. And Clara definitely smiled more than her father did, but she had that same intensity of focus.

Except she was fond of leggings, baggy sweaters, and beanies instead of lab coats.

"Glad you could make it," Clara said sarcastically.

"Some of us have classes."

"Who says you need those?"

Dr. Venture cleared his throat as if to say, *'I do.'*

Clara rolled her eyes. "Some of us get by without it." She was speaking as much about her father as herself. As far as Emmett had heard, Venture had never went to college.

Venture glanced sidelong at her. "Just because I didn't enroll in school doesn't mean I didn't learn everything I could."

Clara held up her hands in mock defeat. "It was a joke, Dad."

The doctor grunted. "I'm sure. Suit up and go to testing chamber two."

Emmett and Clara shared a smirk and exited through the adjoining door.

Clara led the way down the hall.

"I saw a hero today. On the bus."

She paused for breath, then kept walking. "Did you see who it was?"

"No. They... Well, I was on the bus."

"You're losing your touch."

Emmett scoffed. "Do you know the odds of running into a super?"

"Do you?"

"Well, no. But why do you think I keep up with the forums?" Clara chuckled, and Emmett asked seriously, "What's funny about that?"

She called over her shoulder, "It's just that with the crazy tech we get to work with and experiments we get to do, you still can't stop thinking about superheroes."

"You're not the least bit interested in the supers?"

Clara held up a finger. "I didn't say that. I was talking about you."

Emmett shrugged, though she wouldn't see it. "You're right. We do get to play around with some pretty cool stuff... That just means I get to dream a little bigger."

Emmett thought he heard Clara chuckle again, but neither said anything else.

She stopped at the metal door to the testing chamber, grabbed the handles, and spun the release mechanism. The door unlocked with a heavy clang and she pushed it open.

Testing chamber two was a large, domed room, some fifty feet across. It was featureless and almost completely smooth, save for the smaller spherical structure embedded in the center of the floor—it was the heat source that would test their heat sink design, and it was wrapped in coils of refrigerant that glowed with an eerie purple light—

That was different, Emmett realized. They'd changed the refrigerant. They'd been working in testing chamber two for the last few weeks, slowly adjusting the heat sink's design.

The other difference was Clara and the doctor had added batteries in a thin strips overtop of the coils.

"You changed refrigerant," Emmett said idly as he searched for any other changes he might've missed.

Clara smiled, and her father's voice came through the intercom speakers at the top of the room.

"*Why?*" Dr. Venture asked through the intercom. Another test.

"You added batteries," Emmett replied.

"*Correct. Both of you, verify connections.*"

Emmett followed behind Clara as she pointed out the new additions. He listened and studied intently.

It almost seemed like the system was missing something... Emmett just couldn't imagine *what*. Neither the doctor nor Clara had been forthcoming about just what the system was designed for. For all he knew, it might've been some new nuclear design, or a power system for robotics or military hardware—any of those would explain the secrecy.

Emmett worked for Venture, but he was only an intern.

When they were done with their check, both of them retreated to the small, reinforced viewing room where they would be safe from any ambient heat or malfunctions.

Both of them had taken to calling it the "broom closet", since it was only a little bigger than one.

Emmett and Clara filed inside and peered out through the three inches of plastic that comprised the viewing window.

"We're ready, Dad." Clara waited, but no one responded. "...We're ready down here."

Clara sighed and stared out the viewing window, inadvertently stepping closer to Emmett, who was already wedged up against the other wall.

They were shoulder to shoulder now, and the small room felt just a bit hotter. Emmett focused on staring straight ahead. Meanwhile, his thoughts raced.

Was this awkward? He should say something instead of just standing there. That's what a normal person... friend... co-intern would do, right?

"Maybe, uh..." Emmett cleared his throat. "Maybe he went to the bathroom—"

Dr. Venture stepped in front of the viewing window, glaring at him. Emmett jumped.

Venture stepped into the broom closet a moment later. This caused Clara to scooch over another step until she was practically leaning against him.

Emmett tried to catch his breath.

"We're ready now," Venture said. He pushed up his glasses and glanced at Emmett out of the corner of his eye. "What's the matter? Nervous?"

Emmett stayed silent, but swore a smirk crossed the doctor's face. If Clara noticed, she didn't give any indication.

"Begin countdown," Venture said.

TINA counted down from ten, and then the sphere in the center of the room began to heat up. The tubes surrounding it glowed steadily brighter, bathing the room in rolling purple light. Soon the sphere was glowing a molten orange beneath the coils, but even as the heat grew, the purple didn't diminish. The batteries were glowing too, like thin beacons of white.

All three of them watched silently. Emmett wanted to see the readouts later, but so far, everything was going well.

Soon the orange glow from the sphere was completely eclipsed, and TINA said, *"Battery charge steady at one hundred percent."*

"Begin venting excess heat," Venture said.

Emmett looked over nervously. This was new and unexpected, but he stayed silent. The doctor's face was stoic as ever, but Clara's eyes were wide and her smile was even bigger.

Steam erupted from the coils, clouding the room, but soon the steam oozed out in a slow and steady fog.

The team watched intently for another few seconds until the TINA's voice came on again. *"Heat sinks holding steady."*

"Cut the power," Venture ordered.

The power faded from the experiment, but the excitement didn't leave them.

"That's cause to celebrate," Venture said. He'd already turned to leave, but Emmett imagined there was a smile on the doctor's face that mirrored his and Clara's.

Chapter 3

Celebration

As it turned out, Dr. Venture's idea of celebrations was as understated as he was.

There was a small break room near the testing hub—one of the only other rooms Emmett had seen. He'd gotten to sit in it precisely twice, not including this time.

There wasn't much to it: Several cracked leather chairs were arranged to face a wall of displays. The few times Emmett had been in the room, they were always tuned to the major news channels. A small kitchenette occupied the right-hand wall.

Currently, Emmett and Clara sat idly while Dr. Venture put a frozen pizza in the oven.

Emmett and Clara shared a wordless laugh at her father's idea of celebration. Despite the facility they worked in, the doctor had a habit of cutting costs on things that weren't digital or mechanical.

"Tell me again, Dad, why we can't splurge on takeout?"

Venture waved a dismissive hand. "Big Larry's has come a long way since the first frozen pizza. This is gourmet compared to the pizza I grew up with."

Emmett joked, "They didn't have takeout back then."

"Cars either," Venture added, deadpan.

The doctor came over and sat with them, turning intently to the news. Silence settled between them as Emmett and Clara uneasily did the same.

There was ongoing war across the Morrowed Sea, and riots in the South. Domestically, people were in a fuss over the market, though that all sounded like gibberish to Emmett; he'd never been good with economics.

And spliced in with everything were superheroes and villains—the war across the ocean was plagued by warlord supers who harassed the edges of territories and battlefields—sometimes drawing the ire of both countries. Riots in the South were blamed on rogue masks and villains. Domestically, groups tried to pin the stock market dip on the battle between the Summit of Heroes and Antichampions, saying that the Antichampions' increased activity was affecting investors.

Then there were the brawls that destroyed a block of Dramford and Chicby Hills.

Emmett listened, but his eyes were always drawn to the clips of supers and villains. Only registered capes were shown with any clarity. Most photos and video were almost always far away shots of tiny figures—even so, they dominated the screen when they appeared. Lightning arced, fire swirled, and the air quivered around them. Each super felt like they heralded destruction—Emmett wasn't sure if the news meant to depict them that way, but it was the overwhelming impression.

As the moment dragged on, Emmett came back to the silence again, and it felt odd to him. He'd spent a lot of time with the doctor and Clara over the last six months, but most of that time was spent working. There was very little downtime since he'd started working here—pretty much those two other times he'd been invited into the breakroom. So Emmett shifted in his seat, unsure of whether it was a comfortable silence or not.

In the end, he decided it wasn't.

Emmett said, "I've got a project coming up for engineering."

Neither Venture nor Clara responded. They were both watching the news intently. A still shot of the Scarlet King was on the screen. He hovered on the screen, a ball of crackling psychic power. He was an old member of the Antichampions, one who was ousted for over-the-top brutality and rumored to have killed the former hero, Arsenal.

Emmett cleared his throat, "I've got a project for engineering coming up."

The doctor blinked, but it was Clara who turned and answered.

"What are you going to do?" she asked.

"I'm... I'm not sure yet," Emmett replied, leaving out that he forgot about the assignment.

"What did you do last time?"

Emmett reminded her of his variable electromagnetic shielding—a glorified adjustable mesh—and that he couldn't reuse a project from a prior class. It was a maddening rule.

"What about your radio locator that you were working on?"

Emmett paused and considered it. It wasn't flashy, or particularly promising, but Clara was right: He hadn't used that for a prior class. It had been something he'd worked on in his spare time as a way to better track heroes around the city.

"That might work," Emmett conceded. "Thanks."

Emmett briefly thought about using that as an excuse to leave early, but Clara spoke up first, asking if he'd seen the latest *Full Throttle Heart*.

"No spoilers!" he shouted.

Clara had gotten him into *Full Throttle Heart* early in his internship. It was an isekai anime about a delivery truck that gets hit by another truck and subsequently reincarnated in a fantasy world as a sentient truck that transforms into a robot to fight crime. Truck-kun had a habit of shouting *"Time to get isekai'd"* when killing enemies.

It was a satire and comedy, but the last two seasons were getting serious, and Emmett and Clara had been awaiting each new episode with anticipation.

Well, maybe she'd been anticipating it a little more than he had.

When another lull came in their conversation, Emmett asked another hard question.

"Dr. Venture, when am I getting paid?"

The doctor had been watching the news intently—probably zoning out from their conversation. For a moment, it looked like his eyes might've widened in surprise, but it was so fast that Emmett couldn't be sure.

"Knowledge is its own reward," Venture replied.

Emmett swallowed dryly. Rent would be due soon—he had to muster up the courage to remind the doctor that regular people had bills to pay.

Clara laughed sarcastically. "Very funny, Dad. You forgot again, didn't you?"

Venture grunted a laugh. "TINA, please credit two weeks' pay to Emmett's account."

A moment later, she responded, *"Credit delivered."*

"Thanks," Emmett said.

Venture grunted another reply, but was still watching the monitors intently.

Ever since Emmett had known him, the doctor had been a quiet man, but this evening Emmett wondered if it might've been something more. Was the doctor just preoccupied with something... or had Emmett overstayed his welcome? Maybe it was time for him to leave.

As the silence dragged on, Emmett looked at Clara and thought he saw the same uncertainty in her eyes.

But a question came to mind, and Emmett couldn't help but ask it.

"You really like superheroes, don't you, Dr. Venture?"

Even as the question left his mouth, Emmett regretted it, and it felt like the last half of the question had just tumbled out.

Venture didn't respond at first, and Clara looked like her head was frozen looking forward and her face was clenched—like she was trying to be shocked that he actually asked that question.

Venture sighed and tossed Clara the remote control. Then he stood and stretched his arms overhead.

"It's almost past my bedtime," he said. "Clara, be sure to close up the lab before you turn in. Good evening, Emmett."

Dr. Venture shut the door behind him, leaving Clara and Emmett sitting awkwardly.

"It was something I said, wasn't it?" Emmett asked, slumping further down the couch—of course it was; he wasn't sure why he asked.

"It's... complicated," Clara said. "Dad's an engineer, and I'm sure you've realized that some of the things we've worked on are pieces of larger systems... of weapons. Not all of it, but a lot of it.

"I think Dad's afraid that heroes will put us out of work one day."

Emmett had gradually turned, trying to read her face. "You don't sound like you believe that."

Clara turned on the couch to face him, tucking her legs beneath her. "You're right. That's not the whole story. But I'm not even sure *I* know all of it. One day he might tell you more, just don't get your hopes up."

Emmett nodded—at least it wasn't him.

"You're cool with not knowing?"

Emmett's face wrinkled in question. "Yeah, of course. What other choice do I have?"

He'd meant it as a joke, but Clara's face was serious.

"Good," she said, relaxing a little. "Because he does trust you, you know. We both do. It's not every day he takes on an intern, and it's not everyday that he trusts someone to work on these systems with us."

Emmett nodded again. "I get it. You don't have to worry about me."

"Good."

"...He doesn't talk a lot about the past, does he?"

Clara turned away, staring at the screens instead. "He's always thinking about the future. Doesn't talk much about the past, or the present, for that matter." Dejection showed on her face, though she tried to hide it.

"Sorry," Emmett said, without really knowing what he was apologizing for.

"Don't be. Can't change the way things are."

"Yeah."

Silence settled between them, and Emmett took it as his cue to leave. If he hurried, he could catch the next bus.

"I'll see you tomorrow," he said.

"Hope so!"

Cheer bled back into Clara's voice, but she was still staring at the monitors and the supers on the news.

Chapter 4

Homebase

E mmett grabbed his things from the locker room, left the lab, and hustled down the Eastside to the bus stop on 61st Street.

The first and second bus of the day was a mix of passengers—students, workers, and retirees going down town—but this bus was almost exclusively workers going home from Gnosis.

Then he settled in for the long trip back to his apartment by putting on some tunes and getting started on his homework; he couldn't do much, but he could at least map out the rest of what he needed to get done by the end of the night and the next couple days.

When he finally got to his apartment on the West End, Emmett felt like he had a handle on the rest of his evening.

He hopped off the bus and walked the last few blocks to the Woods. It was one of several blocks of apartments that were predominantly rented out to students of the university. Lazy guitar echoed through the apartments, and he passed groups of students under the gazebos.

Emmett hiked up the stairs to the fourth floor, picking up two squashed beer cans along the way—he'd throw them away when he got inside. He opened up room 449 on the top floor and stepped in.

The apartments weren't much, they definitely weren't the Heights, but the Woods had been home these past two years of college. Two bedrooms, living room, bathroom—everything a college student needed, and not a damn thing more.

They had to scrounge for furniture, but at least the Woods let them have free rein, so long as they didn't knock down any walls and repainted when it was time to leave.

And remodel, they did.

Room 449 was decked out in strings of ambient lights, all connected with the TV in the living room and speakers throughout the house. It was currently pulsing red in time with the symphonic music his roommate preferred when studying.

Skeletons of electronics littered what would've been the kitchen table.

Emmett stepped in and shut the door behind him, calling out a greeting to his roommate, Lachlan—who went by *Lock*—but no one answered.

Emmett walked through the small kitchen and living room, and peered into Lock's empty room, but he wasn't there. The living room window was open, so Emmett climbed out to the roof and checked there too, but didn't find him.

Lock kept odd hours—frequently working nights and preferring to sleep during the day—but usually they crossed paths in the morning and evening.

Emmett shrugged and started on his homework.

Emmett had migrated with his laptop to the living room couch. Then he migrated again to the roof, hoping the cool night air would wake him up.

Each apartment block had a small flat section of roof where the air conditioning units sat in rows. Emmett's apartment just happened to be located right beneath it, and their fire escape went directly up to it. Emmett and Lock had stashed folding chairs and a small table up there—their own private balcony.

They rarely went up there in the Summer, but this time of year was perfect.

It was ten o'clock and the bustle on the street was starting to settle down. Emmett had knocked out his daily assignments and started on his engineering project—the radio locator.

It was equal parts design and programming, but ultimately simple. Three antennas were linked together and fitted with directional cones. The computer program helped analyze incoming signal strength and then pinpointed the origin of the signal. Ideally, the cones would turn and the antennas would move. This would make triangulation quicker, but Emmett's program worked well enough with stationary mountings.

Till now he'd only built a small hand-held locator to prove that it would work, but he was going to build a full-sized version for his project—one that he would mount on the roof and could—theoretically—locate a signal anywhere in the city.

There were caveats, of course. His apartment roof wasn't that tall and it wasn't in the center of the city, so skyscrapers would interfere with signals from downtown and signals from across the bay would be weak. But none of that mattered for a school project.

Emmett looked away from his computer screen and rubbed his eyes. He should take a break soon.

For a moment, he imagined leaping rooftop to rooftop, using the locator array to hone in on a superhero transmission across the city. The system on his roof could only get him so close, so of course, he had a smaller system built into his suit. A readout on his helmet guided him closer to the target.

Emmett heard the muffled echo of footsteps on the fire escape and startled out of his daydream. His roommate, Lachlan, popped up with his backpack slung over his shoulder.

"Nice night," Lock called as he walked over.

"You know it."

Lock was a bio major and avid weight-lifter who'd taken to altering his mind as much as his body. Emmett wasn't sure exactly how Lock managed to try out seemingly every hallucinogen known to man *and* hold down his internship at Gnosis, but somehow he did. Probably some combination of just being smart enough and good enough at hiding it.

Lock dropped his backpack on the ground, grabbed another folding chair and slumped down into it, face and bald head still hidden by his baggy hoodie.

"Long evening?" Emmett asked.

"Nah, not tonight." Lock pulled out his vape and took a hit. "Tomorrow night, though, I'm working a concert. So I'll be late."

"Yeah?"

The statement hung in the air like smoke, and Lock didn't answer. That was how he was sometimes—cryptic for the sake of being cryptic. Emmett had learned to ignore it.

Instead, Emmett talked about the radio locator project. Lock listened and nodded along before starting to pull out his own notebooks from his pack.

"...And at the end, I'm going to set up antennas there, there, and there," Emmett said, pointing to the corners of the roof.

"Let me know if you need any help with that," Lock said absently. He had paused his writing and looked up at the sky. It was impossible to see the stars in the city, but up on the roof, Emmett thought he could see them sometimes.

Emmett turned to Lock. "How about you? What are you guys working on in the lab now?"

"Man... just more beauty products." He hesitated before continuing. "Sometimes I think I got into the wrong line of work. Maybe I should've went into engineering like you did."

"At least they'll tell you what you're working on," Emmett replied. "Dr. Venture still won't tell me what kind of stuff we're working on."

"Still think it's weapons?"

Emmett shrugged. "Probably. That's where all the money is, right?"

Lock chuckled. "That and makeup. You still trying to talk to Clara?"

Emmett thought back to their brush in the broom closet. "I don't know. She's hard to read sometimes. Doesn't help that her dad is my boss."

Lock took another drag and waved a finger at him. "You always were good at digging holes for yourself."

Emmett scoffed, but eventually they both laughed.

Lock said, "Remember when getting a date was the craziest thing we had going on?"

"Some of us still have a hard time getting dates." Emmett meant it as a joke—Lock certainly didn't have trouble getting a date—but Lock didn't laugh. He was staring off toward the skyscrapers in the distance.

"I'm just saying, seems like things are getting more complicated."

Emmett watched his roommate, but couldn't see his face behind the hood. "Between school and Gnosis and bouncing? I'm not sure what you're talking about."

"Yeah," Lock said suddenly. "Just senior year. All that. I'm going to turn in. I'll catch you later."

Then he climbed down from the roof, leaving Emmett sitting alone, wondering what he'd said.

It was midnight when Emmett finally stopped working on his project. He'd finished diagramming the design for the radio locator and made a list of all the materials he would need to build the final model.

Instead of going to bed right away, Emmett scrolled lazily through the news sites, looking for more super news and updates. Then he made his way to the various forums that he frequented. Always lurking, never actually posting. *Double Mask*, *Reddest Knight*, and *The Green Machine*... There were other forums, but those three had the best info. Emmett suspected that there were a mixture of heroes, villains, cops, and government agents that leaked information there because there were many stories that often made their way into the actual news days or even weeks after appearing in the forums. But then, for every kernel of truth, there was a pound of rumor and bullshit to search through.

There were two thefts at Aquarius stores, which police were theorizing were actually a string of connected robberies, which the local mob might've been involved in.

Witnesses sighted magic using supers fighting vampires. There was no way to tell if they were involved with a larger cabal or just monster hunters.

Then there was *another* rumor about Paragon retiring from the Summit of Heroes. It felt like this one came up every other month.

There were other rumors from across the country, and other sites with news from across the world, but even on his curious days, Emmett could only take in so much at a time. There was a world of super news out there, and he was just one guy.

With heavy eyes, he opened up his personal database. When Emmett was young, he'd spent his childhood reading about heroes, compiling lists and accounts of their powers. Sure, there were other sites and publicly sanctioned archives that had almost as much information, but Emmett had found discrepancies over the years.

His was more complete.

Public sites often didn't list the known weaknesses and limitations of heroes and villains, and other private forums were often monitored and sanctioned if they listed such things—there had been several high-profile forums that had been forcibly shut down over the years. Now, the main forums quickly and quietly enforced those rules on their members. Talk about the wrong thing, get banned.

Even talking in code wasn't enough sometimes.

So Emmett maintained his own database, encrypted and secure, which focused more on powers and weaknesses of supers.

Emmett scrolled to the Scarlet King, the villain that Dr. Venture had been focused on. He was one of the world's most powerful telekinetics and also a formidable psychic, whose power manifested in violent purple energy.

Emmett scrolled through a dozen photos—all far away or obscured by debris. The Scarlet King wasn't exactly known for staying still for photos.

Why had Dr. Venture been so fixated on them?

The obvious answer was that someone Venture cared about had been hurt or killed by the Scarlet King. Emmett imagined that thousands of people felt that way.

Or maybe... Venture was a cape plotting his next move against an old nemesis.

Emmett chuckled. That was dumb. Why would a cape be making weapons—especially ones that agencies like the Division of Superhuman Affairs often turned against heroes and villains alike?

No, the real answer was simple and tragic. Venture and Clara just hadn't confided in him. Maybe he could ask Clara about it sometime? That would be normal, right?

Emmett fell asleep a few minutes later.

Chapter 5

ATTENTION

The next morning, Emmett was watching the rooftops pass by from the bus window when he saw a missed call from his mom. He must've missed it ringing.

He checked the voicemail.

"Hi Emmett, just calling to say hi and see how you were doing. We're talking about getting together one of these Sundays. Antony has a couple of weekends off from their games. Darryl is figuring out when the grandkids are free. We would love for you to be there too. Text me when would be a good weekend for you to visit. Love you."

Emmett sighed. Classes and work kept him busy, and there were few breaks that lined up for the whole family. He hadn't imagined how little he would see everyone once he and his older brother, Darryl, moved out. And it still frequently blew his mind that he was an uncle. His nieces and nephews grew so much every time he saw them—it even felt like his siblings and his parents were changing each time.

Emmett put a reminder in his phone to check his schedule when he got back to the apartment, then texted his mom back.

Emmett 10:24 AM: *On the bus. I'll check my classes and call you when I get home. Love you Ma*

He pocketed his phone and went back to staring out the window and at the passing rooftops.

Emmett was sure that Dr. Venture would give him time off if he needed it. He just wasn't sure how much he could afford to take off with classes still going.

Either way, Emmett would make time.

On Tuesdays, Emmett had Statistics and his last elective, Modern Government and Applied History. They actually weren't bad—in fact, they were easy compared to Monday and Wednesday.

If anything, Emmett actually enjoyed history class. It was a nice brain break, even if it wasn't his first choice for an elective.

Both classes passed in a blur—

Except for Allison catching him after history. She waited for class to end and for him to walk past her row.

"Hey, Emmett," she said, brushing long brown hair behind her ear and walking beside him, high heels clacking on the floor.

"Hey," was all he could respond.

"So... I was wondering if you wanted to get together tonight and study?"

Emmett's mind went suddenly blank. There was something he had to do tonight—Emmett knew this. What was it?

Then an image hit him—Dr. Venture waiting expectantly for Emmett to arrive before they started the evening's experiments.

"I can't," he stammered. "I have work tonight."

"Oh, well, maybe another night then."

"Yeah," Emmett replied.

Allison gave him a small smile and walked off to join her friends, leaving Emmett walking alone down the hall, listening to the receding clack of her heels.

Allison was just talking about studying, right?

The image of Dr. Venture waiting for him came back—the doctor *and Clara*.

Maybe Emmett was reading into things.

Emmett looked back over his shoulder at Allison's group—and met Allison's eyes as she glanced back at him, too.

He turned back around, and muttered, "Shit." He was never any good at this stuff.

Later on the bus from campus to Eastside, Emmett texted Lock.

Emmett 12:01 PM: *Hypothetically, if a girl asks you to study, is she interested in you?*
Lock 12:02 PM: *Study group? No. Study alone...? Likely*

"Shit." Emmett ran a hand through his hair.

What was he supposed to do with that? Allison was cute... funny... Emmett would be lying if he said he wasn't interested.

But he liked Clara.

Lock 12:03 PM: *Clara or different girl?*
Emmett 12:03 PM: *Different*
Lock 12:04 PM: *I say go for it*
Lock 12:04 PM: *Otherwise you might be waiting forever*
Lock 12:05 PM: *Maybe Clara's Dad will third wheel*
Emmett 12:06 PM: *Funny. Catch you later*

Emmett stuffed his phone into his pocket and sighed. Of all the stuff going on, why did this feel so complicated? Of course Emmett wanted to wait for Clara... but did he, really?

In a way, waiting for Clara was easy, even if it was unknown. It was *safe*.

Even though he was a senior, Emmett still felt like the nervous wallflower he'd been all through grade school. And it sucked.

Lock 12:08 PM: *Don't wait up. Long night tonight.*

Emmett scoffed; no worries there. He was going to spend the night doing homework and wondering what the hell he was doing with his life.

Later that evening in the lab, Emmett and Clara were in testing chamber one, staring at racks of battery designs. The thin strips of batteries hung from the racks and glowed white with varying intensities, making the chamber look like an overgrown alien jungle.

Emmett and Clara went around the room. Each carried a tablet to both download information and make adjustments.

For some rows, this process was quick—like adjustments to input and output charges. These batteries dimmed or glowed brighter in response. Other parameters, like the internal structure, took longer. These strings of batteries would shimmer and flash like light reflecting off water as the changes took place.

But none of them was as dramatic as the testing from yesterday.

Once they settled into their task, Emmett asked, "What do you think your dad is working on?"

Clara glanced at him. "What do you mean?"

"I mean, like while we're down here doing this... Couldn't he make all these changes from upstairs?"

She looked back at her tablet and the rack in front of her. "Maybe. Maybe he values our input."

"He values our input on batteries?"

Clara nodded and got a faraway look in her eyes, like she wasn't staring at the racks but was staring through them.

She said, "We talked a little after you left yesterday. Dad wants me to take a more active role in the company."

"That's good, right? ...Why don't you sound excited about that?"

Clara shrugged. "I kind of like where I'm at right now, you know? If I... Well, it would be more responsibility that I'm not sure if I'm ready for. Business can be intense—from what I hear."

Emmett eyed her, almost chuckling. "We are still talking about technology, right?"

"Yeah," she said suddenly and punching something into her tablet. "What else would we be talking about?"

Now Emmett did laugh, and a hint of a smile crossed Clara's face.

He asked, "Are you sure you want to follow in your dad's footsteps? Is that it?"

Clara paused again, but only for a moment. "No. I'm sure I'm staying in the family business. The stuff we're doing, we're not just building things, we're making a difference in people's lives. I'm just not sure I'm ready to take the leap."

Emmett could respect that last part; he'd often felt the same way. He wasn't exactly the leaping type—maybe he was the wading-in type.

But it felt reassuring to hear that someone else felt the same way.

As the evening went on, it seemed like Clara's mood lifted.

Emmett joked that it was because he was leaving soon. Clara took mock offense.

It was because they had more testing to do—testing both Clara and her father insisted they didn't need Emmett for.

That was fine enough by Emmett. He was already beat. When his shift ended, Emmett bid Clara and Dr. Venture a good night.

Then Emmett rode the bus home. He leaned back against the seat, headphones and music on, and scrolled the super news.

He was tired and had to fight to stay awake.

A pothole jolted him awake.

Emmett shifted in his seat and kept scrolling.

The bus rattled again, and more than a few passengers muttered curses.

An alert buzzed through on Emmett's phone, one that made the breath catch in his throat.

ATTENTION: Super Battle Ongoing. Sighted on Champion Street. Moving East. Take shelter immediately.

The bus shook again, this time violent enough that Emmett had to brace himself against the window and the seat in front of him. Brakes squealed, passengers gasped, and a moment later, traffic up and down the street had stopped.

Everyone on the bus froze, and Emmett realized that car alarms were going off along the street.

Hands shaking, Emmett switched over to his radio app—

"...unknown supers..."

"...teams engaged..."

"...Class three point three..."

"...we're pinned..."

"...moving fast..."

"...send...forcements..."

The rest was a garbled mess, and again the alert repeated, overshadowing everything else—

ATTENTION: Super Battle Ongoing. Sighted on Champion Street. Moving East. Take shelter immediately.

There was a crunch of impact somewhere ahead—metal squealing and concrete shattering. The sound made Emmett shudder. He couldn't tell how far away it was, but it was much too close.

People were running past on the sidewalk now. People on the bus let out a mix of gasps and shouts.

Emmett switched off the radio. His throat was painfully dry.

Several people at the front of the bus demanded to be let off, but the bus driver was already ahead of them. They dashed off, stumbling down the stairs, and joined the growing stream of panic on the street.

More people in the rows were shuffling and pushing to get off the bus.

Emmett didn't move. He was staring at the windshield and the street beyond. Trying to see what was coming.

He didn't know if it would be safer on the bus or in a building... but he knew that depending on the super, they might never make it past the street.

And being caught out in the open might get them killed.

"Stop," Emmett said, but his voice was hoarse and the words came out pitifully quiet.

Only the man next to him heard—he was off and running a moment later.

The alert blared in his headphones again, and Emmett yanked the cord to pull them free.

Another impact rattled the street up ahead. Emmett gripped his phone and seat in front of him. Now it sounded like every car alarm in the city was going off—Emmett's head ringing with alarms and screams.

Sparks showered across the street as a power pole toppled over—just two blocks away! Then lights flickered up and down the block before going out.

"Shit. Shit!" Emmett muttered.

Emmett had heard about earthquakes, though he'd never actually been in one. He knew that sometimes little quakes preceded *the big one*—

That was how the next few moments felt.

A deafening screech sounded through the street. *Something* hurtled through the cars to the right of the bus, cutting them in half and sending them scattering across the street like toys.

It happened so fast that Emmett couldn't see what was going on. He only heard the sound and then felt the roof of the bus caving in as entire halves of cars crashed down on top of it.

Emmett dove to the floor, his scream drowned out by the squealing of collapsing metal and shattering glass. Emmett covered his head with his hands, but shards rained down on him and the floor. He felt dozens of knicks on his knees, elbows, and hands—

But it was all a distant, all a blur.

Then the world flashed white and yellow. And quiet.

Emmett was hurled from the bus. Then rolled in a crumpled heap across the road.

Emmett blinked, eyes blurry with sweat—with red.

He was face down on the street. In the distance, he could just see the smoking remains of his bus. It was cut in two—one half standing on its end against a nearby store. Two other people were laying on the street. They didn't move.

Emmett had to get up. Had to get out of the road. Get to shelter.

It was stupid, and Emmett laughed at himself—his jaw felt numb. Depending on the super, nowhere on the block was safe.

Emmett tried to push himself up, but his right arm wouldn't move. His left arm was pinned beneath his body. Emmett tried to push himself up again, but his whole body spasmed with pain.

He couldn't move. Couldn't get off the street.

Emmett felt a warm pool of liquid forming beneath his chest. A puddle of red. Then he felt cold.

He was going to die on the street.

Somewhere in the distance, Emmett heard the muted impacts of a super battle. One he hadn't even seen.

Something exploded in the distance—a tiny fireball. Emmett wasn't even sure if he heard it or felt it—felt anything anymore.

The last thing he saw was a growing speck in the sky... A car hurtling through the air, growing huge in his vision.

Or maybe it was a truck.

Chapter 6

Waking Up

The first thing Emmett heard was beeping. Steady and quiet.

He woke up to bright lights and in a white room. He was propped up in a bed...

His head swam. Was he alive? How?

The last thing he remembered was lying on the street, unable to get up.

And a truck flying through the air at him.

Emmett tried to sit up and look around, and immediately winced. Pain shot through his right shoulder, down his back, and made his left leg spasm.

He immediately slumped back down in the hospital bed.

His entire goddamn body hurt. Muscles and bones Emmett didn't know he had throbbed like they were alive—like his whole body was on the verge of cramping.

Maybe that's what having a seizure felt like...

Emmett wanted to call out, but just sucking in a deep breath sent stabbing pain through his chest.

So he laid there, focusing on breathing steadily, and finally the pain subsided enough for him to open his eyes and tilt his head.

The first thing Emmett realized was that he was *not* in a hospital room.

Well, he guessed it was, but nothing like any hospital he'd ever seen.

There were empty glass tanks along the wall. Tubes of bubbling liquid stretched across the wall, and cords hung from the ceiling. Behind all that, the walls and ceiling were all bright white.

Across the room, a seam split on the wall, revealing a hidden doorway. It was completely silent, and Emmett only noticed because there was complete darkness beyond.

A person stepped into the room, wearing a bright white containment suit. The glass visor covering their face was utterly black.

Emmett winced and shrank further into his bed.

"What... What happened?" he muttered. "Have I been isekai'd?" He felt utterly delirious as the question tumbled out.

But the person in the containment suit stopped in front of the bed.

"You keep saying it, but I don't know what that means."

Even though the voice was muffled by the suit, Emmett could tell that it was a man's voice... and it was a long moment before he recognized it.

"Dr. Venture?"

"Yes."

Emmett sighed, which hurt, and tried to relax but couldn't.

"This... This isn't a hospital?"

"No. You're in the lab."

"Why? Why am I—"

Emmett looked down at himself. The blanket had fallen away from his chest, and he pulled it further down now.

Instead of a hospital gown, his body was covered in what looked like a thin plastic bag. Beneath the clear shrink-wrap, his skin was an abstract mix of bright red, dark red, and purple.

Everything ached except his right arm. Everything was wrapped in plastic except his right arm. The memory of being facedown on the street came back to him—he vividly remembered not feeling his arm then either.

Emmett's right arm laid beside him on the bed, but it wasn't *his* arm. It was naked metal, the frame and pistons laid bare. Blood dripped through the cords of gray faux muscle; more was caked in the threads—

His blood.

Emmett's head swam, and he laid back on the bed.

And promptly passed out.

Emmett was in and out of consciousness several times, never awake for more than a minute.

When he finally did wake up, Dr. Venture and Clara were waiting for him. They both wore white containment suits, but had taken off their helmets.

"Welcome back," Venture said.

Both of them looked like shit—red eyes and bags under them—like they'd been crying or pulled an all-nighter. Clara managed a small smile.

"How long was I out?"

"Three days," Venture replied.

Clara added, "It's four o'clock. Saturday morning."

The bed was propped up at a forty-five degree angle, and Emmett tried to push himself further up. It was easy. And painless.

Emmett paused and slowly looked down at himself.

His body wasn't covered in a plastic bag anymore. Emmett tugged at the hospital gown that he was now wearing and saw skin beneath—his chest and arms were his normal tan. He looked *normal...*

His right arm looked normal. It wasn't metal.

Emmett lifted his right arm up to look at it closer—looking for scars or discoloration or any evidence of the gruesome sight from the last time he woke up. Nothing looked amiss.

It wasn't until he poked and prodded it with his other hand that he felt the silicone texture and odd shapes beneath the skin.

"It will take some getting used to," Dr. Venture said, his voice breaking Emmett out of his trance.

"What did you do to me?" The question came out half-astonishment, half-accusation.

"What do you remember?" Venture asked.

Emmett recounted being on the bus during a battle between heroes. The bus was hit, and he was thrown from it. How he laid in the street, unable to move.

As he told them, he realized just how out of it he'd been. It felt so distant. Like a bad dream, or like it had happened to someone else and Emmett had just been watching.

"You almost died," Clara said. "We saved you."

"Thanks," Emmett said earnestly. "I just don't understand how. How did you even know? ...Were you there?"

"Not exactly..." Clara said. She looked to her dad, as if unsure of what to say—or what she could say.

Without missing a beat, Venture replied plainly, "I've been keeping tabs on you."

"...What? Why?"

"Our lab deals with some *highly sensitive* research. We can't allow anyone to leak data or materials."

"So you were spying on me?"

Clara interrupted, "No. It's not like that."

Venture sighed. "It's passive monitoring for keywords. No one is spying on you."

Emmett scoffed. "Okay. So if you weren't there... How did you save me?" He held up his hand, then gestured to his body. "How did you do *this*? Any of this?"

Venture said, "We have Fast-Response Drones hidden throughout the city. When there were reports of a battle so close to your location, the closest three were automatically dispatched. They stabilized you and brought you to the lab.

"Then we rebuilt you with Gnosis's research and our tech. Your arm was unfortunate, but it had to be amputated."

Emmett stared at his right arm again, imagining the metal workings beneath—

"Oh shit. It's been three days!" Emmett tried to sit up. "I have to go, or call, or—"

Dr. Venture grabbed his shoulders to stop him, and a flash of surprise and strain crossed his face. "Not yet."

"You don't understand! My folks, they know what bus I ride. If they saw anything on the news—"

"We kept an eye on your phone," Venture said, still visibly keeping him from standing. "Your mom thinks you're home sick. Nothing serious, but enough to keep you in your apartment. Don't forget to tell her which Sunday you're free for dinner."

Emmett relaxed a little and nodded.

"Your roommate, *Lock*, texted too," Venture said, sighing.

Clara added, "We said you were at a girl's place. I... I think he bought it." She smiled awkwardly.

Meanwhile, Venture stared at Emmett with his usually deadpan seriousness, and Emmett felt his apprehension growing like the bottom was dropping out from his stomach.

Venture said, "Lock asked if it was Clara."

Clara's eyes widened. "Obviously, we told him no... but you'll have to make something up when you see him next."

Emmett swallowed dryly. In comparison, death might not have been so bad.

At the request of Dr. Venture and Clara, Emmett slept through the rest of the morning. He eventually relented, if only because he still felt a deep soreness that felt like it was in his bones and because they looked like they needed the rest as much as he did.

It was noon on Saturday by the time Clara and her father came back to visit.

Emmett was glad because he hadn't liked where his mind had gone for the past hour. He couldn't stop thinking about what happened on the street... and what didn't happen.

"Did... Did anyone else from the bus make it?" Emmett asked.

He hadn't known many—any—of them by name, but he remembered their faces. Many of them had been riding the same bus for years. People he'd seen day after day but never talked to.

Dr. Venture was across the room, fiddling with a screen. But now he paused and turned toward Emmett.

"When paramedics respond to an emergency, they aren't told what happens to their patients after they get to the hospital. They do their job, do what they can, and that's it."

"But that's patient confidentiality, isn't it?" Emmett responded. "That's not the same."

"It's for the patient, yes, but it's for the paramedic, too."

"Please. I need to know."

"Some of them survived. Some didn't. Twenty-nine people were killed. Three times that were injured. I haven't cross-checked the list of reported casualties with passengers on the bus..."

Emmett was listening, but again, he felt far away.

Venture had trailed off and paused before continuing. "The attack will be all over the news for the next few days. I suggest you avoid it."

"Can I have a minute?" Emmett asked.

Dr. Venture nodded and turned off the monitor he was working on before leaving. The door hissed shut behind him.

Clara looked from Emmett to the door before walking over to him. "Are you alright?"

Emmett shook his head, afraid of what might tumble out of his mouth if he spoke. He looked at his right hand, remembering how it felt—didn't feel—on the street and when he'd first woken up.

He'd never felt so powerless.

Silence dragged on before Emmett finally said, "All my life, I dreamed of being a superhero, but... When the time came, I froze. I just sat there."

Emmett felt ashamed of himself, like he'd failed the test he'd been waiting for all his life. All he wanted to do was curl up under the blanket and hide. He grit his teeth, choking back tears.

Then he remembered Clara was still in the room with him and he felt even worse—even smaller.

Clara put a hand on his. The glove of her containment suit crinkled softly. "They say there's people that fight and people that run from bad situations... but there's also freezing. It happens. Everyone feels fear, and it takes training to keep your body from doing those three things. Paramedics train. Nurses train. Police, too. Even capes and masks train. Even they feel fear."

Emmett was nodding along, listening, and fighting that feeling of slipping far away again. Trying to stay there and fighting that feeling of being distant.

He almost missed what she said.

Emmett turned suddenly, scoffing. "What do you mean superheroes have to train? Like you would know..."

But Clara just smiled awkwardly. "There's something we have to tell you."

Chapter 7

A Ride

"Your dad used to be a cape?!" Despite the aches, Emmett had swung around so he was sitting on the edge of the bed.

"Yep."

"Which one?"

Clara shrugged. "I can't tell you."

"But..." Emmett tried not to let dejection show on his face.

"It's not like that," Clara replied. "Even though Dad's retired, it's not like he goes around telling everyone what he used to do. Even I don't know all the details. When he gets back, you can ask him yourself."

"What makes you think he would tell me?"

"We already talked about it. Dad feels like he can trust you with more of our research, and... I think he wants some more help around here."

Emmett kicked his feet idly at the white floor. "...What if I wanted out?"

Clara crossed her arms and smirked. "Of course you can leave. We're not going to keep you here. But you don't really want to leave, right?"

She already knew the answer already, but Emmett thought he might also have seen a hopeful look in her eyes. Or maybe he imagined it.

"Oh, of course I'm staying," Emmett blurted out.

The door to the medical lab hissed open, and Dr. Venture walked in. He had changed from his containment suit back into his old lab coat.

"Are you alright now? Good," Venture said without waiting for a response. He glanced between the two of them. "Clara already told you, didn't she?"

Emmett shrugged. "Not *really.*"

"Do you have any questions?"

"Yes! What cape were you?"

Venture sighed. "Something other than that?"

Emmett let out a breath he didn't know he'd been holding. "Well... What happens now?"

"Now you have a choice to make. You can continue to work here, knowing what you do, but only if you swear not to tell another soul about your miraculous survival or what you know about me."

"Done," Emmett said, being sure to look Dr. Venture in the eye.

He hadn't wanted to leave before. Emmett liked working at the lab—and he definitely didn't want to leave now. Not before he had more answers about Dr. Venture's past.

Venture nodded, but his eyes were narrowed. "I'm not sure you understand what I'm asking of you."

"I won't tell my friends, my roommate, my parents, or the rest of my family."

Venture blinked—the closest Emmett had seen to surprise on his face. "And nothing gets logged in your super database. *Nothing.* Do I make myself clear?"

Emmett swallowed, his throat suddenly dry. Maybe the doctor knew more about his life than he originally let on.

"Understood."

Venture relaxed a little and nodded. "Good. That's good—because I can remotely disable your vital functions."

"...That's a thing?"

"The best that Gnosis has to offer."

Clara chuckled awkwardly. "I think he gets the picture, Dad."

Emmett chuckled too. "Can... Can I go back to my apartment now?"

Venture turned and read over the monitor across the room. After a moment, he answered, "Yes. It looks like your new tissue has integrated and your healing is almost complete. You might feel better now, but don't do anything strenuous over the weekend.

"If you still feel like working with us, we can talk more on Monday."

Emmett stood, his legs shaky beneath him. Whether that was from injury or from Dr. Venture's threats, he couldn't be sure.

Emmett rubbed the back of his neck. "Can I get a lift back?"

Dr. Venture's car was a Gemini sedan. Emmett didn't know much about car models, but he knew that it was an older model *and* that the rumble of the engine sounded aftermarket. Venture had upgraded it. Emmett's hunch was only reinforced as Venture pulled out into bustling weekend traffic, the car roaring to life in moments as they slipped from one lane to another.

Emmett sat in the passenger seat while Clara sat in the back, behind her father. It felt like it took forever for his eyes to adjust to the midday sun.

They drove back wordlessly and made the trip much quicker than riding the bus; even when they took the detour around the damage on Champion Street from the battle. Emmett stared at the work crews as they passed.

He was still having trouble processing just how much had changed.

All the technology, all the research... Was that some new direction for Dr. Venture, or was it from past connections as a government-sponsored cape? Were his powers related to technology? Was he an artificer? Emmett's mind raced... How many tech-based heroes had gone inactive in the last ten to twenty years?

He couldn't remember, not without checking his database.

But there were other things that clicked for Emmett: Dr. Venture's hard exterior, for one. Emmett always thought of him as dry, guarded, and a little cold, and recent discoveries had only reinforced that notion. But instead of seeing a hard-ass, Emmett saw someone more akin to a grizzled war veteran.

It even called into question Venture's defensiveness about Clara. Was he just being a dad concerned about a young man being interested in his daughter, or was Venture worried about old enemies trying to get back at him through his family?

And then there was Emmett's apprehension about Clara and her father—not only did he work for her old man, her father was a goddamn super who could probably squash Emmett like a bug.

Everything was different now.

Not to mention that Emmett had almost died. There was that. Maybe it was all those jokes about needing therapy finally catching up to him...

Venture pulled the car into the apartment parking lot, and the surrealness of the situation finally hit Emmett: Dr. Venture—a former cape—and Clara were seeing where he lived. Well, Venture already knew where he lived; Emmett had filled out a work application just like he would have anywhere else.

But Venture had been keeping tabs on him...

Silence dragged on, and before anyone could say anything, Emmett exclaimed, "Well, thanks for the lift!"

As he was about to get out of the car, Dr. Venture asked, "Aren't you going to invite us up for a tour?"

Emmett froze, and Clara chuckled awkwardly.

She said, "You don't have to–"

Emmett replied carefully to Venture, "...Have you already seen my place?"

"No. I said I've been keeping tabs on you. I do not *spy* on you. Besides, I'm interested to see the projects you've been working on in your spare time."

Emmett glanced from Venture to Clara. She gave him a small shrug, as if to say it was his choice.

Without wanting to dwell on it, Emmett said, "Okay. Come on up."

All three got out of the car and Emmett led them to his apartment block. Several groups of students that were hanging out at the pavilion and in front of the block paused their conversations and stared as Emmett's group passed.

For a moment, he was worried that someone might recognize Dr. Venture. He promptly discounted that theory–if Venture was worried about being recognized, of course he wouldn't come out. Students were probably staring because Venture was the oldest one around and looked like a professor–

Which was enough to give any student pause.

Emmett led them up to apartment 449 and, with clammy hands, unlocked the door.

He called out to Lock as they entered, but no one responded. Emmett wasn't sure if that was a good or a bad thing; if Lock was there, it might be awkward for him, but Lock was always good at talking to random people–they could split the awkwardness between them.

"Excuse the mess," Emmett muttered.

Dr. Venture grunted. "My first apartment wasn't much neater."

Emmett gave them the quick tour, which consisted of showing them the small kitchen and living room, then pointing toward the bedrooms and bathroom. He had no intention of showing either Venture or Clara his room, though Clara craned her neck to peer at the door.

Dr. Venture was far more interested in the electronics that littered the room–the ambient lights and the table covered in electronic components. As the doctor stared, Emmett swore he could see something blinking on the lens of his glasses, but he couldn't see for sure.

Meanwhile, Clara slowly took in the sight of everything, staring with the same fascination that she did in the lab.

Suddenly, Venture asked, "What are you looking for?"

Emmett turned. Venture was staring at the pile of electronics, and a moment later realized he was asking about the radio locator. Most of the components were nestled in the pile.

But the way Venture had asked the question made it seem like he already knew the answer.

"Supers," Emmett said. The word hung between them, and the air felt thick with tension.

"Are you still going to look for them?"

"Yes."

After Emmett replied, the gravity of the question dawned on him–*after you nearly died, are you still going to look for them?*

And it didn't change his answer.

Venture nodded, still looking at the pile. "Interesting."

Clara was leaning on the kitchen counter, listening intently.

"Do you think I should give it up?" Emmett asked both of them.

Only Venture answered, and he didn't look at Emmett. "Living as a super isn't as glamorous as the media makes it out to be. It's demanding and violent. And for many, it's scarring and short. Even for those in the periphery. Now you know that better than most."

Venture turned toward him now, his stare icy behind his glasses. "I'm very good at hiding, but I have enemies. Even retired capes aren't one hundred percent safe. If you continue working with us, you won't be one hundred percent safe, either.

"I think you should do what you need to do."

"Nothing's changed for me. My mind is set," Emmett said, his voice much more stoic than he felt.

"Good," Venture replied. "When you come in on Monday, we'll talk more about your *repairs.*"

Venture excused them and led Clara out of the apartment. Clara waved good-bye as they went.

Emmett stayed there for a long while after the door shut behind them.

Dr. Venture's speech stuck out to him—one part in particular: 'If you continue working with us'.

Venture seemed like a man that chose his words carefully... Emmett wasn't sure why, but that seemed like an important detail.

Chapter 8

Venture / Lock

Dr. Venture led Clara out of Emmett's apartment and through the upstairs hall.

Venture wasn't sure what he had expected to see, but inwardly he was relieved–Emmett Laraway was a gifted undergraduate engineering student, both focused and closed off. So far, he'd been trustworthy, and in their short visit, Venture's scans hadn't found any trade secrets locked away on Emmett's network. The young man was a bit naïve when it came to the world and to supers, but nothing that could hamstring him.

"What do you think?" Venture asked without pausing.

Clara walked slightly behind him in the halls, and he had no doubt she understood his question and was giving it the hard consideration he'd come to expect from her.

Too much consideration.

"This isn't a quiz," Venture added. "I want your honest assessment."

"You'll have to teach him a lot."

"*We* will have to teach him a lot; that goes without saying. Do you think he'll join us?"

"...You should've asked him to join us *before* he almost died."

Now Venture sighed audibly. Clara could be as shrewd as her mother.

Venture replied, "There's no point in arguing."

"Agreed."

They rounded the last flight of stairs, and Venture was about to pry more for Clara's opinion, but a student walking down the hall made him pause.

The young man wore a baggy sweatshirt which sloped across his broad shoulders, his eyes quickly scanning Venture and Clara. Venture recognized Lachlan Harris from his prior reconnaissance and because Lachlan worked for a mutual employer–Gnosis.

Venture would've written Lachlan off completely, except that as they passed one another in the hall, Venture's glasses saw even more details about Emmett's roommate.

Lachlan's muscles practically rippled, even beneath the baggy clothes. His body was suffused with Mutagen-X—he was practically oozing it out of his pores.

Lachlan eyed them suspiciously as he passed, but he walked with the confidence of a super.

He wasn't just an intern with Gnosis–he was a test subject. And judging by his Mutagen-X levels, a long-term and promising subject as well.

If Venture had more time, he could've scanned deeper, but a passing scan told him everything he needed to know:

Emmett's roommate was a new super, and unless Gnosis had worked out the kinks in the Mutagen-X compound, possibly a dangerous one.

Both Venture and Clara were silent until they got back into his car and closed the doors.

"Was that Emmett's roommate?" Clara asked.

"Yes."

Clara pulled out her phone and started texting—presumably Emmett. Venture put a hand on her phone to pause her.

"Don't tell him."

Clara put her phone down and stared back in confusion. "But he's a super."

"I know. Nothing good will come from outing him to Emmett though. If Emmett figures it out on his own, or Lachlan confides in him, that's between those two."

Clara looked at her phone again, but set it down without texting again. "And you still want Emmett to work with us?"

"It's an interesting development, but it doesn't change things." Venture backed the car out and started driving out of the parking lot. "Definitely interesting."

Clara shook her head. "I don't think Emmett will see it the same way. Do you think he'll be alright?"

"I could enable his chemical controls, then Emmett could up his own dopamine and serotonin levels," Venture offered.

Out of the corner of his eye, disgust flashed across Clara's face. She replied, "He seemed alright enough."

Venture nodded. So, chemical controls were a step too far in her eyes...

Ultimately, Venture agreed—Emmett wasn't even aware of his baseline augmentations yet.

"I'll keep surveillance on him in the meantime."

Lock kept walking through the apartment hall and resisted the urge to look back over his shoulder as he passed Dr. Venture and Clara Venture. That wasn't hard.

What was hard was avoiding looking at Venture's glasses as ultraviolet readouts ticked across the lenses.

If it weren't for his enhancements, Lock might've slipped–might've looked inadvertently or tripped over his own feet out of surprise.

So Emmett's boss could see in UV...

Two months ago, Lock had stumbled on the fact that Dr. Venture had ties to Gnosis. He was both a prominent customer and a research contributor. No one had been loose-lipped enough to say more than that.

It wasn't *that* weird. Over the last year, Lock had realized that all kinds of people wanted bioenhancement: Everyone from politicians wanting bullet resistant skin to celebrities wanting easy-to-maintain physiques to security and military personnel wanting general physical enhancements.

So, Venture seeing UV wasn't weird–

But Venture's glasses hadn't lit up until Venture passed Lock in the hallway.

Venture had scanned him.

Lock's mind raced as he jogged up the stairwell to the top floor. It wasn't common knowledge that Gnosis was experimenting with Mutagen-X, much less that they were experimenting so freely. Lock was one of dozens of volunteers.

The closer Lock got to apartment 449, the faster he was walking.

When Lock opened the door and found Emmett making a sandwich, he didn't know what to think–

Just a few days ago, Lock thought Emmett was dead. Well, more than thought; Lock had seen Emmett's bus get cut in half. Then his roommate hadn't responded for hours...

"Hey," Emmett said through a mouthful of food.

"Hey yourself," Lock replied, managing a smile. Despite his apprehension, he was relieved to see Emmett alive and well. Lock walked up and hugged Emmett—careful not to squeeze too tight. Emmett hugged him back.

Supposedly, Emmett had spent the last few days at a girl's place...

Lock had believed that shit too–right up until he passed Dr. Venture and Clara in the hall of their apartment.

"So, tell me," Lock said, "who's the lucky girl?"

A mix of surprise and a smile crossed Emmett's face, but he took a solid few seconds to finish chewing. Probably to buy himself time to think of a reply.

"Marianne," Emmett said, covering his mouth.

Lock shook his head and smirked. "Three days... You dog."

Emmett shrugged and took another bite. "Miss me?"

Lock's memory flashed again to the bus, to the screech of tearing metal and the fire.

Lock scoffed. "Nah. Did you just get back? I saw the doc and a girl on the way in."

Again, a flash of surprise. Emmett replied, "Yeah, they gave me a lift. The bus is gone. Did you see that?"

Lock nodded as he walked by, glancing around the room. He did see—he was there.

"I was worried about you, man," Lock said earnestly. "Glad you weren't there. I figured all your talk about wanting to know more about supers finally caught up to you."

Lock sighed—not because of his roommate, but because nothing in the apartment seemed out of place. And he hadn't left anything incriminating laying out in the living room.

Lock asked, "Say, did you give them a tour?"

Emmett took the last bite of his sandwich, stalling again. He nodded. "Not our rooms, though."

Lock nodded. Good.

Cause Lock didn't want the Ventures getting any closer to the apartment. He couldn't trust the doc, but hopefully, he could still trust Emmett.

Chapter 9

Better Already

Emmett spent the rest of the day working on his project and taking breaks to catch up with Lock. Apparently, the concert had gone smoothly, except for a rowdy drunk that Lock got to throw out the gate himself.

He still had trouble picturing Lock as a bouncer—despite Lock's thick build, Emmett knew him too well. He knew that Lock would rather spend his time relaxing and *expanding his mind*, as his roommate was fond of saying.

Lock must have been good at his job, though, because he was never hurting for work.

Eventually, Lock left Emmett to go smoke on the roof, wanting a moment of privacy. Sometimes he offered to share whatever drug he was taking with Emmett—this wasn't one of those times.

Emmett didn't pry.

All the while, Emmett tried to pay attention to his injuries. He still felt a deep ache when he moved, something like a cross between a deep bruise and a bad flu. But it slowly faded throughout the day until Emmett wasn't sure if he was imagining the pain—

He almost died... shouldn't he feel like shit?

When he woke up on Sunday, Emmett couldn't tell he'd been injured at all. He felt fine. Felt good—better, even.

Emmett spent the rest of the weekend working, or at least attempting to. He couldn't help but marvel at his recovery. He almost brought it up to Lock, but quickly stopped himself.

Emmett found himself looking forward to Monday afternoon at the lab so that he could talk to Dr. Venture and Clara about it.

The rest of Sunday evening and Monday morning classes passed so slowly that Emmett felt like he was ten years younger and waiting for his birthday to arrive. He was so excited he could've run from campus to the lab instead of taking the bus.

When he finally got to the lab, he jogged down the halls to the testing hub, where Dr. Venture and Clara were waiting for him.

"I'm better already," Emmett said, patting himself. "One hundred percent. Is that normal?"

"No," Venture replied. Clara glared at her father before he continued. "That's not normal for someone who's been in a serious accident. It *is* normal for your new body."

Emmett looked at both of them. "You didn't just heal me, did you?"

"No. Your new body also has some enhancements: Bones, muscle—enough to handle your new arm."

Emmett's throat felt suddenly tight. "Why?"

"To give you a choice," Venture replied, crossing his arms across his chest. "Bringing you into the fold wasn't the only thing I had in mind... You said you felt powerless. You don't have to feel that way anymore—not if you don't want to."

Emmett felt the realization of what Venture was saying slowly dawn on him—

But apparently too slow for Clara.

"You're a super, Emmett," she said, a small smile on her face.

Emmett looked at his hands, both marveling and feeling somewhat ridiculous because he didn't look any different—he didn't really even *feel* any different. His stomach swam, and he desperately wanted to sit down.

But disbelief and guilt settled on him, too.

"Why? ...Don't get me wrong, I'm grateful to be alive, but this is different. Why me?"

Clara responded, "Why anyone? No one gets to choose to be a super."

Venture added, "You're a good person, a good student, and hard worker. You're a better candidate than most who become supers. And, we need someone else we can trust."

Emmett stumbled over to the holographic table in the center of the room and leaned on it, trying to steady his breathing.

He was a super! What powers did he have? Super strength? Speed? ...He could even register and become a cape!

This was what he'd always wanted, wasn't it?

Screeching metal and fire flashed across his mind again. He'd almost died that day—almost been killed—because of a super.

Did he want that responsibility? What if next time it was him killing someone innocent?

But there was another feeling that stuck out that day: He'd been powerless, lying face down in the middle of the street, unable to save anyone, unable to save himself—

Unable to do goddamn anything at all.

Emmett never wanted to feel that way again.

And instead of just saving himself, maybe he could save other people, too. Maybe Emmett could keep other people safe where some super had failed him.

When Emmett finally met Venture and Clara's eyes, they were both smiling.

Clara said, "Looks like you've made up your mind."

Emmett took a deep breath to steady himself. Underneath his uncertainty, excitement was building.

"So, what can I do?"

Before Clara could answer him, Dr. Venture replied, "You can take the rest of the evening off and make sure this is what you really want."

Emmett felt like the floor had dropped out from beneath him.

"I've already made up my mind."

Venture held up a hand for silence, as much for Clara as for Emmett. "You won't just be working with us, you'll be working *for me*. This isn't danger by association. You'll be expected to fight. Once you go down this path, there is no stopping."

"Forgive me, Dr. Venture, but you stopped being a super."

Venture scoffed. "You're missing the point. It took me twenty years to escape... and I still can't stop."

Venture's words hung heavy in the testing hub, loaded with the weight of a life and decisions that Emmett could only guess at, but felt all the same.

It was Clara that finally broke the silence.

"You should take your time," she said, staring at the center table. "We're not going anywhere."

Reluctantly, Emmett nodded. "Okay. I'll take the night and think about it... but can I help out for a bit? The next bus doesn't come until three."

Dr. Venture agreed to let Emmett stay for another two hours, but work was slow. Since Emmett was still on the outside of their circle of trust, Dr. Venture had relegated their work to systems Emmett already knew about.

So again, Emmett found himself testing heat sinks and batteries. Only this time, he wasn't nearly as excited about the technology in front of him as he was about all the things that lay undiscovered in the rest of the lab.

What other tech did Venture have stored away? Were any of the systems things that he had used during his time as a cape?

Then there was the question of just who Dr. Venture was, and what his powers were.

Emmett and Clara were hunched over the testing formation of testing chamber 2, rearranging strips of batteries between the heat sinks.

He had so many questions, and he was stuck waiting another day!

Emmett groaned audibly with frustration.

Clara raised an eyebrow. "What's wrong?"

"What's wrong? What's *wrong?*" He stared at her in disbelief.

Clara smirked. "I'm not psychic."

Emmett dropped his wrench and leaned on the batteries. "Waiting is killing me."

"I hate to break it to you, but there's a lot of waiting as a super."

"What do you mean?"

"Crimes don't just happen every day, you know. Sometimes you have to wait for intel, or wait in hiding for the villain to arrive. It's a lot like police have to do. Just because you're a super doesn't mean it will be any different. Then there's the research and development. Sometimes we're waiting for parts or waiting for Dad to figure out a missing piece. Lots of waiting."

There was something in Clara's voice that caught Emmett off guard. "It almost sounds like you hate waiting as much as I do."

Clara nodded. "Yep. But that's part of the process."

But Emmett wasn't deterred. He narrowed his eyes. "It almost sounds like you know from *experience*."

Clara glanced at him out of the corner of her eye, so fast he almost missed it. "I do. I just said that even in the R and D stuff, there's a lot of waiting."

Emmett waited, but Clara didn't turn to him—didn't give any indication that she'd heard his accusation.

If her father was a super, was Clara a super too?

He waited another moment before he resolved to get back to work.

Just one more answer he had to wait for.

Chapter 10

The Jump

The last two hours crawled by, and then Emmett left the lab without much of a goodbye—

Which felt weird.

Even if Dr. Venture and Clara hadn't officially accepted him into their operation, even if he wasn't officially a super or a cape... Emmett couldn't help feeling as if everything had changed.

Even if it—technically—hadn't yet.

He couldn't help seeing the lab in a different light. Instead of working on weapons tech, were they actually working on tech for supers? Was the lab underground because it was easier to hide and reinforce that way?

Obviously, Emmett saw the doctor and Clara in a different light too—still unable to shake the nagging suspicion that Clara was a super; 'following in her father's footsteps.'

But as Emmett grabbed his things and left the lab, he realized it wasn't just those things.

As he walked down Champion Street, he realized that *everything* had changed.

He was walking the streets when he should be dead—that was among the first things that hit Emmett. And walking past Gnosis in a body more or less made by them. He had no way of knowing just how much of himself he owed to Gnosis, but he assumed it was a lot. That and Gnosis probably made enhancements for other heroes.

The evening was getting colder, but despite that, Emmett wasn't cold at all—even with the wind. He didn't even feel the need to put his hood up or cover his hands.

Shortly after that, Emmett realized he'd walked past his normal bus stop, but that didn't bother him.

He kept walking, and after ten more blocks, realized he wasn't tired in the slightest.

Dodging and weaving through crowds felt easy, though that might've just been his imagination.

Emmett started jogging. He wanted to run, to sprint, but decided against it. Sprinting down Champion Street was sure to get stares.

He'd never been much of an athlete, but after jogging ten more blocks, Emmett wasn't tired in the slightest.

By the time he crossed into downtown, with the skyscrapers and high rises, a smile was plastered on Emmett's face. He passed electronic ads and news displays showing clips of supers—

One day that might be him.

In a way, it felt like the entire world was different—like he really had been isekai'd. There was a whole new world layered on top of the one Emmett had lived in all his life.

A world that was his. He was a super.

Emmett scanned the high rises as he jogged and the rooftops as he passed from downtown to the West End, looking for supers.

One day that could be him—

Emmett stopped on the sidewalk, dumbfounded and frozen as the crowd passed around him. He barely noticed even as some elbowed past him.

Why did he have to wait for *one day?*

He was a super. That could be him *now*.

Excitement welled up in Emmett until he was laughing out loud like a crazy person. He laughed so loud that people started avoiding him and laughed so long that his stomach started to hurt.

When Emmett finally stopped laughing, as if on cue, he saw a super leap across the rooftops.

Emmett stood there like an idiot, stomach still sore from laughing, looking up at where a super had been.

And decided to follow them.

It took Emmett longer than he would've thought to find a way up to the roofs. He walked five different alleys and across another block before he finally found a fire escape behind a secondhand clothing store.

Thankfully, the alley was empty. The problem was, the ladder wasn't down and the bars were ten feet off the ground. The only way to reach it was to jump.

Before being remade as a super, there was no way Emmett could have made it. Even if he could have, Emmett wasn't even sure if he still would have been able to do a pullup.

He would've been stuck, dangling impotently from the bars until his hands gave out and he fell.

But he wasn't powerless anymore.

Emmett rubbed his hands together, both trying to warm them up and psych himself up.

Then he jumped—

And easily grabbed the bars.

Again he laughed like a maniac, then pulled himself up effortlessly. He climbed over the railing and stood on the platform, looking down on the alley below.

Then he turned and ran up the fire escape stairs to the roof, metal clanking with each step. He pulled his hood up and cinched it taut—it wasn't much, but it would suffice for what he was about to do.

Moments later, Emmett stood on the roof. It was flat like the small section of his apartment roof, except that this roof had pebbles across top of it. They shifted beneath his feet. It was a strange sight, even though Emmett had only ever been on two other roofs in his life—his apartment roof and his parents' roof—and he could see other businesses that had similar designs.

But the strangeness was short-lived and replaced with something ominous or prophetic... like he was standing on the shore and the rocks were all that separated him from something new.

Emmett walked to the edge of the roof and looked across the alley to the next rooftop.

It didn't look *that* far.

Then he peered over the edge—leaned over the edge.

The alley was a long goddamn way down. How high was he? Had he climbed five or six stories?

Emmett's stomach turned, and he backed away to steady himself. Carefully, he stood and counted the windows next door—

Five. He was five stories in the air.

And if he fell... It was five stories to the ground. He wasn't sure how much stronger his new body was compared to his old one, but he imagined falling five stories to the ground wouldn't feel good.

"Don't do it."

"What?" Emmett half-turned, careful to hide his face, and found a woman standing across the roof. She had long, braided white hair, and wore a mix of leather and denim covered in dull shards of mirror. The outfit managed to both be intimidating and strange for a super. She might've been middle-aged—her hair was so bright it had to have been dyed.

"Don't jump," she said.

"Why not?"

"Because it's not worth it."

Confused, Emmett looked at the next rooftop and then peered over the edge again. "It's definitely worth it," he replied, trying to work up the courage to jump.

"You'll regret it."

Emmett scoffed. "No, I won't."

"Yes, you will."

Emmett shook his head and ignored her. He stepped back and took a deep breath. Then he ran to the edge and jumped—

And slammed into something invisible at the edge of the roof.

Emmett bounced back and was sent sprawling across the roof, rocks scattering around him.

He sprung to his feet, expecting pain, but felt more surprised and slightly embarrassed than hurt. If anything, he wasn't hurt at all.

"What the crap!" he exclaimed.

"I told you," the woman said with a shrug.

Emmett walked over to the edge and felt around in the air for what he'd crashed into, but felt nothing. He scoffed again, this time in irritation.

Then he backed up and readied himself to try jumping again.

"You know," she said, "People usually learn their lesson the first time."

"And what lesson is that?" Emmett asked, pausing.

"That they shouldn't throw their life away. That it's a permanent solution to a temporary problem. I don't want to sound cliché, but it's been a long morning, so that's all I've got for you."

Emmett turned. "I'm not trying to jump. I'm trying to *jump.*"

Her face wrinkled in confusion. "I'm not sure I'm following you."

"I'm trying to jump across the alley. To the next roof."

"Oh. Ohhh. Well, that's good, I suppose.... But why?"

"I just got powers. I'm a super."

"But you're not sure if you can jump across an alley?"

Emmett sighed. "No, because you keep interrupting me."

The woman chuckled. "Well, then go ahead. See what you can do."

Emmett glared at her a moment before turning back to the task at hand. It felt like he'd lost all the momentum he'd been building up throughout the day, but he took a deep breath and focused.

Then he ran to the edge and leapt.

For a moment, Emmett's stomach dropped out from under him and it felt like he might not make it.

Then he sailed over the alley and cleared the next roof with almost ten feet to spare. He skidded to a halt on the stones of the roof and laughed.

That had been easy—far too easy.

And freaking awesome.

Emmett turned and found the white-haired woman standing beside him on the roof, taller and much closer than she had been before.

Finally, Emmett asked, "Who are you anyway?"

Her name was Athena, and apparently she'd been a registered cape in Belport for years.

Emmett shook his head. "Sorry. I've never heard of you."

Athena shrugged. "Don't be. Most of us don't make the news. I don't think I'm even listed."

"Really?"

"The Division of Superhuman Affairs doesn't bother to list most of us. There's a lot of supers that don't make it through registration. They either wash out or realize that being a cape isn't right for them. Most of the A-list heroes get credit and the spotlight, which is fine by me. Less people that I have to talk to."

"You're talking to me."

Athena chuckled. "I guess I am. So, newbie, why don't you keep going. I'll stay behind in case you have any questions."

Emmett looked from Athena to the next roof and then beyond. The roofs stretched out across the district like islands.

For a moment, he was torn between asking Athena questions about her powers or testing out his own... For a moment.

Emmett ran to the end of the roof and leapt to the next, and then the next and the next. He cleared each gap easily and kept going without pausing—without even breaking stride. His feet pounded out a rhythm as he ran.

Emmett had no idea how fast he was going, but shingles and rocks and roofs passed in a blur as he hurtled down the blocks.

The next jump was across a street instead of an alley, and he didn't pause to consider just how far it was. Emmett leapt from the edge of the roof—as high and as far as he could.

He hurtled over the street—

But he wasn't going to make it. He'd be lucky if he could even grab the ledge. Actually, it looked like he might crash through a fifth-floor window.

Just as his arc slowed and it looked like he wouldn't make it, Emmett felt like he'd *stepped on an invisible platform* in the middle of the air. He practically tripped over it—

But it was enough that he cleared the edge and fell hard on the roof. Emmett rolled to a stop.

When he stood, Athena was standing beside him.

"Got a little over eager there," she said.

"That was you, wasn't it?" Emmett replied, standing and stretching to see if he'd hurt himself. But he felt fine and brushed himself off.

Athena put out her hand and pushed against an invisible wall. "I can create barriers."

As she pushed, Emmett could just make out a distortion in the air, like looking through thick glass. As soon as Athena stopped pushing, the barrier vanished.

"They're handy for crossing wide streets. Not too shabby in a brawl either. Good for keeping people from jumping off roofs too."

Emmett scoffed. "Thanks for saving me, I guess. I can barely see your barrier. How do you see where to put it?"

"I don't really need to see them. It's kind of like touching your nose with your eyes closed, or like finding your way around your room in the middle of the night."

"So you can't see in the dark?"

"No. Funny enough, that seems like a pretty rare power."

Emmett smiled. "Look, I have to go... This might be weird, but you're the first super I've talked to. How am I going to run into you again?"

Athena crossed her arms, incredulously. "You really are new to this. Do you even have a name yet?"

"Well... no." Emmett hadn't even started thinking of one. He wasn't even sure what his new body could do.

Athena smirked. "Give it some thought. Most days, I like to do some laps around downtown. Good luck coming up with a name. Took me weeks before I finally decided on mine."

Then Athena ran and leapt off the roof. She was gone before Emmett could ask how she came up with her name.

Chapter 11

Burger with Questions

That evening, Emmett finished his commute home in minutes, running across the rooftops and then jogging through the Woods apartments to his block.

He felt like his head was swimming—this time in a good way. He was elated, curious, and apprehensive, and again the feeling of standing on the shore of something amazing hit him like a wall of water.

Emmett tried not to smile like a maniac as he got close. The last thing he needed was to look suspicious or crazy so close to his place.

Conspiratorial paranoia quieted him, and Emmett forced himself to walk through the halls until he got to his apartment. By the time he got to the door, his hands were shaking with excitement.

Shit—what would he tell Lock? Emmett felt like a goddamn madman, and he hoped that he didn't look half as crazy as he felt.

Emmett took a deep breath and pushed open the door.

Dead silence.

He shut the door behind him and glanced around the apartment. Lock's door was open, but he wasn't anywhere in the apartment. Emmett climbed up to the roof and looked around, but his roommate wasn't up there either.

Emmett came back inside and promptly collapsed on the couch.

There he stayed—for about a minute—before Emmett jumped up and forced himself to do *something*. He couldn't stew in his own excitement like this. He had to do something or the day would pass agonizingly slow.

After all, he had a project to work on.

Emmett sighed and got to work.

Thankfully, time flew by as Emmett worked on the radio locator.

This was partially due to Emmett's excitement at taking the project in a new direction. Ultimately, it would take him longer to finish the version he needed for class, but he didn't care—

He was a super now.

Eventually, Emmett would finish a table-top model of the locator for class, but now he was simultaneously working on the rooftop schematics and his portable version.

Both had limitations:

The rooftop model would obviously be much more powerful and could scan across most of the city. It was limited by having all three antennas on the same roof, and by taller buildings that would distort or outright block signals from behind them. This could be mitigated somewhat by software, but no amount of processing could overcome those problems.

The portable model had a much shorter range—just a few square blocks—and ultimately would run into the same interference from structures. But it could move and *track down* a signal.

Of course, he'd always envisioned tying the two systems together—in the same daydream, he was a super, leaping from rooftop to rooftop, chasing villains.

But that wasn't just a daydream anymore.

That could be him *tomorrow*.

So Emmett redoubled his efforts, working on his idealized version of the radio locator: Two systems tied together—the portable locator acting as a fourth antenna for the rooftop system—and a central hub computing and feeding him data in real time.

He spent a good chunk of the day on his laptop, altering and testing code, taking breaks every hour or so to get up and stretch. As the day went on, he would go over to the table littered with electronics and tinker with antennae and wiring.

When Lock got home, it was a little past seven. Emmett had worked straight through dinner and hadn't even realized it.

It wasn't until Lock shut the door behind him and the smell of takeout wafted through the kitchen that Emmett realized just how hungry he was.

Emmett turned, stomach growling and fingers slick with electrical grease.

Lock held up three bags of Burger Shack triumphantly. "Don't worry, I brought you some, too."

Burger Shack was pretty much one of the best fast-food burger places. They weren't fancy, and only had three things on the menu, but what they lacked in variety they more than made up for in quality.

Emmett smiled painfully wide, then ran to the kitchen sink to wash his hands. "Lock with the eleventh hour burgers!"

Lock dropped the bags on the small table in front of the couch, then walked to his room.

Emmett dried his hands and followed the smell toward the living room—but stopped short when he saw Lock through the door.

Lock was changing his shirt, and immediately Emmett noticed two things: His roommate had been hitting the gym and was chiseled like a veteran bodybuilder, *and* it looked like he'd had the shit beaten out of him. His entire upper body was covered in deep purple bruises, and four long gashes stood out—one across his arm still trickled blood. There was even a gash along the top of his bald head.

Emmett winced. No matter how tough Lock was, those were serious injuries.

Lock pulled on another black shirt and turned to see Emmett staring.

Emmett asked, "What happened to you? Are you alright?"

"I'm fine," Lock said, walking past Emmett and sitting down on the couch.

Emmett stared in disbelief. "...Are you sure you don't need to see a doctor or, like, go to the emergency room?"

Lock pulled a burger out of one of the bags, tore open a second to reveal fries, and pushed the last bag toward Emmett.

"I'm sure," Lock replied nonchalantly. "Seriously."

Emmett shook his head and sat down on the other side of the couch. "If you say so. What happened?"

His roommate took a bite of burger and chewed before answering. "Work's a bitch."

Lock proceeded to tell Emmett about a concert he was working at a dive bar downtown. "Couple of drunks got out of hand. One pulled a knife... The band refused to play the show. Canceled and left."

The longer Emmett listened, the less hungry he felt, but he kept eating. Slowly.

A pit was growing in his stomach. Something felt off about Lock's story—maybe Emmett would've believed him, if he hadn't seen Lock's wounds. Emmett was sure that Lock should be in the hospital, especially if those were as fresh as Lock was saying.

His roommate trailed off, continuing to eat... and not talking.

Emmett had the creeping feeling that Lock *knew* Emmett didn't believe the story. It was ridiculous—Lock couldn't read minds...

Could he?

Emmett had seen weirder things over the last few days. His roommate being a super with psychic powers wasn't *that* crazy.

"Anyway," Lock said, "How's the radio locator coming along? You ready to rig antennas on the roof yet?"

"Not yet."

"You've been working on it a lot."

"Yeah," Emmett replied, trying to hide his unease with another bite of burger.

"It's for class right, not for Dr. Venture?"

"Yeah," Emmett replied, a little quicker.

Lock nodded, taking a long sip of his drink. "How's Marianne?"

"Who?"

Lock side-eyed Emmett. "Marianne, you know... Oh, you dog! Don't tell me—"

"No! No, she's good." Emmett lied. "Come on, you know me. I'm not the fling type." Especially not when he had enough trouble keeping track of one imaginary girlfriend.

Lock nodded again, a smile creeping across his face. "That's good. I was beginning to worry that you'd changed. Little ol' Emmett... Changed." Lock leaned back on the couch.

No, of course not. Emmett was exactly the same as he'd always been...

The real question was, was Lachlan still the same guy that he'd always been?

Emmett chuckled awkwardly and focused on eating. His double cheeseburger feeling more and more like a bribe of some kind.

Emmett's questions about his roommate only grew as the evening went on.

Eventually Lock left the apartment again, not bothering to say where he was going.

Come to think of it, it seemed like Lock was working more and more.

Either Lock's work as a bouncer was with a much rougher crowd than he'd been letting on, or Lock had been lying about his job all along.

Emmett wasn't sure he liked either answer.

Full Throttle Heart

Opening

[Montage accompanies opening Narration]

What *is* a truck?

Is it more than the sum of its parts? More than its frame, its cab and wheels? More than its ability to haul boxes and freight?

Is it more than just a truck when it's transporting life saving medicine, or hauling a family and their belongings to their new home? When the heat of its engine warms a blue-collar worker up on the way to work on a cold, cold morning? Or when it dispenses justice to the forgotten corners of a war-torn realm?

An ordinary box truck... No.

This isn't the story of just any box truck.

On Earth 9H, Truck-kun was assembled in an ordinary factory, alongside thousands of its kin. Then it was sold to a big box retailer, transporting big boxes and sometimes smaller boxes all around the country. For years, Truck-kun was a faithful box truck; Faithful to the job, to its driver, and to the cause—delivering boxes.

But Truck-kun was destined for more.

[Theme Song — "Hātofurusurottoru" by Gunpowder Audition — *Full Throttle Heart*, season 1]

[Montage of Truck-kun fighting the Undead Legions of Liquid Shadow]

We spend our days dreaming
—Stirring in our sleep
—Driving through our lives!
Full of octane gas
—Open throttle (we're gonna crash!)
—Can't stop this feeling (in my heart)
Fiercest, only, auto-kun… Truck-kun (Truck-kun!)
Fiercest, only, auto-kun… Truck-kun (Truck-kun!)
Full of octane gas
—Open throttle (we're gonna last!)
—Can't stop this feeling (in my heart)
Approaching certain victory
—Fight the power (unleash the power!)
—Drown out all the cheering fans
—Defeat evil that controls the land

[Hard Cut to Joe's House]

Joe Regular wiped his eyes and started up his work truck on Monday morning. It was still dark outside, and the Spring air was crisp. Joe sat there in the cab, waiting for Truck-kun's engine to warm up, and sipped his coffee. Savored it.

That was the kind of man Joe was—a family man, an everyday warrior. The kind that worked hard, loved deeply, and savored little things as deeply as the big ones.

Back then, Truck-kun could only answer in a rumble of gratitude.

Joe patted the steering wheel of his reliable steed. "It's gonna be a good day, buddy."

Little did either of them know it would be their last fateful work day together.

Joe drove Truck-kun to the Old Factory, the one he'd been picking up boxes from since he was fresh out of high school. There had been other factories closer to the Big City, but Joe liked this one. It was the one his dad used to deliver for.

That was the kind of man Joe was.

Now that Old Factory was the last one in town, the only one that held out against the Big Corporation. All the others had been gobbled up, leaving the Old Factory standing alone against the unflinching tide of Late Stage Capitalism.

[Sad Montage accompanies Narration]

Little convenience stores merged together... Family auto shops were bought out by chains... Skating rinks and diners changed to used car lots and liquor stores... Playgrounds changed from splintery wood structures to unsplintery plastic.

As the world changed around them, Joe and Truck-kun kept driving. Kept working.

That was what they were made to do.

[Cut to Present Day]

That fateful day, Joe Regular and Truck-kun drove their last drive.

They delivered boxes all around town. Joe took the time he could spare to talk with the owners of the stores. Sometimes they shared laughs, other times their struggles. Sometimes they just talked about the weather, but Joe talked with them.

That was the kind of man Joe was.

Meanwhile, Truck-kun kept the engine and the cab warm.

Their next stop was a coffee shop, and as Joe wheeled boxes to the front door, he pictured coffee and mugs and even a coffee maker inside. He didn't know for certain—he never knew—but it was the little things that made his day.

Truck-kun would forever think that it was fate, that the last time he saw Joe was in front of the coffee shop.

The manager had just finished talking about the beautiful weather and handed Joe a complimentary cup of coffee. Truck-kun was on the street, idling.

It was then that a rogue box truck ran a red light, lost control, and careened into Truck-kun. Metal screamed and tires were thrown clear. Truck-kun was T-boned in its driver's side, right where the cab and its cargo hold met—right in its heart.

Joe saw the whole thing through the coffee shop door. Mouth wide and heart pounding, he dropped his fresh cup of coffee. It hit the floor and burst as Joe ran out the door and toward his truck, Truck-kun.

Joe fell to his knees, unable to speak.

Truck-kun was crumpled, its body twisted around the rogue truck, both intertwined in an embrace of death. Truck-kun's frame was shattered, its driveshaft broken, its window pulverized. Gasoline, antifreeze, and hydraulic and windshield wiper fluid drained onto the ground. Truck-kun's engine sputtered its last sputters.

While the bystanders and the other driver were moving away from the wreck, Joe stumbled over to Truck-kun. He leaned on the mangled engine compartment and listened to his truck's final words.

Joe wept, his tears joining the stream of Truck-kun's lifeblood.

In time, the police would come and take statements. Tow trucks would come and haul away the wreckage. The world would keep turning. Deliveries would keep being delivered.

Tomorrow, Joe would go back to work. He would keep going, because that was what he was made to do. Tomorrow, Joe would drive a new truck, but he would never forget Truck-kun.

That was the kind of man Joe was.

Honorable. Silent. Driven.

That was the kind of mentor Truck-kun had. That was the kind of man a truck would try to live up to.

[Commercial Break]

"The standards may change..."

[Quick Montage of people getting ready throughout history:
[Primitive hunter gatherers weaving shells into their hair.
[Ethnically sensitive depiction of warriors shaving the sides of their heads and concubines applying blush.
[Sailors getting matching tattoos.]

"...but the pursuit of beauty..."

[Continue to Quick Montage of people getting ready in modern day:
[Soldiers pressing their uniforms and shining their shoes.
[Businessmen and women adjusting their jackets and ties.
[Men trimming their beards.
[Both sexes applying beauty creams and makeup, dyeing their hair.]

"...is immortal."

[Cut to Gnosis logo — white square with sexless, obscured face staring through]

"Gnosis. The next step in beauty."

Chapter 12

Your New Body

"You didn't let me finish telling you about your new body."

It was Tuesday, and the day had dragged on while Emmett waited for the afternoon to get there.

He was finally standing back in the lab, back in section 006—the same white hospital-like section he'd woken up in a few days prior.

Dr. Venture fiddled with a wall monitor. When he was finished, it showed a 2D genderless drawing of a person with arrows pointing to various body parts. Clara was in a different lab, working on another project—Venture declined to say which.

Venture pushed up his glasses and continued. "As I was saying, you've been given a basic holistic upgrade suite, courtesy of Gnosis. Think of it as the training wheels for manufactured supers.

"Your new body has several enhancements, including enhanced muscular strength, speed, endurance, coordination, and reaction time. Your bones, ligaments, and even your skin are more resilient." As Venture spoke, different arrows lit up with labels and explanations.

"Most of these abilities are at the peak of human athletic achievement and some will surpass even that. You are what's known broadly as a Class 1-0: Minor superhuman capabilities with little to no training."

Emmett's head swam with questions, and he stammered as he thought of where to start.

"Can I train and get stronger?"

Venture chuckled at that, turning back to the monitor. "You can already lift a thousand pounds, run faster and farther than professional athletes. Even without training, you could fight a half dozen unpowered combatants.

"But yes," Venture added, turning back to Emmett. "The compound you've been given is versatile and responds to stress by gradually improving your enhancements *to a point*. You won't be punching out Paragon, no matter how hard you train."

Emmett chuckled. Paragon was one of the leaders of the Summit of Heroes—a bona fide Class 5 super. He could stand toe-to-toe with all of the Antichampions, combined, and his very presence was enough to disarm otherwise catastrophic situations.

Aside from Paragon being the dictionary definition of good, the thought of any *one* super standing against him was *absurd*.

For a moment, Venture shared a smile. "If you train, you will get a little stronger and more capable."

Emmett shook his head, still in disbelief and trying to think of what to ask next. But before he spoke, Emmett noticed something on the display.

"Mutagen-A... Is that what you gave me?"

"Yes."

Emmett nodded. "Gnosis... My roommate works for them. I always thought they were a make-up company. I mean, the military looking building makes sense now. They're really into biomedical enhancements and military applications?"

Venture nodded slightly, and silence settled between them. Emmett wasn't sure if the doctor was pausing for dramatic effect or if he was choosing his words carefully.

Venture said, "Ever since the first supers rose, humankind has been... envious. Some legends say that the first alchemists and mages were inspired by their powers, that humans made the first spears to defend against them. Technology isn't any different.

"Supers give us something to strive for, something to emulate, something to replicate."

Emmett met Venture's eyes, but couldn't bring himself to ask the question that was now on his mind:

Why aren't you a cape anymore?

Venture stared back, eyes hard, as if silently telling him not to ask.

Instead, Emmett asked, "If I'm a Class 1-0 super, does that mean I'm a registered cape now?"

Venture winced as if Emmett had slapped him.

"Did you go through a registration process?"

"No."

"Did you undergo stringent testing and psychological evaluations?"

Emmett nodded. "I understand. I'm not a cape."

Venture pushed up his glasses. "No. You're not. And you would do well to remember that fact. You don't just become a cape and the Division of Superhuman Affairs doesn't approach just anyone to be one either—not unless you have an extremely potent gift.

"If you're going to act as a vigilante, then you'll be what's known as a *mask*. Any actions you take will not be sanctioned by the DSA and the best you can hope for from local law enforcement is tepid indifference."

As Venture spoke, a seriousness bled into his voice that unsettled Emmett. It was a voice of command and determination. In that moment, there was no doubt in his mind that the professor used to be a super.

And he clearly had something against masks.

"You used to be a cape," Emmett said. "Not a mask."

"Yes."

"But you're okay with me being a mask?"

"Perhaps I have... biases. But everyone starts off as a mask. If you stay in the business long enough and get the chance, I recommend you become a cape."

"Why the bias?"

Venture sighed and his eyes narrowed. "There are rules in this business, and I don't mean the rules that capes have to follow. All supers—capes, masks, villains—have certain standards of conduct and rules of engagement.

"We call these the Code. And in my experience, it's new masks that most often break it."

Emmett looked down at the floor—anywhere but looking in Dr. Venture's steely gaze.

Emmett looked down at his right arm. The one that used to be just flesh and blood.

"What about my arm?"

Venture smiled, his intense stare cast aside as quickly and easily as a crumpled piece of paper.

"I was wondering when you would ask."

Dr. Venture led Emmett out of section 006 and across the hall to section 002.

Emmett nearly breathed a sigh of relief when they left the sterile, white halls, and returned to the mechanical bunker-like aesthetic of the rest of the lab. The sensation caught him off guard.

He chalked the relief up to the hospital wing reminding him of his near-death experience. He'd read some accounts of Post-Traumatic Stress Disorder—books on supers and the aftermath of their battles, but also books on war and trauma—so he knew what trauma could look like.

But *feeling it* was something else entirely.

The walls of the hospital-wing weren't just white, they were blinding—almost nauseatingly so, like the few times he'd woken up hungover and braved the bright morning sun to get to class. And they felt oppressively narrow, even though Emmett was sure that they were the same dimensions as the other sections of the lab.

Emmett also knew that he should probably talk to someone about what he went through; he'd heard therapy brought up often enough that the thought occurred to him. But he pushed it aside, hoping that the uneasy feelings would fade.

When Emmett's grandparents passed, it had hurt for a while. For months, if he was being honest. But over time, it got easier. The pain had faded, and eventually it was just something else that had happened in his life. Eventually, he was left with the good memories of them while the pain faded away like a shadow.

Emmett did his best to convince himself that this would be the same, while conveniently ignoring the fact that shadows never truly disappeared.

After all, he was starting a new phase of his life. He would have enough things to occupy his mind between training and vigilante-ing...

Capes and masks didn't go to therapy, did they? The idea seemed kind of silly. It's not like supers fought in the streets every day, but it was more days than not. Fights and violence were integral parts of being a cape or a mask. They probably got used to it. To them, it was probably just another day at school or work.

Better that Emmett get used to the idea now because he knew he wasn't going back.

He wanted this, and he was prepared to train, to struggle, and to sacrifice to live that life.

So he did the best to leave all those other thoughts behind him as he followed Dr. Venture to section 002.

Venture paused at the old camera and display of door 002, tilting his head so it could scan his eyes.

"Thank you for verification. Please step through, Dr. Venture," TINA said. The blast doors of section 002 slid open with well-oiled silence.

"I guess I'm seeing all of the lab today," Emmett said with an equally awkward and excited chuckle.

"Almost," Venture replied.

Section 002 of the lab looked like more of the bunker aesthetic that Emmett was familiar with.

Venture led them through the halls, and Emmett was overcome with the feeling that this wing was *almost* identical to section 003, even down to the layout and monitor-riddled testing hub.

Emmett said, "So, section three is for testing energy-based applications... Section six is biomedical... Section two is mechanical? What's section five, aerospace?"

"Five is our training and simulation room. Four is the armory," Venture replied without looking back.

"What about section one?"

"Living quarters."

Emmett almost scoffed. It seemed ridiculous at first to think about Dr. Venture and Clara living in the lab—almost as ridiculous as a teacher living at school or a cashier living in the store instead of going home.

But now, knowing that Dr. Venture was a former cape in hiding, it made total sense.

Dr. Venture led Emmett to the testing hub of section 002. For a moment, he could almost imagine he was going to a normal afternoon at his internship.

Until Venture told TINA to turn on the displays.

Instead of schematics for heat sinks and batteries, the displays showed a schematic view of Emmett's arm—the skin was gone, showing all the metal, joints, pistons, and actuators in their mechanical glory.

Just like in the display summarizing his body's enhancements, additional details popped up on screen: A blend of tungsten and titanium alloys stood in for bone while electroactive polymers similar to bulletproof fabrics took the place of muscle, tendons, and ligaments.

Emmett read each paragraph with growing entrancement until he came to the section detailing how his arm connected to the flesh and bone of his new body: The metal frame of his arm actually extended into his collarbone, shoulder blade, and a portion of his ribs while the artificial muscle blended similarly into nearby flesh.

Venture must've followed his eyes. "Part of the reason for your other enhancements is that normal bones and muscles couldn't safely support your arm. Even with built-in regulators, all it would take is your arm to bend or exert force in an odd way and you could break your spine. Now there's very little chance of that."

"Wait, wait, wait..." Emmett tried bending his arm around backwards or in circles, but he couldn't get it to bend in any weird way—it felt *normal*. "Are you saying I should be able to bend my arm differently?"

Venture smirked. "Your arm is one of the most advanced prostheses I've designed. *Of course* it's regulated. For now, it will only function as a biological arm

would, which means you're not double-jointed and that its strength is limited to what your physical body can handle. Think of it as a safety precaution."

"Class 1-0."

"Roughly."

Emmett followed the diagram to a zoomed in view of the artificial muscles
that showed dense clusters of polymer.

"And those are nerves?"

"Very good," Venture replied. "They act both to regulate the strength of
the limb and to give you finer motor control."

Immediately, Emmett thought about modifying his arm so he could test
its real limits. Could it push the limits of a class 1 super?

Emmett suppressed a smile—it didn't work.

"What?" Venture asked suspiciously.

Emmett shrugged. "Just thinking ahead."

Venture raised an eyebrow. "Don't get any ideas about disabling the regulators. I'm serious about accidentally breaking your spine. Injure yourself
badly enough and not even Gnosis can make you a cape."

Emmett sighed.

Next time, he thought.

Then something else caught his eye: There were empty pockets in his
mechanical arm.

"What are those?"

Venture fiddled with a setting on the screen, and the schematics of his arm
changed shape. Now it looked thin and malnourished—the muscles nearly
flat against the bones and the joints knobby in comparison.

Venture said, "Your synthetic muscles are much stronger and more effi-
cient than normal ones—even ones enhanced by Mutagen-A." He changed
the schematics back to their original view. "These empty pockets give your
arm a more natural look. They also have other potential uses..."

Emmett was already ahead of Dr. Venture. The empty pockets were reinforced with walls of polymer—they were *actual* pockets.

"I can store things in there!" Emmett said. "Weapons or something defensive..." His thoughts went even faster, thinking of stuffing his miniature radio locator inside.

Again Venture smirked, but this time the smile stayed on his face instead of retreating.

"I thought the same thing. With some experimentation, your arm could be modular—possibly even swapping components out on the fly."

Emmett's heart was racing.

"What do you have?"

Chapter 13

The Code

Emmett followed Dr. Venture through a sealed door and into the next room of the lab, section 002.

"I've laid out several basic modifications for your arm. These are all pieces that would be useful for a new mask."

Four metal tables pushed together in the center of the room and several things were sprawled out on them. The first that drew Emmett's eye was the long whip that curled around the edge of the tables. Then there were several small boxes.

And in the center of it all was a large pistol.

Emmett didn't know much of anything about firearms, aside from the basics learned while playing video games, and he'd never known anyone to own one. It made him feel slightly uneasy seeing a gun in real life.

"Do a lot of capes carry guns?" Emmett asked.

"Firearms aren't looked highly upon, but many supers carry one—especially class 1 and class 2 that might not otherwise have powers effective at range. The Code dictates that we avoid killing our enemies, so you'll only be carrying non-lethal rounds."

That made him feel a little better. Emmett knew that being a cape or a mask would involve getting into fights, but he hadn't thought much more about it than that.

Emmett turned from the mods to Dr. Venture. "So that battle on Champion street... that wasn't normal, was it?"

"No," Venture said quietly.

"Do you have any leads?" he asked without thinking.

"Not yet."

Emmett felt the familiar pit forming in his stomach and he decided to change the subject.

"What is the Code exactly?"

"Think of it as a mix of rules of engagement and decorum amongst active supers. It's the reason why fights between supers tend to be nonlethal and that they avoid excessive damage to buildings and infrastructure. It's not that killing doesn't happen or that particularly heinous supers aren't executed, it's that unnecessary killing would perpetuate. Kill a villain and risk lethal vengeance from their boss or risk them coming after your family.

"Villains that follow the Code can expect imprisonment instead of execution—from capes and from the Division of Superhuman Affairs. It's the reason why the *Vault* is the preferred way of dealing with villains. It keeps the government and supers from outright war on the streets."

Emmett listened intently, mouth hanging open from the realization. He had never heard of the Code, not in any news report or message board.

"Why the secret?"

Venture replied, "It preserves the public's innocence. A mutually assured destruction is what keeps some fringe villains from becoming truly heinous. People don't need to know how perilous that balance is."

Emmett's stomach turned as he listened. Until a few days ago, that had been him—blissfully unaware.

But that wasn't the question that made him feel truly unsettled. He was almost too afraid to ask it.

"...Why doesn't the Summit just take care of those villains?"

Venture raised his eyebrows. "Why don't they?"

Emmett's mouth felt dry. "They can't."

"It's not that simple," Venture replied, eyes falling to the table of mods. "The Summit of Heroes *might* be able to take out some of their enemies... but there's always a chance they fail. Even the Summit have homes and families. Better to play the great game, honor the Code, so that our enemies honor it too."

Venture turned to Emmett. "There's other pieces of the Code, but that's what you need to know for now. Fights shouldn't be lethal and keep collateral damage to a minimum."

Emmett was about to ask about that second part, but Venture pointed to the table.

"Your arm has two main storage areas: One in your forearm and the second in your upper arm. Of course, they're limited in size. Depending on what modifications you want to store, you might be able to store up to three pieces.

"This is what I have for you, so far," Dr. Venture said, and then went into detail about each piece:

The whip was fifteen feet long with a glossy gray pattern along it—similar to the electroactive polymer that made up the muscle in his prosthetic arm, but the whip also had links of titanium running through the center.

Venture slipped on a black glove from his pocket and picked up the end of the whip as he described it. "In addition to being a formidable weapon, you'll also be able to turn the end of it rigid." Venture sent a snap of what Emmett assumed was electricity into the whip, and the end of it wrapped around his wrist. "You can use it as a grappling hook or as a lasso to grapple an opponent."

Next was a thin metal box about a foot long. Venture held it up and again engaged a current from his glove—a metal disk popped out from inside, blossoming into a shield big enough to cover Emmett's torso.

Venture said, "The impact shield takes about a tenth of a second to deploy and can stop small caliber rounds. The alloy is rated to withstand moderate fluctuations of heat and cold, and is resistant to some acids. In short, it will help against most class one and two threats." With a flick of the wrist, the shield folded back up just as quickly as it deployed.

Then Dr. Venture grabbed the cylinder next to it and turned it so that Emmett could see the borehole.

"This is a semiautomatic concealable pistol—a modified version of the forty-five on the table. It fires the same nonlethal 'sledgehammer' rounds."

Venture set the gun mod on the table with a definitive *thunk*.

Emmett sighed. "Well, I still don't know about the gun, but I'll take the other two."

"You don't understand," Venture replied. "These three are suitable for your forearm compartment. Right now, only one will fit."

Emmett's heart sank a little. "But they're modular, right? I can just take all of them with me and change them out when I need them."

Venture smirked. "Not yet. For now, installing or swapping a modification in your forearm will involve minor surgery. They need to be mounted and connected correctly."

Venture walked around the table to another set of components, each of these a small gray box half the size of the other mods.

"These are suited for your upper arm compartment. Smoke pellets for cover and escape, caltrops for evading and disabling vehicles, and a lock-picking kit. These are made to be quickly pulled out for use and refilled later."

Emmett nodded. "The lock-picking kit sounds useful."

Venture eyed him. "Do you even know how to pick a lock?"

"Well, no."

"You'll take smoke pellets and caltrops for now." Venture tossed one of the small grab boxes to Emmett.

Emmett scoffed. "Why give me the option then?" he asked, turning the box over in his hand.

"To show you what's possible. To give you ideas. To get you thinking of what else you can make."

Emmett tried to contain his excitement. Not only was he a super, he was getting to design his own modifications!

He'd already been lucky enough to get a second chance after being left for dead on Champion street. And even though he was only a class 1 super, he'd gotten a general suite of enhancements instead of just one power.

And he had room to grow.

Emmett didn't have to stay a class 1 super. Maybe eventually he could modify himself enough to become class 2 or even class 3.

There were class 4 and 5 supers—namely those in the Summit of Heroes—but that was the big leagues. Most class 4 and 5 supers were aliens, living weapons, or descended from gods. Most were never human to begin with.

Emmett wasn't even sure he would want that kind of power, but he didn't have to settle for *just class 1*.

Emmett tossed the box of smoke pellets back on the table. "Is this the start of my new internship? Making my own modifications?"

"Yes," Venture replied. "Now, which one do you want to test first?"

Chapter 14

Gray Room

E mmett followed Dr. Venture out of section 002 and to the door of section 005, carrying the pile of modifications in his arms. The whip dragged behind him on the ground.

Venture paused at the door, allowing the camera and system to scan him.

Emmett regarded the screen, camera, and speaker next to the door, realizing that these seemed to be the most modern of the entry systems.

"Thank you for verification. Please step through, Dr. Venture," TINA said, its voice coming through with eerie clarity.

Emmett hadn't realized just how accustomed he'd become to the background static of the old speakers strewn throughout the bunker.

"Why did you only upgrade these systems?" Emmett asked as the doors hissed open.

"Makes you wonder, doesn't it?" Venture replied without looking back.

Emmett rolled his eyes. That was code for when Venture wanted him to figure out a question on his own.

Even the lighting system seemed new—white lights came on as they walked, illuminating the hall in time with their steps. It made Emmett feel like he was already a famous cape.

Next, they entered a small locker room, and Dr. Venture pointed him to a black bodysuit hanging on the wall.

Emmett set his armful of mods on the nearby bench, walked over to the suit, and ran the fabric through his fingers. It felt thin and sleek, yet sturdy. He was sure it was some kind of futuristic material that Dr. Venture or Gnosis or the government had designed, but that didn't stop Emmett from suddenly feeling very self-conscious—he'd never worn anything like that before.

"What's wrong?" Venture asked.

"Why is it always leotards?"

"All the supers wear them. And not to be pedantic, but *that's* a bodysuit. Leotards don't have leggings."

Emmett rolled his eyes. "Not all supers wear them."

Venture added simply, "Most do. In addition to being sturdier than jeans and a T-shirt, skin-tight clothing is protected by the body's innate fields—the same forces that keep a shapeshifter's original form or keep a pyrokinetic from burning themselves extend a fraction beyond the skin. That is unless you'd prefer to stash spare changes of clothes around Belport."

"No, that's okay," Emmett replied quickly. "I'll take my chances with the suit."

"I'll give you a minute to put that on," Venture said. "I've taken the liberty of scanning your measurements. The material is form fitting but more durable than any leotard. It should provide some additional protection against any small arms you come up against."

Emmett thought about asking when Venture could've possibly scanned him, but thought better of it. He didn't want to know.

Venture stepped through the door to let Emmett change. Then Emmett set to undressing and pulling on the suit.

...Which wound up taking longer than he thought it would.

The oddest part was the 'shoes' of the suit, which seemed to shrink around his foot and contour to his toes. That was the only easy part. The rest of it felt like pulling sausage casings over his legs, torso, and arms.

Scratch that—the weirdest part was the right arm of the suit, which had cutaways on the back of the upper arm and the underside of the forearm for his storage compartments.

Then he couldn't reach the back zipper.

"Dr. Venture wants to know if you're alright in there or if you fell in?" TINA asked.

Emmett finally succeeded in pulling the zipper up, grabbed his mods, and stepped out into the hall.

Venture chuckled. "It gets easier." Then waved for him to follow.

A few twists and turns later, they stepped into this section's variation of the testing hub. It was similar enough that Emmett recognized it, but the screens were configured differently and there were other additions: Namely, a viewing window that looked out into darkness beyond and a large platform to the right—It was the second thing that drew his eye.

The platform looked like it was made of white bathroom tile, except that the grout in between glowed bright blue. An outfit hung on the wall that at first looked like pieces of a suit of armor. It wasn't until Emmett walked over and realized that they were pieces of a Virtual Reality suit—Helmet and visor, gloves, vest, knee pads, and shin guards.

TINA's voice came through the intercom. *"Which training course would you like me to prepare?"*

Emmett whirled around and looked at Dr. Venture expectantly.

Venture was peering out through the viewing window, hands clasped behind his back.

"Normally, we start with the 'jump' program, but seeing as how you already practiced running across the rooftops of Belport, it's safe to say that we can skip that one..."

Venture trailed off, leaving Emmett feeling slightly awkward about being followed. And defensive.

Emmett set the armful of mods on the center table. "Are you going to follow me all the time?" he asked.

Venture turned, impatience bleeding onto his face. "I meant what I said before. *Passive monitoring.* I have better things to do than listen to your conversations. That's what TINA is for."

"'Passive monitoring' involves listening for specific phrases—"

"That's enough, TINA," Venture said, before continuing. "It's a happy medium between safety and privacy. If you're going to be a mask, then I'm afraid it's non-negotiable. It's the only way my Fast-Response Drones can bail you out if you get in over your head."

Emmett nodded reluctantly. He wanted to trust Dr. Venture—he *did* trust him. But Emmett couldn't shake the fact that Venture had been surveilling him for months without Emmett knowing or the fact that Venture was a former cape with who knew how many secrets.

"I trust you," Emmett said, as much to Venture as to reiterate it to himself. "But I want you to let me in—"

Venture held up a hand. "Trust goes both ways. I'm trusting you enough to bring you into the fold. *Slowly.* Trust me to keep you alive until you can swim on your own."

Emmett nodded. "Deal." Then he turned to the white platform and the VR pieces hanging from the wall. "So, what training course am I starting with?"

Venture chuckled. "That's not for you. That's for me."

Dr. Venture led Emmett through the joining hall and out into a large testing chamber. Instead of solid metal, the walls, floor, and ceiling were made of tiles about six inches square. Each changed color, giving the impression of a wave of light rippling across the room.

Darkness receded into the distance.

Emmett's eyes widened as he realized the true scale of the room—not just hundreds of feet deep, but equally tall.

When all the tiles finally lit up, Emmett and Venture were standing alone in a gigantic white room.

"Impressive, isn't it?" Venture said with a hint of pride in his voice.

"How big is your lab?" was all Emmett could stammer out. He'd brought the armful of mods with him, and clutched them a little tighter.

"Not that big," Venture replied.

TINA's voice came through, seemingly from everywhere at once. *"The Gray Room is only three hundred feet square, but through integrated haptic and visual feedback, it can give the sensation of moving through a space ten times its size."*

Venture answered Emmett's question before he could ask it. "Stick around long enough and I'll show you how I developed them. For now, think of the tiles as holographic and spongy. One day, you might be fast enough to cross a thousand feet in a split second or leap to the top of a skyscraper—the Gray Room should be able to keep up with you until then. As long as you don't learn to fly. Flight is... *harder* to simulate."

Venture turned and walked back toward the door—the one small portion of the room that wasn't slick and white.

"What should I do?" Emmett asked.

Venture muttered something as he walked through the doors, but Emmett couldn't hear what it was. The doors hissed shut behind him and the metal turned into white tiles—

Leaving Emmett alone in the enormous white room.

He set the armful of mods down near where the door had been, and felt a little better having *some kind* of marker in the room.

Thankfully, TINA's voice echoed around him a moment later.

"Loading movement training, lesson two."

"No mods," Venture said, his voice seeming to come from everywhere, just like TINA's did.

Emmett looked around the Gray Room. He assumed Dr. Venture was in the training hub, looking at him through the viewing window, but Emmett couldn't see anything except featureless white walls all around him.

Venture added, "Let's see how you do getting around the city on your own."

The floor shuddered beneath his feet—so subtly that at first Emmett thought he imagined it.

Then tiles began to rise out of the floor.

Emmett watched as tiles rose and shifted, adjusting into walls and platforms. Some even wrapped around themselves, forming cylinders that became faux streetlights. They moved with eerie silence until segments *clicked* into place.

Emmett stood in the middle of the road, watching as a city block rose around him, complete with buildings, alleys, curbs—all of it clad in featureless white. The stretch of city reminded him of the edges of downtown Belport, filled with two and three-story buildings that he'd run across with Athena.

And when the room stopped moving and tiles stopped clicking, the entire room began to flicker like static on a screen. Moments later, the city block flooded with grayscale like a noir movie.

Emmett didn't wait for a signal; he started jogging across the street and toward the nearest alley, looking for a way up to the roofs.

He felt like he should be up high and off of the street.

Emmett ran down an alley, turned a corner, and climbed the first fire escape he found. Then he looked down on the grayscale room from the roof. It was an eerie sight, not just for lack of color; he knew there was something *off* about the skyline of the city and Emmett wasn't sure what. He could see clear across Belport, even see a drab version of the bay in the distance.

Maybe the horizon didn't move quite right—after all, the Gray Room was really only a few hundred feet per side.

He didn't have much time to dwell on it though, because someone else leapt onto the rooftop opposite of him.

At first, it looked like a man wearing a cross between high-tech armor and an old, bulbous diving suit, but the joints were far too thin for a person to be inside.

Dr. Venture said, "This is my training robot."

As Venture spoke, two things happened: The robot shifted color from dull gray to white, blue, black, red, and back to blue, and Venture's voice shifted until it came only from the robot.

"See if you can keep up," Venture said, and the robot waved exaggeratedly for Emmett to follow.

He did.

Even with the faux grayscale of the room and the weirdly silent steps of the blue robot just in front of him, Emmett quickly lost himself in the joy of his newfound powers. For the second time in two days, Emmett found himself racing across the rooftops of Belport.

He easily kept up with Venture's robot, even as it changed course—turning left, right, or completely around and running back the way they came.

"Not bad," Venture said.

"Easy," Emmett corrected. He wanted more.

Venture scoffed through the robot. "Very well."

The robot ran faster, weaving across the roof of a third story building while grayscale Belport stretched out around them.

Then it bolted—running toward downtown.

For the first time since using his newfound powers, Emmett felt his heart pump and his chest heave as he sprinted to catch up. His feet pounded and alleys passed beneath him in a blur as he hurtled from rooftop to rooftop.

The robot ran toward a four story building, the face of it stretching up another ten feet above them, and it leapt—

Practically exploded from the roof, soared clear up to the top, and disappeared over the edge.

Emmett was only a few steps behind and wasn't about to stop now.

Emmett ran to the edge and jumped, arms outstretched.

The side of the building passed in a blur and then he saw the top of the building—right before he slammed chest-first into the wall. Emmett gasped and clung desperately to the ledge of the roof.

He hung there a moment, catching his breath, while the blue robot stared at him from across the roof.

Emmett swore he heard Venture chuckle.

The robot crossed its arms. "From now on, you'll spend an equal amount of time in here training as you do working in the lab. You need to learn what your body is capable of so you know what risks you can take, who you can fight, and when you need to run."

Emmett nodded, then hauled himself over the ledge. The ease of it caught him off guard, and he stumbled as he stood.

"Again."

Chapter 15

Personal Touch

E mmett spent the next two hours chasing after the blue robot.

At first, Emmett had doubts about how much he would enjoy training in the Gray Room, but after the first few minutes Emmett had lost himself in the simulation and in the game—

Which was equal parts amazing and frustrating.

As awesome as it was hurtling across rooftops with superhuman speed, Emmett felt like a kid who'd just had the world's most enormous and awkward growth spurt. Several times he slipped when trying to turn or overstepped the edge of a roof and fell two stories to the gray street below.

It took him almost half the time just to work out that he could, in fact, leap up a full story from one rooftop to a higher one, but only if he remembered to slow down before he reached the edge. Otherwise, he would be moving too fast and slam into the side of the building.

After the full two hours, Emmett was leaping from one roof to the next, climbing and falling from different heights with a coordination that he'd never known.

During one of their breaks, Venture admitted that this was due to his new body—not only was he more coordinated than any unenhanced human, but his body would also learn and adapt much quicker.

The highlight was following the robot as it leapt off a fourth story building.

Emmett was only a few steps behind but skid to a halt. He peered over the edge of the roof in time to see the blue robot skid a few feet down the side of the wall before leaping across the alley and skidding down the opposite building. It did this once more, skidding and leaping to the opposite wall—each time slowing its descent until it landed in the alley below.

The robot looked up at Emmet, seemingly waiting for him to try.

Emmett breathed deep, took a few steps back, and leapt across the alley. He'd been so used to leaping clear across to the next roof that he slammed into the side of the building.

"Shit," Emmett muttered as he fell, gray tiles passing concerningly fast in front of his face.

He pushed off awkwardly, hurling himself back toward the original building and slammed shoulder-first into the wall.

By the time he turned and pushed off again, the floor was right below him.

Emmett managed to land feet-first, but tripped and careened into the ground. Again, the breath was knocked out of him and it was a moment before he tried to stand.

Flashes of that night came back to him—when he was laying in the middle of the street—feeling like he couldn't move.

Emmett grit his teeth. He wasn't there now. The floor was gray. He was in the Gray Room. *He wasn't there.*

He rolled over and forced himself to stand. Emmett's shoulder ached from landing on it, and his knees didn't feel great either, but he was still in one piece.

Better than he'd felt that night, dying in the street.

The blue robot nodded to him, and Venture said, "It will get easier."

Emmett stared at the robot, realizing that Venture wasn't just talking about running and jumping and relearning his body—Venture knew.

"I still think you're psychic," Emmett muttered.

"No. But I've seen enough trauma to know what it looks like. Emmett, this life will never be easy."

"I know," Emmett said, trying to put the conversation past him as quickly as possible. "Let's keep going."

"...Very well."

Emmett caught the robot five times in those two hours.

Two of those times he got lucky, and Emmett suspected that Venture let him catch up during the other two. One time, it felt like an honest win.

The last time, he followed the robot over the edge of a roof and fell on it as it tried sliding down the side of a building. Both of them had fallen the last two stories to the ground, Emmett landing on the robot in a twisted heap.

Emmett wished he would've just landed on the ground—landing on the robot hurt even worse. Whatever it was made of was not soft *at all*. And Emmett had landed on his one arm that was still flesh and bone.

Emmett rolled off of the robot and used the nearby alley wall to push himself up.

"That's enough for today," Dr. Venture said, his voice bleeding back into the open air.

"No," Emmett stammered. "I can keep going," he added, clutching his aching shoulder. And he still hadn't gotten to test out any modifications yet!

"We have work to do in the lab, and you're not a machine. You will still need ample time for rest and recovery."

The gray walls of the faux city descended, their tiles shrinking back into the floor with eerie clicks. A square opened in the floor and the blue robot also disappeared beneath the Gray Room.

Emmett watched, heart aching at the possibilities of his upcoming training.

When all but the highest gray roofs had disappeared, Emmett turned to find a single doorway opening across the room. He grabbed his unused pile of mods and exited, following the dimly lit hall back to the locker room, and changed before going to work.

Dr. Venture was waiting for him just down the hall in the training hub—standing on the white platform and removing the shin guards of the VR suit.

Emmett stared while Venture removed the last pieces and tidied them up on the wall.

"You were controlling the robot?"

"Not the entire time. The robot has several autonomous programs, but I felt like you needed a personal touch."

"Thanks, I think."

Clara's voice sounded through the intercom. "He means there isn't a beginner mode."

Emmett scoffed. "Nice of you to join us."

"I would have, but I've been over here setting up our experiment in section three."

Venture replied, "Point taken. We're on our way."

Emmett followed Dr. Venture out of the hub and down the hall, feeling like he'd missed something.

"Is she upset because we lost track of time?" he asked.

Venture grumbled. "Possibly."

Emmett knew enough to leave the topic alone.

Since learning that Dr. Venture was a retired cape, Emmett hadn't given much thought to the relationship between Venture and Clara—but he imagined there was a lot more going on than he thought. Was Clara following in the family tech business and the family cape business? What powers did she have?

Venture didn't offer any more insight, and Emmett didn't ask. They walked in silence through the halls, and Venture informed Emmett not to bother leaving his stuff in the locker room anymore; it wasn't necessary. Then they continued to the testing hub of section 003.

Clara was waiting for them, arms crossed and face wrinkled like she had tried to hide her impatience and given up halfway.

"So," Emmett said awkwardly, "where are we starting?"

When Clara didn't answer right away, Dr. Venture added, "Well?"

Clara turned and started walking toward the next hall. "We're set up in testing chamber two. I need help checking the heat sinks and connections."

Emmett looked to Dr. Venture, but he had already turned to one of the monitor screens and didn't say anything. So Emmett took that as his cue to follow Clara.

He jogged to catch up.

Once they were down the hall and out of earshot of the testing hub, Emmett asked, "Hey, is everything alright?"

Clara didn't respond—didn't even acknowledge his question.

Moments later, they emerged in testing chamber two, the large domed room with the spherical reactor in the center, wrapped in coils of glowing, purple refrigerant and layered in batteries.

Emmett followed Clara to the center of the room and paused to look over the experiment.

It looked exactly the same as the last set up, even down to the layout of the batteries. There had to be something different...

"Did you change the power output?" Emmett asked.

"Yes."

"Increased?"

"No," Clara replied. "Lower output, longer duration. Looking for higher overall stress tolerance."

As much as Emmett listened, he was watching Clara.

"Is everything alright?" he asked.

Clara turned and stared at him, face flush, as if the answer was obvious.

"Do you want to talk about it?"

"No. I need—I want—to get back to work."

"Alright," Emmett replied, slightly defeated. He'd never seen Clara irritated like this before...

And a part of him was worried he might've done something that caused it. He thought back to his earlier questions about Clara and her dad. Maybe their relationship wasn't what he thought: Maybe Clara didn't have powers after all.

Maybe Emmett had unwittingly stumbled between a retired cape and his pow-erless daughter. Emmett imagined that would do a number on both of them.

Emmett suppressed a sigh. Hopefully Clara just needed some time and she would talk later.

Clara did not want to talk later.

She seemed content to focus on the heat sink experiment.

If anything, 'focus' wasn't an intense enough word. Clara seemed captivated by it.

Emmett wasn't sure why and he was afraid to ask. He was also hesitant to ask why Dr. Venture had been silent throughout the four tests they ran.

Emmett imagined Venture was watching the experiments—he always did. But he didn't even chime in to celebrate the final test—not even when Clara herself finally seemed to cheer up.

They'd lowered the power output by 75% from their previous maximum out-put, but the heat sinks and battery overflow lasted seven times as long.

Emmett and Clara were standing in the broom closet, watching the final test wind down. Clara breathed a sigh of relief.

Emmett smiled. He resisted saying anything—he was just glad she was in better spirits.

"Does that mean we're celebrating with Big Larry's gourmet pizza again?" Emmett asked.

Clara chuckled. "No. I'm done. I'm going to sleep."

Clara said goodnight and then left Emmett standing in the closet with more questions than answers.

Not the least of which was: What was the missing system in the reactor, heat sink, and battery set up? What was it made to run?

Chapter 16

Wrong Side of Town

E mmett was about to walk out of the lab when Dr. Venture stopped him in the hallway outside of section 003.

Venture stood ominously in front of Emmett, blocking his path. "Before you go, we need to talk."

Emmett swallowed dryly, wondering if it was related to whatever was eating at Clara.

"You'll be allowed to train here with the understanding that you don't neglect your studies. Your work in the lab and your classes take priority. Heroics is a young person's game. You'll be retired and normal much longer than you'll be a cape or a mask."

Emmett sighed, slightly relieved to be hearing this speech instead of something more serious... but also slightly annoyed to be hearing *this* speech.

Emmett nodded, trying his best to keep a serious face. "Anything else?"

Dr. Venture pulled something from the inside pocket of his lab coat and tossed it to Emmett, who caught it.

A silky gray mask. The fabric felt thick and weighted to the touch, almost like it was filled with a thin layer of sand.

"If you're going to go running around the city, you should wear that. The fabric is specially made to alter your face shape so that you can't be identified through cameras.

"It's not foolproof," Venture continued. "You'll need to vary the routes you take to and from your apartment. Get a spare phone for emergencies and leave your normal one at home. Wear layers of generic clothes that you can ditch at a moment's notice. Your identity is one of the most precious things you have. Guard it."

Venture sighed and his eyes narrowed—somehow he looked even more serious than he already did.

"If you become an active mask, you'll need to keep your nose clean and keep to the Code. Don't give anyone a reason to follow you too closely. If you screw up too many times or too badly, capes or DSA will track you down. It's much easier for them to find you than it is to hide from them.

"And that will affect our relationship."

Venture's final words echoed and hung heavy in the hallway.

Emmett understood. It wasn't just his ass on the line—it meant that his actions could affect Dr. Venture and Clara, too. Not to mention his family.

Emmett rolled the mask over in his fingers, tracing the seams and the strange material. Now it felt even heavier in his hands.

He nodded.

Venture turned and walked away.

With the warning fresh in his mind, Emmett jogged down Champion street. He passed his normal bus stop and kept going, breathing deep and savoring the chill evening air.

The last of the sunset was red in the sky when Emmett made it to the West End and climbed the first fire escape he found.

Emmett stood on the roof, looking out over the city of Belport and deciding where to go. He'd make his way home eventually, but Emmett felt restless—

And without giving it too much thought, he started leaping across rooftops, heading south toward the bay.

Most of his time in college had been spent between the Eastside and West End. The former was where the majority of prominent companies had located their factories and warehouses—Gnosis being one of the biggest. The West End was made up of various middle income housing blocks, including Emmett's block in The Woods.

The North side of Champion street and Belport was exclusively upper income housing—the Heights. Coincidentally, the portion of Belport that Emmett was least familiar with.

But as Emmett leapt from rooftop to rooftop, running toward the bay, he couldn't actually remember the last time he'd actually been on the south side of town. The bay and the surrounding area of Belport were *touristy*—built up and gentrified over the last ten years. Pushing out almost all the lower income housing into stretches of slums that lined the highway.

He was crossing into one of those stretches now, passing above and perpendicular to the L train rails. Rows of graffiti covered, cramped apartments stretched up and down Eighteenth Street. Somewhere down the street, shouts were punctuated by a bottle shattering.

Emmett took one look across the street and realized that he wouldn't be able to just jump across—the highway was four lanes wide. He would have to climb down and cross on foot.

He took a deep breath and peered over the side. No fire escape... But the alley behind the building was empty.

Why not put his training to use?

Emmett took a few steps back and leapt off the roof. He sailed across and hit the side of the building, sliding down a few feet before springing across to the opposite wall and repeating the process.

It was a short drop, and moments later, Emmett was standing in the middle of the alley, savoring victory.

He pulled his hood up and set out toward Eighteenth Street, walking quickly and purposefully—mask still on.

He had to walk the block to get to a crosswalk. Nervousness bubbled up in him. Back in high school he'd went with his old friend Manny to the docks, then made the mistake of trying to cut through the slums so they could catch the bus back to the West Side—they didn't make it far before they got mugged, right there on Eighteenth. They wound up begging for change and calling Manny's parents from a payphone, back when those were still a thing.

It was hard not to think about that as Emmett walked down the street, trash crunching beneath his shoes. The L train rattled in the air as it passed.

Despite his nerves, Emmett couldn't help but look around. He passed boarded-up stores and others with barred windows and reinforced doors. Shouts echoed from a nearby apartment, and across Eighteenth a drunken brawl spilled out of a bar.

There were other people walking, minding their business, keeping their heads down, but most seemed completely unfazed by the commotion.

But there were two people that drew Emmett's eyes: Two men walked toward him wearing masks.

The one on the left was the taller and broader of the two—standing a head taller than Emmett and the other one. He wore a skull mask, and platinum blond hair hung out from behind it. His denim jacket was covered in patches and frayed ends.

The second was rail-thin and wore a dark green tracksuit and a matching mask.

For a moment, Emmett wondered if they were posing as supers. It was rare, but he'd read about it. Usually, it ended poorly for someone claiming to be a super when they really weren't.

But there was something about the way the two guys carried themselves that made Emmett *sure* that they weren't bluffing. Both of them were supers.

The stranger thing was that despite all Emmett's years living in the city, he'd never seen masks walk the street. Was that normal on this side of Belport?

Emmett did his best not to look at the two supers as they passed. And as far as he could tell, they didn't pay him any mind either.

Emmett stopped at the intersection and waited for the light to change before making his way across. Soon he'd be back on the rooftops and racing toward the bay.

Emmett slipped into the nearest unoccupied alley.

"Well, well, well, what do we have here..."

Emmett turned to find both of the masks staring at him from the alley entrance.

They walked toward him, the man in green walking just in front.

"Haven't seen you before," Green Mask said. "You lost boy?"

Emmett suppressed his urge to scoff at the comment and met the eyes behind the mask. Emmett felt a little more confident; Green Mask didn't sound any older than he was.

"Just passing through," Emmett replied.

The hulking man in the skull mask scoffed. "Lost *and* stupid."

"These are our streets," Green Mask said. "And you've taken up enough of my time. Toss me your wallet and then get the fuck out of here." He held out his hand expectantly.

Emmett stared them down, ignoring the sweat dripping down his neck. He could run or he could fight... And Emmett didn't particularly like his odds being outnumbered and facing two unknown supers.

Emmett slipped his hand into his pocket like he was reaching for his wallet—

Then he bolted down the alley.

A breath later, he'd leapt up to the fire escape and then leapt up again to the next roof.

Emmett sprinted across the roof, heading in the direction of the bay, but something slammed into him from the side and sent him sprawling across the tar.

He rolled to a stop and looked up to see Skull Mask standing across the roof.

"Did I say you could leave?"

Skull Mask sprinted across the roof—covering the distance in a blink. Emmett had assumed his enemy had some generic spread of super strength similar to what he had with Mutagen-A, but Skull Mask was on a whole other level—

It was everything Emmett could do to get his hands up in front to block the next attack.

Skull Mask pummeled him, and Emmett tucked his arms in close and backed away frantically. His head was knocked to the side, the wind knocked out of his chest—it didn't matter how he tried to guard himself, Skull Mask was punching *through* his blocks.

It didn't help that Emmett didn't know how to fight. He'd been in precisely one fight: On the playground in elementary school. For as strong and as fast as Emmett felt now, he had no idea what he was doing, and Skull Mask was stronger *and* faster than he was.

Emmett tried to swing back, but Skull Mask lunged for him, grabbing his arm and pushing him backward toward the edge of the roof.

He slid back until his foot caught on the outer ledge of the roof, and Emmett caught a glimpse of the alley below, gasping in panic. Emmett wrenched his arms down and pushed forward with all his strength.

With his feet against the ledge, he had enough leverage to push Skull Mask back several steps.

The two fighters paused, staring each other down.

Then Green Mask appeared from behind his ally.

"I didn't plan on working this evening," he said, holding out his arms out in front of him. Dark smoke rose from the roof and then rushed toward Emmett in a wave.

Emmett recoiled, his first thought that the tar of the roof was on fire. But as the smoke reached him, wisps of it coalesced into tendrils and then into hands, reaching toward him like ghouls climbing out of black waves.

He shivered and was already turning to run when the first hand reached him, grabbed his ankle, and held him in place. Emmett wrenched his leg, but it wouldn't budge.

More hands grabbed his left wrist, clutched his legs and waist, each ice cold to the touch.

Then something slammed into the side of his head, sending Emmett sprawling across the roof. His vision swam—the dark fog was everywhere, blotting out all but the black of the night sky directly above him.

Skull Mask strode out of the smoke, cracking his knuckles. He smirked and added, "It's almost not fair."

Emmett rolled to his feet, but icy hands seized him and held him in place—Everything but his right hand.

Skull Mask swung and Emmett tried to block, but he was fighting one handed. Punch after punch slammed into Emmett, and even the few that managed to get his right hand in front of still sent him reeling.

Every time he was knocked back, smoky hands grabbed him and held him still.

The next punch sent Emmett sprawling to the ground. Blood dripped onto the tar and Emmett's face and mask felt wet with it. Desperately, he rolled onto his back, trying to scooch away from his attacker—to the edge of the roof—anywhere else. Icy hands grabbed him and pulled him down as Skull Mask knelt down over him.

"Don't worry, rookie," he said. "I'm not going to kill you."

Emmett brought his right hand up in front of his face to defend himself.

From somewhere in the smoke, Green Mask said, "We got a stubborn one."

Skull Mask's face wrinkled in irritation. He hauled back and punched down at Emmett's face.

Emmett turned to the side, barely avoiding the next two swings.

Skull Mask grunted in frustration and grabbed for Emmett's neck, trying to choke him.

Emmett grabbed his wrist and squeezed.

The next thing he heard was Skull Mask scream in pain, followed by bone crunching—

Skull Mask's wrist snapped in his hand.

Emmett's eyes were almost as wide as his attacker's and it was several moments of struggle before Emmett realized what he'd done. All that time, he didn't let go.

Skull Mask was clutching his broken arm and trying to pull away, but he was still sitting on top of Emmett. Emmett pulled, using leverage against him. His mechanical arm won out easily, and a moment later, Emmett was holding Skull Mask by the throat.

Skull Mask pawed impotently at Emmett's arm and at Emmett's face, but he was clearly overcome with panic.

He wasn't sure how hard he could squeeze without breaking the guy's neck, but he wasn't about to let up.

Emmett sneered, "Let me go. Let me go. Now!"

A second later, the smoke vanished, and the rooftop slums of Belport came back into view.

"Alright, alright, man," Green Mask said. He stood across the roof, holding his hands up in surrender. "Don't do something you're gonna regret."

Emmett grit his teeth and pushed himself up, all the while not letting go of Skull Masks's throat. Blood dripped down the front of his hoodie. His whole body shook with adrenaline and rage.

Emmett hauled Skull Mask to his feet and glared at the two supers. Without thinking, Emmett shoved him toward Green Mask.

Skull Mask was hurled backward across the roof, skipping backward like a stone across a pond, and careened into Green Mask, taking them both over the side of the roof.

As surprised as Emmett was, he didn't stay. He ran and leapt to the next roof, running as fast as he could toward the bay.

He only made it two blocks.

Out of nowhere, a suit of armor materialized in the air. Hot streams of air billowed from the foot thrusters and across the roof, causing Emmett to step back. It hovered in front of him—humanoid, sleek, and matte gray.

Emmett stared at the newcomer, half in awe and half apprehensive. He doubted they were working with Skull Mask and Green Mask—but it would be a bad time to be wrong. Unconsciously, he squeezed his mechanical arm.

The figure lowered themselves to the rooftop and their thrusters cut off completely.

"You can relax," she said.

Even though her voice was slightly muffled and obscured by static, Emmett immediately knew who it was, and he almost collapsed with relief.

CHAPTER 17

Armor and Footsteps

"You can relax," she said again. "They're not coming after us."

Emmett had run another four blocks across the rooftops, and only stopped when they were definitively along the boardwalk and out of the slums.

Clara had flown beside him with her cloaking system engaged. During that time she'd shimmered like a mirage, but otherwise been completely invisible. When they finally stopped to rest, her suit shimmered and became its normal understated gray.

Futuristic was the best word Emmett could come up with to describe it. It looked like a fighter jet pared down and molded into a suit of armor. At the same time it was understated, walking a line between subtle and commanding—if it had any weapon systems loaded then they were hidden and hidden well.

It reminded him of the former cape, Arsenal, but then there were a dozen other big league tech-based heroes.

Emmett was so captivated by Clara's armor that he'd almost forgotten about his injuries.

Almost.

He was looking over her shoulder connections and helmet, when he reached up to scratch his chin and promptly winced at the pain.

"You look like shit," Clara said.

"Thanks," Emmett muttered.

"But nothing's broken and you don't have any internal bleeding."

"How can you be sure?"

Clara tapped her helmet. "There's a lot of tech crammed in here. The medical suite is one of the least impressive."

Emmett breathed deep to laugh and promptly winced at the pain in his ribs. He was torn between wanting to know absolutely everything about Clara and her armor, and wanting to pass out.

"You owe me an explanation," he finally said. "You know that, right?"

Clara snorted. "I had a bet with Dad what you would do first: Ask questions or ask me to fly you home."

Emmett smiled. The moon was hanging full in the sky and reflecting in the calm water of the bay. It was a beautiful night...

But Emmett wanted to go home.

"How about you walk me home?"

Clara reached for the side of her armor and a small compartment clicked open. She pulled something tiny out and tossed it to him. An earpiece.

"Wear that, and we can talk. I'll be in stealth mode, right beside you."

Emmett put on the earpiece and marveled at how it seemed to shrink and conform so it fit flush to his ear.

Then Clara's armor shimmered and vanished. Emmett felt a gust of heat as she took off from the roof, but even that seemed muted.

Emmett started jogging parallel to the bay, heading west.

Occasionally, he thought he heard the muffled sound of her thrusters, but no matter how many times he glanced over his shoulder, Emmett didn't see Clara's armor.

Clara's voice came through the earpiece. "Do me a favor and keep your eyes on the city. Less chance of you giving away my position."

Emmett scoffed. He couldn't even figure out where she was—

But maybe other supers could.

Emmett kept his eye on the city.

"So, what questions do you have?" she asked.

Emmett leapt from one roof to another, stuttering on his landing from the dull pain that seemed to travel through his whole body.

"You're... You're not mad at me, are you?"

"No!" she said quickly. "Why would you think that?"

"Well, you seemed like something was bugging you in the lab today. I thought maybe I spent too much time in the Gray Room training. You said nothing was wrong, but then you let those two supers kick the shit out of me. So, I thought maybe you were mad after all."

Clara chuckled in his earpiece. "I was in the neighborhood when I got the alert that you were in combat. By the time I got there, you already had the bruiser by the throat. You were fine.

"But you're right. I was short with you. I've, uh, been burning the candle at both ends, between patrolling the city and keeping up with Dad's research."

Even though Clara sounded upbeat, she sounded as tired as he felt.

"That's where you were yesterday? You know," he said, "your dad would probably give you a break if you asked for one."

"Yeah... he would. And that's why I can't. Dad needs a break more than I do."

Emmett frowned. In that regard, Clara sounded just like his mom—always taking care of others and not taking enough care of herself.

Clara continued, "It's not like I can take a break, anyways... Someone has to teach you how to fight."

"Was it that bad?"

"From what I saw... Yes."

Emmett chuckled awkwardly. "Good thing I have *two teachers* then."

He paused at the edge of the next roof to consider how he would cross Eighteenth Street. Emmett wasn't exactly keen on climbing down and walking across the street again, seeing what happened last time.

Clara must have seen his face.

"Don't worry," she said. There's not another super for three blocks. Back of the alley is clear."

Emmett nodded, then went to the backside of the building and leapt down to the alley. His legs spasmed when he landed, and he sucked a breath in through his teeth.

"Don't suppose you've got an extra suit of armor I can use for next time?"

"Do you really think we have these just lying around? Because we do, but none that will fit you comfortably."

Emmett chuckled, stuffed his hands in his pocket, kept his head down, and crossed Eighteenth as inconspicuously as he could. If nobody looked directly at him, maybe they wouldn't notice the blood that caked the front of his hoodie.

"How about an extra hoodie?" Emmett asked.

"Did Dad give you the talk about having extra clothes?"

"Yep."

Emmett headed toward the nearest alley and jumped up to reach the fire escape, gritting his teeth as he hauled himself over the bars.

The clangs of the bars startled a couple making out at the end of the alley, and they quickly left.

"Woops," Emmett muttered.

Moments later, he was at the top and running across the roofs toward the West End.

"So are you going to tell me why you feel like you can't take a break? Are you trying to live up to your dad or something?"

"...Sure. Let's go with that."

Emmett scoffed a laugh. "You couldn't sound more unconvincing if you tried."

Clara didn't answer, and Emmett was left alone with the sound of his feet pounding on the roof.

"That *is* part of it," she finally said. "Dad wasn't just any cape."

"Still not going to say which?"

"Not out here."

Emmett's pace faltered, and he suddenly felt much more self-conscious about their conversation.

"Worried about someone eavesdropping?"

Clara snorted a laugh. "There are supers that can hear a pin drop across the city, see in UV, and read minds. Yes. I'm always worried about someone eavesdropping, and you should be too."

"Fair enough."

"But Dad and I are artificers. That part should be obvious from the armor... We don't have super strength or psychic power. My dad made almost all of his tech—quite literally made himself the cape that he was.

"A large portion of supers inherit their powers from their parents, but it's a different story for artificers. We're not limited by inheritance from our parents, or our strength or psychic power. We're just limited by what we can create.

"That's what I have to follow. That's what I have to live up to."

Emmett listened intently—relating without completely understanding.

Up until that point, he thought it had been rough enough that his parents wanted him to graduate college so that he would have more opportunities than they had. He couldn't imagine what it would be like if one or both of them had been capes and he was living in their shadow.

Now, on top of all that, she was going to teach Emmett to fight too?

Not that he wasn't grateful—Emmett would take all the help he could get.

When silence had settled between them, Emmett added, "Let me know if there's anything I can do to help."

"I appreciate it. For now, just focus on keeping up."

Emmett stopped near Hosta Street on the West End. He would climb down from the roof and walk the rest of the way.

He pulled off his blood-soaked mask and took up his blood-stained hoodie. He'd bunch them up and carry them under his arm.

Emmett turned to a random spot in the sky and asked, "How do I look?" He smiled, sure that he had blood in his mouth.

Clara's voice came through the earpiece. "Better, but take some spit and wipe your face. Otherwise, people are going to think you're an axe-murderer. ...On second thought, just wipe your face because your mouth is still bleeding."

Emmett chuckled and smiled for real. "Thanks for walking me home."

"Don't mention it."

There was the slightest gust of warm air telling Emmett that Clara had flown off.

Even though Emmett knew he wouldn't see her, he searched the sky anyway. A few seconds later, he gave up and climbed down from the roof to finish his walk home.

Emmett kept his head down as he reached the Woods. Thankfully, there were only a few students out on the lawn and Emmett didn't catch anyone staring at him as he passed. He didn't relax until he got to his apartment.

A wave of exhaustion overcame him as he opened the door—

Followed promptly by dread.

Emmett stood in the doorway, waiting to hear if Lock was home. It hadn't even crossed his mind to think of an excuse to tell Lock.

But Emmett didn't hear anything. He shut the door behind him and crept toward the bathroom.

The apartment was empty. Lock's room was empty.

Emmett heaved a sigh of relief and set to cleaning himself up in the bathroom. He stripped his hoodie and shirt off and tried not to dwell on the bruises that covered his ribs. Then he wiped the blood off his neck and face and found his right eye was swollen and blue.

"Shit," Emmett muttered.

He went and grabbed an ice pack from the freezer and popped a pain reliever, hoping the swelling would go down by morning.

Then he shut his door, crawled into bed, and promptly passed out.

Chapter 18

Give Me a Reason

Emmett spent most of Wednesday's classes alternating between trying to concentrate and staring at the clock on the wall, watching it tick away—

Waiting for his time at the lab—

Waiting until he could train in the Gray Room.

Waiting.

Waiting.

By the time his Machine Design Class let out that afternoon, Emmett was tempted to sprint to the lab.

Instead, he rode the bus.

Emmett wasn't supposed to draw attention to himself. At first, he assumed that just meant varying his routes across the rooftops, but there was more to it than that. Emmett couldn't just stop taking the bus home, just like he couldn't just stop going to class.

So, somewhat begrudgingly, Emmett boarded the afternoon bus toward Eastside and sat in an empty row.

Emmett tried to get comfortable but his heart was pounding and his hands were clammy—

It had been the same every time he'd taken the bus this week. Ever since that night.

He pulled up his playlist of Lime Profond and put in his headphones, focusing on taking deep breaths and on the steady hum of the wheels and the engine of the bus.

Dr. Venture had been right: It wasn't going to be a quick process to get over that night.

You almost died, Venture said. *Go easy on yourself.*

After a few minutes of concentration, Emmett pulled out his phone and pulled up the forums—something to take his mind off how he felt.

Besides, he did miss keeping up with the news, and it was hard to scroll or listen to something while running across the rooftops of Belport.

Most of the forums were hit or miss, but Emmett paused at the stories that were either corroborated by mainstream news or expansions on those articles:

Vicious Battle between Long-Time Rivals Tryptarch and Vincent Black.

One-Two Punch of Embezzlement and Security Breach for Gnosis Corporation. A list of villains and masks followed that had possible connections to Gnosis.

War between Shian and Catalina Escalates with Threats of Nukes and Supers.

Gruesome Vampire Attack in Midtown Wardenton. Public Demands Retribution. An anonymous poster linked evidence that members of the city planning committee have ties to the Felwardens and the Cabal of Jesiré, speculating that the wardens and the cabal are in breach of the ancient pact.

Tremors in Deep Sea Trench Believed to be Harmless.

Disgraced Cape, Porcelain, Wanted in Connection with Champion Street Attack.

Emmett's stomach dropped. He clicked on the link, reading the scant update about the accident—his accident:

Former Cape, Porcelain, also known as Christine Daws, is wanted for questioning in connection to last Tuesday's attack that left a wake of destruction across Belport's downtown, injured sixty-three, and killed five. Porcelain was caught on camera, fleeing the scene. The other three supers have not been identified. The Division of Superhuman Affairs asks for anyone with information to come forward. All four supers are approximately Class 2 and 3, and are considered extremely dangerous.

Emmett had never heard of her before—this wasn't surprising, though. Only the most powerful supers were household names, and very few supers seemed to want 'celebrity' status. So a lot of Class 3 and under supers flew under the radar.

Emmett probably knew more low-level supers than most people did, but he had really only categorized supers in his own city of Belport. There were thousands of other supers—probably millions—spread out across the globe.

The last thing that caught his eye was that the article was from two days ago.

Did Venture know? Did Clara? When were they going to tell him?

Emmett immediately began searching for information on Porcelain. The DSA's website was a good place to start.

At the top of her page, it showed several pictures of Porcelain during her time with the Summit of Heroes. She wore a white mask and bodysuit that covered her entire body, making her look like a bald white mannequin.

Porcelain – Christine Daws. 28 years old. Former Registered Cape with 7 years' service. Dishonorable Discharge.

Current Designation: Active Villain. Power Designation Class 2.3:

Class 2.0 – Multiple powers with high destructive potential, requiring multiple superhumans to respond.

Class 2.3 – Abilities listed above, including negation powers, requiring special consideration or a coordinated team of responders.

Powers include Self-Duplication. Versatile Energy Manipulation, Limited Reality Manipulation.

Current Location: Unknown.

Emmett scrolled through the rest of the meager information, searching for any other pertinent information. Her last known whereabouts were from two years ago and across the country. Her former nemeses were deceased or retired, and no accomplices were listed.

Then again, the DSA's website wasn't exactly the best source of information—

The forums were.

Emmett was about to scroll the forums when the driver announced his bus stop.

Emmett sighed and reluctantly pocketed his phone.

Maybe there was an even better source of information...

Emmett descended the stairs of the lab, shoes echoing on the concrete.

"Dr. Venture is waiting for you in section five," TINA said.

Between the excitement of heading to the Gray Room and his questions about Porcelain, Emmett felt his heart skip a beat.

Emmett didn't waste any time changing into his bodysuit and heading to the training hub. Dr. Venture and Clara were talking around the holographic table. They stopped when he came in.

"So," Venture started, folding his arms across his chest, "you made some new friends last night."

Emmett should've realized that Dr. Venture would bring it up. He rubbed the back of his neck. "About that... I was just going to the bay."

Venture frowned but didn't say anything. Clara shrugged as if to say something between *sorry* and *better you than me.*

"At least you had your mask on," Venture finally said. "I expect you to work extra hard today."

"I... I have a question first."

Both Venture and Clara turned toward him.

"Why didn't you tell me about Porcelain?"

Clara turned and looked at her dad as if she didn't know what Emmett was talking about.

Venture pushed up his glasses. "I wasn't going to—*not yet.*"

"Why not?"

"What would you do?" Venture asked plainly.

"Track her down. Question her. Find out why she was there that night and who else was with her."

Venture nodded. "I should've expected that you would want to... We're keeping a lookout for her. When we find her, Clara will be the one to make contact."

"Okay. I'll hang back then."

"You won't be going," Venture replied.

Clara smiled, a small and reluctant gesture, like she'd known exactly what her father was going to say.

Emmett scoffed. "I won't get in the way."

Venture's eyes and voice were firm. "You won't be going."

Emmett's eyes fell to the floor and he clenched his fist in frustration.

Venture continued, "Even if you were at a proficient level of training, it would be too dangerous and too personal—"

"What if I get to that level?" Emmett asked, meeting Venture's eyes. He didn't look away.

Venture's glare softened, then he gestured over his shoulder to the Gray Room. "Give me a reason to consider your request."

Emmett stood at the edge of the Gray Room as white tiles rose from the floor and created an approximation of Belport.

Two blue robots stood beside him—both identical.

Before he'd left the training hub, a second white platform and second set of VR gear had emerged from a hidden compartment. Both Dr. Venture and Clara were hooked in and controlling their own robot.

TINA's voice echoed through the room. *"Loading combat training, lesson two."*

"Nervous?" Clara asked.

Emmett nodded. He'd been trying not to think about it.

"Watch and listen," Venture said as both robots stepped forward and faced each other.

"Lesson two is all about basic combat training. You'll recognize some of it as a mix of introductory boxing, as well as basic martial arts striking and grappling techniques. These are staples for a reason, and at your current power level, they are the techniques that will serve you best. Most new and Class one supers neglect the basics. At lower power levels, technique is an equalizer."

Clara added, "But don't get cocky. Technique will only help so much."

Dr. Venture cleared his throat. "Let's begin."

For the next two hours, Venture and Clara alternated between demonstrating and running Emmett through drills:

How to throw a punch and a kick were both relatively simple. Within the first few, he realized the importance of recovering quickly to a guard position—after Clara punched him across the chin with a robotic fist.

In the first few minutes, Emmett realized that his body wasn't just stronger and faster than before. His coordination was also noticeably better. He'd never been a gifted athlete, but he already felt like he—or rather his body—had a solid grasp on the fundamentals.

When Emmett asked about this, Venture confirmed that Mutagen-A enhanced 'muscle memory' and large-scale locomotion. It would not, however, help much with fine motor movements—he wouldn't learn the guitar any quicker than before.

Funnily enough, for as strong and as fast as Emmett felt, he noticed that his flexibility didn't seem any better.

Venture said, "Mutagen-A won't help with that." The way he said it made Emmett think that there were other Mutagen compounds that did different things, but the thought was quickly pushed aside by Clara's flurry of punches.

Clara added, "Don't bother with high kicks. Keep them below the waist or for defending yourself when you're on the ground."

Grappling was next:

Venture said, "Grappling has all to do with leverage and your center of gravity."

Venture demonstrated this by showing various shoves, hip throws, trips, and take-downs on Clara's robot—then demonstrating the same moves on Emmett so that he could see how they felt.

Only then did Emmett get to try the moves out for himself—

And began to realize that they felt *weird*—like their weight was changing in the air.

Emmett paused after the third hip throw. "It doesn't feel right when I pick you up. It's like the robot gets lighter all of a sudden."

Ventured replied, *"That* is the first reason why combat between supers is fundamentally different from normal fighting: Much of the advantage of enhanced strength relies on leverage. Keep your feet planted firmly on the ground, and you maintain your strength. But if someone picks you up off your feet, you lose almost every benefit.

"What's more, you weigh 183 pounds and 4 ounces. Regardless of your strength, once you're off your feet you will be thrown around as if you weigh 183 pounds and 4 ounces."

Emmett thought back to fighting the two masks on the roof of the slums. Emmett had managed to shove Skull Mask so hard he tumbled off the roof—even though the guy easily outweighed him.

Then again, he'd used his mechanical arm to do it.

Emmett looked down at his right hand and squeezed, trying to feel the metal and composite flexing beneath the skin.

Again, the feeling of being powerless came back to him. He should've died on Champion street, and even though Skull Mask said he wouldn't kill Emmett, it sure felt like he was going to. The Code hadn't felt like much protection, at all.

He'd nearly died twice in a week!

He was sick of feeling powerless. Sick of being at the mercy of other supers.

Emmett made himself a promise: He would learn to fight and defend himself. Learn how to make his body and arm better and stronger. He would do whatever it takes, and he wouldn't stop until he didn't feel powerless again.

Chapter 19

Time to Spare

After two hours of combat training, the chest cavity of Dr. Venture's robot opened, and it pulled out the long gray whip.

Emmett's eyes widened. He'd been so preoccupied with training that he'd forgotten about his mods.

The robot walked over to Emmett and held out the whip.

"How do I, uh…"

"Hold out your right arm." Thin, wiry fingers slid out of the robot's fist as it reached for him.

Emmett kept his arm as still as he could, despite the cold touch of the metal and the tiny pinches that felt like static electricity as it touched his skin.

A moment later, the skin on the inside of his forearm bulged in the shape of a cylinder, and then slid open—the extra skin sliding over the back of his forearm like two panes of glass.

Emmett shivered.

Ever since the accident, his right arm had felt almost exactly the same as his real one—it moved the same as a real arm, felt pressure and pain the same as a real arm. Only a handful of times had he remembered that it was, in fact, mechanical. Even then, he couldn't *feel* a difference. It was only when he poked at the compartments and felt the shape beneath the 'skin' was different that he really knew.

But now, staring at a cylindrical, flesh-colored gap in his forearm, it was like his mind couldn't process what was happening. *It felt like a hole*—like a missing tooth.

"You'll get used to it," Dr. Venture said. "...I think."

Emmett chuckled awkwardly. "So, you don't have any mechanical limbs with weapon storage in them?"

"No. Now watch carefully, and hold still. This is how you secure a modification in your arm."

The robot pressed the end of the whip into the gap and toward a bundle of connections toward the elbow. With a quick twist, the base of the whip *clicked* into place.

Immediately, Emmett felt the whip—not just where it connected to his forearm, but felt the entire length of it as if it was an extension of his arm.

It felt like an extra finger.

"Holy shit," Emmett muttered.

His hand jerked slightly, and the end of the whip twitched.

Emmett moved each of his fingers, one by one, and watched as the end of the whip twitched slightly each time.

Dr. Venture said, "Try holding the whip and then moving it. The whip is made of similar materials to your arm and so it will be strong enough for any Class one or Class two super you engage with, but holding it will prevent extra stress on the connections.

"In addition, it will take time for your brain and nerves to adjust to any new modification. Holding the whip will help your brain shunt attention from your hand to the whip so it can divert more attention to the modification. One day you'll be adapted enough that you'll be able to move it like an extra arm or nimble enough for it to be an extra hand, but holding the whip will help you in the meantime."

While Dr. Venture talked, Emmett did as he suggested, gripping the 'handle' of the whip and trying to move it around again. Immediately, he felt a difference.

It felt like an arm that had woken up from numbness after being laid on the wrong way. Emmett could feel the individual linkages like bones and could curl the whip around into coils and S's. He curled the end of it so that the whip rose into the air until the tip of it looked him in the eye like a snake.

Emmett smirked, giddier than he'd been in years—than all his time working for Dr. Venture.

"How do I—"

Emmett had been about to ask how to fold the whip and hide it in his forearm, but he didn't have time to get the question out.

The whip began retracting—each link shrinking back into the one before it like a collapsible pole. Emmett watched as the fifteen foot whip condensed to just under a foot long and then slipped into the gap in his forearm. The covering of skin slid back into place a moment later.

The entire process took just under two seconds.

"Wow," was all Emmett could manage. He looked his forearm over in disbelief.

It had gone back to that eerie feeling of normalcy—except for the miniscule feeling of extra weight in his forearm, like he was wearing a watch or a wrist brace.

Venture added, "The extending and retracting the whip should get faster and easier too as your body gets used to it."

Mentally, Emmett commanded the whip to extend, and the process reversed itself—the whip uncoiled link by link until it was lying on the street of the Gray Room again.

"So, uh, can I test it out yet?" Emmett asked, trying not to seem overly eager. Meanwhile, the end of the whip twitched with anticipation.

"You and Clara will test it. Start with movement drills. I'll be back later." A square opened up in the tiles and swallowed Venture's robot.

After Dr. Venture and his robot left the Gray Room, Emmett turned and found Clara's robot looking at him expectantly.

Emmett's whip twitched—mirroring his own eagerness. "So what's it going to be?" he asked. "Combat training? Movement training?"

"How are you feeling?" she asked.

Emmett paused and shrugged. "Alright enough, I guess."

Clara's blue robot stared at him for a long moment, and Emmett felt like she was reading into what he said—which was odd because all he saw staring at him was a featureless blue face.

Clara added, "Because you went from looking like you were having a flashback to wearing that same brutal determination you had when you were choking out Zanté on the roof."

Emmett stared at her in disbelief and confusion. "Oh, that was Skull Masks's name?"

"Yep."

"Oh..."

"You didn't bother to look him up?"

Emmett shrugged again. "I was hoping I wouldn't run into him again."

Again, he felt Clara staring at him, and Emmett wished he could see her face instead of the expressionless robot.

Emmett told her as much.

"You couldn't keep up with me," she replied.

"You mean your suit..."

"Besides," she continued, ignoring him, "we're going to run into them again. Dad thinks he has a lead in the Champion street attack."

Emmett's eyes widened. "Go on. I'm listening."

The robot shook its head. "Dad thinks we have time to spare. First, you need to finish movement training and combat training."

Emmett groaned. She was right. Venture was right—and Emmett had no desire to get beaten two times in a row by the same supers.

But he wasn't happy about waiting. The end of the whip twitched, mirroring his internal struggle.

"Fine," Emmett said through his teeth. "What's next?"

"Loading movement training, lesson three," TINA said.

Clara added, "Let's work on moving around the city using your whip. Honestly, of all the tools Dad scrounged up for you, it will wind up being the most versatile. It's also going to take that much more practice to get used to."

Clara's robot ran across the white-tile street and leapt two stories up to the top of the nearest building. Then she waited expectantly for him.

Emmett retracted the whip and then extended it again, feeling like he was flexing and stretching the limb—like he was limbering up.

He ran toward the closest single story building, and when Emmett was close, he jumped and extended the whip—a motion halfway between throwing a ball and shot-putting it. The whip hurled upward like a spring, stretching to its limit as the end sailed over the top of the building.

It curled around the lip of the building and felt like Emmett was grabbing on with his fingertips.

He stood there, staring up with satisfaction, before wondering what he was supposed to do next.

Emmett tried retracting the whip, hoping that it would pull him up, but he could feel the mechanisms inside the modification resisting—it was a whip, not a grappling hook.

So Emmett tried climbing up by gripping the whip and 'walking' up the side of the wall—

The whip lost its grip on the roof, and Emmett fell on his back.

Clara snickered from the rooftop. "Just haul yourself up. You have super strength, remember?"

Emmett sighed and stood. He threw the whip up again and grabbed the edge. This time he pulled with both hands and hurled himself up to the rooftop. Then he turned and looked back down at the floor in disbelief.

"You're still only 183 pounds, remember?" Clara said. "It's a lot easier to do a pullup now."

Emmett nodded, still processing the information. In his best shape, he'd been able to do precisely two pullups. Now he could do them one-handed.

"That's better," she said. "Now, let's see if you can keep up."

Emmett spent the next hour chasing Clara's robot around the Gray Room. And it quickly became clear that Dr. Venture had been toying with him the last time they trained.

He didn't catch Clara—not once. Not even by accident.

As they ran and leapt across the faux city, Emmett slowly got more proficient with his whip, which in turn forced him to learn even better coordination with his body. Soon he was leaping two stories upward at a time, leaping up one story and using his whip to grab another fifteen feet up.

He practiced leaping from windowsill to windowsill by his fingertips and even managed to use his whip to do the same. The end of it was amazingly strong and versatile in that regard, being able to contort itself to grab the slimmest of ledges and nooks.

Emmett also revisited leaping back and forth between the sides of the buildings in an alley, skidding down the walls to slow his descent. By the end of the afternoon's practice, he was confident enough that he could leap off the roof of a ten story building and land safely—provided there were two buildings for him to slide down.

Even though Emmett never caught Clara's robot, her mood seemed to improve as the afternoon went on, and before long she was cracking jokes—mostly at his expense.

When he fell—"The ground won that one."

When he slammed into the side of a building—"You're not supposed to use your face."

Others were more generic, like "Good thing you're smart."

Eventually Emmett was laughing too.

Training with Clara was the best time he'd had in a long time.

But then Clara's robot stopped suddenly on the roof of a three-story building, and Venture's voice sounded through the room.

"That's enough for today. Emmett, meet us in the training hub."

Emmett retracted his whip. Then he jogged out of the Gray Room while the grayscale representation of Belport and the Clara's robot disappeared behind him.

Dr. Venture and Clara were waiting for him in the training room.

Clara gave Emmett a small smile as he entered. Venture didn't.

"That's enough for today," Venture said, hands clasped behind his back and eyes hard.

Emmett wanted to argue. He was sore, sure—every muscle in his body felt like it had a hot coal buried in it, but he could've kept going. He *wanted* to keep going.

But all Emmett could think to say was, "I'm not that sore."

At that, Venture smirked, quick and fleeting. "It might not feel like it, but your new body needs rest and sleep—almost as much as your old one did. Your muscles will recover faster and your coordination will improve faster too.

"Go home, rest, and take care of the classwork you've been neglecting. Doctor's orders."

CHAPTER 20

Venture

D r. Venture rubbed his eyes and adjusted his glasses.

He'd been watching Clara and Emmett train—

Clara and Emmett.

Venture still wasn't sure if he was okay with that. Then again, there was still a chance he was getting worried over nothing. A few years ago, Clara had confided in him that she was gay, and Venture had never heard anything to confirm Emmett's interests—

Aside from that text message from *Lock.*

Venture sighed and pushed it out of his mind. At the end of the day, it wasn't *his* business—Narine would have reminded him of that. Smugly.

Instead, Venture had muted their incoming comms and focused on assessing Emmett's progress visually while monitoring the Mutagen-A in his body.

In the training hub, Venture was surrounded by monitors and readouts, and he practically drank in the information. After all, he'd had decades of practice parsing mountains of data.

He had a 'knack' for it—a term for minor powers.

There was still speculation on whether knacks could technically be classified as powers in the normal sense. Most knacks were extremely niché and not useful for combat, and so knacks went unnoticed by all except the most discerning supers and catalogers.

Emmett's body was responding beautifully to the initial dose of Mutagen-A. Virtually every aspect of his physiology had been affected, and he was well beyond what a peak athlete could do.

Emmett was firmly a Class 1 super, one with minor superhuman capabilities. Now, even with only two days of training, he could probably be classified as Class 1-1. If he applied all the modifications to his arm that he was able to, Emmett could very well rank in Class 1-2.

If he was crafty enough with all his different enhancements, he might even be able to *punch up* a weight class. Technically, that would make him Class 1-3, even if negation powers were normally required for Special Designation -3; it wasn't normally so much the idea of punching up as it was *dragging your opponent down to your level.*

And then there was the possibility of going even further...

If Emmett's body bonded so readily with Mutagen-A, then he might very well find himself in one of Gnosis's many programs, skirting the limits of what human biology was capable of.

Then again...

Venture's prosthesis technology had turned a proverbial corner. It had connected far better to Emmett's nervous system than any other system Venture had conceived of. Emmett's arm could, quite literally, rewrite what was possible with prosthetics and weapons systems—

Imagine: Weapons platforms controlled at the speed of thought.

Venture chuckled to himself as he watched Emmett and Clara silently leap across the Gray Room. On the other screens, readouts showed internal stress forces, protein acclimation, neurochemistry and electrical potential, and dozens of other measurements in real-time.

It was all nominal.

Emmett had a promising chance ahead of him, assuming he didn't get mixed up with the wrong supers—a mask like Athena, for instance.

She was a capable Class 3 super. One who'd been offered registration three times and turned it down three times. No one turned down being a cape. In all likelihood, she was hiding something. The question was just how damning the secret was.

And why Emmett hadn't mentioned Athena yet.

So far, she was a harmless contact for Emmett, but Venture would keep an eye on them...

What really mattered now was Emmett: What he decided to do, and, more importantly, how far he decided to go.

Assuming his body continued reacting well to successive mutagens, Gnosis could take him all the way to Class 3, that much had been documented and leaked.

But Gnosis might be able to take Emmett even further. Venture long suspected there was research that was secured so well that even he couldn't access it. Who knew how powerful their other test subjects really were.

Then again, Venture was certain that no matter how strong Emmett's biological body got, he could make an arm to match it. In fact, Venture wagered that his tech would always beat out biology.

After all, only a handful of supers from their planet had stood toe-to-toe with Venture's best sets of armor.

Venture focused on Emmett as he chased Clara's robot across the faux rooftops. The young man was shrewd and hungry. Who was to say that he would stop with biology?

It was a morbid thought, but what if Emmett saw the eventual limits of his biology—even the Mutagens—and decided to start becoming more mechanical?

What if, indeed.

Venture rubbed his temples again, his eyes aching from staring at screens all day, and not helped by his old corneal implants.

Even Venture had added or swapped out parts of himself for technology. He hadn't been able to say no... but at least he'd been able to stop.

What would Emmett do?

The young engineer had found himself in a crossroads of potential, and Dr. Venture couldn't wait to see what direction he went.

Eventually, Dr. Venture pried himself away from the screens and walked toward section 003. His excitement for Emmett could wait; he still had to test adjustments on the heat sinks for Clara's armor.

That was the much more pressing concern.

Venture walked through the halls of section 003 and entered the secure storage wing. The heavy metal doors slid open with a familiar hiss—

Something only he would recognize.

Each door in his lab was similar enough, all made by a long-defunct subcontractor of the Summit of Heroes, but each door had its own particular tone and cadence. Nothing more than slight nuances of manufacturing, but they were there if you knew what to listen for.

Ever since Clara's powers emerged, Venture had spent more and more time in this particular part of section 003.

His wife, Narine, had wanted to see the world when they retired from the Summit of Heroes. Venture had agreed, somewhat reluctantly.

He was a cape, damnit. Why should he give that up? It's what he was born to do. He relished the fights, the close calls, helping civilians—all of it. He relished it and needed it...

But by the time retirement was close, Venture was beyond tired. It was more like physical, mental, and existential exhaustion. He was ready to give it all up and travel with her.

Maybe traveling would cure the rift that had been building between them. Maybe it would give Venture and Narine a chance to reconnect and fall for each other all over again.

Venture's quiet resignation had smoldered.

Both he and Narine were excited.

In the secure storage wing, Dr. Venture walked past holographic displays of armor components—some that had originated in his own power armor, and many more iterations of designs for his daughter's suit. Each cast the room in dismal grays.

"TINA, show me the most recent successful test combined with Clara's newest armor. Highlight for compatibility and display necessary changes."

The colors of the holographic displays changed. Incompatible armor glowed red—as expected, that was most of the room. A handful of pieces stayed gray;

those would be suitable, but not ideal. Only a handful of components glowed blue, like gems in a sea of red—

Like a path laid out for him.

Four components that were compatible with the new heat sinks. Another dozen gray components that were adequate, for now. He would adjust them later.

For every choice we think we have, there's really only one optimal path. One correct path.

In time, Clara would see that. Just as Emmett would. Just as Venture himself had seen it.

Instead of rearranging the displays, Venture walked to each of the blue components individually:

Thrusters and weapons systems were well within operating loads, so long as Clara wasn't too heavy-handed with power output. The new heat sinks and regulators would help with that.

Most of the armor layers themselves were also compatible—ballistics, pressure shielding, integrated medical system, and, of course, heat shields. The joints and all the necessary actuators and polymers were fine as well—the armor's strength, speed, and augmented reaction time.

Finally, Venture passed the fine instrumentation systems—sensor arrays, mapping, and targeting systems. The onboard medical system was unaffected, but then it was one of the most reinforced to begin with.

It was different from the armor he had worn. In so many ways, it was better—it had to be because anything less couldn't handle her power.

Venture stopped in front of the strings of heat sinks. The hologram hung in the air like dead lights without a tree to hang on. So understated... and this was the piece that her entire armor hung on.

No matter how Clara's power developed, Venture would find a way to improve her armor and keep her safe.

All he had to do was listen to the data.

Data never lied.

CHAPTER 21

Lock

Lachlan jogged the West End streets of Belport, concentrating on the steady rhythm of his shoes on the pavement.

He went right past Gnosis's sprawling concrete headquarters, not stopping until he reached a set of unmarked buildings on the far end. To the uninformed, the warehouses probably looked like storage.

Lock jogged between warehouses until he came to a secret doorway on the outer wall. Hidden sensors scanned his tracking chip, and the door slid open for him.

Three guards greeted him, each wearing black unmarked uniforms. Lock felt the almost imperceptible touch of a psychic as they read his surface level thoughts but it was impossible to guess which of the guards was responsible.

It didn't really matter.

It had been six or seven months since they'd brought Lock in through the main gate. Since then, it had been back alleys and secret entrances.

And other things.

They escorted Lock down a darkened set of stairs to the laboratory beneath Gnosis. All the while, Lock tried not to think about how much the entire Gnosis underground reminded him of a horror film:

Pitted concrete walls, dim and flickering lights, smells of must, dried blood, and bleach. No matter how much Gnosis tried to scrub away the evidence, Lock's senses didn't miss a thing.

The smells... didn't bother Lock as much as they used to. Even the bleach.

He reached out and ran his fingers over one of the larger red stains in the concrete—there was no doubt it was blood. Lock could taste the residual iron through his skin.

Lock felt the gentle psychic touch two more times as he's escorted through the halls. *It's not personal*, Lock reminded himself. They're just worried about getting more blood on the concrete.

After all, Lock's mutations were some of the *best controlled* of all the test subjects.

The guards took Lock all the way to a small medical room. Clean plastic sheets covered the walls like a murder scene waiting to happen, and stainless steel boxes lined the edges of the room.

Lock sat down on the edge of the hospital bed, paying no mind to the leather restraints.

He didn't have to wait long.

Two nurses came in wearing full surgery gear—heavy frocks, face shields, masks, and gloves. Some of the blood on their frocks looked fresh.

That was all but confirmed when the nurse's voice shook.

"Verify your identity, please."

"Lachlan Harris. Code 50927."

She must've had a bad time with the last patient.

"Roll up your sleeve, please."

The nurses were careful not to look him in the eye and not to stare at him.

Without further ceremony, the nurses went to work. They pulled several tools and vials from the steel boxes and began taking samples from him.

Not all of which were created equal. The needle they used to draw blood barely felt like a pinch compared to the needles they used for bone marrow and spinal fluid. The deep muscle tissue extraction wasn't fun either; it involved an incision in the skin, followed by thin forceps to cut a strand of bicep from the middle of the muscle belly.

Lock turned off his pain receptors for all of it. He had tried toughing it out the first time—he wasn't going to make that mistake again.

The nurses were done with him in ten minutes.

Then Lock was ushered through more concrete halls and down more stairs. Deeper below Gnosis. Deeper into the Mutagen Program.

He tried to map it out in his head. Lock wasn't sure if they were still below the headquarters or if they were somewhere else beneath Belport.

Deep enough that their fights won't affect the substructures of the city.

Lock waited in another concrete room—this one was still lined in plastic and fluttering with nurses. This time the nurses jabbed him with shots, adding things instead of taking samples away, each containing microscopic testing diodes that will deliver real-time data to watching scientists.

Meanwhile, Lock watched the single television monitor on the wall.

Over the last few months, Lock had seen over ten other mutants fight, each one stranger than the last: Basic telekinetics, psychic criers, acid-spewers, extendable bone blades, and one that could only be described as an eldritch horror—if their dozens of tentacles ended with spear-tips instead of suckers. There were even a few that looked like vampires, complete with pale skin and fangs, and another that might've been given a variant of Mutagen-X.

Gnosis was trying to make their own supers but they all just turned out... wrong.

Lock wasn't sure exactly which mutagens equated to which powers—some letter designations and mutagen precursors were supposedly benign in appearance, like super strength, healing, enhanced senses, and wrinkle reversal. Some of these singular precursors were rumored to be available in mass for world leaders, military special forces, and even celebrities.

Lock, himself, had been given a dozen different injections and the only ones that had been named were Mutagen-A, the baseline mutagen by which all others were compared, and Mutagen X.

The latter was supposedly Gnosis's newest and most promising blend. The rest of the *letters* were a glorified freakshow.

Even the precursors were just a front. Gnosis wasn't in the business of health or security. They were in the business of making weapons.

And business was only getting better.

Steel doors at the end of the room opened and three more guards appeared, this time wearing light power armor—Gnosis's proprietary model: Hardened impact plates, actuator enhanced joints, and personal rebreathers. They ushered him down the hall. Lock obliged.

He rolled his neck and shrugged his shoulders, loosening himself up for his coming fight. It was more mental preparation than physical.

Lock followed the long hall to a twin set of steel doors, made to keep the sometimes noxious biological weaponry from escaping. The final door opened, and Lock caught the pungent remnants of acid lingering in the air.

The arena was some two hundred feet square and nearly as tall. The left half was divided into a three level parking garage, while the other half was completely open air. Concrete blocks and dividers littered both sections, simulating the occasional barricade or parked car to hide behind. All the surfaces were either pitted, scored, stained, or filled in with fresh white concrete.

Gnosis had tried to design a singular arena so that they didn't give advantage to any one kind of powerset. For their simple and brutal testing, Gnosis mostly succeeded.

To Lock, it looked like an abstract painting.

In the center of the open area, fresh red blood stood out. The loser had a bad time... Depending on the Mutagen, they'd live.

Across the room, another set of metal doors hissed open.

A young woman staggered in, her hands pressed against her face. Her hair floated above her, like clumps of bright red seaweed floating in the tide. Her scalp was bleeding and droplets flowed upward and dissolved into mist above.

The guards behind her had weapons pointed at her and shouted desperately into their comms for whoever was in control to close the door.

She didn't pay any mind as the door hissed shut.

She sobbed, and Lock waited for her to finish.

A booming voice sounded from the speakers above. "Subject 61565 AND Subject 50927, your fight will now begin. It ends with grievous injury, incapacitation, or death."

Only then did the young woman look up. She scanned the room, recognition flashing across her face before her eyes settled on Lachlan. Her shirt had a large red heart on it, the same color as her hair. The collar was matted with blood.

Lock kept his face expressionless and kicked his shoes off.

Heart-girl's face twisted into a grimace equal parts anger and pain. She screamed, but the sound was muted by whatever twisted power she was about to unleash. Her hair grew, spreading out in a blood-tinged crescent until it was fifty feet wide.

The strands coalesced into a dozen thick limbs. They pierced the floor and lifted Heart-girl up until it looked like she was hanging in the mouth of a giant red spider.

Then she scurried toward him.

Lock sprinted toward the left side 'parking garage' of the room. He deadened his sense of pain and willed the tips of his fingers and toes to grow into a bastardized mix of sharpened nails and bone spurs. He leapt up to the nearest column, his claws hooking easily into the concrete, and climbed up as quickly as he could.

In less than a breath, Lock was on the third level. He stood ready, his muscles coiling like they had minds of their own.

He waited and listened to the *tick, tick, tick,* of Heart-girl as she climbed hair-first up the wall. The image made Lock take a step back from the edge; no matter how advanced his biology was, it was hard to suppress his lingering psychology.

A moment later, red spidery limbs crested the top of the parking garage. The tips of each limb jabbed into the concrete like ice picks, and left behind bloody impacts. Heart-girl followed, her body hanging lifeless like a marionette. Her face was slack-jawed and blank, except for her eyes, which stared unblinking at him.

Lock crouched, his own claws digging into the concrete.

A spear of hair shot toward him, and Lock leapt upward. He contorted in mid air, hitting the ceiling feet-first, and then sprung toward his target. Heart-girl ambled out of the way, defending herself with a flurry of red tendrils.

With superhuman reflexes, Lock seized one of the red tendrils, but it slipped through his hand—the blood that coated her hair was slick and his hand came back wet.

Lock hit the concrete and tumbled across it. Tendrils followed, slashing and stabbing at him like a dozen separate weapons.

Lock dodged all of them.

He lunged for Heart-girl and she backpedaled across the third floor of the parking garage. Lock slashed at her attacks, severing the first few tendrils, but her hair regrew as quickly as it fell.

Meanwhile, other tendrils speared through Lock's shoulder—another through his thigh. His blood coagulated instantaneously. The tips that didn't recoil immediately, Lock slashed through with his claws.

It was one thing to fight a super that moved like a semi-normal human, but with an atypical target, it was too easy to be surprised by a sudden, unexpected counter attack. If Lock hadn't just fought a similar mutant, he might've been afraid. Heart-girl wasn't much different from the eldritch horror from last time—they both moved like insects and protected their torso.

Lock had no doubt he was going to win. He just had to get close enough to Heart-girl to end the fight.

He waited, biding his time.

Heart-girl retreated toward the wall. Lock already knew she would try to scale the wall and fight from the ceiling. Up there, she would have better reach and mobility.

Lock didn't plan on letting her get there.

Heart-girl was still backpedaling, desperately trying to fend him off. Lock let her think it was working.

Heart-girl dug her first few steps into the wall and started to climb.

Lock seized the next tendril, quickly wrapping the length around his palm. This time, when he squeezed, the hair didn't come free from his grasp. At the same time, the claws on his feet dug into the floor.

He pulled. She stabbed. Lock grabbed another handful of hair, then he pulled in earnest.

Lock wrenched Heart-girl free from the wall and spun, whipping her around like a catapult and slammed her into the wall. A dull thump echoed through the parking lot—like a sack of laundry hitting the ground. The whole motion took less than a half second. The hair slackened around Lock's hands.

But Heart-girl still stood on spidery-red limbs. She was cocooned in hair, only a sliver of her face visible behind the curtain of red.

Lock didn't waste a breath.

Keeping hold of her hair, Lock pulled again and leapt at the same time. He rocketed toward Heart-girl and caught her in a flurry of slashes, cutting her body free and severing nearly all the hair from her head.

Catastrophic damage was the only way to reliably beat someone with accelerated healing.

By the time Lock's assault was over, Heart-girl was nearly bald. The hair that was left on her head was short and quivered—still alive. She dropped to the ground, clutching her hands to her chest.

He could've brought the parking garage down on her, but he doubted Gnosis would appreciate the destruction.

"It's over," Lock said, glancing around the ceiling. He wasn't sure where the cameras were—they were small and hidden, but Lock knew they were watching.

They were always watching.

Lock turned and started walking to the edge of the parking garage before leaping off and continuing to the exit.

"And next time, give me a challenge."

Chapter 22

Trust / Lock

E mmett took the bus home Wednesday night.

Part of him wanted to run home across the rooftops of Belport, but his entire body was sore from training in Gray Room. Emmett sat down on an empty seat in the middle of the bus and tried to stretch his legs out without moving them too much—

Whatever muscles were in the back of his thighs were tight and felt like they would cramp up any second.

Between that and Emmett's apprehension about running into an enemy super again... it really hadn't taken much convincing.

So Emmett scrolled his phone, figuring out just what assignments he had to get done tonight for class. That way he could go to sleep that much quicker...

Emmett stared at the screen, eyes widening.

He'd missed a discussion and a quiz in his Product and Process class—Professor Quinn's class.

For the briefest moment, Emmett considered asking her for mercy. He'd been in an accident and wound up in the hospital. *Technically,* it was the truth, except that there was no record of him at either place.

It wasn't enough to flunk him, but Quinn was a hard enough professor already—Emmett wanted all the buffer he could get going into the final project

"Shit," Emmett muttered. Missing those assignments didn't do him any favors.

Emmett kept going, adding to his to-do list and then started on the reading that he could do on the bus.

The apartment was empty when Emmett got home. Lock was out late again.

That was fine by Emmett. It saved him from answering anymore questions about Marianne—his girlfriend that didn't exist.

Emmett sighed, rubbing his neck as he walked to his room and then tossing his keys and wallet on the side table.

He didn't care for the *sneaking around* part of being a super. He didn't even have a superhero name, and here Emmett was, already lamenting having a secret identity!

Emmett would have to keep his life secret from Lock, from his classmates, even from his family, and Emmett could already tell it wasn't going to sit right with him.

It made complete sense to keep his identity a secret—any enemies he made wouldn't be able to come after his family or friends...

But couldn't he confide in someone? ...Tell just one person?

Emmett chuckled at himself.

His younger brother Antony might be able to keep it a secret, but if his best friend Sherman ever got wind of it, he would probably blast it on the very same forums that Emmett frequented.

Emmett dismissed his older brother Darryl as quickly as he did Mom and Dad—all three of them would worry themselves sick.

Lock... Could he trust Lock?

Emmett shook his head.

Maybe.

But he didn't know what circles Lock ran in, not anymore. If he was mixed up with the wrong crowd and let Emmett's name slip... It wouldn't be good. Emmett didn't want his roommate getting hurt on account of knowing Emmett's secret.

It was decided: Of course Emmett couldn't tell Lock the truth.

Emmett sighed and settled in for hopefully a short night of homework and a good night's rest.

It was four in the morning when Lachlan got home to the apartment.

He glanced around for Emmett, but didn't see him in the common area. A moment later, Lock heard his roommate snoring quietly from his room.

He shut the door behind him and locked it, taking care to do it quietly.

Then he pulled back his hood and walked to the sink to wash his hands.

Lock turned the faucet lukewarm and set to wiping his opponent's blood from the creases of his hands. His fingertips were already scabbed over with normal flesh.

As the blood was washed away, it took the metallic taste with it—the taste of blood.

A few months ago, the sensation of tasting through his hands, especially blood, had disgusted him... Maybe it still should, but it didn't. Lock had made peace with it. He couldn't change what he was—not anymore.

Lock dried his hands off and walked to his room. His door was opposite of Emmett's, and Lock paused with his doorknob in hand—staring at Emmett's door.

Curiosity was getting the better of him. That or the mutagens were fucking with his head.

Something smelled *off* in the apartment.

Lock shut his door quietly, changed into shorts and a T-shirt. His stomach was completely healed, with only hints of scars remaining where Mr. Wendell had stabbed him with the screwdriver a half-an-hour ago. His shirt and hoodie had holes in them, but they were just that—just holes.

He tossed his black clothes aside and laid down, trying not to pay attention as his muscles writhed with a life of their own, like worms crawling beneath his skin. It made him feel like a walking corpse—like a deadman balloon.

He felt the urge to look at his body in the mirror, to see the changes, but he'd thrown away the mirror from his room weeks ago. The bathroom mirror was harder, and he had to purposefully keep from looking in it when he went to the bathroom or showered.

It was a long minute in the dark before the urge to see his reflection passed.

Lock cracked the window beside his bed and pulled out his box of pipes and Gnosis-grade narcotic. Then he set to smoking a blend made especially for him. Gnosis hadn't even told him the name of it, but it was enough to knock out three people.

Lock slept until 10 o'clock Thursday morning—

Basically hopped up out of bed.

He had to admit, getting a restful night's sleep every night was almost worth the horrors he endured getting to this point.

Lock stood in his room, waiting. Listening.

And when he didn't hear any sign of Emmett or any noise at all, Lock walked out of his room and into Emmett's.

The apartment smelled *off*.

And Lock already knew why.

He knew, but he had to be sure.

The smell wasn't something that any normal human would be able to catch, but Lock wasn't normal. Not anymore.

His sense of smell was closer to a hound dog than a human's.

Lock walked around Emmett's room to his laundry hamper and grabbed the shirt on top. Apprehensively, he pulled it to his nose and sniffed—already knowing what he was going to find.

He recoiled immediately.

Emmett's shirt reeked of Gnosis's mutagens. His pores were probably oozing it.

Lock smelled the shirt again. It was Mutagen-A; he was sure of it, and the smell was so potent because Emmett's body was taking to the mutations extraordinarily well.

But there was something else... something that Lock couldn't discern.

And it was stronger on the right arm of his shirt.

Lock stood in Emmett's room, smelling his roommate's dirty shirt for much longer than he would ever admit, but he figured out what was off about the smell:

The right arm of Emmett's shirt didn't smell normal. It barely smelled of Mutagen-A.

Lock's mind raced as he thought of the possibilities.

Venture had saved Emmett that night on Champion street. Lock hadn't seen exactly how, but he knew that the doctor specialized in robots. Now, Lock also knew that Venture had dosed Emmett with Mutagen-A—*without* the approval and guidance of Gnosis...

Maybe the Mutagen wasn't taking as well as he originally thought. That was a very real and very dangerous possibility.

Gnosis didn't like failures.

But that wasn't the only thing wrong with Emmett's shirt. The right arm didn't even have the underlying smell of sweat. It smelled... *fake.*

Had Venture rebuilt Emmett's arm?

Lock stared at the shirt. *That would explain it.* He sneered and chucked Emmett's shirt back in the hamper.

So, Venture was turning Emmett into his own little pawn... Using Gnosis's proprietary mutagens and his own technology. After all these years of being a fanboy, Emmett finally had a chance to play hero. It wasn't a stretch to imagine Emmett running across the rooftops like a naïve brat.

One day that would probably put Lock and Emmett at odds, and, well... Heroes tended to retire early when they went against Gnosis.

Lock shook his head and went back to his own room to get changed for the day. He threw on another set of black pants, black shirt, and another black hoodie. His muscles rippled with anticipation, squirming beneath the fabric with barely contained strength.

Then he pulled up the encrypted window on his phone while he waited for Gnosis to send his next job.

And he contemplated telling his boss about Emmett...

Not yet, Lock thought.

Not yet.

Full Throttle Heart

A Whole New World

[Truck-kun waking up in a strange forest]

Truck-kun's engine rumbled to life, the revometer visibly trembling. The last thing it remembered was that rogue box truck barreling toward it... Joe's wide-eyed face through the coffee shop window... The sound of screeching metal and busting glass... Joe falling to his knees in anguish...

That was one crazy nightmare!

Truck-kun rolled forward, its tires gripping dirt. It sprayed fluid on its windshield and wiped, trying to get rid of the haze.

Wait, that wasn't right...

Dirt?

Truck-kun spun its wheels, kicking up dirt. That definitely *wasn't right*. There wasn't any dirt in the city.

Its engine revved and its revometer flicked with uncertainty. Finally, Truck-kun's window cleared enough for it to see.

It was in the middle of a forest, surrounded by enormous, towering trees. A blanket of moss stretched out between them. Realization settled on Truck-kun's metal frame—not just that it was a long way from city streets, but that it was also alone. Not even distant bird calls helped to shake the unease spreading through its engine.

"Joe?" Truck-kun grumbled in desperation.

Where was Joe?

"Joe?" This time it was Truck-kun's own voice that gave it pause.

"Joe..." The voice came out in a deep rumble, like Truck-kun had just woken up from a deep slumber. In a pang of sadness, it reminded Truck-kun of Joe's own voice early in the morning, before Joe had his second cup of coffee.

"Is this real?" Truck-kun wondered aloud, as much to its newfound voice as to the strange surroundings.

Only silence answered.

Not knowing what else to do, Truck-kun put on its flashers and drove cautiously through the forest.

[Montage of Truck-kun driving through the forest:

[Craning its high beams up to see just how tall the trees are.

[Passing empty meadows and streams.

[Illuminating ancient, overgrown statues of warriors in strange armor.]

It was at the second such statue, of a man wearing large, boxy armor and standing proudly, that Truck-kun stopped to rest. It had driven for hours and not met another soul in the forest. There weren't even any radio stations to keep it company.

The sun was getting low behind the trees, casting the forest in gloom. A beautiful bluebird flew down from the trees and settled on Truck-kun's roof. Joe would've taken it as a sign, and Truck-kun resolved to stay there until the next morning.

Truck-kun didn't work nights.

Truck-kun's engine hummed wearily, and it turned toward the statue—its headlights casting the shadow in a harsh light. Again, it thought of Joe, and how the driver looked walking outside on those cold, cold mornings back home... wherever home was.

"I miss you, Joe," Truck-kun rumbled.

"WHAT THE HELL!?"

The box car startled, its engine rumbling with shock. It turned around and backed up to the statue, high beams scanning the forest for danger. But as Truck-kun searched the treeline, it didn't see anything at all—

Except for the statue, and an equally frightened bluebird perched atop it.

The bluebird craned its head, regarding Truck-kun through the bright lights.

Truck-kun flicked its high beams off to be polite.

"Was that you?" Truck-kun asked.

For a moment, the bluebird looked equal parts scared and offended. The bird ruffled its feathers. "Of course it was—who else would it be? I thought you were a statue." Its voice was surprisingly gruff, like a used car salesman who'd smoked a pack a day since they were twelve.

"I'm not a statue. I'm a truck."

"I don't know what that is."

"It's what I am," Truck-kun replied confidently. Then, because it wanted to know more about the strange forest, it asked, "Do other animals talk in this strange forest?"

The bluebird let out a horrid cough that made Truck-kun wince. It was only after the bird finished that Truck-kun realized it had been laughing.

"Buddy, everybody talks in this forest. You got a lot of dummies where you come from?"

Truck-kun shook his cab. "I come from an honorable city."

"Likely story. Listen, uh... Say, what's your name?"

"My name is Truck-kun."

"Well, I'm Al. Nice to meet you. Now beat it. This is my statue."

Truck-kun glanced from the statue to the bird. "Weren't you just content to sit on my head?"

"Yes, but that was then. This is now. Now beat it. Everybody knows only one bird to a statue."

"But I'm not a bird."

"And you're not a statue either." The bluebird ruffled its feathers and settled onto the shoulder of the statue, as if the argument was settled.

Truck-kun turned and looked out across the forest again. But as its light cast spooky shadows among the trees, its decision only became more certain.

"I am staying," Truck-kun said.

"Buddy, I don't know if you heard me, so I'll speak slowly this time…"

The bluebird trailed off just as an enormous silhouette appeared in the distance. It stared at Truck-kun with two blood-red eyes.

The creature plodded forward ominously, Its hulking form becoming even more prominent. It was an enormous bear with shoulders as tall as Truck-kun's cab. Its claws gouged the earth and saliva dripped from its deadly looking fangs.

"That's a dire bear," Al, the bluebird, whispered. "And that's not a small one. If you try to run, be sure to zig-zag. If you can soil yourself, do it—sometimes that will deter them… Sometimes."

"What else can I do?"

"You can't fly, can you?"

"No."

The dire bear plodded forward with the inexorability of an apex predator. Truck-kun had never seen a creature so big other than fellow automobiles, nor one so angry.

It lumbered all the way up to Truck-kun, stopping just a foot away from its headlights. Then the bear reared up on its hind legs, its head rising up even higher than the top of Truck-kun's box.

Truck-kun saw the world in slow motion—just like it had during that fateful crash.

The dire bear bellowed and lunged forward, slashing at Truck-kun with the entirety of its bulk and power. Truck-kun heard the squeal of the bear's terrible claws on its metal hood. And it felt nothing…

It felt nothing. Nothing at all.

Truck-kun was unharmed.

The bear roared again, undeterred, and reared back to strike again.

Something within Truck-kun stirred, something deep within its engine—within its heart. A power it had never known. Truck-kun's body began to change.

[Cue stylized view of Truck-kun transforming from its normal truck form to its truck warrior form].

Truck-kun's entire body transformed! Its wheelbase contorted, its wheels shifting to become feet while the rest of its wheelbase became legs. Its cab rose up until it was a torso. At the same time, its storage box unfolded, becoming armor plates that sheathed its limbs.

Truck-kun was tall enough to look the dire bear in the face, and the bear's eyes grew wide and it let out a confused growl.

Truck-kun hauled back and punched the bear in the face.

The dire bear was thrown back, skidding across the dirt. It lay crumpled in a heap, unmoving. Dead.

Truck-kun stared in confusion at its slain enemy.

"WHAT THE HELL?"

Truck-kun startled and turned to face the statue, and the shocked face of the bluebird.

"How did you do that?" Al demanded. "That was a dire bear! I don't know if you know this, but dire bears aren't just any old bears—they're dire."

"I'm sorry," Truck-kun said, both to the bluebird and to the bear. Truck-kun hadn't meant to kill it.

"Don't be sorry! That was awesome. You were just like, *get outta my forest* and then *WHAM!*"

Truck-kun looked at the slain corpse of the bear with a mix of relief, confusion, and sadness. It should've known what would happen—it should've known!

No animal could stand up to unflinching, unfeeling steel.

Chapter 23

Types of Supers

Emmett napped on the bus to class and then dozed off again on the bus to the lab. He'd done homework until almost three in the morning before he finally gave up and went to sleep.

His older brother Darryl used to say that as he got older, it got harder to pull late nights. Emmett hadn't believed him until now.

At the bus stop near the lab, Emmett wondered if it would be any easier to pull an all-nighter if he was doing something related to being a super rather than doing schoolwork. Would it be easier to stay awake patrolling the city, chasing a villain, or staking out their lair?

Did supers get bored?

Emmett scoffed. He couldn't imagine getting bored while he was running across the rooftops of Belport, or while training in the Gray Room.

Just thinking about training made him walk a little faster across the West End to the lab.

A few minutes later, Emmett was in the Gray Room beside Clara's robot while white tiles rose up out of the floor.

"I've been meaning to talk to you," Clara's robot said.

Emmett turned, tensing up unconsciously—it was only a few words away from that infamous phrase, 'we need to talk'.

"About what?" Emmett asked.

"Follow me."

The robot jogged away and then leapt up to the top of a second story building. Emmett followed, leaping halfway up, grabbed the edge of the roof with his whip, and hauled himself up the rest of the way.

He tried not to smile too hard with satisfaction as he climbed over the edge and retracted the whip back into his forearm. The whole movement felt so easy and natural, and for a moment he forgot all about 'we need to talk'.

It was hard to believe that he'd only had one day of movement training with the whip.

Dr. Venture was right about Mutagen-A enhancing muscle memory. It made Emmett even more excited about the rest of his training.

And curious about what Gnosis's other mutagens were like.

Clara cleared her throat. "What did you do wrong Tuesday night when you fought Zanté on the roof?"

"Oh..." Emmett wasn't sure what he had expected, but this wasn't the worst thing or the best thing she could've brought up.

"...I'm not sure," he said in earnest. He got the crap beat out of him, so there was probably a lot that could've been better.

"You should've run: You were outnumbered, and fighting two unknown supers. As soon as you realized that Zanté, er Skull Mask, outclassed you, you should've run. But that's not the worst—he gave you an easy out and you didn't take it."

Up until that point, Emmett had been trying not to feel like he was getting a talking to from his mother.

"Wait... What *out* did he give me?

Clara's robot stared at him, and let out an exasperated sigh. "He tried to throw you off the roof."

"How is that an out?!"

"Next time, let them throw you off the roof."

Emmett shook his head. "Clara, I don't know what you think would happen to me if I fell off a roof, but I can't fly."

"Think, Emmett... You already knew that Zanté was stronger than you. If someone outclasses you in close-quarter combat, the last place you want to be is within arm's reach of them."

"It was a two-story building!"

"And you have super strength!"

Emmett stared at Clara's robot, feeling like a frustrated and rapidly deflating balloon.

She must've noticed. "It was only a two-story building... Sorry. Sometimes I forget what it's like to be new at this."

"It's okay. It didn't even occur to me when I was up there." Emmett peered over the edge of the building, down to the faux street below. "It really wouldn't hurt?"

The robot shrugged. "It might feel like falling on your back and getting the wind knocked out of you, but I'm pretty sure you wouldn't break anything."

Emmett chuckled, still looking over the edge. "Pretty sure—"

Clara pushed him from behind, and Emmett toppled over the edge of the building.

He yelled in surprise, his heart already pounding. Eyes half-closed, he twisted, trying to orient himself to land, and hit the ground a moment later—

Feet first, rolled across the ground, and sprung to his feet.

Then Emmett stood on the ground in disbelief.

He'd just managed to land on his feet, like a cat. And it hadn't hurt his legs at all—the rolling was probably unnecessary.

Clara was right: Falling off a two-story building wasn't enough to hurt him.

Clara called from the rooftop. "Not bad. Now get back up here."

They spent the next hour running through combat drills in the Gray Room: Punches, kicks, blocks, grapples—

All of it was easier than yesterday.

Emmett tried to push aside the excitement and disbelief. Turned it into an incentive to focus that much harder on his training.

If he could learn faster than a normal human, then he resolved to train harder than a normal human.

Emmett concentrated on every punch, every kick, every move.

Clara's robot squared up with him on top of the gray two-story building. Emmett ducked and weaved around blue punches before countering with his own. His fists clanged against its metal torso.

That was something else—the robot's metal felt soft, almost forgiving, with each punch. Like the robot's strength and durability could change as easily as the tiles shaped the faux city around them.

A punch glanced against Emmett's chin, quickly bringing him back to the moment.

He retaliated with three more punches—not bothering to slip Clara's counter punch. The blue first hit him directly in the face, but Emmett leaned into it and followed up with his own—

Emmett punched *hard*, throwing all his weight into it and hitting the robot in the head. The impact echoed through the Gray Room and Clara's robot stumbled backward across the roof.

Emmett didn't follow. His vision swam from taking a direct hit.

Thankfully, Clara didn't move either.

Clara laughed. "That was a gamble."

"Thanks," Emmett muttered, planting his feet to keep the room from spinning. "I think."

"You know you're going to be one of the weakest in a fight, right?"

"I... Well, no. I didn't know that."

"You need to remember that," Clara said sternly. "You're only class one, and a new one at that. You won't be the strongest or the fastest. And you won't be the most experienced or have the best technique."

Emmett winced. He knew that—of course he did. He just didn't want to think about it.

But he would have to get over that fact. He was one of the weakest *right now*, but he wouldn't always be.

Emmett wouldn't stay weak forever.

Emmett swallowed his pride and asked, "So, what am I supposed to do?"

"You have to fight strategically. Don't get into a fight with an unknown super. Figure out any weakness or exploits they have: For instance, pyrokinetics might be weak to extreme cold, certain mutations might be weak to sonic waves, or other artificers might use tech that we have counters to."

"What if they don't have a weakness?"

"Most won't," Clara replied, "but at the very least, you need to know what powers they have. That way, you can protect yourself or directly counter them. For example, I would never get within arm's reach of someone like Zanté who has super strength. I would stay in the air and fire from range."

Emmett smirked. "Must be nice to be able to fly."

Clara laughed, her hard tone finally softening. "It is."

Emmett thought back to Tuesday night on the roof—to Green Mask.

"What about psychics?"

Clara didn't answer right away. She made Emmett wait until they were done training and both back in the training hub.

She was hanging up the rest of her Virtual Reality suit when Emmett came in. He tried his best to look at random displays and not at Clara's tank top. Emmett swallowed nervously.

"Where's your dad?" he asked, remembering Venture's tendency to pop up suddenly and unannounced.

"He's working in section four. Didn't say what he was working on. I think he wanted some time to himself."

"Doesn't he get a lot of that already?"

Clara chuckled quietly. "Yeah, I guess so."

A moment later, Clara slipped her baggy green sweater and beanie on and pulled up the center table's holographic display. She pulled up four separate columns and filled each with information.

"There are a bunch of different ways to classify powers," Clara said, "but since you're working with us, you're going to learn our system.

"First, the Augmented supers—these are the ones that make or conjure their enhancements. Artificers like myself who use technology, or mages or artifact wielders that use magic. It amounts to the same thing. Sometimes these items can grant the wielder powers like those from other categories.

"Next are the Physically Enhanced—body or mind. They're stronger, faster, smarter or have better senses than a normal human.

"Then there are the Kinetics—those whose powers can affect others. Psychics, telekinetics, elementalists, illusionists, all fall into this category. Even things like flight, reality and time warping count.

"Last are the Anti-Powers—those that negate other categories of powers. These can be broad, like being physically invulnerable, or more specific, like immunity to fire and heat. They also include specific immunities. Magic blessings are sometimes like this—like you're immune to a specific weapon heirloom of an ancient family."

Emmett nodded along, looking over the columns and listings that hung in the air.

Clara shuffled the columns to the side, and pulled up the Division of Superhuman Affairs' familiar bullseye logo.

"The Class ranking system used by the DSA is good for broadly describing threats, but it breaks down on a granular level. Certain powers are better at countering others, and so a psychic and an artificer will fare differently against someone like Zanté or you—even if they're all the same class rank.

"So as important as it is to familiarize yourself with the Class ranking system, it's not enough. You need all the information you can get before going into a fight. That means research, reconnaissance, and countermeasures."

"Okay," Emmett said, trying to take in all the info. "But how do I counter a psychic?"

Clara shrugged. "There's not a lot you can do. You can practice mental grounding exercises. Or you can run."

"Is that what you and Venture did?"

"No. The helmets of our armor are shielded against most psychic attacks, but you can't really have eye holes or even air holes. Every opening makes the shielding less effective."

Emmett joked, "I guess I'll just have to ask your dad to make me a suit, then."

Clara scoffed. "Fat chance. He didn't even want to make me a suit. Dad wanted me to make it myself."

"What changed?"

Clara turned back to the holographic display. "I didn't have time." Before Emmett had a chance to ask Clara to explain, she said, "Psychics are one of the hardest counters you'll come up against. They don't have to touch you to hurt you. I suggest you run."

"...That's it? Just run?"

Clara shrugged. "Unless you turn yourself into a robot, you're always going to be vulnerable to psychic attacks."

Emmett frowned, unsatisfied with her answer.

It seemed like every power set had a counter, and Emmett liked the idea of being able to prepare for a battle.

Again, he thought back to the other night on the rooftop—how Green Mask had made the world feel small and claustrophobic. As far as psychic powers went, Emmett imagined that was probably the least horrifying.

He wasn't sure about turning himself into a robot, but there had to be something he could do to defend against that. If Emmett really was going to defend himself and make it so he never felt powerless again, then he would need to find something to counter psychics. Even if it meant making his own armor suit.

"Come on," Clara said, signaling for them to get back to training. "You've got a lot of practice before you worry about that."

Reluctantly, Emmett agreed.

CHAPTER 24

Classwork and Classifications

E mmett rode the bus back to Eastside and spent the rest of Thursday evening trying his hardest to work on classwork and not get distracted by superhero stuff.

It mostly worked.

He caught up on the readings and discussions he had to finish—weekly busywork. Then he worked on his final project for engineering, setting up the desktop version of his radio locator.

By the time midnight rolled around, Emmett had pushed aside the piles of electronics on the kitchen table and had finished the wiring on the three desktop antennas.

The next step would be to test the antennas and calibrate the software, but Emmett needed a break. So he climbed out the window to the fire escape and went up to the roof.

It was brisk and quiet up on top of the building, and Emmett basked in the calmness. He stood on the roof, staring up at the night black sky.

Eventually, Emmett remembered that he'd went up without a hoodie, but he wasn't that cold. He checked the weather on his phone and realized that it was, in fact, almost freezing tonight.

So, he wasn't just stronger and faster... his new body also tolerated the cold better.

Emmett chuckled.

Everything had changed, yet here he was enjoying the solitude of the roof, just like before.

When Emmett was ready to turn in, he didn't just go to sleep. He laid in bed, looking over the DSA's Class system.

Clara had sent it to his phone under the promise that he get his work done first before he pored over it.

The Class system was based on overall power level from Class 0 all the way to Class 5.

Class 0 — Normal Human Capabilities

Class 1 — Minor Superhuman Capabilities

Class 2 — Medium Destructive Capabilities, damage potential up to a city block

Class 3 — Major Destructive Capabilities, guaranteed city block potential with possible need for evacuation

Class 4 — Guaranteed City-Wide Destruction. Possible risk to multiple cities. Evacuation takes priority.

Class 5 — Threat of Continental Destruction. Possible World-Wide Fallout. Containment takes priority.

Emmett had heard about the basic Class listing from his time frequenting the forums.

The more interesting part, were the secondary distinctions that were used in conjunction with the system. Up until this point, Emmett had just thought of the Class system as a way to rank supers—almost like grades at school.

That wasn't it at all.

The Division of Superhuman Affairs was concerned about *combating rogue supers*—the Classes and distinctions were all about giving strike teams information about the super they were facing.

For Class 1 supers with minor powers:

Designation 10 *(pronounced 1 0)* – New Hero with Minor Powers and little skill/training in their use

Designation 11 *(pronounced 1 1)* – Single Power or Minor Powers NOT exceeding a single squad's ability to take down

Designation 12 – Multiple Minor Powers NOT exceeding a single squad's ability to take down

Designation 13 – Single Power or Minor Powers AND Negation Powers, might require special consideration OR multiple superhuman responders

Designations for the other classes were similar:

Designation 0 seemed to be flexible—describing a lack of training or a Single Power that could be easily countered.

Designation 1 pertained to Single Powers that could not be easily countered.

Designation 2 was reserved for Multiple Powers, or those with High Skill and Destructive Potential.

Designation 3 warned that the super had Negation Powers—something that effectively allowed them to "punch up" above their power class.

Emmett thought back to what Clara had said about the ranking system. He could see its usefulness for quickly conferring information. If he was a Class 1 super next to a battle between Class 3's, then he would know immediately to get away.

But Clara was right that they needed more information. The Class system wasn't enough. They would also need to know what power their enemy had, that way they could counter it.

Emmett rolled over in bed, thinking of possibilities before he drifted off to sleep.

Government of the Allied States
THE DIVISION OF SUPERHUMAN AFFAIRS
Threat Classification System for
Superpowered Individuals

CLASS 0 — Normal Human Capabilities

Designation 00 – Unpowered/untrained Civilian

Designation 01 – Trained Human, otherwise unpowered.

Designation 02 – Peak Human Performance and Peak Training in multiple areas

Designation 03 – Human in possession of an Artifact OR Negation Power that makes them a threat to Superhumans

CLASS 1 — Super with Minor Powers:

Designation 10 – New Hero with Minor Powers and little skill/training in their use

Designation 11 – Single Power or Minor Powers NOT exceeding a single squad's ability to take down

Designation 12 – Multiple Minor Powers NOT exceeding a single squad's ability to take down

Designation 13 – Single Power or Minor Powers AND Negation Powers, might require special consideration OR multiple superhuman responders

CLASS 2 — Super with Medium Destructive Capabilities (up to a city block). May require evacuation:

Designation 20 – Minor Powers with High Control or High Destructive Potential, requiring a Single Superhuman Responder

Designation 21 – Single Power (as above) requiring Multiple Superhuman Responders

Designation 22 — Multiple Powers (as above) requiring Multiple Superhuman Responders

Designation 23 — Single Power or Multiple Powers (as above) AND Negation Powers, requires special consideration OR a coordinated team of multiple superhuman responders

ADDENDUM: All Threats labeled Class 3 or above require Coordinated Teams of Multiple Superhuman Responders. At these levels, normal human responders should focus on evacuation or quarantine of affected areas.

As a general rule, Class 3 Threats and Above should only be engaged by Equivalent Power Levels, preferably with Multiple Supers of equivalent or greater power.

Normal human responders and Lower Ranked Supers SHOULD NOT ENGAGE threats of the following magnitudes unless given direct approval from a commanding officer OR they are under mortal threat and evacuation is not possible.

CLASS 3 — Super with Guaranteed city block potential, up to risking an entire city. Will require Evacuation of affected areas:

Designation 30 — Single Power with High Destructive Potential BUT that is easily countered or negated

Designation 31 — Single Power (as above) that is NOT easily countered, or additional Minor Powers that complicate engagement

Designation 32 — Multiple Powers (as above) ALL with High Skill or High Destructive Potential

Designation 33 — Single Power or Multiple Powers (as above) AND Negation Powers, requires special consideration OR preparation

CLASS 4 — Super with Guaranteed City-Wide destructive potential, possibly risking multiple cities. Evacuation takes PRIORITY:

Designation 40 — Single Power with High Destructive Potential BUT that can be countered or negated

Designation 41 — Single Power (as above) that is NOT easily countered, or additional Minor Powers that complicate engagement

Designation 42 — Multiple Powers (as above) ALL with High Skill or High Destructive Potential

Designation 43 — Single Power or Multiple Powers (as above) AND Negation Powers, requires special consideration AND preparation

CLASS 5 — Threat of Continental Destruction, World-wide fallout implications. Containment takes PRIORITY:

Designation 50 — Single Power with Overwhelming Destructive Potential WITH possibility of being countered or negated

Designation 51 — Single Power (as above) that is NOT easily countered, or additional Minor Powers that complicate engagement

Designation 52 — Multiple Powers (as above) ALL with Immaculate Skill or Overwhelming Destructive Potential

Designation 53 — Single Power or Multiple Powers (as above) AND Negation Powers, requires special consideration AND preparation

ADDENDUM: Active Class 4 and 5 Capes, Masks, Villains, and Threats Otherwise Unspecified
CLEARANCE DENIED
INFORMATION REDACTED

ADDENDUM: Active Quarantine Zones
CLEARANCE DENIED
INFORMATION REDACTED

ADDENDUM: Dormant OR Contained Quarantine Zones

Greenspire (CONTAINED) — Sovereign Forest and Refuge ruled over by the self-proclaimed Seelie Court, consisting of Lord Sumac, the Heiress of Lies, Winter's Bane, and the Changeling Horde.

The Seelie Court maintains a respected border and ceasefire agreements with neighboring states.

The Deep Ones (CONTAINED)— Multiple Sovereign Cities circa 10,000 feet under multiple oceans. Telepathic Collective.
Ceasefire maintained with Terran Societies.

OTHER INFORMATION ABOUT DORMANT and CONTAINED QUARANTINE ZONES AVAILABLE UPON REQUEST

ADDENDUM: Possible Extinction Level Threats
CLEARANCE DENIED
INFORMATION REDACTED

Chapter 25

Getting Ahead (Of Yourself)

It had only been a week since Emmett had gotten his new body and powers, and it was only getting harder to pay attention in his classes.

He spent most of engineering and machine design classes doodling in the margins of his notebooks: Mostly mod ideas for his arm.

Venture had said that eventually Emmett could swap things out on the fly, but the more he brainstormed, the more he realized he wanted all of these things: Smoke pellets, caltrops, the lock-picking kit (even if he didn't know how to use it), and those were just the beginning.

What about the Impact Shield, concealable pistol, or plastic explosive, a sonic weapon, taser, or cutting torch? Then there were med kits, homing tags, remote controlled drones, miniature EMP devices, heat-vision or night-vision goggles.

Even things that appeared situational at first might have multiple uses:

Flashlights — Seeing in the dark. A high-powered light could also be used to blind an attacker

Portable Oxygen — Underwater diving. Also useful against airborne toxins

Even his whip was the same way—useful for climbing and grabbing items out of normal reach. Possibly useful for combat and grappling. Eventually, if he got fine enough control of the whip, it could be an extra hand.

Emmett had been so engrossed in his doodles that he'd nearly gotten caught by Professor Quinn. He hadn't seen her move from behind her comically oversized desk. It was only when she was a few steps behind him that he registered her footsteps.

"I hope you're concentrating on your studies, Mr. Laraway," she muttered as she passed.

The close call helped him focus—

For a little while.

In machine design class, Emmett started thinking of ideas for his super alias.

And came up blank.

Thinking of a name was so much harder than thinking of random ideas for mods!

He planned on having a bunch of different mods with him or at least be able to swap out a bunch at a moment's notice.

Arsenal would've been an awesome name, but of course, that was already taken.

Emmett perused the forums, looking for inspiration for names while his machine design professor droned on.

Funnily enough, there had been several capes and masks named *Arsenal* over the years (even one villain), but most people only remembered one.

Even similar names like *Ammo, Battery, Barrage* and *Ordinance* were all taken by power armor-wearing supers. Then there were variations on the 'arsenal' theme, like *Captain Dakka, Shock and Awe,* and *Lead Debt.*

Even gadget-themed names were taken: *Gadget Jim, Gismo, The Wondrous Inventor,* and *Token Surprise.*

There already seemed to be an overabundance of Mutant-centered ideas. Armor and Mecha themes were dried up. Futuristic names were everywhere, and robot names were overdone.

The professor announced the end of class and startled Emmett back to reality.

Emmett had assumed thinking of a name would be easy. But it was just one more assumption about supers that he was wrong about.

Clara laughed heartily as Emmett and her robot ran across the faux rooftops of the Gray Room.

"You're going about it all wrong," she said.

Emmett leapt across an alley and slung his whip upward to reach the next roof. "What do you mean?"

"It's like picking a nickname. You don't get to pick your own nickname. Well, maybe you could, but that's not how it should be done."

Emmett hauled himself upward and met Clara on the roof.

"What's your name?"

"Arsenal."

Emmett scoffed and waited for Clara to say that it was a joke. "...No shit?"

"No shit."

Well, that was one more *Arsenal* that he'd heard of. Now Emmett definitely couldn't take that name.

"Do me a favor?" Emmett asked.

Clara's robot leaned uneasily on its feet. "What did you have in mind?"

"Help me think of a name."

Clara laughed. "Sure thing."

A moment later, Venture's voice came through the intercom, "Coming up with a name should be the last thing on your mind."

Moments later, a second blue robot hopped up to a nearby rooftop and landed with an ominous clang. Venture spoke through it. "You've done well with movement training, so today we'll focus on combat training, lesson one."

Emmett tilted his head in confusion. "I'm already on lesson two, though."

"We skipped that," Venture replied, "but now it's time you learned the most important lesson that a new hero can learn."

TINA's voice echoed through the room. *"Loading combat training, lesson two."*

It might've been Emmett's imagination, but he swore he heard a subtle hum coming from inside both robots. The bright blue color of both robots morphed into blood red.

Venture continued, "The most important lesson is learning how to survive against a more powerful super."

"Don't you mean fight?" Emmett laughed nervously.

Clara's robot shook her head. "No. No, he doesn't."

Venture said, "Lesson one is running away."

Emmett grumbled to himself. That definitely wasn't the lesson he'd been psyching himself up for.

Venture added, "You can start running now."

The robot sprinted toward him.

Emmett froze, watching as it leapt across the alley and landed beside him—moving eerily like a person.

Venture's robot swung at Emmett, a blocky red fist coming toward his face.

Emmett ducked and felt a breeze pass over his head.

He swung back with his left—punching the robot in its torso. A clang echoed through the Gray Room and his arm shook with impact. Emmett winced at the pain in his knuckles.

But the robot didn't budge, and it already swung again, punching down at him.

Emmett lurched backward, dodging it easily. Then he lunged forward and swung with his prosthetic right arm.

This time the clang of metal on metal was so loud Emmett gasped and recoiled.

Again, the robot didn't so much as stumble or tremble—it didn't seem phased at all.

Now it reached toward Emmett with both hands and seized him around the torso. Emmett was lifted off the ground, squirming to get away but unable to free himself.

Emmett's heart beat faster, and he pummeled the robot's spherical helmet. Clangs echoed through the room, but nothing phased the robot.

Venture's voice came from the robot again. "I said you can start running now."

Then the robot hurled Emmett across the block.

Emmett crashed into the side of a building, the impact knocking the breath from his lungs. Dazed and disoriented, Emmett fell toward the alley—fingertips scraping for window ledges or anything to stop his fall.

On a whim, he hurled his whip upward and managed to snag the edge of the roof—swinging instead of crashing to the tiles below.

Emmett barely had a moment to catch his breath. Both red robots leapt off the roof and landed behind him with loud clangs.

Emmett ran, and the robots ran after him.

Clang, clang, clang. Clang, clang.

Within moments, Emmett could hear them catching up, so he turned the nearest corner and started weaving his way through back alleys, hoping they would lose sight of him.

It almost worked.

As soon as he got one turn ahead of them, Emmett slipped around a corner, pressed his back against the gray wall and tried to breathe as quietly as he could.

One of the robots turned the wrong way and continued running, its clangs growing distant.

Then he heard Clara's voice above him on the rooftop. "Over here!"

She leapt off the roof, meaning to land directly on top of him.

Emmett's eyes went wide and he stepped out of the way.

But the robots were split up—this was his chance to *do something*.

Emmett reached out with his whip, and instead of grabbing onto a ledge, he aimed for the robot's leg. The whip wrapped around its ankle and Emmett yanked on it.

He pulled the feet out from under Clara's robot, and it landed on its back with a crash.

Laughter echoed from Clara's robot. "Not bad—"

Emmett kept hold of her ankle, spun, and hurled Clara's robot as hard as he could. She careened down the alley, soaring a full block before she hit the ground and tumbled even farther.

Clangs sounded from behind Emmett as Venture's robot turned the corner. It didn't pause.

"I thought I told you to run," Venture said as the robot barreled toward Emmett.

"I don't like running."

Emmett lashed out with his whip, and Venture's robot blocked, expecting the whip to hit him in the chest.

But Emmett grabbed his ankle and pulled.

For the second time in roughly six seconds, Emmett spun and hurled a robot down the alley—cackling like a madman as he did.

Venture's robot didn't smack into the other one, but Clara had to leap out of the way to avoid it.

Emmett turned and ran.

Again, he weaved through alleys to put as much distance as he could between them.

Even if Emmett couldn't fight them, he wasn't powerless. He still had modifications that they didn't have—

Well, one.

Instead of stopping around a random corner, Emmett kept running until he found a two story building, then leapt up the side and grabbed the roof with his whip. He pulled himself up until he was right below the edge of the roof and stayed there.

Emmett wasn't sure if he should curl up in a ball or flatten out against the wall—either way, hopefully Venture and Clara would be looking for him on the ground.

Sure enough, one red robot ran through the alleys, missing him completely.

Emmett smiled, still trying to be as quiet as possible as he hung in the air.

Maybe this lesson wouldn't be so bad after all...

Emmett listened, but couldn't hear anything else moving, save for the one robot running away from him. So he resolved to lower himself to the ground and keep running.

Emmett extended his whip as far as he could and then released the ledge—

But he didn't fall.

He looked up and saw a red robot holding the end of his whip.

Clara's voice came through the robot. "My turn."

If Emmett knew how to detach his whip, he might have. But he didn't.

The world became a blur of gray as Clara hurled Emmett across the Gray Room. He was in the air so long his stomach turned and he nearly retched.

Then he skipped across the roofs like a stone before crashing to a halt. He lay in a heap and seconds later, he heard the clang of robots running toward him. Fast.

But they sounded distant. Felt distant.

Where was he? Was he on the roofs of the Gray Room... Or was he on the street again?

No—the tiles beneath him were gray. This wasn't the street. He was training. He was safe... kind of.

Emmett groaned and pushed himself up.

But the robots were already on top of him.

Thankfully, they didn't attack.

Venture said, "You have a very different definition of running than I do."

Emmett chuckled awkwardly and rolled his shoulders, trying not to wince. He definitely felt that throw.

Clara added, "Hiding wasn't a bad idea. You were just unlucky that I found you."

Venture said, "Fighting wasn't a bad idea, but it's a gamble each time you fight someone more powerful than you. But now that's out of the way...

"Again."

Chapter 26

Tag, You're It

Emmett spent the rest of Friday evening in the Gray Room, struggling to find a difference between running and fighting.

Emmett still didn't like running.

He blamed it on reading too many comics and watching too much anime. There was nothing heroic about running from a fight.

Clara and Venture's robots were definitely stronger than him, but they weren't *that strong*. Emmett wasn't even sure if their current settings would qualify as Class 2 supers.

They weren't so strong that Emmett couldn't get an advantage, at least for a few seconds.

The problem was that each time he figured out a new way to use his powers, his training, or his whip to get an upper hand, Clara and Dr. Venture were quick to overcome it. Maybe they didn't want him to get complacent and resort to the same trick...

But it almost felt personal, like they didn't like Emmett beating them.

He almost said as much after Clara's robot grabbed his whip and hurled Emmett through a wall and into a faux building. Tiles quaked around him and Emmett had to quickly run out before the rest of it collapsed on top of him.

Emmett found himself longing for an exploit or an outright cheat that could level the playing field. But this wasn't a video game—there were no codes or exploits. His opponents weren't bosses that could be cheesed or bypassed.

Granted, there were supers with negation powers—something that Emmett planned on researching heavily when he got the chance. But Emmett didn't have anything like that, and he doubted Venture or Clara did either.

Besides, even negation powers weren't a trump card. Emmett knew that most negation powers were limited and only affected a set number of other powers.

Then again... Emmett wasn't limited like other supers. He could swap out his mods.

Eventually, Dr. Venture bowed out for the evening, leaving Emmett alone with Clara's robot.

"How about we change things up a bit?" she asked.

"What did you have in mind?"

Clara's robot was standing next to Emmett when it reached out and tapped him on the shoulder.

"Tag. You're it."

Then the robot sprinted away, its color quickly turning blue.

Emmett laughed and followed, chasing her across rooftops while gray Belport passed by in a blur.

They were heading downtown, and the buildings were getting steadily taller. Clara's robot leapt easily from roof to roof and up two stories at a time. Emmett was able to follow, using his whip to keep up.

Soon they were ten stories up, and the architecture began to change. So far, the city skyline had risen and fallen in orderly 'steps' of a story or two at a time. But now skyscrapers rose up... well, like skyscrapers—the difference in height from one block of buildings to the next became five stories, ten stories, or more. Flat roofs gave way to jagged peaks.

Emmett chased Clara up the 'steps' of the skyline, and now they were barreling across the tops of ten-story buildings, and running right toward a sheer wall of skyscrapers.

Breath caught in his throat as he tried to calculate what Clara would do.

The blue robot ran to the edge of the roof—

And jumped down over the edge.

Emmett didn't slow. He ran right up to the edge, and paused just long enough to see Clara sliding down the side of the building, friction slowing her descent.

Emmett jumped and didn't ride the wall.

He plummeted, picking up speed, falling toward Clara like a bullet.

Six stories—

Five stories—

Four—

Clara glanced up at Emmett then the robot twisted and pushed off the side of the building. She soared across the alley, slammed into the opposite wall, and continued riding the side of the building to the alley below.

Emmett missed and began to scramble, digging his fingers into the tiles of the building—desperately trying to slow himself. His whip lashed out and plunged into the wall, trying to do the same thing.

Emmett cut gouges into the tiles, but slowed himself just enough.

He landed feet first, and tiles cracked beneath him as Emmett tucked and rolled across the ground. It hurt like shit and Emmett was dizzy when he finally stopped and stood up, but he'd survived.

He'd jumped off the side of a ten story building and survived.

Emmett doubted anything could wipe the smile off his face.

Clara's robot strolled over. She was laughing too. "You're having way too much fun."

Emmett and Clara went back and forth across the Gray Room, playing the most awesome game of tag ever. Each time their roles switched, the color of Clara's robot changed—red for pursuer, blue for target.

They left the skyscrapers of faux downtown and ran back toward the West End and more manageable heights.

Emmett might not have caught her every time, but he was proud to say that she didn't have any easier of a time catching him.

Especially once Emmett realized he could go *inside* buildings.

He was chasing Clara's robot, when she leapt down to the street and then barreled through the wall of a nearby building. Emmett followed her inside and found tiles rising, reforming to make fake shelves and display racks like the inside of a convenience store.

They weaved through aisles, Emmett only a few steps behind. Then Clara grabbed the end of a display rack and toppled it, causing row after row to topple over like dominos.

Emmett jumped, then slung his whip to grip the end of a rack and pulled himself through the air—across the room.

Clara's robot leapt straight up, crashing through the ceiling and onto the second floor. Emmett followed through the gap. Clara leapt through a window and outside onto the next roof.

Emmett couldn't be sure, but it felt like the robot was running even faster.

Emmett followed her back out to the rooftops, an idea forming in his head.

When Emmett reached the edge of the roof, he used his whip to grab the edge, then leapt and pulled at the same time—slingshotting himself through the air.

He gained almost an entire rooftop. Now Clara was only one roof ahead.

Emmett kept running and grabbed the edge of the next roof, slingshotting himself again—

This time, as hard as he could.

Emmett soared through the air, eyes wide, startling himself with speed.

Clara's robot glanced back, and if she would've paused any longer, Emmett would have flown right into her.

But Clara ducked, half-hanging over the edge of the next building and let Emmett sail overhead. The next building was a story shorter, and so Emmett sailed the length of another entire roof before he landed.

By the time he turned and backtracked, he saw Clara's blue robot waving from almost three entire blocks away.

Thankfully, she waited for him to run over.

"You have good intuition," she said. "But what was your mistake?"

Emmett shrugged. "Using the same move twice in a row?"

The robot shook its head. "You spent too long in the air. You can't fly, so every second you spend in the air, you're a sitting duck."

Emmett found himself nodding along. "Alright, that makes sense. But what happened to that whole thing in the Code about not causing excessive collateral damage?"

Clara chuckled. "Eh, a few convenience store shelves are nothing. Besides, when you're running for your life, all bets are off. Get away from the threat, however you can—screw the Code."

Emmett nodded. That was easy enough to remember.

"There are other powers we can simulate," Clara's robot said.

"Like what?" Emmett asked. They were still standing on the faux roofs of the Gray Room.

The robot shrugged. "Pretty much anything. Pick something."

Emmett stood there a moment, dumbfounded. A part of him wanted to see Green Mask's psychic power again. Then there was Athena's forcefield power or any one of the powers that Porcelain had, but that might be too much to ask for—Porcelain was not only out of his league, but off limits. And there were literally hundreds—probably thousands—of other powers and combinations of powers.

How was he supposed to choose?

Emmett sighed in defeat. "Surprise me."

Clara's robot stared straight ahead, as if she was having trouble deciding too.

Then fire erupted from her hand.

Emmett immediately threw his hands up, shielding his face. Heat poured over him—so hot and so thick that for a moment it felt like she'd thrown a bucket of boiling water at him. Emmett winced and backed away.

Thankfully, the heat died down enough for him to peer through his fingers.

Clara's robot held a flame in its palm—not just a flame. That didn't do it justice. It looked like a spear of molten plasma nearly four feet tall. It didn't flicker like fire, but ebbed and rolled like water.

But as Emmett watched, the fire *changed*—shrinking in height and lessening in heat. The movement changed too, turning from molten liquid to normal, flickering flame.

"Sorry..." Clara said, her voice muffled by the wind rolling off of the fire—Emmett had been so distracted by the heat that he hadn't noticed at first. "Sometimes I forget what the settings are left on."

A moment later, Clara was holding a ball of fire half a foot tall in her palm. Emmett finally lowered his hands.

"Thanks for dialing it down. I'm only Class one, remember!"

Clara chuckled. "I remember."

Emmett stared at the flame in the robot's palm, still feeling apprehensive. His heart was still thumping in his chest—he hadn't been that scared since getting his ass kicked on the rooftops... or maybe even since the Champion street attack.

He was going to have a hard time forgetting that fire.

"It's not going to cook me or burn my clothes off, is it?" he asked.

"I don't think so. I turned it down to something you *and* your suit can handle. So don't worry."

"Easy for you to say."

"Hey Emmett... You can start running now."

Emmett chuckled until Clara's robot turned red.

She aimed her palm toward him. Then he leapt to the side. Fire erupted in a wave from Clara's robot, cooking the spot where he'd been standing a breath ago.

The heat might not have been as overpowering as when Clara first conjured it, but it was still HOT, and every fiber of Emmett's mind and body screamed at him to get away from it.

He sprinted for the edge of the roof, but even as he ran, Emmett already felt more fire chasing him. He couldn't just leap across to the next roof; he wouldn't make it—

So he dropped over the side, grabbing the gray wall with his whip and swinging down the street.

Emmett swung, detaching his whip, then hurling it forward and grabbing the next building. It wasn't pretty—Emmett lurched hard in the air and struggled not to spin around like a top—but he didn't fall.

He even managed to glance back over his shoulder in time to see Clara's robot leap off the roof.

Fire erupted from her hands and feet, halting her in midair. A split second later, Clara was rocketing toward Emmett.

Emmett spun back around, mid-swing—stomach dropping. He wasn't moving nearly fast enough to outrun her. Besides, she was flying—he wasn't.

Emmett commanded his whip to release, and he fell three stories to the narrow street below. He hit the ground and then charged toward the nearest window—busting through and tumbling into the faux building.

Fire blanketed the street outside—the entire street.

Emmett didn't have any time to gawk.

He recoiled from the heat and shuffled farther into the building. Gray tiles rose up around him, simulating convenience store aisles and displays. Emmett kept going, running toward the back of the store.

He needed to get distance from Clara, but to do that Emmett needed to get out of sight of her.

He just hoped there was an exit in the back.

The hallway turned and branched: There were three doors. Emmett pushed on the first—it opened to a small room that would've been a storage closet in the real world. Then he pushed on the middle door—it opened to another street.

That was where he should go.

But Emmett didn't want to run.

The sound of fire echoed through the store, and Emmett knew he only had a moment before Clara's robot found him.

He kicked the exit door *hard*—so hard the hinges shattered and it skidded across the gray street.

Then turned and slid into the storage closet as quickly and shut the door as quietly as he could.

Emmett didn't want to be directly behind the door in case Clara blasted it. So he stayed a step away from it. And he waited.

Waited in the soft light of the Gray Room tiles while the sound of fire faded and footsteps grew louder.

For a moment, Emmett hoped Clara would run right past him and down the street. Then Emmett could run the other way. It would be an easy win.

But the footsteps stopped right outside the closet door.

Shit.

Emmett only waited for a breath, and it felt like he'd waited entirely too long. That was all it took to make up his mind.

Emmett threw himself at the door—through the door—and at Clara's robot. As hard as he could.

Both Emmett and the door slammed into her, and all three went careening into the opposite room: A second storage closet that felt even smaller than the first.

But that could've been Emmett's imagination.

They both sprawled to the ground.

Emmett scrambled toward the robot, hoping to attack before it could blast him. He lunged—half crawling, half punching. Clara turned and saw Emmett's right fist swing wildly toward her.

The robot burst into flames. In an instant, it was encased in a thin, swirling shield.

Too late, Emmett's fist connected with the robot's head. It twisted and slumped against the floor, then rolled backward—raising both its palms.

Emmett chased after it, swinging again.

His right hand connected again—

And exploded with pain. Even though it was made of metal, it felt like he'd dipped his hand in molten lava. Jolts raced up his arm like electric skewers had been shoved inside it.

As his punch landed, Emmett crumpled to the floor, clutching his arm. Desperately, he rolled away and into the corner of the wall.

By the time Emmett opened his eyes, Clara's robot was looming over him. The fire was already gone.

A moment later, the pain faded from his hand and his arm. His fist was red, tender, and felt tight—bending his fingers hurt.

"You're a stubborn bastard, you know that?" Clara said, offering a hand—her left hand.

It was a long moment before Emmett took it. She pulled him to his feet.

Emmett grit his teeth. He was tired of getting beaten. Damn tired.

"Maybe one day I'll learn my lesson."

Chapter 27

It's... Going

Emmett took his time walking down the hallway to the training hub. His right arm still ached from the *first time* he tried punching Clara's fiery robot. Now the rest of his body ached too: It felt like he'd spent the last hours of the evening running for his life and getting burned alive...

Which Emmett supposed he had.

He walked into the training room, muscles tender and skin feeling raw beneath his suit.

Clara was unhooking the last of pieces of her VR gear and slotting them back into the wall. She turned, half wincing, half smiling.

"I got you good that last time. Your face looks sunburned."

Emmett said sarcastically, "It's not so bad, you should try it sometime."

Clara shook her head. "I've had more than enough close calls with fire. Next time we'll practice with a different power set. That is one advantage you will have over other heroes, you know—you can simulate their powers here. You just have to make sure you get good intel."

"So which super was I fighting against just now?"

Clara turned around, examining the VR gear again. She looked at the visor, maybe looking at a log of some kind.

She answered while looking at the visor. "We don't usually pull info from just one super, even if you wanted to train against a specific one. Even the best data is incomplete. Any super worth their ranking is always trying to improve their techniques and stretch their abilities in new ways. So we don't just take data

from one pyrokinetic: Today you were fighting against techniques from
Blond Bombshell, Liquid Red, and *Instaflame.*"

Emmett's mouth dropped open. "Isn't Instaflame a Class three super?"

"Yep," Clara replied, hanging the visor back on the wall. "We can adjust
the strength of each ability, though. If you were fighting Instaflame at full
strength, you wouldn't have made it off the roof."

Emmett believed it. He'd seen plenty of records of Instaflame's battles—always the aftermath. Bystanders didn't tend to stick around his battles to film.

But something else Clara said piqued Emmett's curiosity.

"...Can supers get more powerful?"

"Sure. It's easier for some power types: Artificers like us, for instance, but
others can too. When a super first gets their power, they're not going to be
very good at using it, right? But as they practice, they'll get better. Someone
with super strength will become more coordinated. Someone with psychic
powers might increase their range or be able to concentrate longer."

"But there are limits, right?" Emmett asked.

Clara thought for a moment before nodding. "Yes. Super strength will
only grow so much, and someone with pyrokinesis won't spontaneously
develop negation powers, but you would be surprised how much training
and creativity counts. That's part of why the Code says *do not fuck with a
veteran super*—they won't just have three or four moves. They'll have dozens
of techniques and surprises, and they'll be quick with every single one of
them."

Emmett nodded. It made sense even before Clara laid it out like that, but
he had a hard time believing anyone would be stupid enough to pick a fight
with a veteran super—some new pyrokinetic going up against someone like
Instaflame.

Just training with Clara had made Emmett realize how much he had to
learn, and she wasn't a veteran super—she wasn't even a pyrokinetic. Worst
of all, she was probably taking it easy on him!

Still, every super had their limits. Even someone as powerful as Instaflame.

But artificers weren't limited like that.

Emmett glanced between his mechanical arm and Clara.

He'd been given Mutagen-A, and Emmett would bet that there were other Mutagen formulas out there. That was tempting, but he was more intrigued by mechanical possibilities.

Maybe Emmett could talk Dr. Venture into helping him make his own set of armor? And in the meantime he could keep upgrading his arm... It was a shame he didn't have *two metal arms*—then he could carry even more mods. But Emmett wasn't about to cut off his other arm, though.

Clara raised an eyebrow. "You've got a crazy look in your eye."

Emmett chuckled. Despite feeling like he'd been worked over, he actually felt great.

He felt like running across the rooftops all the way home.

"Hey..." Emmett said, rubbing the sunburn on the back of his neck. "Do you want to go out tonight?"

Clara's eyes widened. So did Emmett's.

"What I mean is, do you want to go run around the town together? I mean, the rooftops."

Clara's face turned as red as Emmett's face felt. Meanwhile, he would almost rather be cooked alive.

"I... can't," she said, glancing awkwardly around the room.

Emmett tried to keep his face straight, but inwardly, he was cursing himself. Of course Clara couldn't just go *run around the town* with him—why had he said it that way, anyway? She probably had her own training to do; Her dad was probably listening in to their conversation; And she was a super! He was barely a newbie...

Or Clara thought Emmett just asked her on a date. *That wasn't what he'd meant...* not really.

Clara was his friend, and he didn't want to mess that up.

Clara cleared her throat. "What I mean is, I'm looking for leads on Champion street. And you can't come with me."

"Oh..."

Somehow, Emmett felt both relieved and devastated.

"Okay," he finally said. "Just let me know what you find."

Clara nodded reluctantly, but Emmett already knew: It depended on what she found, and if Dr. Venture would allow her to share it.

The air felt thick and awkward, and Emmett wasn't about to overstay his welcome.

"I'll see you Monday," Clara said. She gave him a small smile.

Emmett did his best to return it. "Yeah."

Emmett waved goodbye to Clara and left the lab. He didn't see Dr. Venture on the way out.

Once he got outside, he pulled his hoodie up and walked the streets of Eastside, enjoying the cool Friday night air—

At least until he got a few blocks away. Then he turned and took a detour a few blocks North. Emmett would take a long way home tonight, going between the high rises in the middle of the city and the high-class homes of the Heights—taking Dr. Venture's advice about varying his routes.

He was even wearing a new blank, gray hoodie—he'd gotten it and several other nondescript clothes from a nearby thrift store the other day.

When Emmett felt like he was far enough away from the lab, he turned into an alley and pulled on his mask. He'd washed the blood out of it since his unfortunate run in with the two masked supers in the slums.

It felt surreal putting the mask back on—Emmett swore he could still smell the copper of his own blood even though there was nothing on it.

Surreal—and *right*.

Emmett smiled, then leapt up to the nearest fire escape and climbed to the roof.

Then he started running.

Emmett didn't stop until he'd ran almost ten blocks—

Until he ran across Athena.

He'd almost run right by her.

Athena was sitting against the ledge of a roof, one that was covered with gravel. Her white, braided hair lay over the shoulders of her leather jacket, and she skipped stones across the roof—No. They skipped across the roof but never touched the ground. She was bouncing them off her transparent force fields.

"Hey," Emmett said.

Athena looked up and smiled. "Nice mask. I was beginning to worry that maybe you'd missed a jump... Did you get some sun today?" She pointed to his cheeks.

Emmett chuckled. "Something like that. What are you doing up here? Killing time?"

"Waiting for you."

Emmett glanced around at the neighboring roofs. Athena still hadn't sat up, and she hadn't been facing East. She wouldn't have seen him coming. So unless she had super hearing or some other power...

"Did you know I was coming?"

"Yep," Athena replied, skipping another stone through mid-air.

"How?"

"Premonition, future-sight, visions... Call it what you want."

Emmett's eyebrows raised. "That is pretty cool," he replied—the understatement of the year.

Athena shrugged. "It has its uses, but it's not perfect. Hence the confusion the last time we met."

So, she'd seen Emmett at the edge of the roof, but hadn't known he was a super. Why else would a normal person go up to the roof and look down...

It was a dark joke, but now it all made sense.

Emmett chuckled.

Athena finally stood up and fixed her jacket. "Yeah, can't say I've had that mix-up before. So, how's your training going?"

Emmett took a step back and cleared his throat. It hadn't been that long since he'd seen her, but he'd forgotten how tall Athena was—Emmett was barely taller than her shoulders, which meant she must've been six feet one or two inches tall.

"It's... going," Emmett finally said, realizing that he couldn't just tell Athena about the lab.

She smiled anyway and snapped her fingers. "Good instinct. You don't have to say anything more than that if you don't want."

Emmett considered his options, and didn't see any harm in telling her *what* he'd been practicing.

"...A lot of running away from things."

Athena's face wrinkled in consideration. "I guess that's as good a place to start as any. But you don't sound very happy about that."

Emmett gave her a half-hearted smile. "It's a good place to start."

"Uh huh," Athena replied, totally not convinced. "Look, in another thirty minutes or so, a delivery van is going to pull into the loading bay of the building we're standing on. Except they're not dropping off groceries—they're carrying knock-off mutagen compounds."

"Like the kind Gnosis makes?"

Athena crossed her arms and looked at him incredulously. "Yes, but how do you know that?"

Emmett tried to keep a straight face. "I read... a lot."

"Uh huh. Well, like I said, it's a knock-off brand, and I could use some help destroying their supply."

Now Emmett's eyes widened in excitement—far too quickly to pretend otherwise. "Yes."

CHAPTER 28

Knock-Off Brand

Emmett took a minute to stash his phone and wallet on the roof of a nearby coffee shop, hiding it in a crevice of the air conditioning unit. Then he backtracked to the warehouse roof, keeping an eye out for any guards as he leaped across the rooftops.

While Emmett and Athena waited, crouched in the dark on the edge of the warehouse roof, Athena explained how she'd been tracking the new mutagen variants.

"There's a group of us keeping tabs on shipments. We'll get word a day before a van arrives, destroy the contents, interrogate the drivers... So far we haven't had much luck—the drivers know about as much as we do. Most of the time, they don't even realize what they're transporting."

"What's so bad about these mutagens?" Emmett asked.

"Well, Gnosis has some respect for the scientific method and human experimentation, and I stress the word *some*; whoever is making these knock-offs doesn't."

"How'd they even break into Gnosis?" Emmett saw the main compound more often than most. Calling it formidable was an understatement.

Athena shrugged. "Gnosis reported a security breach to the papers, but they were extremely tight-lipped with the details."

Emmett nodded, looking from the alley behind the warehouse to the surrounding rooftops. "Speaking of security... There's not a lot of security here. Is that normal?"

Athena sighed. "Yes. At first it seemed like whoever stole from Gnosis didn't learn their own lesson. I thought it was ironic…"

"…But?"

"We've destroyed twelve shipments so far, and there's still more that we've missed. They're not bothering to defend them because there's plenty more that make it through. It's a numbers game."

Damn. That was a depressing thought.

Athena must've seen the look on his face. "Cheer up. Even tigers only catch ten percent of what they hunt."

"That doesn't really help."

Athena chuckled. "Did you think of a name yet?"

Emmett stared down at the alley, dumbfounded for a moment. "No. Still thinking."

"It'll come to you. Speaking of, I think this is our guy." Athena ducked lower and pointed down toward headlights—a nondescript white van driving into the alley. "We'll wait for them to open up and give us a look at the cargo before we drop down. Do you need a hand getting down from the roof?"

Emmett shook his head, not taking his eyes off the van. It was only three stories down, but his heart was pounding.

"I can get down on my own," he finally said.

"Good. Move when I move and watch my back."

"Says the woman with precognition."

"It's not *that* kind of precognition. Now listen, there's usually two to four in a van and these guys are probably armed, so be careful. Some carry guns—I'll take them. If you see a gun, just get away or get behind something."

Emmett nodded along, even though this was only his second mission and even though never practiced working as part of a team before. It all seemed straightforward enough.

But that didn't reassure him.

In the alley below, the van had backed up to a loading bay door and two men in coveralls got out of the front seats. They walked around to the back, opened up the van doors, and started unloading white boxes.

"Let's go," Athena said, and leapt over the edge.

Emmett was right behind her, grabbing the edge of the roof with his whip to slow himself down.

Athena landed in a crouch beside the van, making the three-story drop look effortless. The two nearest men startled and dropped their boxes—one turned to run away while the other reached for a gun on his belt.

Emmett watched the scene as he descended: The guy that turned to run slammed face-first into an invisible barrier, and the second aimed his gun at Athena.

"Get out of here, cape!" he shouted.

Simultaneous shouts came from the warehouse and the front seats of the van—

Emmett didn't catch any of what they said, though, because the passenger-side door opened, and Emmett could only focus on the pistol the person was carrying. It positively gleamed in Emmett's vision.

Emmett threw himself at the passenger-side door, careening into it shoulder-first. The impact knocked the passenger backward and crumpled the door inward. *Gunshots went off behind him.* Emmett bounced off the door and saw both men struggling in the front seats—he'd knocked one on top of the other.

A man behind the van shouted and then flew through the air and slammed into the opposite wall of the building. He slumped to the ground, unconscious.

Time seemed to slow down for Emmett—he watched dumbfounded as the two men in the van recovered and pushed open the driver's side door. He felt like he was moving through molasses.

"Gun!" Emmett shouted.

A moment later, the two men were hurled into the same wall and crumpled on top of the other unconscious bad guy—like they'd been shoved by an invisible forcefield.

Emmett winced at the impact, but turned back to the van. He kept his back to the side and slid around to the back of the van.

Athena was hunched over one of the crates, rifling through vials of liquid—ambers, browns, reds, and greens. Cold, smokey air seeped over the edges.

"Give me your phone," Athena said, without looking up.

It wasn't until Emmett rounded the back of the van that he realized she was talking to one of the men—the one who tried to run away. He clutched his bloody nose and was sitting in the back of the van.

"Here, take it!" he shouted, voice muffled. With a shaky hand, he tossed Athena his phone.

It skidded off the van and Athena caught it with her power, then slipped it in her jacket pocket.

"Huh... that's different," Athena muttered. She pocketed three different vials.

Then the man screamed.

Seven more bad guys in coveralls appeared in the loading bay, each aiming a pistol or a rifle at Athena. They fired.

Emmett only had time to recoil—wincing at the erupting cacophony of gunfire. For the moment Emmett shut his eyes, he was blind and deaf.

He might've screamed for Athena, but he couldn't hear anything but ringing in his ears and the faint popping of gunfire.

Distraught, Emmett peered cautiously through his fingers and saw Athena, still hunched over the white container of vials.

She looked up at Emmett, smiled, and said something to him—maybe *"I think that's it"*.

Pops of gunfire sounded again, and this time Emmett didn't wince. Muzzles flashed and Emmett watched as a hail of bullets slammed into Athena's invisible forcefield and fell harmlessly to the ground; she'd blocked the entire loading bay.

Emmett's mouth was open in disbelief.

He walked over and knelt down on the other side of the case. "You can block bullets?" His voice still sounded faint to him, even though he was shouting.

"That's why I said for you to get out of the way."

Emmett still couldn't believe it, but he found his gaze dropping to the open container of vials. And found his hand reaching inside it.

He already had Mutagen-A in his system... Could he take something else? It was probably a stupid idea—who knew what would happen if he mixed mutagens. Emmett could already imagine Dr. Venture saying the same thing.

But it wasn't like Emmett was going to use any of the vials *now*. He could be a little patient. Besides, even if Dr. Venture talked him out of it, maybe Venture could help track down the origin of the compounds.

Emmett paused. The vials were only a few inches away from his fingers. He looked to Athena for approval.

Athena was already looking at him, her face a mix of apprehension and concern.

"I'm not your mother," she finally said. "I'm not going to stop you, but I think it's a bad idea. You'll need to keep them on ice, and for gods' sake don't take more than one at a time."

Emmett quickly grabbed two of each color vial—ten in total and stuffed them into his hoodie and his trousers.

The men fired another impotent barrage at Athena's barrier, making Emmett flinch.

"Do you have everything you need?" Athena stood, eyeing down the guards.

"Yes."

"Good." Athena turned and swept her hand toward the van, and an invisible forcefield shattered all the crates and the interior of the cab. Metal screeched, wood and glass shattered, and mutagens sprayed across the van and the pavement.

Emmett jumped back in surprise, shielding his face.

Athena grabbed him by the shoulder of his hoodie to get his attention. "Step exactly where I step."

She started *running upward* like she was bounding up huge invisible stairs... which Emmett supposed she was. Emmett followed, keeping his eyes on her shoes. It was even more nerve-wracking than walking a balance beam; Emmett kept his whip ready because it felt like he might fall at any second.

Moments later they were back on the roof and sprinting toward the center of the city, crossing the coffee shop roof so that Emmett could grab his stashed items. Emmett clutched the vials as he ran, trying his best to keep them from clinking together.

Two blocks later, they heard the first police sirens.

"Down into the alley," Athena said. Emmett followed her off the roof, using his whip to drop to the ground. "Now change up your disguise."

Emmett pulled off his hoodie and wrapped all the vials inside it, along with his mask. He made sure to keep his face turned, so it was hidden by his hair and by the darkness of the alley.

Athena slipped off her dark leather jacket and flipped it inside out. It was plain red leather on the inside. Emmett hadn't realized that it was reversible; it couldn't have been comfortable—the original dark side had shards of mirror woven into it...

Athena finished by wrapping her long white hair into a bun and slipping on a beanie.

It wasn't until Athena was done changing her disguise that Emmett realized her jacket *shouldn't* have been able to flip inside out like that.

Athena noticed him staring and said nonchalantly, "It's a magic coat."

"Oh."

"One day I'll tell you the story, but for now, we need to split up. Are you okay going home from here?"

Emmett nodded. "Yeah, I think I'm good."

"Alright, see you around," Athena replied, giving him a quick nod. "Next time you can tell me about that arm." With that, she walked down the alley, leaving Emmett holding his hoodie full of Gnosis knock-off contraband.

Emmett let out a sigh that he didn't know he'd been holding.

Well, that was something.

Just when Emmett was about to start walking home, Athena stuck her head around the corner and said, "Don't forget to think of a name!"

Chapter 29

Part-A

Emmett jogged the rest of the way to his apartment, hoping that he looked completely normal—like a guy out for a jog at 11 o'clock at night.

Even though jogging was easier than it had ever been, Emmett's heart was racing the entire way home. By the time he got to the Woods apartments on the West End, Emmett was a bundle of nerves.

He just wanted to make it to his room without talking to anyone—without any luck Lock would be out tonight, too.

It seemed like *everyone* was out tonight—the gazebos and lawns of the Woods were littered with students. Maybe it wasn't anymore than usual; it was Friday night, after all.

There was even someone lighting fireworks; three quick pops of light shone over the apartments.

Emmett kept his head down as he passed the gazebos and breathed a sigh of relief—a small one—when he got to the steps of his apartment building.

He'd made it.

A wave of exhaustion hit him, and Emmett couldn't wait to lie down and go to sleep.

Emmett walked up to door 449, took out his keys, and froze—

There was music coming from inside, and not the stuff that Emmett or Lock normally listened to.

And people were talking inside.

Oh shit. Lock had people over.

Until then, Emmett was going to stuff the vials in the bottom of the ice maker or even in a random food box; he would've used something Lock didn't like to minimize the chance of him stumbling on the vials—at least until tomorrow when he could take the vials to the lab.

But it wasn't like he could just walk in, say hi, and start stuffing the vials in the freezer. What if Lock or one of his friends were in the kitchen? *Oh, don't mind these, they're just knock-off Gnosis, not the real thing.*

Emmett turned and kept walking. He didn't know what else to do. At least this would buy him a few minutes to think.

He walked across the hall to the next set of stairs, meaning to go down a floor and circle back.

The vials were supposed to stay cold, so the freezer was preferable, but maybe he could hide them somewhere else in the meantime. His room might have to do. The only problem was, Emmett wasn't sure if they had a spare lunch bag in the apartment, much less anything insulated.

Emmett chuckled defeatedly to himself. Maybe one of Lock's friends brought a cooler. *Hey, mind if I use that?*

Maybe the roof? Emmett shook his head. It wasn't supposed to be cold tonight, so it was the same problem as his room.

Maybe he could put them in a plastic bag and put them in the toilet tank. Emmett felt like he'd seen that in a movie once. The water was cold-ish and he could dump ice in too. At least there was no chance of anyone looking in there.

...Welp, it might have to be the toilet.

Emmett finished his lap of the third floor and went back up. Then he went to room 449 and opened the door.

Lock had people over.

Emmett was hit by a wall of sound when the door opened. There was a group talking in the kitchen who all simultaneously turned to greet him. Emmett gave a half-hearted nod as he tried to process what he was seeing. There were even more people in the living room. All looked like they might've been college students, wearing a mix of hoodies, polos, and dresses.

Emmett wasn't big on parties, but he'd been to a few—enough to realize that's what he was looking at now.

Lock wasn't just having people over. Was he having a party?

His stomach turned and his hands felt clammy. Immediately, Emmett clutched his hoodie tighter.

Normally, he would've been equal parts annoyed and confused that Lock would throw a party without telling him. They'd always been solid enough roommates that they checked with each other before bringing people over—especially this many people.

And here Emmett was, standing in the kitchen clutching vials of knock-off Gnosis mutagens.

Emmett looked over the room again. He didn't see Lock.

And the bathroom door was closed.

Alright, next plan—keep the vials in his room. That would have to do for now. Thankfully, Emmett's bedroom door was cracked and the light was off.

Emmett muttered, "excuse me," as he shuffled into the kitchen. Carefully, he pushed aside the couple of empty liquor bottles on the counter and set down his bundled hoodie so that the vials didn't clink together, then grabbed a soda from the fridge. He grabbed the largest cup they had in the cabinet, filled it with ice, and grabbed a plastic sandwich bag from the nearby drawer—several bags.

The whole time hoping that his face wasn't actually as red as it felt and that no one could see his heart thrumming in his chest.

Then Emmett scurried to his room and flicked on the light—

And came face to face with a woman sitting on his bed. She'd been scrolling her phone and now stared at him with a wide-eyed expression.

"This... This is my room."

Her cheeks turned as red as Emmett's. "I was just checking my phone. Needed a break from the party."

"That's okay," Emmett stammered, trying to reassure her and think of an excuse to get her out. "But, uh, I need to change."

"Oh! Okay," she said, jumping up and hurrying past him.

"Wait! Is Lock around?"

She paused and glanced around the living room. "I guess he's still up on the roof."

Emmett nodded, quickly shut his door, and locked it. Then he collapsed on his bed, sighing deeply.

Now he'd made it. He could stash the mutagens somewhere safe for the night. And it had only been a little awkward getting in the apartment and to his room.

Emmett dumped the ice from the cup into the plastic bags, then tucked the vials, ice, and a can of cold unopened soda into a spare hoodie. Then he shoved the hoodie under his bed and between his storage boxes. It would last at least until everyone had left.

He tucked his mask and burner phone in the mattress cover, then laid back on his bed, exhausted and in disbelief.

What was he going to do now? Emmett didn't feel ready yet to go out and talk to Lock, much less random people. He thought about trying to sleep and talking to Lock about the party in the morning, but there was no way he was going to fall asleep with everything going on—as if on cue, two more pops of fireworks echoed through the Woods. And it wasn't like he could get any work done—all his stuff was either in the living room or out on the roof.

So Emmett pulled out his phone to kill some time.

And immediately saw he had missed messages:

Lock 6:12 PM: *Hey. Going to celebrate with friends tonight. Don't wait up.*
Lock 7:39 PM: *Cool if a few of us hang at the apartment?*
Lock 8:31 PM: *People coming back to the apartment. Be there around 9:30.*

Emmett sighed. He hadn't even thought to check his phone—he'd been too busy training in the lab and then knocking off that shipment with Athena.

Well, at least Lock had tried to get a hold of him. He texted back:

Emmett 11:46 PM: *Missed your texts. I'm back. Chilling for a bit.*

Then he scrolled the forums, going through *Double Mask*, *Reddest Knight*, and *The Green Machine*, looking for any information about the mutagens or their knock-offs.

There wasn't much, which didn't surprise Emmett—big companies like Gnosis would scrub any leaked information. He managed to find one thread on *Double Mask* talking about mutagen variants, but all of the posts and user info had been deleted.

Emmett groaned in frustration, lay back on the bed, staring at his ceiling.

He could always ask Dr. Venture... Venture said himself that he was familiar with Gnosis. Not to mention the fact that he'd somehow procured a dose of Mutagen-A to save Emmett's life.

Maybe Venture could analyze the samples and figure out something about their origins...

There was always the chance that Venture would be mad about Emmett taking the vials in the first place and that he would try to talk Emmett out of supplementing his diet... But if he could help Athena out then it would be worth it.

Oh, yeah... He'd have to tell Dr. Venture and Clara about Athena. Emmett had forgotten to mention her.

Oops.

Emmett lounged in bed until midnight before he was calmed down enough to venture outside his room.

The party was still going, and Lock was still nowhere to be found. So Emmett waded through the living room, past the half-dozen people talking, to the fire escape and climbed up to the roof.

Emmett found Lock and several others talking on the roof. They had pulled out folding chairs and were gathered in a circle, vaping, drinking, and carrying on.

"What's going on," Lock said, waving Emmett over. "Guys, this is my roommate, Emmett. *The engineer.*"

Emmett walked over sheepishly with his hands stuffed in his pockets.

Lock's tone made Emmett think his roommate had been enjoying his party—not to mention the empty bottle of rum beside his chair.

Lock introduced the other three: Manton, Carter, and Jessie. Manton met Emmett's eyes from behind a thick beard and an equally thick pair of glasses; he and Lock had known each other from biology classes. Carter smiled from behind the popped collar of a stylish long coat, their features sharp and androgynous. Jessie hid behind a baggy hoodie. Lock knew them both from Gnosis.

They were celebrating Jessie's promotion.

Emmett tried to keep a straight face. "Cool. And congratulations."

Jessie let out a loud woo, cupped her hands together, and then threw something upward. A small bundle of light sailed high into the night air and popped.

"So that was you earlier..." But Emmett had seen her hands... No fireworks. No lighter. "How did you do that?"

Jessie peered out from behind her hoodie and flashed a smile.

Lock smirked. "Jessie's *special* like that."

Emmett's eyes widened, and Jessie nodded quickly, like she was a kid on a playground sharing a secret. She cupped her hands together, and this time Emmett watched intently as a tiny flame peeked out from between her fingers. She hurled it up into the air and it popped overhead.

Carter leaned over and elbowed Lock. "He doesn't look impressed. You said he would be impressed."

Lock gestured at him. "Man, this guy here is a bona fide super *fanboy*. Or at least I thought so." Then Lock's face suddenly turned blank and unreadable. "Guess, I was wrong."

"It's not that..." Emmett muttered. "It's cool. I just had a long day. Tell you about it later—" He turned to Jessie. "You're not worried? I thought most *people*... you know... hid their powers?"

Carter interjected. "Why should she hide?"

Lock replied, "We're all friends here. Emmett's cool."

Emmett shrugged and said to Carter, "Most supers wear masks, don't they?"

Carter raised an eyebrow. "Maybe they shouldn't."

Manton rolled his eyes behind his glasses. "Oh, don't start that again. We were having a nice night, and you had to go and get political."

Carter added, "There's nothing *wrong* with reevaluating things we take for granted, even things about ourselves."

Jessie made another firecracker with her power and tossed it overhead. It popped a moment later.

Lock chuckled—clearly inebriated and in better spirits than everyone, except maybe Jessie. "What Carter is trying to say is that the world's backwards. Why are supers the ones skulking around at night and in masks? Hiding from normal people."

There was something menacing about the way Lock said '*normal people*'—even beneath his jovial inebriation. And it almost made Emmett shudder.

Emmett asked, "What else would supers do?"

Manton rolled his eyes again. "Don't get them started. I beg of you."

Jessie giggled. "Manton, you're just sad 'cause you're normal."

Lock held up his hands. "Fine. Fine. No more supers *or* politics."

Jessie threw another firecracker into the air for emphasis.

Chapter 30

Lock

Lock woke up Saturday afternoon to the sun peeking through a crack in the curtains. He wiped the sleep out of his eyes and sat on the edge of the bed. He winced at the headache and massaged his temples.

So... he could still catch a hangover—it just took him three bottles of rum now instead of one.

Thankfully, only Manton, Carter, and Jessie had seen him chugging straight out of the bottle and they already knew Lock was enhanced. They didn't give him any grief.

He didn't have to hide from them.

Emmett on the other hand...

Synth music was playing quietly in the living room. No doubt Emmett was working steadily on his radio locator project. Lock could picture him hunched over the table, surrounded by electronics. The man was a machine like that, always working.

If only Emmett would've stayed like that—It would've been so much easier if one of them was normal. But no, Emmett had to go and get shot up with Mutagen-A.

Emmett had to go and fuck it up.

Lock reached into his nightstand and grabbed pills for his headache, then he pulled out his pipe and something for his nerves.

He inhaled deeply, letting the powerful drugs take the edge off his changing body. All the while, he looked at his bedroom door, toward the living room and Emmett beyond.

Emmett was lucky. Lock wasn't sure how Venture had gotten Emmett a dose of Mutagen-A, but at least he'd started with that and not something else from Gnosis. Not all of their mutagens were created equal—even turning into a monster wasn't the worst that could happen with a bad reaction.

To make things worse, there were other nefarious parties that were making their own alterations to the mutagens and selling them on the street. Rumor was, there was a mole in Gnosis. The company poured resources into the problem—not just finding the mole, but trying to keep it quiet.

It was barely working.

Lock knew because Carter knew, but it had only been a few weeks since the first reports and now everyone at Gnosis was whispering about it.

Sooner or later, the news would piece things together. Lock had seen enough of the other mutagens that he knew there wasn't really a string of vampire attacks in Wardenton; Gnosis and the media were covering up for mutagens getting onto the street.

Lock's burner phone beeped, and he pulled it out from under his pillow.

Simon 3:04 PM: *Work has been moved up to 5:00 PM today. Location 2D. Be in position by 4:30.*

Lock 3:05 PM: *Received.*

Lock stood and got dressed, throwing on slacks and khakis. Ones he didn't particularly care for. He slipped a black hoodie on overtop, all the while trying to suppress his frustration.

This was the third time in a row *Simon* had moved a job last minute. And he still had the gall to tell Lock to be there early.

Lock wasn't some punk. He always got there early to scout a job.

That was part of why Gnosis had recommended Lock in the first place, and why he was paid so well for his services: Powers, discretion, adaptation... and ability to put up with client's bullshit.

The only problem with today is that Lock had to leave in the next few minutes to get to South Central Station early.

Once Lock was ready to go, he left his room and went to the kitchen to grab a protein bar. He nodded to Emmett, who looked up from his pile of electronics at the table.

"How are you feeling today?" Emmett smirked. "You looked like you were feeling good last night."

Lock's headache was already subsiding, but he made a show of rubbing his temples. "It was good. You should've come back early and hung out with us."

Emmett chuckled awkwardly, looking at the pile of electronics like it was going to save him. "Yeah, I got hung up with work."

Lock nodded and kept a straight face.

Right. At work. With Dr. Venture.

Right.

"Don't work too hard." Lock smirked and turned for the door.

"Hey... I'll catch you later."

Lock didn't turn. "Maybe." Then he left the apartment and headed for South Central Station.

Lock and Emmett had been close for most of their time at Belport University, but that all changed junior year when they both got their internships—Lock with Gnosis and Emmett with Dr. Venture.

Both of them had joked that it was a big step. *Real jobs,* they said. They'd even joked that they wouldn't see each other much anymore—at least they'd been right about that.

But neither of them had known what they were getting into. How could they?

Maybe that was why Lock was mad about Emmett taking Mutagen-A; it wasn't that Venture had dosed him without Gnosis's guidance, or that Emmett might be in danger of mutation or being found out...

Lock had been keeping his own powers secret from Emmett for over a year now, and now Emmett was keeping his own secrets.

It felt like betrayal, despite the hypocrisy.

But it had started even before that.

Lock had missed hanging out with his roommate.

Lock had grown up on the rougher side of Belport, and he hadn't had the luxury of keeping too many friends. It was hard to do that when you were keeping your nose clean and staying out of trouble, all so he could get into Belport University. All so he could get out of the slums.

Emmett had been the first real friend Lachlan had. Now Emmett had betrayed him.

It wasn't fair.

Lock wasn't supposed to be the one getting left behind. He wasn't supposed to have friends. It made it easier to leave when he didn't.

Lock walked down the streets of Belport, head down, hands stuffed in his hoodie. Silent. Reminiscing. Wondering where he went wrong. Seething.

Yeah, he felt like a hypocrite, but the difference was Lock was better at hiding his powers. Emmett probably still thought he was a bouncer.

In contrast, Lock had figured his roommate out the night of the Champion street attack. Emmett spent the night with some random chick he'd never mentioned—*right*. It was such a shitty cover story that Lock had been insulted.

He'd been relieved too, that Emmett hadn't been on the bus that night when it'd been cut in half. And it was funny just how short-lived that feeling had been.

Now, Lock was just angry.

It had been easy to pretend that everything was the same when Lock was only keeping his own secrets... When he was the only one lying.

Lock arrived at South Central Station at 5:20 PM. Ten minutes to spare. He leaned against a pillar near the East entrance, hoodie tucked under his arm.

His left eye twitched. It was hot and noisy down here, and Lock wished he had his pipe to take the edge off his powers.

South Central Station was underground. In almost every way, it was a surveillance nightmare. It was one of the wider platforms in Belport, well-lit, and absolutely packed with people. It was one of the last places they should be meeting at, which meant Simon had chosen this platform in spite of those reasons.

It meant Simon was worried about the client he was meeting, and he was trusting that client's better judgment not to start shit in the middle of a crowded station.

Hopefully that trust was better placed than Lock's had been.

A few minutes later, Simon walked down the stairs of the East entrance, wearing an obnoxious three-piece suit and carrying a large handbag. This time he'd darkened his complexion, and opted for tits, and long, almost shining black hair. It took Lock a few seconds to recognize the shapeshifter—he always came to these things wearing a different body.

There was no hiding his smell, though. He sweat too much, and no matter which cologne he wore, he always put on too damn much.

Or the swagger he walked with.

Lock smirked. Simon met his eyes and tried to hide his dejection.

"How is it you can always tell?"

Lock shrugged. "Maybe you're not as good as you think."

Simon smiled and scoffed, thinking Lock was joking when he wasn't.

There was a thought—a shapeshifter that was actually conscientious enough to hide their scent, and change their demeanor and accents. Too bad every shapeshifter Lock had met was sloppy.

A man and a woman followed Simon, both walking with the confidence only supers had. Enforcers—both dressed in black business casual, meant to be as forgettable as possible. That was the way to blend in without a mask—be as plain and forgettable.

Simon didn't look at either of them. "Stay close," was all he said.

Lock and the two other enforcers followed at respectable distances, then took positions around the subway platform. Lock leaned against the nearby pillar and waited.

A few minutes later, Lock spotted another unassuming group walk down the opposite stairs—

It was almost funny to think that no one noticed them: Four men with military haircuts and dark clothes, one of which carrying a briefcase. Even when they split up, their eyes scanned the crowd. To Lock, it was painfully obvious that they weren't there to catch the train.

But then, no one seemed to notice the group or Lock's group. No one paid any mind as Simon and his contact exchanged the briefcase and the bag with only a few words, then walked away.

None of the other groups or families or travelers noticed. No—they just weren't looking. They didn't *want* to see Simon or Lock, or any of the other enforcers or supers. They didn't want to see what was really going on.

Lock knew this because he was much the same. He didn't know who Simon or his contact worked for. Didn't want to know what businesses Gnosis contracted their experiments out to, or what Emmett had been doing with his newfound powers.

Simon walked past Lock and joined up with the other two enforcers. They would escort Simon to wherever he was going.

Lock kept his eye on the crowd and watched Simon out of the corner of his eye as the three walked up the East stairs and back out into Belport. Thankfully, today's job went off without a hitch.

Easy money.

CHAPTER 31

Clara

Clara had found her father in the hub of section 006—the biomedical wing—staring intently at a cluster of monitors. He didn't so much as turn when she entered.

"I have a lead," she said.

"A lead on what?"

"Porcelain."

Her father still hadn't responded by the time Clara walked over to him. She looked over his shoulder at the readouts.

The screens were absolutely covered with information—charts, diagrams, graphs, and wave patterns, all scrunched together like tightly packed building blocks.

It was so much to take in that Clara only got a vague idea of what her father was mulling over:

Emmett.

The metal arm was a dead giveaway.

He flicked the power of the monitors, turning them dark. Then he spun around in his chair to face her.

"What's this—"

"Why are you so interested in Emmett?" she asked, cutting him off. She hadn't meant the question to come out so harshly.

"I'm monitoring his progress. Mutagen-A may be Gnosis's best-tested formula, but there's always the chance of anomalies."

Clara narrowed her eyes. Dad didn't lie frequently, but he was fond of omitting parts of the truth.

Venture sighed and added, "I'm also looking at ways he might progress, both biologically and mechanically. Emmett has a unique opportunity. His body is taking extraordinarily well to Mutagen-A, and his prosthetic arm is a breakthrough of neural integration—it might very well lead to breakthroughs for other parts of your armor."

It had been a while since Dad had been so excited and hopeful. He got that way when he found a solution to a problem.

Clara felt queasy, and she had a lump in her throat that felt like it would climb out if she spoke.

She managed to ask, "Is it safe?"

Venture's eyebrows wrinkled in concern. He'd seen right through her pitiful facade. "Of course it's safe. Mutagen A is Gnosis's best tested formula, and I'll monitor him every step of the way."

Clara grit her teeth. She *hated* that people could tell when she was upset. If there was only one thing she could change about herself, it would be that.

Venture moved like he was about to stand up, like he was going to offer her a hug—

"Don't," Clara said quickly. "I'm fine."

"Clara, you're not jealous, are you? Because it doesn't—"

"I'm not. I just think you should ask Emmett first."

He nodded sullenly. "I plan on it. It will be his choice what direction he goes."

Clara felt her chest clench again. "Then I *am* jealous."

"Why?"

"Because you're giving him the choice."

Clara turned and walked away before her father could reply. She called back from the hall. "I'm going out."

Clara stormed off to the armory—section 004—feeling hot and angry. She stopped in front of the blast door and controlled her breathing while she waited for TINA to scan her.

A moment later, TINA's voice came through the old speaker. *"Greeting Clara, what exosuit would you like prepared for you?"*

She should've expected the question—No matter how old Clara was or how many times she'd entered this wing, TINA always asked it. Still, it didn't help Clara calm down.

"The only one he lets me wear."

The double doors hissed open, and Clara disappeared down the winding halls.

The Venture armory was the second most secure wing of the lab, second only to Clara and her father's living quarters.

Every system of the wing was isolated and redundant, including TINA. This meant that even if an enemy breached the outer defenses of the lab or somehow gained access to other sections, the enemy was still locked out of the armory.

When Clara was young, she'd thought her dad was paranoid to put so much thought into the lab's networks and sequestrations. Then, when Clara was eleven years old, sorcerers from a splinter cell of the Felwardens breached the lab. TINA and the lab's countless defenses stalled them long enough for Dr. Venture to return. If not for all the defenses, the sorcerers might've killed Clara... Well, they would've tried.

Now Clara walked the winding halls and entered the armory proper. The hallway ended, giving way to a metal catwalk. The metal walls blossomed out in all directions into a gigantic, spherical room three hundred feet in diameter.

The walls of the armory were far too blocky. To Clara, it looked like giant metal gears were embedded in the walls—frozen and unmoving. Each outcropping of metal hid an exosuit.

The catwalk ended in the center of the room, hanging in the center of the sphere.

As Clara reached the center platform, she turned to her right and watched a small door open in the wall. Then her armor floated out from it and across the room to the platform. When Clara was a little girl, she had asked her father how exactly the armory worked, but he'd never given a straight answer. The closest that Clara could tell, TINA levitated the exosuit over to the center platform.

It was odd to witness—unsettling even, sometimes. As many times as she'd watched the suit float across the room, it was still *weird*.

Weird like the Gray Room. Like they didn't belong.

Her suit set down on the center platform, sleek and stealth gray, and the back hatch opened, silently beckoning her in. Clara climbed inside and the hatch closed behind her.

Most suits, including Clara's, were designed in almost 1:1 proportions with the user's body—the exception being the forearms and hands. Rather than slipping her hands into gloves, Clara's hands rested in the end of the suit's forearms, her fingers wrapped around tightly-packed switches—this allowed the user to control both the hands and internal controls for various subsystems with their fingers.

The next thing Clara felt was the cool, subtle touch of mesh as the pockets in the lining of the suit filled with pressurized gel. These acted as a cushion to disperse impact and as environmental filters for toxins and extreme heat (on top of the heat sinks for the systems). Thin tubes in the helmet helped force air through the gel and into a solidified *pocket* around Clara's nose and mouth.

As the exosuit cocooned her, the main system responded to Clara's presence—regulators funneled her power to the dozens of systems and subsystems. For a split second, Clara saw the world only through the small ballistic window of her helmet, but even that closed once the exosuit booted up.

A breath later, her Heads Up Display (HUD) appeared on the inside of her helmet—her electronic window to the outside.

Blue text appeared: ALL SYSTEMS OPERATIONAL

Clara flicked the switch to engage her thrusters. Even through all the dampening and shielding, she could feel the heat and power funneling from the rest of the suit to the thruster systems that wrapped around her legs and feet.

THRUSTERS ENGAGED

Years ago, Clara disabled the TINA's onboard voiceover for everything except alerts, opting instead for text displays in the HUD. She preferred to hear the ambient sounds of the city and the wind rushing around her as she flew.

A passage opened up in the ceiling of the armory, and Clara rocketed toward it.

The sound reminded her of fire.

Clara raised her arms overhead as she flew through the passage, weaving through twists and turns as it passed through the underground of Belport.

STEALTH SYSTEM ENGAGED

The matte gray of her suit vanished in a mirage—hiding her not just from sight, but also hiding her radar and heat signatures, and masking the sound of her flight.

Clara soared more or less invisibly across the night sky of Belport.

An hour ago, one of Venture's drones spotted a super matching Porcelain's description—white mask, white bodysuit—and sent the location to Clara and Dr. Venture.

Her father had been too busy to notice.

Clara followed her guidance system to the coordinates on the outer limits of the Eastside, past the old factories and warehouses. Few were still in operation. Most were boarded up like wooden bandaids over grungy brick and broken glass.

Despite the squalor, it wasn't completely empty. There were small fires that transients huddled around and small flashes of power as low-level supers fought. The police and the capes turned a blind eye to most of it, since keeping brawls relegated to the abandoned areas of the city spared places citizens actually cared about.

The drone waited atop one of those warehouses, using the same stealth tech as Clara's suit.

Clara scanned the building as she approached, her HUD showing an overlay of the building's interior. It was completely empty and quiet, except for three homeless people sleeping on the second floor.

That was fine with her—it was completely empty where she needed to go.

Clara hovered near the roof, then followed the drone through a broken fourth-floor window. She set down and followed the drone as it floated through the dusty hall. The world turned a sharp green as her visor automatically switched to a low-light view, and exhaust gas and dampeners cushioned her steps. Clara walked the abandoned hall like a ghost.

Of all the places in Belport... Why had Porcelain come here?

Was she hiding out after the Champion street attack? Had she been meeting a contact?

Clara followed the drone into a large room with a window overlooking highways that led out of the city. At one point, newspapers had been stuck to the enormous window, but now they were peeling down in sheets and littered the floor. The panes that were visible were cracked and broken.

The drone stopped just inside the door. Its onboard scanning was much more detailed than her own, so Clara patched into its feed.

SCANNING SUITE ACTIVATED

Immediately, Clara's HUD was overwhelmed by a wall of blue. She fumbled the controls, dialing back the sensitivity. Eventually, the solid blue turned to a cloud and then to a haze.

Porcelain hadn't just been here—it looked like she'd fought for her life!

Every smear of blue was Porcelain's residual power signature. The haze of blue that enveloped the room was actually dozens of smaller clouds that had congealed together. Now that Clara had dialed back the intensity of the data, she saw the ground littered with blue crystals.

She stooped down and rifled through newspapers until she found one of the crystals—it was a shard of white glass, exactly matching the chemical signature of Porcelain's other remnants.

Clara shivered with unease.

"Are you seeing this?" she asked, trying to keep her voice even.

"Yes," Venture replied through her headset. *"I'm setting the drone to scan for other power signatures."*

The drone's internals whirred quietly as the drone scanned the rest of the room.

Clara knew from experience that the scan should only take a minute.

Three minutes passed.

"What's wrong?"

"There's no other power signatures there except for Porcelain's. I had the drone repeat the scan to be sure."

Clara looked around the room, once more feeling a pit of dread. Even though her HUD would automatically alert her to any movement in the building, Clara couldn't shake the feeling that she wasn't alone.

"What does that mean?"

"I don't know. Do a visual search of the room, grab samples, then return to the lab."

"Sure thing." Dad didn't need to tell her twice.

Clara dialed back the blue highlights in her display and searched with only her low-light view. She walked the length of the room, taking in the ruin and the... atrophy. Shards of porcelain crunched beneath her suit.

The room felt heavy, like Clara could feel the weight of the air or maybe the battle pressing down on her. The weight of loss.

Of something broken.

Chapter 32

As the World Turns

Emmett spent Saturday trying to focus on schoolwork. It wasn't easy.

He topped off the mutagen vials with fresh ice and pushed them back under his bed. Even after Lock woke up and rushed out of the apartment, Emmett tried to keep from fixating on the vials—

There wasn't any point. Emmett wasn't about to take any of the mutagens blindly. He'd wait until he could take the vials by the lab on Monday and ask Dr. Venture to analyze them.

And he really did have schoolwork to do.

Last night didn't help his concentration either. Emmett kept going back to his conversation on the rooftop with Lock and his friends—how carefree they'd been about Jessie showing off her powers.

Emmett had excused himself after only a brief conversation. He blamed it on being tired, but in truth, he'd just felt awkward about the whole dynamic—Jessie's showing off her powers wasn't normal. Even if they were on the roof, it was still a public place. It went against everything Emmett knew about supers.

Then there was Carter's comment that supers shouldn't have to hide. Lock had even agreed!

Emmett still wasn't sure how he felt about it... Especially now that he was a super.

Supers hid to protect themselves and their families. Maybe Carter and Lock thought they didn't have anyone to keep safe... but that was ridiculous.

Then there was something else Jessie said to Manton: *"Manton, you're just sad 'cause you're normal."*

Did anyone else in their group have powers? Carter probably did, considering her views on hiding... But what about Lock? They all worked for Gnosis, except for Manton...

Emmett stared idly at the table and the mass of electronics sitting on it.

That would be something, wouldn't it? Emmett went and got an internship with a retired super, and wound up becoming one himself. Lock got an internship with a company *quite literally* making supers... What if Lock was a super, too?

Emmett chuckled bleakly.

What were the odds of that?

On Sunday, Emmett topped off the ice on the vials and left for his parents house across the city. Lock had come home late and still wasn't awake by the time Emmett left.

Instead of jogging to his parents' house, Emmett opted for his usual routine of taking the bus.

His parents lived in a rowhouse in a small neighborhood just outside the Heights. It was a quiet place, lined with chain-link fences and patches of lawn, seemingly full of other folks his parents' age. It was an older section of Belport that had managed to escape both the sprawl and gentrification of other areas.

Emmett got off the bus and walked the blocks of rowhouses until he came to Hayden Avenue, then walked down the block—to the home he'd grown up in.

Emmett's childhood home was in the center, brick-faced and almost indistinguishable from the surrounding block—except for the strawberry knick knacks sitting in the window.

He walked up and punched in the door code on the keypad, then let himself in and hollered a greeting. It sounded like everyone was in the kitchen at the end of the hall.

His older brother, Darryl, peeked out from the kitchen, sporting a wide smile half-hidden behind his bushy beard. The collar of his button-up was already loose—he must've gotten stuck working from home before coming to mom and dad's. "There he is. Late, as per usual. Man, I hope you read blueprints better than you read a clock."

Emmett groaned and met him halfway down the hall for a hug. "Must be nice, having your own car."

"My own car. Hah! It's the family's car. I'm just the chauffeur."

As if on cue, one of Darryl's kids ran past—too quick to identify.

"Hey, no running in the house!" Darryl turned and stormed after them.

Emmett shook his head and walked down the hall, past the photos hanging on the wall of him and his brothers when they were young, and into the kitchen where most of the family had gathered. He answered their greetings and leaned against the kitchen wall.

Mom and Emmett's youngest brother, Antony, were preparing dinner. Mom was getting a pot ready for instant potatoes and putting the finishing touches on a roast, moving with a whirl of purpose. Tony was at the end of the counter, chopping vegetables for salad. His kid brother looked bigger every time Emmett saw him. Antony was a junior at Rutherford High, and played tight end on the football team... or at least Emmett thought that was the position—he could only remember that Antony played defense.

Dad was sitting at the kitchen table, staring intently at his phone—likely doing a crossword puzzle. He chimed in to the conversation without looking up.

Darryl's wife, Maci, was in the living room, booting up the old GameBox for the kids—the same one that Emmett and his brothers had played for the last ten years. His two nephews were huddled in front of the TV, controllers in hand and intense looks in their eyes. They were perpetually toddlers in Emmett's eyes, even though they were both in elementary school now. The oldest boy, Martie, waved sheepishly to Emmett. Emmett waved back.

It might keep the kids occupied until dinner.

Darryl walked back into the kitchen and slumped down at the table across from Dad.

So Sunday at the Laraways began in an earnest and orderly fashion.

Updates were first:

Darryl lamented not being able to get a raise at the office, but at least the kids were both in school now and they didn't need to pay for daycare anymore. Maci's government job was going well, which helped.

Dad was counting down the days until retirement with the steadfastness of a soldier on the front lines. *'How long until retirement, Dad?' 'Two years, two hundred and sixty-four days, and this morning.'* Meanwhile, Mom was the opposite, she loved her teaching job and said she never wanted to retire.

Meanwhile, Emmett had started to sweat.

So, it turns out that Dr. Venture, you know, my eccentric inventor-mentor, is a retired hero and gave me superpowers. Also, I almost died. I forgot about that. It's okay though. I'm totally fine. Better, actually.

Also, I have a metal arm. I met another mask. I can leap across rooftops, and I got shot at! It's okay though. I'm totally fine.

Yeah... Emmett couldn't tell them any of that.

So, when expectant glances turned to Emmett, he shrugged and stammered out what he could tell them: About classes and his radio locator project.

After his short update, Dad eyed him suspiciously. "Keeping those grades up?"

"Of course."

"That's my boy," he replied, turning back to the puzzle on his phone.

Emmett looked to his kid brother, and on cue Antony updated them on his recent games—excitedly mentioning his multiple sacks and interceptions.

The youngest nephew, Justin, ran into the kitchen, shouting, "I won! I won!—"

And promptly got intercepted by his grandpa, who snatched him up absently with one arm. "What did we say about running? *What did we say about running?*" he asked, jostling the boy. Justin was giggling too much to answer—

Until grandpa put him down and Justin ran back toward the living room, exclaiming, "No running! No running!"

Darryl watched the boy go with a look of defeat.

"I blame you," Maci called good-naturedly from the living room.

So it went. They talked about work and school and the grandkids until dinner was ready. And the longer the day went on, the more silent Emmett became. At one point, Mom asked about Lock, and Emmett responded that Lock had been busy working and studying before Emmett deflected back to Darryl and the grandkids.

The less Emmett said, the less chance he'd accidentally say something he wasn't supposed to. It wasn't the first time he'd felt self-conscious about sharing something with his family. Emmett had always been an *under-sharer*, but this time was clearly different—not just for the superhero nature of it.

Maybe it was the magnitude of getting powers or of almost dying. Maybe it was how getting powers felt like it affected everything in Emmett's life...

Yeah, maybe that was it. Everything was different now.

It reminded Emmett of when his grandparents died. It had been a car crash—sudden and unexpected. Emmett had to go pick up groceries for Mom because she was so distraught. Dad still had to work. Up until they got the news, it had been such a normal day.

Emmett had barely kept it together himself as he wandered the aisles of the grocery store. Everyone else was just going about their lives because it was a normal day *for them*. As much as he wanted to, Emmett couldn't just stop in the middle of the aisle and tell someone that his grandparents had died.

At one point, Emmett stood in the middle of an aisle, unmoving, while shoppers browsed and shuffled around him. All he wanted to do was stop and the world just... kept going.

That day, it had been hard not to feel spiteful at all the normal people going about their day while Emmett felt like his chest was turning inside out. All he wanted to do was stop and plant himself out of spite while the world kept turning around him.

While today felt so similar, it wasn't quite the same...

Emmett tried to listen, tried to participate, but he felt walled off from everyone. Like every minute that passed, every back and forth that he didn't participate in was placing another brick between him and the rest of his family.

He decided *that* was the part that felt strange. Any other time something was eating him, Emmett told himself that the feeling or the situation would pass. Even his grandparents' deaths had gotten easier with time. In time, it was just like walking past a picture in the hallway.

But being a mask wasn't something that was just going to go away. This was Emmett's life now, and he needed to make peace with it.

Thankfully, dinner was the quietest part of the afternoon; it was hard to carry a conversation over Mom's cooking, but the nephews carried enough of it for everyone, talking about elementary school.

After dinner, Emmett busied himself rinsing off dishes and loading the dishwasher. It was his usual chore, but it was a welcome reprieve today.

While he did dishes, the rest of the family cleaned up, and Mom packed leftovers for Emmett and Darryl's side to take home. She saved the rest for Dad and Antony, joking that they would make short work of whatever was left behind.

Emmett would never admit it, but he was ready to get out of there. He held off until Darryl's family was ready to leave, for fear of eating and running, then made his rounds hugging everyone goodbye.

He was the first one out the door.

"Hey, man," Darryl called from the door as he tugged both nephews along with him. "Do you want a lift home?"

Emmett shuffled awkwardly. "It's okay. I'm going to take the bus back."

Darryl nodded. For a moment, he looked concerned, but it passed as quickly as it came. "Next time then."

Emmett forced a smile. "Next time."

Then he walked down the block, waving to the car when Darryl and the family passed.

When Emmett was far enough outside the Heights and the buildings were growing taller, he climbed up to the roofs and started the long jog home.

Chapter 33

The Illusion of Choice

"Let me get this straight... You've been a super for a little over a week, and you want to take another mutagen already?"

Dr. Venture's eyes were narrowed and focused on Emmett. There might have been a hint of a smile on the doctor's face, but somehow that unsettled Emmett more.

Until that moment, Emmett had been dying to get to the lab so he could confer with Dr. Venture and Clara about the mutagens. The weekend had dragged, classes had dragged. Even the jog over to the lab had taken forever. Emmett had practically barged into the medical wing and dumped the vials onto the center table.

Now Emmett felt like a kid who'd gotten caught sneaking candy before dinner.

"That wasn't the *only* reason I took them. It was a reason... but not the only one."

Venture glanced again at the vials in the grocery bag and shook his head. "And Athena just let you take them?"

The name made Emmett's throat go dry. "You already knew..."

"I'm keeping tabs on you, remember?" Venture's voice was level, as if he wasn't concerned about that detail at all. "Now, answer the question."

"Right," Emmett replied, still processing the fact that keeping secrets would be harder than he thought. "Well, she hesitated. Told me that she wasn't my mother, and not to take more than one at a time."

Venture nodded and turned back to the vials. "She's right on both counts... I'm not against you taking these, but you'll need to give me time to analyze them. We'll need to make sure that you won't have an adverse reaction with the Mutagen-A already in your system, especially considering that these aren't exactly Gnosis-approved."

Emmett leaned on the table, looking over the cold, multicolored vials. "Have you seen anything like this before? Athena said that there's a lot of these shipments."

"I've heard rumors, both from outside and inside Gnosis."

Emmett regarded Venture curiously. "What do you do for Gnosis? And how do you have a lab underneath their parking garage?"

Venture scoffed. "They have a parking garage above my lab. I was here first. As for what I do... Makes you wonder, doesn't it?"

Emmett rolled his eyes. "It does. I'll add it to the *mystery* pile."

Emmett spent the rest of the day training in the Gray Room and doing classwork at night. Tuesday was more of the same.

It felt like Lock was avoiding him. Emmett hadn't spoken more than two words to his roommate since the party. Lock was always working late or sleeping in. Emmett hoped that he hadn't said something stupid at the party and made things awkward with Lock and his friends.

Clara also seemed tight-lipped during their trainings, even leaving Emmett early to go out by herself in the city.

He asked if it was another lead on Porcelain, but Clara said that she couldn't say. Emmett guessed that her dad had sworn her to secrecy, but she wouldn't confirm it.

Eventually, Emmett quit prying—each time he asked, Clara's face twisted into a frown like she didn't want to keep it from him.

At least she didn't seem to get a kick out of keeping secrets like Venture did.

It was late Tuesday. Clara had already left the lab, leaving Emmett to train alone against auto-piloted robots. After an hour or so, Emmett gave up playing tag and walked out of the Gray Room in frustration.

He could only train for so long. Wasn't he supposed to be out there doing *something?* Clara was.

Dr. Venture met him in the main hallway.

"Follow me," was all he said.

"There are five compounds." Venture pointed to the five vials on the center of the biomedical table before continuing. "Unfortunately, you don't have that many choices."

Venture went on to explain each of the vials:

He pointed to the first vial, one the color of blood. "The first compound is a modification of Mutagen-A, designed to stimulate platelet and soft tissue production. In short, it would increase your healing factor by an additional factor of two to three. Unfortunately, it also stimulates tumor growth. You'd heal faster, but also kill yourself in the process. Therefore, I'm denying that choice."

The second vial was a swirl of unmixing red and brown. "This increases the density of the dermal and subdermal layers of tissue. In short, it would increase the strength and resilience of your skin."

Emmett frowned. He could already hear the disgust in Venture's tone. "What's wrong with it?"

"It would also change the appearance and texture of your skin... Something akin to the scales of a crocodile. In light of that, I'm denying this choice as well. Appearing normal is an advantage you shouldn't give up."

He didn't give Emmett time to voice concern before going to the third vial, which seemed to swirl with a mix of greens. "This was an interesting compound. It allows the body to create different chemical compounds not unlike those of the poison dart frog and other amphibians. Some were poisonous, even lethal, while others were hallucinogenic. Good for killing or disabling an opponent, depending on how the compound is secreted."

"That doesn't sound bad... What?"

Venture sighed. "Poisons are... frowned upon. Unless you want to look like a villain, I'd advise against this one."

Now Emmett couldn't help but groan. "So this is like one of those video games where there's multiple choices, but the outcome is the same?"

"Something like that."

Emmett held his hands up in defeat. "So why give me the option?"

"I knew you would ask what the others did. So I told you."

"...Fair enough."

Venture continued to the fourth vial, one that almost seemed to glow bright green. "This was another interesting compound. It helps amplify the body's innate electric field, even to the point of generating an impressive electrical charge. Think of the shock of an electric eel."

Emmett nodded. That was more like it. "...What's the catch?"

"No catch. I ran five simulations with each compound. These last two were completely safe."

"Okay. What about the last one?"

Venture gestured to the vial with swirling amber liquid. "This is perhaps the simplest one. It stimulates division of the rods and cones found in the human eye—specifically the rods. It will even stimulate the growth of UV and infrared receptors. It won't be as dramatic as wearing night vision goggles, but simply put, your low light vision will improve by several factors. You'll be able to see well in everything except absolute darkness."

"That... is not as cool as the other options."

Venture smirked. "Not as flashy, but infinitely more useful. And we might be able to revise the formula in the future."

Emmett looked over the vials again. He only had two options, which was disappointing, but at least the fourth option seemed useful. Emmett was already thinking ahead, stunning opponents with an electrical charge—maybe even at range with his whip.

Venture cleared his throat.

Emmett looked up, defeated. "What now?"

Venture explained, "Of the two options, I suggest you go with vial five—low light vision. If you're considering option four, I'll just say that's something we can duplicate with tech rather easily."

Emmett did his best to keep a straight face. "I can't take both, can I?"

"No," Venture replied flatly. "Your body will take time to acclimate to each new mutagen. We need to see how you react before you take a second vial."

"Is there any chance that we can modify the other compounds so that they're safe to take?"

Venture met Emmett's eyes, and this time there was a hint of satisfaction on his face. "Not without Gnosis's help, and I'm not keen on them asking questions."

Emmett nodded. "Fair enough." Then his decision was already made. "Can I take it now?"

Venture nodded. "So long as you're willing to hang around for another hour to make sure there aren't any side effects."

"Hah! I'd stay the night and have a sleepover if I needed to."

Venture didn't laugh, didn't even crack a smile.

"Or not."

Venture handed him the vial. "I'd swallow it quickly."

Emmett took the vial and was about to ask why when he uncorked the top and got a whiff. It smelled like pure gasoline.

He gagged and asked, "You're sure this is okay to drink?"

Venture smirked and nodded.

Emmett eyed the vial suspiciously before forcing himself to drink it. He wanted to get stronger, and taking a shot of something nasty had to be one of the quickest and easiest ways to do it.

He remembered what Lock told him once about pinching his nose when he took a shot of liquor to make the taste less intense. Emmett pinched his nose and tilted the vial all the way back.

Pinching his nose didn't help in the slightest.

The mutagen burned all the way down like he'd swallowed red-hot coals. Emmett tried to breathe and it felt like flames were shooting out his nose.

It was everything he could do to set the empty vial down and grab onto the table while he hacked up his lungs. By the time he was done, his eyes were watering fiercely.

Meanwhile, Venture was wincing with laughter. "You college kids."

Emmett didn't stop coughing for a full minute after drinking the vial—long enough for Venture to leave the room and come back with a water bottle.

Emmett sipped on it, savoring the cold sensation.

Finally, mercifully, he stopped coughing.

"Good stuff?" Venture asked. He smirked, and Emmett realized he was asking about the mutagen.

"That was horrible," Emmett whispered. "Not even Lock could take a shot of that without coughing. Are all of them that bad?"

Dr. Venture turned toward the monitors. "No. Most of Gnosis's formulas are administered intravenously."

Emmett looked apprehensively at the empty vial on the center table. "I can see why. So, how long should it take before I notice an improvement?"

"The body's incorporation of the mutagen should happen on a parabolic curve." Venture mimicked the arch-shape with a finger. "It will take a day for your body to break down the compounds. You won't notice anything at first except for some gastrointestinal discomfort. Once your body starts incorporating the mutagen, changes should happen rather quickly. Your eyes will make more rods and cones, your optic nerve will acclimate, and you'll notice a sudden improvement in your low-light vision. Then improvements will taper off as your eyes finish changing and your nerves optimize. In two to four days, the mutagen should be fully integrated."

"Can I keep training?"

"I don't see why not. If it were your bones that were changing, I would say to take a few days off. Maybe don't get into too much late night trouble."

Emmett chuckled, trying to hide his excitement. "I'll try not to."

Even if seeing in the dark wasn't a flashy power, getting a new ability was enough to lift his spirits and shake off the last of the taste of the mutagen.

Athena had said that seeing in the dark was a fairly rare power... maybe it would be more useful than he first thought.

Emmett glanced at the other mutagens on the table. "Why would anyone put these on the streets if they're going to kill or disfigure their host?"

"Money or power," Venture responded. "It always comes back to those two things. Usually money." He turned to Emmett. "Sit tight. I'll be back within the hour. If you feel anything more than an upset stomach, let TINA know."

Chapter 34

Venture

D r. Venture strode quickly through the halls to wing 002 where Clara was waiting. He'd asked her to check on the analysis of Porcelain's samples. Apparently, the results were compiled.

Venture entered one of the half dozen testing rooms of the mechanical wing. Apertures lined the walls, each one specifically tailored to test different properties of materials—chemical markers, tensile strength, energy absorption, psychic refraction... Among other measurements useful in analyzing the remnants of supers.

Clara was waiting for him beside the monitors. When she met his eyes, her face was hard.

"I don't like lying to Emmett," Clara said.

Venture frowned. She'd left Emmett's training early, using the excuse that she was going out into the city. Emmett naturally assumed it was something to do with Porcelain—in that respect, he wasn't wrong.

No amount of excuses would make Clara feel better though, so Venture tried the best thing he could.

"You won't have to for much longer."

Clara crossed her arms. "You've said that before."

He didn't know what to say, other than Emmett needed more time. The boy still wasn't ready—not to deal with Class 2 supers.

So Venture said nothing. He kept his face emotionless and turned the monitor toward him and examined the data from Porcelain's samples in the warehouse.

"There were traces of Porcelain's energy powers and her negation powers in the building. The signatures were strong enough that we can refine our search algorithm...

"Judging by the energy signatures and the sheer amount of fragments you found, it's safe to say that Porcelain got into a fight, but we don't know if she was the instigator or was under attack. Either way, there were no other energy sources or traces of tissue or armor—no evidence of any other super.

"All of the samples are molecularly identical, which means that she indeed used her self-duplication powers in the fight, *and* that no one was copying her powers; otherwise, there would've been a second signature."

"Dad, that was a lot of debris. How many times can she use that power?"

"TINA, are there any records of Porcelain's limits?"

"There are two fights in the DSA records. Both suggest that, in this instance, Porcelain was pushed to her limits."

Clara groaned in frustration, her hands already balled into fists.

Venture offered quietly, "We'll find her next time. Faster."

"Dad, she's our best lead to the Champion street attack. Our *only* lead—"

"I know," he said sternly. She didn't need to remind him. Venture understood all too well how much this meant to her and Emmett, and there was more riding on their investigation than just closure for them.

Venture collected himself before continuing. "The only thing we can do now is wait for her to use her powers again. TINA, what's the new range on our scanners?"

"Range increased by three hundred percent. Accuracy of the scanning algorithm within ninety-seven percent."

That was better than Venture had hoped for; even Clara seemed to relax a little at the boost in their systems. With any luck, they wouldn't find traces of Porcelain next time—they would find her. Then they could get some answers.

Venture said, "The next batch of scanners are ready for placement. Could you—"

"Yes," Clara replied quickly. "I'll do it."

She left a moment later, leaving Venture to check on Emmett.

Soon Clara would be flying across Belport, secretly placing scanners along the rooftops, adding to their detection web. He would send a message from TINA to concentrate on the warehouse district—the last sighting of Porcelain.

Clara probably already knew, but these things bore repeating.

Dr. Venture took his time walking back into section 006, the biomedical wing. By the time he got back to Emmett, the hour wait period was up.

Emmett was sitting on one of the benches along the wall and looked up eagerly when Venture entered.

"How are you feeling?"

"Fine," Emmett said, patting his chest. "A little heartburn."

Venture looked him over. In so many ways, Emmett was the pinnacle of health: His normal values—blood pressure, heart rate, vitamins, hormones, and the like—were that of a professional athlete. His bone density and body composition were equally impressive.

Emmett looked like he'd filled out, like he wasn't a young man anymore, but actually a man—everywhere except that baby face of his. The shaggy hair didn't help.

Despite the changes, despite all Emmett's training, when Emmett met Venture's eyes, the retired cape couldn't see him as anything else other than a kid.

Just like Clara.

Neither of them should be supers. Neither of them would ever be ready—not ready enough.

"You need a haircut," Venture muttered, turning to look at the data readout.

"Thanks, Dad," Emmett replied sarcastically.

"One kid is enough, thank you."

Venture took his time looking over the data, the graphs and data points that showed Emmett's body absorbing the mutagen and starting to incorporate it into his DNA and tissues. Venture was looking for something wrong.

He didn't find anything.

Emmett could go home. There wasn't any reason to keep him.

Venture sighed and was glad when Emmett didn't pry or didn't notice.

In so many ways, there was little Venture could do to stop things or even to delay them. So many things were out of his hands. All he could do was guide them and hope for the best.

One day Emmett would truly be a mask—one day, maybe even a cape.

One day Clara wouldn't need to wear an exosuit anymore.

Maybe it was the dad part of him that was terrified of both prospects.

Venture dismissed Emmett, then went back to the break room near the 003 testing hub. There were other break rooms, but since the three of them had done so much work recently in 003, it was the best stocked break room.

He turned on the news while waiting for the oven to preheat and grabbed a Big Larry's pepperoni pizza out of the freezer. He scrolled through channels while the oven preheated, then put the pizza in and set a timer for twenty minutes.

Then Venture collapsed one of the cracked leather couches.

It was another few minutes before he circled through all the channels and came back to the channel for the Belport Bulletin.

Most of the coverage was still stuck on the war between Shian and Catalina on the other side of the world. It had only escalated in recent months, and now both sides were throwing around threats of nukes and supers. It was bluster, of course. Both weapons risked Mutually Assured Destruction.

That wasn't to say that low-level supers weren't involved. Class 1 supers and *knack* abilities often went undetected, whether in everyday life or in warfare. And Class 2 and Class 3 supers would be involved patrolling the borders of the war, staving off attacks from warlords who didn't share the restraint of *civilized countries.*

Venture grumbled to himself. There were things he didn't agree with politically—the war itself, for one, and the siphoning of talent from other countries.

Most people wouldn't think to ask why Class 3, 4, and 5 supers were usually affiliated with developed countries and why only low-level supers harassed the edges of Shian and Catalina. It was by design.

All part of the Code that the Summit of Heroes and other super organizations enforced. Recruitment, retirement, or imprisonment.

The news cut from foreign to domestic issues, the number one of which was always the stock market. Ultimately, every big event, foreign or domestic, ended with *'and how will this affect share prices?'*

Venture scoffed and glanced at the oven. A part of him wanted to watch the news, if only to see the spin that the government was putting on current events, but Venture had better ways of staying updated. And he still didn't smell pizza, so he had time to kill.

He changed from the news to his own system, and then to his access to the Summit's systems. The feed on the TV changed to several browsing windows, which Venture flicked through with the remote. Since *retiring*, he wasn't a full member, but he still had access to some of their systems.

The most powerful supers on Earth monitored countless things—only some that the public would ever hear about. Most of the things the Summit dealt with would never be known to the public: The conquerors of Alpha Centauri, frozen bioweapons, ancient evils, and more.

The threats the world faced were as varied and as numerous as the heroes that protected it... and they would drive a normal person mad. That was the world that Clara and Emmett were getting into.

The smell of pizza finally reached him. It wouldn't be long now.

Venture rubbed the stubble on his chin as he contemplated the feeds.

He nearly scrolled to the Summit's archives, but he didn't need to. Didn't need any help remembering the Scarlet King. Venture remembered them all too well.

Soon things would change. Soon Clara and Venture wouldn't have to stay in hiding anymore.

A part of Venture couldn't wait to bring Emmett into the fold. Together, maybe the three of them could succeed where Venture, alone, had failed. After all, the best part of being on the Summit of Heroes was being part of a team.

And now, Venture had people that he could trust.

Chapter 35

Different Powersets

Emmet ran home across the rooftops of Belport Wednesday evening and spent the rest of the night hunched over his kitchen table, working on his radio locator project. It was the beginning of March now—already halfway through the semester.

He already noticed a difference in his low-light vision when he needed to pee in the middle of the night. His room looked so bright Emmett thought he'd left a light on. It was a long, groggy minute before Emmett realized that he had, in fact, not left any light in his room on, and that the new mutagen was already affecting his vision.

Emmett could see all the patterns on his comforter and on the clothes in his laundry basket. He could make out the posters on his wall and even the wood grain on his dresser—the only odd thing was that his new night vision was in black and white. He couldn't make out color at all.

No, that wasn't quite right... There was a soft glow to some things so faint that Emmett almost didn't notice it. Venture had mentioned that his eyes might develop new receptors for UV and infrared light—that must be what he was seeing. His skin was the brightest example; it almost seemed to glow faintly.

Emmett was fine with that, though, and spent several more minutes looking around his room in awe before he tried to go back to sleep.

After Thursday morning classes, Emmett found himself back in the Gray Room. He stood on a featureless rooftop, facing Clara's robot.

"We're going to try a different powerset today," Clara said through the robot. "Are you familiar with Lord Sumac?"

Emmett chuckled awkwardly. "You mean the sovereign ruler of the Greenspire forest? Class five, plant-based powers?"

"That's the one."

Emmett had seen news footage of Lord Sumac's battles—clips of him plucking helicopters from the sky, collapsing buildings and single-handedly fighting off the Summit of Heroes.

The last time they trained against a random powerset, Clara had used abilities from Instaflame... Lord Sumac might actually be even worse.

"You're going to tone his abilities down, right?"

Clara laughed through the speaker. "You know, I do actually enjoy our training. I don't want to stomp you so bad you give up."

He smirked and shrugged. "I'll just start running."

Clara's robot shimmered and turned blue, as it did when signaling Emmett to chase it. Simultaneously, a section of tile raised up from the tiles of the roof, forming a one cubic square box. This turned golden, and Clara stooped down and picked it up. The roof tiles slid together to fill in the gap.

"This is your objective," Clara said, gently tossing the cube for emphasis. "Try to get it."

Emmett didn't need any further goading—he'd been ready for a change in their training. Not to mention a powerset like Lord Sumac's was way different from anything he'd trained against so far.

Emmett took a step forward and nearly fell flat on his face.

Vines were growing up from the tiles and had wrapped around his ankles—they were stark white with hints of green and stood out against the rest of the Gray Room. Individually, they were no thicker than a pencil, but they were growing impossibly fast and converging on his feet.

Emmett reached down and easily snapped the first vines, then leapt across the roof toward Clara's robot.

The one edge that Emmett had in this fight, compared to other powersets Clara had used, was that Emmett was already familiar with Lord Sumac's powers.

This was commonly referred to as Lord Sumac's *grasping vines* and they were relentless. Emmett knew that as soon as he landed, more vines would sprout, forcing him to keep moving.

Meanwhile, Clara's robot turned and ran.

Emmett chased her across the faux rooftops of the Gray Room.

Despite his increased speed and stamina, she kept half a rooftop ahead of him with no sign of slowing down. It wasn't surprising, most supers Class 3 and higher were stronger, faster, and more resilient than normal people, even if their powersets weren't based on physical strength.

It meant that Emmett was going to need to do more than just mindlessly chase after Clara though, if he was going to catch her.

So when Emmett neared the end of the next rooftop, he lashed out with his whip and snared the edge. Then he jumped a few steps early and pulled as hard as he could on the whip—*slingshotting himself forward.*

He hurtled through the air, gaining on the robot, and ready to do the trick again.

But by the next jump, Clara was ready for him. As soon as she cleared the roof, vines erupted into the air, creating a barrier between them.

Emmett groaned and stopped his whip mid-swing. His run stuttered, then he humped upward, trying to hurtle the vine wall as it grew steadily higher—just clearing it.

As he sailed over the vines, Emmett lashed his whip downward. The tip struck the roof and dug into the faux brick. Then Emmett hauled himself downward, landed, and continued running without missing a beat.

Ahead, Clara was already growing barriers at the next several roofs like she was raising a hedge maze on the skyline of Belport—each seemingly faster and taller than the last. Thicker vines whipped toward Clara's robot, hoisting it up and over the walls.

Emmett reached the next vine wall and again leapt up and over. This time, instead of hauling himself back to the roof, he lashed onto the next vine barrier and hauled himself toward it. Immediately, the vines of the wall grabbed for his whip, but it was easy to pull it free. Emmett flew across the roof—ten feet in the air—

But he was already falling and wouldn't clear the next roof. As quickly as he could, Emmett grabbed the opposite edge of the wall with his whip and hauled himself sideways—going around the wall instead of over it. His arc was wide and wild, but Emmett swung again, grabbing the next vine wall and hurling himself upward and across the roof again.

He passed over another two roofs using this S-pattern, swinging across the roof and around the already towering vine walls.

And the next time Emmett swung around, he lost sight of Clara. The robot had seemingly vanished in the middle of the air.

Emmett looked around frantically as he swung across the alley and saw Clara's robot falling between the buildings—plummeting toward the street. Emmett followed—lashing his whip to the nearest building and hurling himself downward.

He tucked and slammed into the robot feet first.

It had been a gamble—Emmett tried to slow himself by grabbing the wall with his whip, but it was too little, too late. Both he and Clara's robot slammed into the ground. Even landing feet first, Emmett was sent sprawling and stopped hard up against the corner of a building.

He smiled in spite of the fierce pain in his shoulder and side, because he *heard* Clara hit the ground with a crunch.

All his joy vanished though, when Emmett pushed himself up and saw the robot standing in front of him, clad in thick, barkskin armor.

He'd forgotten about that one. *Barkskin* was one of the most common abilities plant-based supers tried to develop, and for good reason.

Emmett was on his feet, just in time to dodge a heavy first. Clara punched and kicked at him, and Emmett could hear and feel the extra weight behind each strike. The only thing saving him was his faster speed.

Even that wasn't enough though, because new vines sprouted from the street and the walls of the alley. Some reached for Emmett, trying to grab his ankles and his wrists. Others threaded together, making a wall behind Emmett to keep him from escaping.

Even though Lord Sumac's abilities were toned down, Emmett found himself almost overwhelmed by the sheer number of abilities Clara was throwing at him—so much so that he almost missed the fact that she was no longer holding the golden cube.

It was hanging in a cluster of vines three stories above him. She must've ditched it on the way down.

Emmett backpedaled as he dodged the robot's armored punches and kicks, but was dangerously close to the vine wall behind him. Deciding to test his strength against Clara's barkskin armor, Emmett struck back, punching fast and hard. His fists *cracked* against the thick wood, the sound echoing through the alley and pain shooting through his hands.

But no matter how hard Emmett punched, Clara's robot didn't so much as flinch in its attacks. In addition to the bulk that the armor added, its feet were probably anchored to the ground by roots.

Emmett was left with only one other option:

He ducked and opened the compartment on the back of his upper right arm—the skin separating with a thought—and pulled out two smoke pellets. He threw one at the ground and it exploded into a cloud of dense gray—nearly black—smoke.

For a moment, Emmett was completely blind. The smoke was so thick he couldn't see even an inch in front of him and could barely hear the crunch of Clara's armor on the street. Emmett didn't dare even try to breathe.

Then Emmett leapt up, easily clearing the smoke and leaving his enemy behind. He lashed out with his whip, grabbed the wall, and hurled himself upward. Vines reached for the whip, but he was already ascending quickly.

Emmett smirked, thinking he'd won—

Until the gray sky dimmed and looked like it was falling. Simultaneously, all the vine barriers above them collapsed, sending a tidal wave of writhing faux vegetation toward Emmett.

There was no way he would beat the vines to the golden box.

Eyes wide and breath held, Emmett hurled his whip through the largest opening in the mass and grabbed the faux brick behind it. And when he felt tension, Emmett pulled as hard as he could.

He rocketed upward, just barely threading through the hole in the vines—several thorns catching on his arms. He made it, and the mass of foliage tumbled past him.

In fact, it was everything Emmett could do to catch himself on the edge of the roof before overshooting. He kept his whip embedded until he steadied himself, then planted his feet and leapt off the wall toward the golden cube.

A breath later and Emmett grabbed the cube, and grabbed the edge of the roof to keep from falling. Emmett had been about to leap away with the cube, but the vines around him faded. The alley below cleared, leaving Clara's robot, sans-bark, and slow-clapping.

Emmett hung there for a moment longer, triumphant.

"That was awesome!" Emmett exclaimed as he dropped to the alley, chest still heaving from excitement and exertion.

Even though Emmett had had good showings in training before, there was something different about this victory. Maybe it was the fact that Emmett knew how potent Lord Sumac's powerset was, or that he'd managed to use his abilities differently. Either way, it truly felt like a *victory*, instead of just surviving.

Clara's robot stood across from him in the alley, hands on its hips and laughter leaking through. "I honestly thought I had you at the end."

"I thought you did too! How did you even know where I was?"

"The vines. I could feel where you went each time you touched the vines."

Emmett smacked himself in the forehead. Of course, she'd been able to see him. He should've remembered that from Lord Sumac's powers.

"Don't feel too bad," Clara continued. "It's easy to forget that supers won't just have extra powers, but extra senses intertwined with them: Lord Sumac can see through his vines. Psychics can sense the mind of someone nearby, even if they're cloaked or invisible. Sorcerers can sense other magic users and relic users.

"It's even more than that, though. Changelings and shapeshifters are adept at spotting their own kind because they know exactly what *tells* to look for. Vampires or supers with heightened senses can smell when another super has recently been in a battle by the traces of blood left on them. Even time and reality warpers can sense the *scars* in the world left over from other warpers.

"There are as many different senses to keep track of as there are different types of supers. *But...*" Clara paused for emphasis, holding up a robot finger. "There are ways we can cloak ourselves with technology, turn the senses of supers against them, and even mirror their senses."

Emmett was listening intently as Clara monologued, his mind already spinning with possibilities. He'd already been thinking about his own abilities—how he could use additional mods and upgrade his capabilities—but now there was so much more.

Why did he have to be limited by mutagens or even mods, when he could be using the senses of other supers?

It was a long shot, of course—it had taken Emmett over a year to develop the newest versions of the radio locator... and if he was being honest with himself, it still wasn't quite finished. Something like reverse engineering the senses or abilities of other supers was bound to take longer...

But even as Emmett had that epiphany, another realization hit him suddenly. One that couldn't wait for the end of training.

CHAPTER 36

What About...

"What about a utility belt?" Emmett asked.

He'd already wrapped up training for the evening and had basically dragged Clara to section 002. Now she stood across from him in one of the many storage rooms. The overhead lights reflected harshly on the scattered metal tables.

His mind had been racing too much to explain to Clara on the way over. Emmett wasn't even sure he could explain what he was thinking—it had taken him the several minute walk to section 002 to realize what he'd figured out.

Dr. Venture's voice came through the speakers. *I'm on my way over. I think I found something that might be useful for you.*

"So, what are you thinking?" Clara asked, arms crossed expectantly. "Did you think of something you could've used against Lord Sumac? Because if that's the thing—"

"Not just Lord Sumac," Emmett said, leaning on the cold metal table. "I want something for everyone."

Clara chuckled, then she realized he wasn't joking. "There's hundreds of different types of supers—probably even more than that. You'd be lugging around an armory."

"Not necessarily," Venture said. He walked in, carrying an overflowing box of components, and set them on the table with a *thunk*. Then he began pulling pieces out and setting them on the table.

"Clara is right," Venture continued, "that there are more powersets than can be countered, probably more than can be properly categorized. However, that doesn't mean they don't have overlapping weaknesses."

It took several minutes for Venture to empty the box. He narrated each item he pulled out and set aside: Flares, flashbangs, first aid coagulate, folding knife, powdered minerals, hand taser, dog whistle, steel mirror, noise maker, cell/radio jammer, portable, high-powered flashlight, gas mask, portable rebreather, capsaicin spray, tear gas pellets, cutting torch... Emmett lost track somewhere around then.

"And lastly, your lock-pick set... that you don't know how to use."

Venture tossed the cardboard box unceremoniously to the floor and stepped back. Electronics and components covered all four tables, reminding Emmett of his apartment kitchen table.

Now that Emmett saw all the gadgets laid out in front of him, he paused, voice caught in his throat. Where was he going to start? He had known at one point... Hadn't he?

Even Clara was wide-eyed as she looked over the room full of gadgets.

Dr. Venture cleared his throat and pointed to one table, and two objects in particular: A slender container and a utility belt.

"Start here. This container is a mock-up of your upper arm storage. You're limited, but you can rearrange it as you see fit or modify it with access rails—whatever you need to. I suggest you use your arm for things you absolutely want to keep on your person."

Venture turned over the utility belt. It was made of shiny black fabric, with slightly thicker material around the pockets. "This is your standard utility belt. By the time you load it up, it will be too bulky to wear under anything except a hoodie, but you can carry it in your backpack for quick access. Obviously, you won't be able to take everything here with you, but you might be able to modify or shrink some of these items."

"I'm looking forward to what you put together."

The last line caught Emmett off guard, and he turned to Dr. Venture.

"You're not going to help?"

Venture pushed up his glasses. "I'll be around if you have questions, but between you and Clara, you should be able to figure everything out."

Then Dr. Venture turned and walked out of the room, leaving the pair to gawk at the pile of gadgets.

Emmett and Clara spent the rest of the evening going through the gadgets, prioritizing them, and figuring out which ones would fit.

In the end, he prioritized items based on those that would counter the senses of *most* supers. Thankfully, things that affected sight, hearing, touch, and smell would give him an edge against the majority.

Flares won out over flashbangs. Since Emmett planned on keeping his utility belt with him all the time, he decided carrying miniature bombs around all day probably wasn't the best idea. Flares could also obscure infrared and double as lures for an ambush.

The collapsible gas mask won out over the portable rebreather for similar reasons. Carrying around pressurized oxygen would make him vulnerable to fire-wielding supers.

Noise-makers were also an easy decision. They were loud enough to disorient an attacker and also emitted high pitch frequencies for more *animalistic* supers.

In spite of his new low-light vision, Emmett grabbed an adjustable, high-powered flashlight at Clara's insistence. It would help him see color, if needed, and also could temporarily blind attackers.

The small cell phone and radio jammer had its uses. It might not be effective against mechanical opponents, but it could stop someone from calling for back-up.

Emmett took all four baggies of powdered minerals—silver, sand, a mix of moonstone and quartz, and a mix of quartz and different gemstones. Apparently, these had uses against magic-wielding supers.

The steel folding mirror was useful against light-based supers and could also help Emmett see around corners without getting blasted by ranged energy powers.

He also found room for the folding knife, hand taser, and several doses of first aid coagulate. Last, he stuffed in the lock pick set.

Emmett decided to keep the smoke pellets in his upper arm compartment because the majority of low-level supers relied on sight. The smoke was also dense enough to block infrared and potent enough to obscure his smell, at least for a time. He kept the caltrops in his arm too, if only because he didn't have time to decide where else to put them.

When he was done with the compartment in the back of his upper arm, he closed it with a click and the seam disappeared within his synthetic skin.

After everything was decided, both Emmett and Clara leaned against the middle table. Most of the gadgets had found their way back inside the cardboard box, but there were still a few that lay scattered about.

All in all though, Emmett was satisfied with his new belt.

Emmett picked up the black utility belt and swung it a few times, feeling the weight distribution. Then he put it around his waist and buckled it. It was probably three to four pounds—not heavy, but definitely noticeable around his waist and over his training suit. Emmett understood now what Venture meant about keeping it in his backpack. Even if it was slim enough to hide under most clothes, Emmett wasn't sure if he would want to wear it all day.

Emmett turned and struck a pose, crossing his arms over his chest. "How do I look?"

Clara smirked. "Finally, kind of like a hero."

Emmett chuckled. "*Thanks.* But also, seriously, thanks for working with me in the Gray Room and with the mods just now."

Clara's face softened, suddenly a mix of serious and sympathetic. "Sure thing. But I only helped. You're doing most of the hard work—pushing yourself, learning, adapting. That's all you, Emmett. You should be proud of it."

Emmett nodded, feeling both relieved at the acknowledgment and a little awkward at the compliment. He had been working hard, harder than he'd ever worked at engineering or anything else. Because he wanted this more than he'd wanted anything else. Being a super was a dream come true, and there was absolutely no way Emmett was going to waste even a minute of it.

It was a moment before Emmett could say anything because he was afraid his face might crack if he did.

Finally, Emmett said, "Maybe Venture will finally let me come with you on a mission."

Clara smirked. If she noticed Emmett's tumultuous emotions, she didn't say anything.

"About that... I think Dad's warming up to the idea."

Emmett sighed with relief and muttered, "About time. I was worried I'd be his age before I got to go."

Clara chuckled awkwardly. "Dad's just... overly cautious like that. A scientist through and through. Don't take it personal. He treated me the same way when I started with this hero stuff... He still treats me that way, and it's been..." She must've seen Emmett's face because she added, "Don't worry. It won't be much longer."

Emmett met Clara's eyes hopefully. There was a part of him that was already quaking with excitement, but the rest of him didn't want to get his hopes up.

"You seem super sure about this."

"Soon I'm going to need some help." Clara shrugged. "There's a reason why heroes work in teams."

Chapter 37

Alias, Pythia

A city is nothing without its foundation.

Beneath the bustle and gleam of Belport's skyline lies a framework of concrete, steel, piping, and wires, subways, electricity, and plumbing.

So much unseen. So much taken for granted.

And beneath even the skeleton and nerves of Belport, beneath the urban sprawl, lies the ruins of all that came before: Demolished brick from the industrial era, wattle and daub from the colonial era, tanned skins and bones from primitive nomads long forgotten.

The modern world was built atop the ruins of old, and not just physically, but in ideas and institutions as well. Heroic myths gave way to masks, capes, and villains. Windows to the outside traded for televisions and illusion. The bricks of providence laid by the hands of the poor upon their own backs—all at the direction of their lords.

What was a president or a CEO or a cape, but a lord by some other title?

Pythia walked the downtown streets of Belport, philosophizing silently to themself. The collar of their long coat was turned up and their pace was quick.

In a twisted mirror of the city, Pythia too was a product of those that came before. Poetry, philosophy, public school teachers, long dead professors, dusty books, bright screens...

And like all those that came before, Pythia wasn't afraid of asking questions. They weren't afraid of change. They weren't afraid of a reckoning.

The question was: Are the supers the skyline, or are they the foundation?

Like all great minds that came before, Pythia formulated a hypothesis and resolved to test it.

Pythia followed Burton Street through the bustle of downtown to the Tempest Solutions building and passed through the revolving glass doors.

The lobby was impressive by *normal* standards. The whole of it was clad in stone and metal, like an ancient palace. Pythia's heels clicked on the granite tiles and sunlight glinted off the enormous metal Tempest Solutions logo that covered the back wall. They walked past security and the dozen front desk clerks to the lobby elevators.

Pythia boarded the nearest elevator along with two businesswomen. None of them spoke—preferring to ride upward in anonymity.

Tempest Solutions wasn't Pythia's destination. Nor were the 45th or 46th floors that they pressed, nor the 26th or 67th that the other passengers selected.

Pythia was going to a space between.

The elevator rose, and shortly after, the first passenger stepped out on the 26th floor. But as the elevator neared the 40th floor, the compartment began to shimmer.

A moment later, Pythia *appeared* to get out on the 45th floor—

Pythia actually disembarked on a demiplane between floors 45 and 46.

This building's iteration of the Donjon Club.

The elevator doors opened to a sprawling nightclub bathed in futuristic opulence. Neon lasers flickered in time with thumping bass. An illusion of the aurora borealis dominated the upper walls and the ceiling. Streams of mist fell in columns and pooled across the floor. Directly ahead, a dance floor filled with people and flanked by booths and lounges where the other attendees mingled, most holding drinks that glowed like miniature stars. On the outermost walls, more booths rose up like the side of ancient step pyramids.

The attendees of the club were simultaneously the strangest and most mundane of all. Everyone in attendance wore business or casual clothes, no different from anywhere else in Belport. And they were all supers.

Supers playing pretend.

A lithe woman with bright pink hair and pantsuit greeted Pythia as they entered. Pythia turned and lowered the coat over their shoulders expectantly. The hostess took their coat, revealing long white gloves and a sleeveless purple evening gown that shimmered in the lights.

"Welcome to the Donjon Club. Please mind the rules and enjoy your stay."

Pythia glanced up at the top of the archway in front of her, reading the engraved reminder and creed of the Donjon Clubs:

No names. No powers.

The only names allowed here were single use, disposable monikers.

"Doff thy name," Pythia muttered.

Today they would be *Juliet*.

Then Juliet tried her best to relax and look natural in a wholly unnatural place. She sauntered past the dance floor and the surrounding booths, deciding to find a spot in one of the lounge areas perched on the upper wall. Juliet climbed the stone stairs, scanning the crowd as she went.

There were two parts to their plan, and Pythia had just completed arguably the most difficult part:

Getting into the Donjon Club without raising any alarms.

There were dozens of Donjon establishments all throughout the world, all run by a shadowy cabal of sorcerers, illusionists, and reality warpers as old as myth. Each club was a fortified demiplane, completely separate from reality, and only accessible by *privileged parties*—in modern day, this meant supers.

But Pythia—Juliet—wasn't interested in who ran the place. They were only interested in who was there.

Hopefully, the intel was good...

Even more than that, Juliet hoped no one talked to her. Any other night, they might have enjoyed the opulence and anonymity of this place. But tonight, Juliet needed to concentrate.

She tugged idly at her long white gloves, trying not to think about their silk-like material or the poison hidden just beneath the skin of her fingers.

It had been a gamble, one that ultimately Pythia—and their boss—agreed to.

Each Donjon plane and its cabal masters used magic to detect any uses of power by its attendees—no matter how strong or subtle. As such, Pythia couldn't create their poison *while they were in the club*.

So Pythia made it hours ago, before they even crossed into downtown.

It sat now, just underneath the uppermost layer of the skin of their fingers and kept in place by Pythia's focused will. It was a delicate exercise, like holding fresh, crumbly snow between the fingers. Hold too loosely and the poison would ooze through their pores. Hold too tightly and it might very well slip into their own bloodstream.

Pythia reminded themself to breathe as they ascended the top of the stairs and found an almost empty platform. Up here, an L-shaped leather couch and a small table overlooked the club.

Juliet sat on the edge of the couch, ignoring the couple on the other side. The two men leaned on each other, whispering flirtatiously and occasionally laughing to themselves.

Meanwhile, Juliet scanned the crowd until she found her target.

Thankfully, it didn't take long.

Ricardo Olivera sat with a small group on a mid-tier platform across the club. Ricardo talked animatedly on the couch—clearly having a good time. Even from far away, Juliet could see the glint of his smile. He was dark and handsome.

Ricardo Olivera, alias Amarque. Member of the Summit of Heroes.

Pythia's face felt flush, equal parts from finding their target and seeing the man.

It was another few minutes before Ricardo glanced in Juliet's direction, and Juliet made a point to meet his eye. When he did a double take, Juliet was sure to smile, coyly.

Twice more, they connected across the club before Ricardo excused himself from his friends and went down to the bar. He ordered two drinks and brought them both up to Juliet's platform.

Men were too easy.

As he approached, Juliet took in the rest of him. He wore a well-tailored suit, no tie, and he was broad shouldered, a stature expected from a physically minded super, not a reality warper.

Ricardo smiled when he reached Juliet's couch. "You looked thirsty, but I wasn't sure which you would prefer..." He indicated the drinks, one bright green, the other a deep red. "Melon prosecco or cranberry bourbon?"

"I'll have the prosecco and the company," Juliet replied, not bothering to look at the other drink. It was important to maintain the illusion that Juliet was a bachelorette that knew what she wanted... which was intimately close to the truth.

Meanwhile, Pythia wondered why a man who could have anything would limit his choices.

Ricardo nodded to the couple on the other end of the L-shaped couch and sat an arm away from Juliet. He had a distinguished air about him—the kind of confidence born from true power. Even so, Ricardo seemed to take in the sight of Juliet carefully, even delicately.

Juliet sipped on her drink with muted enjoyment; it really was quite good. Though she could only enjoy it so much while concentrating on holding the poison in her skin. Ricardo seemed pleased at her reaction and tried his own drink.

"I wonder what you would say if I didn't want either."

Ricardo waved away her concern. "I would ask what you were in the mood for, and bring it to you, salvaging my dignity along the way."

Juliet relaxed on the couch and into the act. "Surely a refusal wouldn't harm your dignity."

"Any man who says they don't covet the smile of a beautiful stranger is a liar."

"Something tells me smiles aren't hard to come by."

"No, I suppose not, but the intrigue of a stranger is." Ricardo smirked and sipped his drink.

Juliet pressed her luck. "You must live quite the life if nothing surprises you." It was taboo to pry into a super's identities while in the Donjon Clubs, but Juliet was bold.

"That's why I'm here," Ricardo replied, toasting his glass to the club. "No names. No powers..."

"All surprises."

"Exactly! What about you... Why are you here?" Ricardo leaned attentively toward her.

Juliet leaned forward to match him. "I'm looking for something different. Though a surprise would be nice too."

"Why stop at one?"

As he spoke, Juliet flushed and took his hand, rubbing her thumb over his knuckles, then rubbing his wrist and just up his sleeve. Poison that she'd been holding onto seeped through the special material of her gloves and into Ricardo's skin.

He wouldn't notice until it was too late.

"I'm going to freshen up," Juliet said, standing and leaning over closer to him. She ran her other hand behind Ricardo's neck, releasing the rest of the poison before leaning over to whisper in his ear. "Don't go anywhere."

Beside them, the couple laughed, and Juliet winked at them before descending the stairs.

With any luck, Ricardo was watching her go, intent on waiting for her to return—for a promise unfulfilled.

She passed the bar and turned like she was going to the restrooms, but stopped at the front desk to ask for her coat. A moment later Pythia put it on, hiked the collar, and left Juliet and the bar behind.

Pythia walked quickly.

There would be a few minutes before Ricardo felt the effects of the poison. And a few minutes more before downtown Belport was destroyed.

Chapter 38

ATTENTION

Emmett went out on the rooftops of Belport earlier than usual that Thursday night. As per usual, he slipped into an alley, donned his mask, turned his hoodie inside out and wore it overtop of his backpack. Then he buckled his utility belt and climbed up to the roof.

He was excited about the belt, but he couldn't really use anything... not without getting into a fight.

Clara had *explicitly* warned him not to do that, and it had taken a solid five minutes of reassuring her before Clara believed him. Emmett suspected part of the reason was because Clara wouldn't be able to help him out if he got into a jam—she had her own things to do across the city.

For the most part, Emmett was content just running across the rooftops, cackling to himself like he was ten years old again and playing hero.

Emmett did glance off to the South, toward the slums just before the bay. There was a small part of him that wanted to go back to the slums for the chance of running into Zanté and Green Mask again. Emmett had no doubt that he'd surprise them in a rematch. But he kept a level head.

After all, just because he enjoyed training in the Gray Room didn't mean Emmett was looking for a fight; Clara had often reminded him of the difference between those two things. Not that he needed it—his beating on the rooftop of the slums was still fresh in his mind.

And Emmett wouldn't admit it, but a part of him was still apprehensive about Green Mask and his darkness powers... or psychic powers. He'd searched the databases for information on Green Mask, but hadn't found anything. There usually wasn't much on lower-level supers unless they were particularly famous or well connected. Green Mask was neither. So Emmett had no idea of knowing whether his new low-light vision or any of his countermeasures would be effective against Green Mask.

He was nearing the edge of downtown when the rooftop shook, stopping Emmett in his tracks. He crouched low, heart racing. At first, he thought something was wrong with the building, but as the city went still and quiet around him, Emmett's apprehension grew. Maybe it was the start of an earthquake—they were rare, but weren't unheard of in Belport, and being on the roof probably wasn't the best place to be.

The moment dragged on until Belport had grown so quiet that the only sound was Emmett's increasingly panicked breathing.

Emmett was frozen with apprehension. Whether there was an earthquake or something else, Emmett couldn't bring himself to move. If anything, he kept crouching lower, making himself as small as possible.

Something was wrong—so very wrong. Like the beginning of a nightmare.

Not even Emmett's newfound strength or his metal arm reassured him. He glanced across the skyline of Belport, waiting to see a building fall or an explosion or a super blot out the sun.

When it finally happened, Emmett could only watch with wide-eyed, open-mouthed horror.

Chunks of buildings broke away—not just the roof Emmett was standing on. The entire skyline of Belport seemed to crumble *and fall upward*. Pebbles and bricks and chunks as big as cars. Though gravity didn't feel any different, it looked like the world had suddenly been flipped end over end. Roofs, rubble, power lines, water from busted sprinklers—everything rose into the air like smoke.

And all of it was completely silent.

Emmett stumbled as chunks of the roof shifted beneath his feet and floated away. The shock of the moment was gone, replaced again with panic.

He ran, keeping an eye on his footing as sections of roof lifted away. His heart was pounding and his breaths were deafening as he ran. He leapt across to the next roof, lashing his whip to the section that hadn't evaporated yet and hauling himself across.

Emmett sprinted South, running across evaporating buildings, toward the only part of the city that looked unscathed. Toward the bay and the slums. He didn't stop, not when the sky was dappled with wreckage, not when he was running past shocked civilians looking up in horror where their ceilings had been only moments ago.

He didn't stop, not until he got to the slums and the sounds of Belport traffic came back. It was so subtle at first that he almost missed it.

Until a massive boom echoed across the sky.

Emmett skidded to a halt on the roof and spun around. Again, his mouth dropped open—

A tiny silver blur streaked down to Belport like a missile, ramming through the wreckage-filled sky. It was so fast, at first Emmett thought his eyes were playing tricks on him. A moment later, he recognized the super—Paragon.

Wonder and awe overcame Emmett and his heart beat quickly now for a different reason:

Whatever had happened—earthquake, bomb, or renegade super—it didn't matter anymore. Paragon was here. He would take care of it.

Three shockwaves washed over the city—the gusts of wind so fierce they almost knocked Emmett off his feet. As the wind subsided, Emmett finally heard the *crack* of the third impact; whatever phenomenon had kept the city absolutely silent was seemingly undone with Paragon's third attack.

Then whatever had happened was over. Like it had never happened. *Like nothing had ever happened.* Emmett shook his head in disbelief—the sky-line of Belport was untouched. The sky wasn't blotted out by wreckage. Rooftops weren't falling back to the ground. It was like everything had been undone in a literal blink of his eye.

Sirens blared in the distance, and Emmett thought he heard shouting over the normal lull of Belport traffic. He hadn't imagined it—there were too many sirens—and an alert was going off on his phone. He could imagine what it said: Some combination of **ATTENTION** and *take shelter immediately.*

Any other time he would've wracked his brain to figure out what had just happened—which supers had been involved and what powers had been used. But Emmett still hadn't moved from that rooftop in the slums.

There hadn't been any warning. It had been too late. Way too late.

For a moment, Emmett was reliving that night on Champion street. Paralyzed and cold with fear. Emmett couldn't do anything but stare, dumbfounded, at the sight of the immaculate downtown.

So much power.

No wonder the Code was a thing. No wonder the strongest supers and villains kept away from populated areas—*they were walking natural disasters.*

Clara—

Clara was out there somewhere. Did she say what side of town she was going to? He couldn't remember.

Emmett glanced across the skyline, fumbling for his burner phone and trying desperately to recall where his friend said she was going.

He'd been so preoccupied that he didn't hear the footsteps on the roof behind him. Didn't turn around until it was too late.

Something hit Emmett upside the head so hard that he tumbled across the roof—

He came too, sprawled facedown on the tar. Hands seized him by the arm and leg, and lifted him up into the air. Still groggy and weak, Emmett writhed in the air, trying to free himself from the grip of this new attacker.

"Must be your unlucky day," a familiar voice said.

Emmett finally peered down and saw the edge of the roof and the alley four stories below—

Saw the alley rushing up at him.

Emmett lashed out with his whip, felt it dig into the bricks and wrench his metal arm and shoulder. Still half awake and unable to control his descent, Emmett slammed into the brick wall, then fell the rest of the way to the alley.

Emmett came to on the cold asphalt, gasping. He'd landed on his side or maybe his back—everything throbbed with pain. His whip retracted, scraping across the ground. He blinked away tears and saw the sliver of sky above.

Hurriedly, he pushed himself up in time to see two familiar enemies standing at the end of the alley, one wearing a green mask, the other wearing a skull mask.

Chapter 39

Round Two, Fight

Emmett managed to push himself up on shaking arms and legs to face his enemies across the alley.

Green Mask leaned against the wall, arms crossed overtop of his dark green tracksuit. "You sure you're up for this?" the rail-thin man asked his counterpart.

Skull Mask—Zanté—stood in front. His old denim jacket creased around his muscles. He nodded to Emmett, his platinum blond flicking with the movement. "I'm still not sure how this punk got one over on me." Zanté rubbed the brace on his wrist for emphasis.

Emmett stared them down and grit his teeth.

Up until a minute ago, he would've been confident kicking the crap out of them. Emmett had won the first time, and now he had his utility belt. But now he was also recovering from being sucker punched and thrown off a roof.

Instead of shaking off his fall, Emmett stood straight, not wanting to look weak. Not sure what else to do, Emmett quipped back at them.

"Is your arm healed yet?"

Zanté chuckled and flexed the fingers of his injured arm. "Healed enough, freak."

The word caught Emmett like a smack in the face.

"What did you say?"

"You heard me," Zanté replied. Before Emmett could say anything, Zanté sprinted toward him, closing the length of the alley like a freight train.

A spark of anger had been lit within Emmett, and he lashed out with his whip, swinging down in a wide, violent arc. Zanté blocked it and kept running, his stride barely flinching.

Emmett pulled his whip back and braced himself, ready to dodge out of the way if the big guy tried to tackle him. Instead, Zanté skidded to a halt in front of him and unleashed a torrent of punches. Emmett's hands were already up and ready.

Last time they'd fought, Emmett had been in precisely one fight—in elementary school—and it had showed. Zanté was stronger, faster, and experienced. He'd pummeled the shit out of Emmett that night on the roof.

But Emmett had spent the last week training against Clara and Venture's robots. Instead of blindly hiding behind his own hands, Emmett bobbed and slipped Zanté's punches. Emmett smirked, even as some of those punches packed enough force that even a graze was enough to send him staggering back.

He was doing it—he was standing toe-to-toe with Zanté. With a super that outclassed him.

Emmett struck back when he could. Zanté's punches were wild, almost careless, but nothing Emmett did seemed to hurt the big super. Emmett's smirk quickly turned to frustration.

What was he doing wrong? Even Emmett's punches with his mechanical hand didn't seem to affect Zanté.

It wasn't until Zanté got the upper hand and punched Emmett hard enough to send him reeling, that Emmett finally got mad and finally figured out what he'd been doing wrong.

Emmett snorted, trying to shake off Zanté's last punch. When the big super lunged for him, Emmett ducked under the punch, dug his heels in, and swung his right hand as hard as he could. His punch hooked Zanté in the side with so much force it knocked him sideways.

Zanté slammed back-first into the wall and Emmett almost lost his own footing. He'd felt the impact of the punch through his shoulder and chest—through his whole body.

Fighting out here on the street wasn't the same as fighting in the Gray Room. Emmett had been afraid of Zanté, and that fear had caused him to hold back.

That time Emmett had punched like he meant it, like when he'd tried to knock out the training robots.

Pieces of brick fell around Zanté as he pulled away from the wall. He grimaced in a mix of surprise and anger, and the big super redoubled his assault.

This time, Emmett was ready.

Emmett ducked, bobbed, and weaved, trying to stay light on his feet, and when Emmett saw an opening, he struck hard with his right hand. He fought like a bullwhip, flowing and loose until he struck, and each punch echoed through the alleyway.

Emmett didn't even bother punching with his regular arm.

An uppercut to the stomach nearly took Zanté off his feet completely, but then the big super managed to grab Emmett by the throat. He lifted Emmett up and pinned him to the wall—holding Emmett's throat with one hand and pinning his mechanical arm to the wall with his other. If anything, it felt like Zanté was putting all his force on Emmett's wrist.

Emmett's feet dangled helplessly, and he kicked at Zanté's stomach, but the super didn't budge or release his grip.

Zanté's eyes were wide and blood seeped from his lips where Emmett had gotten a good shot in.

He seethed, "You'll learn, freak."

Again with that word.

In the beginning, Emmett's excitement at fighting and testing himself had been a smoldering flame—little more than burned out coals. Then he'd gotten angry and stopped holding back and that fire within him had kindled into a roaring fire... But Emmett didn't know what to call this.

It was like the insult had dumped pure gasoline on him.

Even though Zanté had Emmett's mechanical arm pinned against the wall with all of his strength, the limb pushed forward. Somehow, Zanté's eyes went even wider. The big super groaned with effort, but Emmett's limb pushed forward with inhuman strength.

Meanwhile, Emmett concentrated on his attacker's shifting weight and concentration.

As soon as the pressure slackened around his throat, Emmett braced himself and pushed off the wall. Caught off guard, Zanté stumbled backward and released Emmett.

Emmett fell toward him and punched him in the face. A *crack* echoed through the alley and both fighters fell to their hands and knees on the ground.

Emmett had hoped that would be enough—*he'd been sure* that would be enough. His whole damn body hurt—everything except his mechanical arm, anyway.

But Zanté raised his head and glared at Emmett. Blood dripped from his mouth. There was no longer rage or anger in his eyes. There was something else, something that worried Emmett even more:

Desperation.

Without thinking, Emmett asked, "Is that all you got?"

Zanté roared and charged at Emmett, his hands and feet slipping on the concrete at first before he barreled forward.

Emmett dodged to the left, anchoring his whip into the opposite wall. When Zanté missed his tackle, he tripped over the whip and hurtled end over end down the alley.

Emmett glanced back at Green Mask while his partner crunched into the opposite wall. The thin man waved—he was still leaning nonchalantly against the wall, as if he was content to wait.

Fine. Emmett wasn't going to give Green Mask time to change his mind.

Emmett turned and ran toward Zanté, who was already rising to his feet. The hulking super growled and scrambled toward him. Emmett reached into his upper arm compartment and grabbed a handful of smoke pellets, then hurled them down the alley. Black smoke erupted, instantly filling the alley.

There was a single breath where Zanté skidded to a halt and groaned in confusion.

Emmett didn't stop running.

At the last second, he just made out the silhouette of Zanté in the darkness. Emmett launched himself fist-first. His mechanical knuckles hit Zanté's chest like a rocket and the big man crumpled to his knees.

Before Zanté could get up, Emmett hauled his right hand back and punched him in the face. The *thump* of impact shook Emmett's whole body. Zanté recoiled and spat blood, but wasn't done yet.

Emmett punched again and again with his right hand, not bothering with his left—not letting Zanté get up. After who knows how many hits, Zanté finally collapsed onto the ground.

Emmett leaned against the wall of the alley as the smoke cleared, staring down at the big man. He heaved a sigh of relief that Zanté stayed down and another that the super was still breathing.

The last thing Emmett needed was to accidentally kill someone.

Emmett was exhausted. His joints ached from the impact of his punches. His lungs burned. And he wasn't done yet.

Slow clapping echoed through the alleyway. "You are a stubborn one," Green Mask said.

Emmett grit his teeth and turned, only to find darkness billowing through the alley like flood water. In moments, it had swallowed everything in blackness and Emmett had to reach a hand out to make sure the brick wall of the alley was still there.

"People think strength is everything," Green Mask said from somewhere at the end of the alley. "Strength and technology, whatever you got going on with that arm of yours. But do you know what one of the oldest fears of mankind is? Do you know what *everyone's* afraid of, from the highest super to the regular people? Darkness."

Last time they fought, Emmett had been able to see a little—enough to see Zanté as he pummeled the crap out of him. But that had been a different power.

This time, there weren't any hands of darkness reaching for Emmett. It was like Green Mask had instead channeled all of his power into making the alley as dark as possible. Emmett tried his flashlight, but even its light was swallowed up.

For a few moments, Emmett couldn't see anything at all. It was like his eyes were stapled shut or he'd plunged into black water. Even though Emmett knew it was only because of Green Mask's power, a part of him was deathly afraid that he'd been blinded and Emmett had to struggle to keep from panicking.

Until his eyes adjusted.

Emmett's eyes weren't magic. He still needed light to see. Luckily, even on the darkest night in Belport, there's still more than enough ambient light. Green Mask's power must've blotted out even more light than that—maybe even 99% of all light—but it didn't block everything. And there was still the trickle of UV and infrared that he could see.

The fraction of light remaining was enough that Emmett could see the faintest outline of the alley walls and the featureless silhouette of his enemy at the end.

Once again, Emmett struggled to keep his composure, only this time it was to keep from smirking or staring directly at his enemy.

"You feel it, don't you?" Green Mask continued. "That fear. The same fear the first humans felt when they came down from the trees and scurried back up before night fell."

The silhouette walked steadily closer. Emmett feigned being blind—kept one hand on the wall and his eyes darting around the alley. Kept up the act.

"It's too bad—"

This time, the voice came from behind Emmett. He started and spun around, but saw nothing but the outline of an empty alley behind him.

"—You've got spirit, boy."

Emmett glanced around again and found Green Mask's silhouette hadn't moved at all. He was still walking steadily toward Emmett from the same end of the alley, even though his voice was coming from elsewhere.

Emmett pretended to follow the voice while also hiding that he was impressed with Green Mask's trick.

"You just came to the wrong side of—ugh!"

Emmett had turned and punched Green Mask in the stomach, catching him mid-monologue. The thin super dropped *hard*. He lay in the fetal position, wheezing.

Immediately, the darkness vanished. Even though the alley was only dimly lit, Emmett winced and shielded his eyes until they adjusted.

Again, Emmett found himself leaning against the bricks for support and looking down at his fallen opponent. He'd punched with his right hand... Emmett wasn't sure what other powers Green Mask might have, but super strength clearly wasn't one of them.

Thankfully, Green Mask wheezed, "Fuck you, man," and Emmett took that as a sign that his enemy would live.

Emmett leaned over. "You too. Look, I'll try to stay away, and you guys... Just leave me alone."

That would have to be good enough. Emmett didn't know what else to say and he certainly wasn't going to monologue about his victory. He felt like shit.

So Emmett turned, ready to climb back up to the roofs and run home, but he immediately froze where he was standing. It'd already been a long day and Emmett had already been through way more emotions than he'd planned on.

But now he was looking up at the sky, mouth wide—equal parts in awe and apprehension.

A man hovered above the alley, cloak billowing in the sky. His skin was albino white and his suit was a gleaming silver. His long white hair hung still and lifeless, as if the wind itself didn't affect him. He glared down at Emmett, eyes narrowed and *glowing* red.

The most powerful super in the world.

Paragon.

CHAPTER 40

Like a Child

Paragon. Savior of the World.

His presence alone was enough to send villains running. He was nigh-invincible and his strength was without limit. Fast enough to catch bullets and outrun missiles. His eye rays burned hotter than the center of the sun.

The first time Emmett saw Paragon was when he was five-years-old. He and his family had been huddled in front of the TV—Emmett and his older brother Darryl sitting on the floor as close as they could. Mom and Dad sat on the couch behind them, clutching young Antony. Paragon had single-hand-edly redirected an asteroid that was on a collision course for Earth.

There were other supers that could've done it, given more time to prepare—even a few governments had hastily cobbled together rockets in case Paragon failed. It was an unnecessary precaution.

Paragon **never** failed.

Paragon was a Class 5 super, a flying nuclear deterrent who literal gods were afraid of. A being so powerful, he spent his time fighting natural disasters instead of other supers.

Despite all his feats of power, the most impressive thing about Paragon was that he was a hero of the people, that he was on *our side*. He was a benevolent force for good. In all the news clips Emmett had seen of his idol over the years, there had been plenty of emotions on the hero's face: Grins of satisfaction and humor, steadfast determination, genuine surprise, teeth clenched resolve, and even sorrow.

But Emmett had never seen Paragon angry.

He was floating fifty feet above a slum alley of Belport, glaring down at Emmett. His eyes were narrowed and glowing red—the air around his face boiled with power.

Emmett tried to speak, tried to say something. Anything. His throat was dry and his mouth wouldn't move.

Since he was a kid, Emmett had dreamed of meeting Paragon. He'd dreamed of *this moment*. Of being too awestruck to speak to his idol. Of Paragon smiling and telling him that it was alright to be nervous. Sometimes in his dreams, Paragon would crack a joke and make Emmett laugh, and Emmett would forget all about being nervous in front of the world's most powerful super.

Emmett wasn't awestruck. He was terrified.

Any moment, Emmett expected the air around him to heat up. And that would probably be the only thing he felt. Just a little heat. His metal arm probably wouldn't even be left behind.

And Emmett couldn't even mouth the word he wanted to ask:

Why?

Why was his childhood hero looking down on Emmett like he was a villain? Why were Paragon's eyes red with anger? Was Paragon going to execute him?

What did I do?

Something beyond even childlike fear welled up in him. Something akin to primal, incomprehensible terror—not of running from a bear or staring down the barrel of a gun, but of watching a tsunami or an avalanche bearing down on him.

Emmett's mouth wouldn't move—he could barely even breathe.

Finally, Paragon spoke. It had felt like hours of fear but couldn't have been more than a minute. He looked down on Emmett like an angel of judgment, eyes still blazing red, and said two words.

"Go home."

Emmett heard him, clear as if Paragon had whispered in his ear. He staggered back, nearly tripping over Zanté as he did. Both of Emmett's enemies were still recovering, but were now quickly scrambling to their feet and heeding Paragon's command, just like Emmett.

Emmett stumbled past them, not paying attention to where he was going at first, only that he was moving *away* from Paragon. He ran out into a side street, knocking over a trashcan in the process. Only then did he take a second to get his bearings and start jogging West down whatever street he was on.

After he'd jogged three blocks, Emmett glanced over his shoulder and to the sky. There was no sign of Paragon.

With trembling hands, Emmett pulled his hood up, pulled off his mask and stuffed it in his pocket. No one around paid him any attention. They were paying more attention to the sirens in the distance. Emmett had completely forgotten about *the event* on the rooftops of midtown. Whatever had happened, it had been enough for Paragon to show up and for most of the city's police to mobilize after.

Emmett continued to walk West. Head down and hands stuffed in his pockets. He was halfway home before the sirens slowed down and breathing returned to normal.

Occasionally, he wiped the tears from his eyes.

Emmett skirted the border of slums on his way home, wanting to stay as far away from the downtown area as possible. He was about halfway home, and the sirens were a distant afterthought.

No matter how many times Emmett glanced over his shoulder and scanned the night sky, he couldn't shake the fear of being followed.

Of Paragon hanging ominously in the sky above him.

So, when Emmett made it to the subway station on the edge of the West End, he went down the steps and into the subway, thinking that being underground might ease his nerves. Then again, Paragon could see through solid walls—he could probably see thirty or so feet through the roof of the subway.

It was a little warmer in the station but still cool, and thankfully, the station wasn't crowded. Emmett found a spot along the back wall to rest, taking off his hoodie and backpack...

And his utility belt. Emmett had completely forgotten he was wearing it and his hands trembled as he unbuckled it and stuffed it in his backpack. All this time, he'd had his hoodie on overtop to hide his pack, but now he put them back on like a normal person. Not like someone playing hero...

Emmett couldn't even bring himself to put his backpack on. He clutched it tightly and slumped down on the floor with his back to the wall.

What was he doing? Running around playing hero like a goddamn child. Emmett wasn't five anymore.

Who was he kidding? People didn't just become supers. Sure, he had taken a mutagen (or two), but that didn't make him a super.

Emmett had even won his rematch with Zanté and Green Mask—*decisively*. An hour ago, he would have been proud of that.

But it didn't make him a hero.

None of it did. And nothing would.

No amount of training would change the fact that Emmett was just some punk kid playing hero.

Paragon, himself, said as much. He might've said *'go home'*, but that wasn't what Emmett heard.

'Go home, child.'

Emmett held his backpack tightly in his lap while quiet tears fell on it. He tried not to think about what had happened, tried not to think of anything at all, but he couldn't help feeling like the subway was collapsing around him. Like he was impossibly small and suffocating while a dream collapsed around him.

Emmett didn't know how long passed on the floor of the subway, only that he was startled by someone sitting down next to him.

"Hey..." Clara's eyes widened for a second when Emmett looked up at her. "What happened?"

Emmett wiped his face on his sleeve and swallowed dryly. As happy as he was to see her, he was suddenly very self-conscious of how puffy and red his eyes felt.

"I, uh... Did you see what happened to downtown?"

Clara nodded. "I was in the warehouse district, but I saw. I think everyone in the city could see it."

"Well, I ran from downtown when everything happened. Ran straight into Zanté and Green Mask. I won... But then Paragon appeared. I don't know what he did downtown, but after that he found me... He just hovered in the sky looking down at me with his eyes glowing red. He told me to 'go home', but I... Clara, I thought he was going to kill me and I don't know why."

Emmett clamped his mouth shut, afraid to keep talking. He squeezed the fabric of his backpack.

Clara whistled in surprise.

For a minute, neither of them spoke. Emmett kept his head down, watching the feet of pedestrians mulling about the subway station.

Finally, Clara cleared her throat. "They still don't know how it happened." Her words hung ominously in the air until she continued.

"Amarque lost control. They're a reality warper—that's why everything *looked* like it was the end of the world until Paragon stopped them and then it was suddenly fine again."

Emmett nodded. He knew about Amarque... He'd just never imagined how powerful they were. It looked like the entire city of Belport had been crumbling.

Ignoring power level, reality warpers came in two flavors: Temporary and permanent. The former could usually affect larger areas, but those supers could only affect reality while actively using their powers. The second type could concentrate long enough and hard enough to make permanent change.

The thing was, Amarque was a *permanent warper.*

If Paragon hadn't intervened, the destruction to Belport would've been very, very real.

Clara continued, "No one's sure what happened to Amarque, but now they're in a coma. Paragon..."

Whether Clara didn't want to finish that statement or couldn't bring herself to finish it—it didn't really matter. Emmett knew what she meant:

Paragon put Amarque in a coma to stop them. Which meant that two things:

Amarque had been forced to stop. Either they had lost control of their powers or had turned into a villain.

And *Paragon just put down one of his best friends.*

Slowly, the reality of the situation dawned on Emmett. "I... I think I get it now," he muttered.

"It's not your fault," Clara said, leaning her shoulder against his. "After some-thing catastrophic, capes get sent around to keep the peace; they tell the riff raff to knock it off, you know? Paragon was so pissed he took it upon himself to deliver the order.

"Paragon wasn't mad *at you*, Emmett. He was just mad. I would be too—I can't imagine having to fight you or one of my friends."

Emmett just shook his head. He understood, and he agreed with Clara but... "You didn't *see* him."

Emmett couldn't shake the sight of Paragon hovering above him with glowing red eyes. It felt like it'd been burned into his vision.

Clara put a hand on his knee. "You're right. That must've sucked."

Emmett snorted, then promptly wiped his nose. "Yeah, it did."

"But it's okay now. Paragon's gone and it's not like he's going to remember you, at all."

Emmett chuckled and pushed her hand away. "Okay, you can stop making me feel better."

"Come on, I didn't mean it like that!" Clara feigned offense. "I was going to walk you home, but *clearly* you're fine."

Emmett met her eyes and tried to manage a smile that wasn't pitiful. "I'd like the company."

Clara looked away quickly. "Alright, fine."

Clara looked up at the night sky as they walked. "You know, I can't remember the last time I walked this far. You're not taking the bus anymore?"

Emmett adjusted the straps on his backpack and glanced up at the sky before pulling his hood further up. He hadn't seen anything in the sky, but it was hard to shake that feeling of being watched.

But he was starting to relax, at least a little.

The two of them had walked a few blocks West, passing boutiques and restaurants. The smell of bread and cigarettes came and went with the wind.

"I still take the bus. Sometimes."

Beside him, Clara went back to taking in the sights, sounds, and smells of Belport. "I can see why you walk. There's so much to see!"

Emmett chuckled. "Who said I walk? I've been taking the rooftops."

"Oh. The rooftops are nice too, it's just... There's a whole city down here."

Emmett regarded Clara for the first time since she'd rescued him from his wallowing on the floor of the subway station. She wore a thin, workout style sweatshirt and beanie over her head. It was cold enough to see their breath now, so her outfit must've been much warmer than it looked.

"You sure you don't want my hoodie?" Emmett asked. "I don't really need it since, uh, since that vial. I don't feel the cold as much. It just feels weird to walk around in a t-shirt when it's obviously cold outside."

Clara shook her head. "This outfit's all custom and much warmer than it looks. But thanks."

"No problem." Then, thinking back to her comment, added, "You guys don't get out much."

"No, we don't."

Emmett had been about to say *'I can tell'*, but something in Clara's voice made Emmett pause before jabbing at her.

Instead, he tried a lighter joke. "How do you guys get groceries?"

Clara chuckled. "Sometimes Dad runs out to the corner store... Usually he just gets them delivered."

Emmett snorted. "Sorry, I can't picture him wearing anything but his lab coat. So he's still looking like his usual serious self while wandering the freezer aisle with a stack of frozen pizzas."

"You know he can hear you, right?"

Emmett's mouth went dry and he stumbled on the sidewalk. "...Really?"

"...You should see your face right now."

Emmett elbowed her playfully as they walked. "You got me. Don't let it go to your head." Then he added, "You know, there's still like twenty blocks to go. Are you going to make it or are you going to need to fly me home?"

That time Emmett meant it as a jab, but Clara just smiled. "My suit's following us, cloaked and flying a randomized perimeter. After I escort you home, I'll suit up and fly back."

"My hero."

Their conversation devolved even further after that, with good natured jabs and talk about *Full Throttle Heart* and other anime.

As much as he joked, Emmett was glad for Clara's company. Even if the walk home took three times as long as usual, Emmett didn't mind—he didn't even notice.

Full Throttle Heart

A Small Hero

Truck-kun drove through the dark forest, its tires deftly weaving around trees and over their thick roots. Its headlights pushed aside the oppressive darkness and the rumble of its engine pushed aside the stifling quiet.

It had left the body of the dire bear behind, and tried to do the same with the memory of the short but brutal fight. In that respect, Truck-kun failed.

It wasn't the first time Truck-kun had slain an animal. Before this, there were bunnies, birds, and even a deer. All of them smashed on its steel bumper or crushed beneath its tires—each reduced to roadkill.

Yet there was something different about slaying the dire bear.

It didn't know whether it was because of the surprising transformation Truck-kun had suddenly taken at the start of the battle—raising up to twice its height and transforming into some miraculous design somewhere between truck and human. Was it because Truck-kun was in this miraculous place, or was because all those times before, Joe had been at the wheel, guiding Truck-kun to its destination? Or was it because the dire bear had been the first to attack...

"I still can't freaking believe it," Al, the bluebird, said from its perch atop Truck-kun's cab. He waved his wings and gestured wildly as he talked in his gruff voice. "That was the most amazing—the most stupendous—the most outrageous—never in my life seen anything like it..."

The bluebird had insisted on accompanying Truck-kun since its battle with the dire bear.

Despite all of Al's praise and reassurance that the dire bear was both demonstratively evil and dire, it didn't assuage the feeling deep within Truck-kun's engine—within its heart.

[Sad Montage accompanies Narration]

Nothing made of flesh and bone could stand up to unflinching, unfeeling steel. Had all those animals slain before just been preparing Truck-kun for something? Had they been preparing Truck-kun for this strange new place?

Or maybe slaying the dire bear was different merely because Truck-kun had saved the life of Al, the bluebird.

Truck-kun quickly decided that wasn't the case, and that it wished the bluebird wasn't riding on top of its cab.

[Al's singing overpowers the Sad Montage]

"He's the greatest hero in all the land
"The chosen one,
"The bee's knees,
"The dire bear's death rattle...
"Truck-dude is the greatest!"

Truck-kun made a defeated sound with its horn. It wanted nothing more than to ask Al to stop singing, but Truck-kun felt guilty—after all, Al had done nothing but praise the truck since.

Truck-kun might not have minded, if Al's singing voice wasn't worse than his regular voice—sounding like a trash disposal gargling marbles.

Wherever this strange journey would lead, it was going to be a long journey with Al. Especially if the bluebird kept singing.

Truck-kun spoke up. "Al, what are you doing in the forest all alone?"

The bluebird stopped suddenly (for which the truck was grateful). Al cleared his throat. "Oh, man, this is embarrassing. I don't know if I should tell you."

"Why wouldn't you tell me?"

"Because you're *the greatest hero in all the land.*" Al sang that line for emphasis, making Truck-kun wince. "I'm just a bird... a, uh, single bird."

There was a pang of sadness in the bluebird's gruff voice, like a note of a single bell that had fallen into the disposal along with the marbles.

"Are you lonely?" Truck-kun asked.

"Yeah, you could say that."

Truck-kun slowed and cast its high beams around the gloomy forest. There weren't any other animals around. In fact, there wasn't any other bird song at all out here. This was strange; Truck-kun had driven through plenty of country roads, through forests and by city parks in its time with Joe, and they were full of birds...

"Al, there aren't any other birds out here."

"I know, Truck-dude."

Truck-kun slowed to a complete stop. "Then why are you out here all alone?"

Al's voice quivered. "I... I... I have a horrible singing voice, okay? I'm a shame to bluebirds everywhere."

"I'm sorry, Al. Surely... surely your voice isn't that bad."

"Oh, it's bad." The bluebird croaked. "The Princess of Thatlandia ordered archers to shoot at me, and the Bishop of Otherlanden called me a blue devil!"

Poor Al wept, his tears wiping away the bird poop beneath his perch.

That *was* bad, Truck-kun admitted silently. It thought back to its time with Joe, and though he'd accidentally cut off cars on the freeway and double-parked once before, Joe had never offended royalty or men of the cloth.

"What do the other birds say?" Truck-kun asked.

"They... they laugh at me! Why do you think I'm single and wandering the dark forest?" Al sobbed horridly for a few moments before finding the fortitude to continue. "I'm out here trying to find my singing voice... or magic, you know? They say there's fey that grant wishes and demons that kind of do the same... Alright, let's be real. I'm desperate and lazy, so I'm hoping to find something magical. I thought if I wandered around long enough, I would stumble on *something.*"

Truck-kun's steel heart softened a little at hearing Al's despair. It had to admit that the bluebird's voice was extraordinarily bad—the kind of grating that no amount of practice could possibly fix. Magic was Al's only hope.

As much as Truck-kun wanted to make it back to Joe, the pitiful bluebird sitting atop its cab needed Truck-kun's help.

"I'll help you," the truck said, startling Al out of its misery.

"Oh, Truck-dude, you will?"

"Yes, Al. I'll help you. And my name is Truck-kun."

[Outtro — Slow, Instrumental version of Theme Song — "Hātofu-rusurottoru" by Gunpowder Audition]

[Outtro Still Shot of Joe driving Truck-kun on the highway. Al is flying beside them and singing. Both Joe's hands are off the wheel because he's covering his ears.]

[Local Commercial Break]

[Camera view of the Belport Bulletin anchor desk. Bethany Wonder sits alone at the desk, her dyed hair and dress both a deep blue. Bethany taps her papers on the desk and strikes a smile for the audience.]

"Is it time to talk peace? Conflict between Shian and Catalina escalates with threats of nukes and supers. When will the vampire menace in Wardenton be caught? Those questions and more this morning during the seven o'clock block. But for now we're joined by our eye on the street, Johnny Armour.

"What do you have for us, Johnny?"

[Camera switches to a news reporter for Belport Bulletin on downtown Champion street. It's nighttime and the bright, colorful lights of downtown are on. The reporter is wearing a thick red scarf that he keeps pulling down to talk.]

"As you can see behind me, restoration is almost finished on Champion street after the battle between supers left the city's thoroughfare devastated. Repair crews have been working around the clock, and the Summit of Heroes is continuing their investigation into the attack that killed twenty-nine and left over eighty wounded.

"With the Summit of Heroes on the case, you can rest assured that the perpetrators will be brought to justice."

[Camera switches back to the anchor desk.]

"Thank you, Johnny. Be sure to tune in at ten for more news. Remember, the Bulletin is on your side."

Chapter 41

[Not] Superhero 101

E mmett barely slept at all Thursday night. Between everything that happened with Paragon and Amarque's accident downtown, then talking with mom on the phone, and waiting for Lock to come home, Emmett was a mess.

Emmett heard his roommate finally come home around three in the morning, and Emmett must have fallen asleep shortly after—

Suddenly, daylight seared his eyelids.

Emmett rolled away from the light and grabbed his phone. The first thing he noticed was the alert saying that classes were canceled today due to the accident, and that it was already eleven o'clock.

Even though he was exhausted, Emmett forced himself to get up.

He had to get to the lab.

Emmett took the bus, which was emptier and slower than usual. Streets were closed down and several checkpoints were in effect downtown. Emmett couldn't remember ever seeing the police out in force like this, and he even saw several unmarked cars that could only belong to the Division of Superhuman Affairs.

Whatever had happened with Amarque yesterday had the city spooked and on high alert.

Dr. Venture and Clara were waiting for Emmett when he walked into the hub of the mechanical wing, section 002. They had both been looking at wall monitors and turned to greet him.

Clara's eyes were red. She looked tired, but Dr. Venture looked *exhausted*. Even though Venture perked up when Emmett arrived, his shoulders sagged.

"You guys didn't get much sleep," Emmett said, but Venture's glare made him immediately regret the remark.

"Thank you for stating the obvious," Venture replied.

Clara's eyes said much the same thing.

Emmett cleared his throat awkwardly. "So, what happened yesterday?"

Venture turned back to the monitor on the wall. "At approximately 8:34 p .m., Amarque lost control of their powers. The event lasted almost three minutes. Thankfully, Paragon intervened before the warp could stabilize and reduce downtown Belport to rubble. Amarque is currently in a coma at an undisclosed location, most likely outside of Belport."

Emmett watched as several of the wall monitors showed footage of the event—chunks of buildings crumbling and falling upward like a child turning a snow globe upside down.

It was different seeing it on a screen and it took Emmett a moment to process how he felt.

Seeing it from so far away, some of the rubble was as small as a pixel, but *Emmett had been there*. He'd run away from downtown. Those tiny bits on the screen were pebbles, bricks, chunks as big as cars, and whole floors of buildings.

Seeing it now, it just looked so... sterile, compared to the pandemonium of actually being there. It was mesmerizing and horrifying.

Emmett still couldn't get over the fact that it had been the work of *one super,* accidental or otherwise. One person did that.

"Why did it happen?" Emmett asked, tearing himself away from the screen.

Both Venture and Clara regarded him, like they'd been studying him as he'd been studying the screen.

Venture replied, "That's the big question: What happened to Amarque?"

Clara added, "All we know is what the Summit has shared through official channels."

Venture crossed his arms. "There was nothing on his person or in his blood to suggest foul play. He'd been drinking, but his blood alcohol levels were nonexistent by the time he was scanned."

Clara said, "There are poisons and toxins with short half-lives."

"Then there's no traces. No evidence."

Emmett came over to the central table. "Where was he when it happened? What about cameras?"

Venture said, "He was at the Donjon Club. It's an establishment that caters to supers. They don't have cameras in the club, but the Cabal of Otanh have ways of keeping tabs on who comes and goes. Unfortunately, Amarque nearly destroyed the club, and the cabal had their hands full just keeping the plane from collapsing."

Emmett raised an eyebrow. "The plane? Like a plane of reality?"

Clara rolled her eyes. "Each club is on a separate demiplane, tucked away outside our reality. The clubs are managed by the Cabal of Otanh, a collection of reality warpers, sorcerers, and illusionists. Emmett, try to keep up."

"That sounds *awesome.*"

"It is," Venture replied with a smirk.

"When do I get to go to the club?"

Venture's face turned hard. "After we figure out why Amarque nearly destroyed it."

Clara replied, "Please. The club is overrated and the Cabal of Otanh is a glorified fraternity."

Emmett chuckled. "Sounds like someone's bitter they didn't get invited."

Clara scoffed, but Venture spoke up. "We have several theories to work off of, but there's still a lot that we don't know.

"Theory one: Amarque lost control through some fault of their powers. If so, the threat is already contained, though there is a chance their condition might deteriorate.

"Theory two: Someone provoked Amarque. I doubt someone openly challenged him, especially in the middle of the Donjon Club. And I doubt he would purposefully retaliate in such a manner.

"Theory three: Amarque was compromised by a nefarious actor—whether through poison or mind control. This would be difficult, considering the safeguards of the club, his specific power set, and hundreds of witnesses, but isn't outside the realm of possibility."

Emmett listened intently until Venture was finished. "So theory two is out, and theory one doesn't really matter... Are you guys considering number three, then?"

"Yes."

Clara leaned against the center table. "But as Dad said, there's no traces. No evidence."

"So, what can we figure out?" Venture asked. He glanced at the two of them like an expectant teacher, and Emmett felt like he hadn't missed class after all.

"Motive," Emmett suggested. "We can figure out the motive, then that will help us narrow down suspects. But shouldn't the Summit be investigating this?"

"They are," Venture replied. "The Summit, the Cabal of Otanh, the DSA... and so will we. If someone did poison or mind control Amarque, then this is a major assault on Belport, the Summit, and a violation of the Code. What could've been the targets?"

The three of them proposed several targets, one after another: Amarque, the Summit, the Donjon Club, the city of Belport, or any potential attendee of the Club or downtown business.

Venture said, "I doubt the target was some other individual in the club or downtown. There are a multitude of easier ways to assassinate someone that don't require manipulating one of the most powerful supers in the world. Even if a single business was the target, there are easier, less messy ways."

Clara added, "But what if they were trying to assassinate another super?"

Venture rubbed his chin. "Possible, but my point still stands. There are easier ways to take out a fellow super."

Emmett was taken aback at how carefree Venture spoke about assassinating supers—not just the ease with which he proposed the violence, but that it *would be easy* to take out a super. Emmett thought back to Venture's lecture about the Code and felt like he understood the rules a little better.

Emmett said, "So then they were after Amarque, specifically, or the Summit, or the Donjon Club."

"Or the city," Clara said solemnly.

Emmett glanced at both of them expectantly, but Venture didn't refute the idea. "You think it could be terrorism?"

Venture sighed. "We can't rule out the possibility."

"What about *'it always comes back to money and power'*?"

"Power," Venture said simply. "That's the end result of terrorism."

Silence hung in the room and uncertainty hung on their faces.

Finally Emmett said, "We don't have much to go on, do we?"

"No," Venture replied. "We'll have more when Amarque wakes up. I've asked the Summit to notify me when they have something else to go off of."

"So what do we do in the meantime?"

Venture gestured to the wall monitors and information sprang up about Porcelain. Pictures, video highlights, and bulleted information covered the wall, reminding Emmett of a noir movie with a mystery tacked up on the wall or spread out haphazardly across the floor.

Despite the gravity of the day, Emmett couldn't shake the strange appearance of Porcelain's mask and bodysuit. It looked like they were investigating a missing department store mannequin.

Venture said, "We already have our own case to solve: Porcelain's involvement in the Champion street attack."

That brought Emmett back to the moment.

Emmett steeled himself. "If I'm going to be involved in this... I want to know what happened that night."

Venture met his eyes, and for a moment, it felt like Venture was challenging him, but he nodded.

"That night, Porcelain and an unidentified villain were engaged with two members of Summit of Heroes. There's been little information released and the rest of it's been suppressed. The DSA has a gag order in place."

A knot had already formed in Emmett's stomach.

Attacks in the city were rare, but not unheard of. He knew now that was because of the Code. But for the Division of Superhuman Affairs to cover it up...

Venture continued and the words hit Emmett like a truck: "Your bus was hit by a member of the Summit."

Emmett swallowed dryly. "What?"

The question slipped out, and Emmett didn't know why he'd asked. He'd heard Venture perfectly. There was no mistaking what he'd said.

A hero had killed him—killed five people and injured dozens. And the DSA was covering it up.

"It was an accident," Venture said, startling Emmett. "And that cape is being reprimanded."

Clara turned in frustration, as if she'd already grilled her dad with the same questions and knew what his answers would be.

"Who was it?"

Venture replied, "I can't say, because I honestly don't know. By the time the Fast-Response Drone reached you, there were other supers present and I had to prioritize between getting involved and saving your life."

Emmett nodded. His fists were clenched, knuckles white. "You know who else was present?"

Venture frowned, but the retired cape didn't look sad... he looked disappointed. "I will not be telling you which supers were there." The statement fell with the weight of a gavel.

"Why not?"

"So you could do what, exactly? So you could question them?"

"Well, yeah."

Venture's voice rose. "You think they would give you answers that they won't give the public? You're not a cape. You're not one of them, Emmett."

Emmett didn't know what to say. He stammered and a dozen things tumbled out silently.

Clara spoke up, "Maybe so he could get answers and get some closure, *Dad.*" Disdain dripped from her voice, but Venture didn't flinch.

"This is *not* a game," Venture said, struggling to keep his voice even. "The incident downtown and on Champion street... We've found ourselves staring down problems too big to take chances with. This isn't some introductory superhero 101 course."

Venture sighed. "I know what it's like to want answers... and I sincerely hope that we'll get them in time. But not like this. Even if you manage to find answers, it's not worth the chance of getting on the wrong side of the Summit. There are enough dangers without making enemies of them, too."

Neither Emmett nor Clara said anything.

Emmett was still frustrated. He didn't want to wait—*he shouldn't have to wait.*

But that was the joke, right? How do superheroes spend 90% of their time? ...Waiting for shit to happen.

Venture said quietly, "I'm not asking for you to trust the Summit or anyone else. I'm asking for you to trust me."

Venture was looking at Clara when he said that last line. Again, Emmett felt that pang of realization that there was something deeper between father and daughter, but now he knew better than to expect answers anytime soon.

Emmett wasn't *just* caught between the Summit of Heroes and some villains, or Porcelain, or anyone else. He was caught between Venture and Clara, too.

Chapter 42

Keeping Secrets

Emmett and Clara spent the day training in the Gray Room. Any other day, it would've been a nice change from the earlier—getting lectured by Dr. Venture about the nature of trust, waiting, and finding answers. The Gray Room should have been cathartic.

It was for one of them, at least.

It was Clara's opinion that Emmett should spend his time training against as many different powersets as possible. So, each time Emmett and Clara's robot started fighting, Emmett found himself facing a completely different super. They were all scaled down to Emmett's level, of course, but that only helped so much when every battle was new and unexpected.

Clara sounded giddy, though Emmett wasn't sure if it was because she was getting to use so many different powers or if it was using those powers *against him.*

The first powers Clara used were glass and silica-based powers, which were almost impossible to escape from. Windows could be shattered and turned into a storm of shards, turned into obscuring sand, or melted and reformed into weapons.

Light Sculpting was difficult to fight outside and reminded Emmett of Athena's powers. Light itself could be forged into barriers and weapons, or magnified into beams. Emmett needed to fight indoors as much as possible, and ultimately dealt with these first two sets of powers in the same way: By luring

Clara's robot inside a building and using tight hallways and low-light to his advantage.

Clara even used a negation-super against him—one specializing in tech-negation. Emmett had come to rely so much on his mechanical arm for attacks and his whip for movement that this was a wake-up call for him. Instead of using his whip to climb, he was forced to leap to windowsills to climb higher buildings and fight one handed when he did get close enough to engage.

Summoners were next. These types could conjure anything from a massive single ogre to a pack of wolves or flock of bats. Either way, Emmett had difficulty, though the bigger the enemy, the more he could lean on his increased speed and ability to climb. Though when an ogre hit him, it *really* hurt.

General telekinesis came after, and this was both the power that varied the most in difficulty and that Emmett had the most fun fighting. Clara took her time ramping up the difficulty, at first only using telekinesis to throw the odd object at Emmett while he chased her robot. Slowly, her fighting style became more complex. Soon, the robot was throwing chairs like boomerangs, changing direction mid-jump while pestering Emmett with clouds of debris that buzzed him like wasps. By the end, Emmett felt like he was fighting three opponents at the same time—Clara's robot was fighting hand to hand while simultaneously assaulting him with random objects.

Emmett sat down on the roof to catch his breath. "No—no more."

The robot put its hands on its hips, and Clara's laughter echoed through it. "That's all you've got?"

"For right now. Give me five."

It didn't take quite that long. After only a minute, Emmett was already feeling good enough to start again.

He looked up and found Clara's robot still hadn't moved. It was still looking down at him expectantly.

"So... Are you going to talk to me about what's going on between you and your dad? Did you guys have a fight or something?"

Clara didn't answer. Her robot didn't move at all.

Emmett sighed. He hoped he hadn't pressed his luck by asking. "It's just... seems like something happened. It's been kind of... awkward."

Still nothing.

Emmett's face felt even more flush than it had from working out. "You don't have to talk to me about it if you don't want to. I'm just offering, I guess. You've never really talked about having a lot of friends, so I was... So I was offering, I guess."

Silence dragged on, and Emmett tried to hide his growing distress. He stood up and paced to the edge of the roof, fingers laced on top of his head.

"Sorry," Emmett said. "Forget I said anything."

A few moments later, someone landed on the roof beside Emmett, startling him. Clara tossed her sweatshirt and beanie on the roof, then stood ready with her hands on her hips. Emmett was taken aback at her sudden appearance and her training outfit—it was rare to see her without her sweatshirt and beanie... It was even stranger to see the metal armor she wore overtop of her outfit: Metal boots, gloves, helmet, and sparse frame that wrapped around her joints. It looked like her exosuit, only stripped down do the barest essentials, like a car without any paneling.

"My eyes are up here," Clara joked.

Emmett felt his face turn another shade of red and cleared his throat. "I've never seen you wear this one." Thankfully, he'd been looking at her exosuit and not her.

"This?" Clara held up her hands for emphasis. "This is just what I wear when I don't need all the extra armor. Who were you talking to a minute ago?"

Emmett glanced back at the robot that still hadn't moved. Now he knew why and felt even more ridiculous.

"I *thought* I was talking to you. I was just wondering what's up with you and your dad. It's been awkward."

"Has it?" Clara's face wrinkled in concern. "Sorry. I guess it has been pretty obvious."

"You can talk to me about it, you know," Emmett offered. "But I get it if you don't want to. No pressure. I just figured I would offer."

"Thanks," Clara said, managing a smile. "It's mostly just about him not trusting us."

"Us?"

"Well, me. But also you. With all the stuff that's going..." Clara sighed in frustration. "I guess I was just hoping that we were getting to the end of all the secrets."

Emmett raised an eyebrow. "I know he's keeping secrets from me—about what super he used to be, about Porcelain, maybe even about what really happened on Champion street... But what's he keeping from you?"

"About what really happened to Mom." Clara's shoulders sagged like it took an enormous amount of effort to tell him... maybe even just to give voice to it.

"Clara... I'm not sure I understand what you're saying."

"Mom was a super, too. And she's gone." Clara turned and looked out over the faux city of Belport. "I can't even tell you the *official story*."

"...Because that might affect your dad's cover story?"

"Yep. Dad's a retired hero and if I tell you the story about Mom, then you might put the rest of it together... All that matters is, the official story about Mom is bullshit, and the only one that can tell me the truth, won't." Clara's fist shook at her side. "I know we have more important things going on right now. I just thought... I just thought Dad might finally tell me."

Emmett stepped up beside her on the edge of the roof, wishing he could think of *something* to say. "Sorry," was all he could find.

Then a moment later, he added, "Let's go around the city. I'd like to see what that suit can do."

Clara nodded and wiped her eye. "Yeah. Let's go."

Emmett ran across the white rooftops while Clara flew beside him.

Her training exosuit was a marvel. She flew mostly with the thrusters in her boots, but at slower speeds, she stabilized and compensated with the thrusters in her gloves. Despite the bare bones frame, it had all the speed and maneuverability of her normal suit.

Emmett commented as much, then asked, "How did you shrink the power source?"

Clara stopped and hovered beside the roof. "Most of our suits use modified fusion reactors. This one may look the same, but it, uh, has a lot less power."

Emmett chuckled. "That wasn't convincing *at all*. Come on, what's up with the suit?"

Clara shrugged. "It's pretty close, but definitely different. And check this out." Clara aimed an outstretched palm at him. Air shimmered around the glove.

Emmett had the sense to jump out of the way just before a pulse of heat blast through where he'd been standing a moment ago. He quickly stood and looked at the crumpled tiles on the next building over.

"What was that for?" Emmett asked, only half laughing.

"Just keeping you on your toes." She held up the glove and wiggled the metal fingers. "The suit can fire kinetic blasts. It's a similar process to how it flies—taking fusion heat energy using a laser to super-heat air. By adjusting the laser, we can adjust the explosion, changing the range and power of the blast."

The near miss was all but forgotten as Emmett gawked at the suit's tech.

"That. Is. Awesome."

"Yes, it is." Clara aimed her gauntlet at Emmett again, and they took off across the Gray Room in another game of cat and mouse.

Since he wasn't sure if Clara had any powers beside her suit, Emmett focused on escape instead of fighting back. He didn't want to hurt her accidentally.

It was only a few minutes before Dr. Venture's voice came over the intercom—

"Porcelain sighted. Clara, Emmett, both of you report to the armory immediately for deployment. I repeat, Clara, Emmett, both of you report to the armory for immediate deployment."

Emmett and Clara glanced at each other, and without saying a word, took off out of the Gray Room and down the hall.

Chapter 43

We Just Want to Talk

E mmett sprinted after Clara to the armory, section 004, feeling like his heart was beating in his throat. Not only was he finally getting to go after Porcelain, he was going to see the armory.

Despite his super speed, Emmett felt like he was chasing Clara through a dream, like he was moving through water or syrup. He barely heard Clara call for TINA to prepare her suit.

They ran through familiar twists and turns as the layout of section 004 mimicked the halls and hubs of neighboring sections, but no amount of imagination could've prepared Emmett for what he saw when they reached the depths of the armory.

The hallway turned into an open air catwalk which extended out into the center of a massive spherical room several hundred feet across. The walls of the room were blocky, like the steps of an ancient pyramid, but at the same time metal and not nearly as uniform. The longer Emmett stared, the more it reminded him of an abstract drawing—something made to play tricks on the eye. Maybe it was made to hide the true structure beneath...

Emmett didn't get a chance to ask because Clara was already at the end of the catwalk and yelling for him to hurry up.

"You can gawk later," she said.

Emmett ran over to the center of the room, his eyes still struggling to take it all in. There was something clearly different about the armory. Like the Gray Room, it didn't fit with the rest of the bunker.

Everything else Emmett had seen looked like normal technology. Cutting edge—sure. Futuristic—totally. But the armory and the Gray Room... they felt otherworldly.

"If you told me that your dad was an alien, I would believe you."

Clara scoffed, and then quickly wiped the spittle from her lips.

Emmett followed her eyes across the enormous room and his jaw dropped.

A compartment had opened in the wall of the armory, and Clara's exosuit floated out of it. *Floated over to them.*

Emmett couldn't do anything but watch and grow progressively more dumbfounded by the second. There wasn't any platform moving the suit. There weren't any wires holding it up. It wasn't even being piloted remotely or automatically. It just floated and set down gently on the platform next to Clara.

Was it anti-gravity? Magic? ...Was Clara telekinetic?

"Don't ask," she said, glancing back at him. "I don't know how the armory works or how TINA interacts with it."

Clara's comment brought Emmett back to the moment, and his attention focused on the exosuit. It was sleek and almost form fitting, with just a hint of hard edges to suggest armor. Emmett found it beautiful—like a mix of classical statue and deadly weaponry.

His admiration was dwarfed by his curiosity, though. Emmett wanted to examine the suit, even tear it down and dismantle it. Wanted to figure out how it worked, and then make his own.

One day. One day...

The back of the exosuit opened, Clara climbed inside, and the hatch closed behind her. Emmett watched jealously as the suit hummed to life.

Something else across the room caught Emmett's eye. A large metal box floated toward them, sleek and dark, about ten feet tall and six feet wide, and almost completely square. It looked like a glorified suitcase compared to the exosuit Clara used.

Emmett couldn't help but chuckle. "What is that?"

Dr. Venture's voice seemed to echo from the walls all around them. *"One of my Fast-Response Drones. Now get in."*

As if on cue, the drone set down on the catwalk and split open like the doors of a giant closet, revealing a glossy mesh-covered interior.

Behind him, Clara's suit rumbled with life. "Now's not the time to be shy."

Emmett swallowed and awkwardly climbed in, trying not to think about how dark and completely enclosed he was about to be.

The doors closed around him, sealing Emmett in the dark. The mesh felt cool and squishy beneath his hands, and then Emmett felt it close in around him to encase his legs, his hips, stomach, chest, and arms. By the time the gel crept up the back of his neck, Emmett was struggling not to panic.

He couldn't move his legs or his arms—he couldn't move at all. Even his head wouldn't turn—not even as gel solidified around his face and Emmett felt cool air around his mouth and nose...

He could still breathe.

He could still breathe.

"Try to relax," Venture said. His voice filtered through the gel, sounding almost ethereal. *"The gel is to keep you safe from any impacts, toxins, and extreme temperature changes. You don't need to do anything except enjoy the ride."*

Emmett sighed and wrinkled his face, feeling the gel give slightly around his mouth. "I can talk... What happens if I pee myself?"

"Don't do that."

Clara added, "If you two geeks are done, let's go."

There was a soft rumbling from outside that Emmett could barely hear through the gel, then a slight lurch—such a small movement that Emmett thought he'd imagined it.

TINA's voice came through a moment later. *"Following exosuit."*

Emmett waited in absolute darkness, but couldn't tell if anything was happening.

"Are we moving?"

Clara laughed over the intercom. "Yes. It's probably good that you can't see this part. The speed is hard to get used to."

Emmett sighed. "I'll have to trust you on that."

Flying across Belport was much quicker than Emmett expected, even sitting in a pitch-black drone.

TINA's announcements came one after the other:

"Exiting Lab..."

"Target locked..."

"Approaching..."

"Nearing drop point..."

By the time TINA announced, *"Prepare for drop,"* it felt like only a minute had passed.

The drone split open, and Emmett winced at the lights of the warehouse district. Then it unceremoniously dumped him onto the roof.

Emmett tucked and rolled, his enhanced reflexes making up for the surprise. Behind him, the drone was already engaging its cloaking system.

Despite how dead the warehouse district was, it took Emmett a moment to adjust. All his senses had been muted in the drone. Now even the sparse lights and muted sounds of the traffic felt overwhelming, and he shivered as he felt the night air.

"Come on," Clara said, her exosuit shimmering in the air beside him. "She's two buildings over on the top floor. It looks like there's an open window we can go through."

Emmett nodded. He leapt across the roofs to follow.

They were on the far Eastside of the city—the old warehouse and business district. It was the first time Emmett had been on this side of Belport, and he was taken back by the squalor. Buildings looked like they were being held up by wooden boards and a prayer. The roof creaked beneath his feet.

Clara flew into the fourth-floor window of the next warehouse, visible only by a shimmer and the hum of her thrusters. Emmett followed, using his whip to swing after her.

Inside, the warehouse looked like it had been hit by a natural disaster. Papers and splintered office furniture lay strewn about. Walls were crumbling or completely knocked down—graffiti covered the parts that were still standing. The smell of mildew and old smoke lingered in the air.

A crash came from down the hall, like shattering glass.

"That's her," Clara whispered. "She's alone in the building. Stay behind me, but stay close."

She kept the suit's cloaking engaged and stepped out into the hallway. Dappled light filtered in through broken windows, but otherwise the building was dimly lit and without power.

Emmett actually didn't mind that part; he could see just fine.

"What's the plan?" Emmett asked, peering around cautiously.

"Talk to her... hopefully. Otherwise, subdue her and bring her in for questioning."

Clara crept forward down the hall. Emmett followed, twitching his mechanical fingers for reassurance. He hadn't forgotten that Porcelain was a Class 2 super—

Class 2.3, actually. Which meant she could *punch up* even higher than Class 2.

A shuffle of paper beneath Emmett's feet brought him back to the moment. He followed Clara's shimmering form down the hall, focusing on where he was stepping. Despite its armor and bulk, somehow Clara's suit moved in complete silence. It took focused effort for Emmett to do the same.

Another crash came from a room at the end of the hall. White shards tumbled out of the room.

Porcelain was definitely in there.

Clara disengaged her cloaking and the sleek gray of her suit appeared. She stepped into the doorway, hands raised in a nonthreatening manner.

"Porcelain, we've come to talk to you. It's okay. You don't have to be afraid. We're just here to talk—"

An explosion tore through the air—bright white and a sound like shattering glass.

Emmett recoiled as it erupted from the room and pushed Clara back. White shards sprayed across the floor and past Emmett's feet. As quick and violent as the explosion was, it was over in a millisecond and reminded Emmett of a flashbang grenade.

Clara was still standing defiantly. She'd been pushed back a few feet, but otherwise her suit looked unharmed.

"Fine," Clara said. "Let's do this the hard way."

Clara disappeared into the room and chaos ensued. Impacts echoed from the room—squeals of metal, crunching glass, and more flashes of light.

For a moment, Emmett didn't know what to do. If Clara got overwhelmed, how much help would he really be? Emmett wasn't sure if she was a Class 2 or maybe even a Class 3 super, but she had to be higher than his lowly Class 1.

Maybe he could sit just outside the room, ready to surprise Porcelain if she tried to run...

It was a short-lived brainstorming session, because a moment later Porcelain ran out of the room—

Then another—

And another.

Three Porcelains turned and ran straight for Emmett.

He barely had time to process before the first Porcelain lunged for him. Emmett recoiled and blocked her first punches, and immediately regretted it—not only did the super look like a white marble statue, she was as solid as one too. Each punch felt like getting hit by a club and sent Emmett stumbling back a step.

His mechanical arm fared better, and Emmett was almost able to block direct hits with it, but he was wary of stressing it too much against her.

Porcelain was powerful, and even Venture hadn't been privy to all of her combat data. She might have even more tricks she could pull out.

Immediately, Emmett stopped trying to block and focused on avoiding or redirecting Porcelain's strikes. She may have had super strength, but it didn't seem like she had the speed to back it up, while Emmett realized he had both. He was able to stay a few millimeters ahead of her.

At least until the other two duplicates reached him.

Emmett backpedaled wildly to stay away from all three. Meanwhile the sounds of battle in the other room hadn't stopped. Worse, Porcelain didn't seem to be running—she seemed content to fight Clara and Emmett at the same time.

Emmett reached into his upper arm compartment for a handful of smoke pellets and threw them at his feet. They exploded, blanketing the hallway in smoke.

Out of desperation, Emmett slipped the folding knife from his utility belt. He crouched and slipped to the side so his back was against the wall. When the first

Porcelain appeared in the smoke, Emmett lunged, but the knife scraped across her side. He tried again, stabbing straight into her stomach, but the blade broke in half. Out of options, Emmett punched, driving his mechanical fist into her side. A crack sounded through the hall as her body splintered. Porcelain turned, half crumpling as she lunged for Emmett, but he slipped out of the way.

A second Porcelain came at him as more explosions sounded in the other room. Emmett slipped her punch and retaliated with one of his own, sending her sprawling away.

The third lunged straight for him, and Emmett reached out reflexively to push her away. His hand found her throat and for a moment, she paused, as if realizing her mistake.

"We don't want to fight you," Emmett said. "Stop! We don't want—"

Emmett's vision went white and he felt hundreds of pinprick stabs all across his skin—from his face down to his legs. There was nothing left in his hand; Porcelain was gone.

He pawed at the air, deaf and blind from Porcelain's explosion except for the ringing in his ears.

Haze came back into view, right before something hit Emmett in the side of the head—sending him sprawling across the hall. He couldn't tell if the smoke was swirling or if his vision was swimming from the blow, but Emmett clawed his way up from the ground.

The two remaining Porcelains came at him with crazed fury, and their lack of coordination was the only thing that allowed Emmett to survive the onslaught. He slipped under one while her punch gouged chunks out of the wall, then ducked behind her to keep his enemies stumbling over one another.

Despite his panic, Emmett noticed the duplicates were cracking and beneath their stony white skin were cybernetics that sparked with electricity... It caught Emmett so off guard that he nearly took a punch for it.

Emmett's ears hadn't stopped ringing, and he could see faint flashes of light behind the veil of smoke—Clara was still fighting other duplicates. She wasn't coming to help.

Another duplicate slammed into Emmett from behind, and the impact brought him back to the moment. Emmett stumbled while it wrapped its cold stoney arms around his chest.

Emmett's vision went white again and he rolled across the ground. He expected pain, but there was only a dull burning ache all across his back that felt distant and blurred like his vision. His ears were ringing again.

More flashes in the distance—

Another up close.

The world was a haze of light... But somehow he could still see the glistening metal and wires beneath the cracks in Porcelain's skin.

Maybe there was a reason after all why Venture wanted to keep him away from this mission.

Darkness bled in from the edges as Emmett started to lose consciousness.

Shit.

Chapter 44

Clara

Clara spun around, using a mixture of punches, kicks, and kinetic blasts to dispatch duplicates of Porcelain. Her targeting HUD flashed red in the corners of her vision, alerting her to duplicates trying to strike her from behind.

Meanwhile, Porcelain retaliated with her own punches and kicks, which clanged against Clara's exosuit so hard that she could *feel* the impact through the metal and diffusion mesh. Then there were the explosions—Porcelain's two main powers were creating duplicates of herself, then causing those duplicates to explode in a hail of light and shards of herself.

The explosions actually weren't that dangerous to Clara—they weren't strong enough to puncture her exosuit. They were disorienting, however, and each blast took a split second for her HUD to refocus, prolonging the fight that much longer. Clara was more frustrated than anything—

Until she heard explosions in the hall, followed by Emmett's screams.

Clara cursed herself. She'd been going easy on Porcelain, still hoping that the super would stop fighting. But she wasn't even speaking anymore, let alone slowing down. It was like she was crazy.

Clara's fingers adjusted the controls of her suit and multiple sets of blue text flashed across her HUD:

COMBAT THRUSTERS ENGAGED

Clara became a blur as extra thrusters opened up along the shoulders, hips, knees, and elbows of her exosuit. The same kinetic blasts that shot out of her palms now powered her punches and kicks, turning them into jet-propelled attacks.

She was no longer contained to the suit's mechanical movement—Clara felt like she was moving at the speed of thought.

Instead of cracking Porcelain's duplicates, chunks of them shattered completely with each of Clara's strikes.

But it still wasn't enough. Porcelain made duplicates as fast as Clara destroyed them—faster even.

DECREASING HEAT SINK POTENTIAL

Clara redoubled her effort and fought her way to the door. Even more power flooded into the suit and the alloy squealed under the forces as Clara pushed it to the max. Heat poured off of her suit and mixed with the atomized powder of duplicates, clouding the room with steam.

Porcelain *had* to be getting tired—there was no way she should be able to keep this up.

But neither could Clara.

SYSTEMS OVERLOADING
POWER DISPERSAL RECOMMENDED

If Clara had one weakness, it was that she had so much power inside herself that it was hard to wield. Like bringing a fire hose to snuff out a candle.

Again Clara's fingers flicked across the controls. Her hands—her whole body—trembled with power, and her skin felt like it was on fire. She adjusted the controls of the suit, sending all the excess power to her kinetic weapons.

But as warnings continued to flash across her HUD, Clara realized it was too little, too late. She screamed in frustration. Her suit was already activating its most powerful failsafe to keep from melting down.

CONCUSSIVE DISCHARGE

Thin slivers opened all across Clara's armor and promptly began to glow. She'd seen the protocol once before, when her dad vented the power from a leaky fusion core. The openings exposed the heat sinks that ran like wires under the surface of the armor.

For a moment, the room was bathed in an almost otherworldly glow.

Even though Venture had explained the science of what happened next, Clara only knew the aftereffects:

Three explosions sounded—

The first two explosions sounded like the *thunk* of a heavy gear turning, and marked the deposition of all the surrounding air into a dense, near-solid state. To Porcelain, it would feel like all the air in the room rushed toward Clara and suddenly became as thick as mud.

The third explosion turned the rest of Clara's excess energy into a bomb.

The process was supposed to mitigate the damage—keep it contained to the size of a small room instead of a city block.

The duplicates of Porcelain closest to Clara disintegrated in a cloud of white dust. Then further copies turned into a hail of shards. The walls, floor, and ceiling of the room crumbled—

Clara dove into the hall as the room collapsed behind her. The knees of her exosuit screeched as she skidded across the floor and then staggered to her feet.

POWER LOW

"No shit," Clara muttered between ragged breaths. Her muscles burned like she'd just sprinted for a mile.

The suit's discharge failsafe didn't just drain excess power from the suit, it also took a fair amount of power from Clara herself—an unfortunate side effect of the safeguard. Now, instead of feeling like the firehose of unlimited power, Clara now felt like the dwindling candle.

Across the hall, Emmett was surrounded by white rubble and half a dozen duplicates of the enemy. The front of his suit was peppered by white shrapnel and streaks of blood. His eyes were closed and he flailed to defend himself as he retreated.

Somehow, despite being blinded, outnumbered, and outmatched, Emmett was still on his feet.

The small swell of pride that Clara felt was dwarfed by her panic and anger at the sight of her friend against the ropes.

You stubborn fool, Clara thought. He never did know when to run.

POWER TO KINETIC WEAPONS

Clara redoubled her effort, letting her emotions stoke her power. Kinetic blasts flew through the hall, cracking and punching through enemies.

If she could just get Porcelain's attention and get her away from Emmett...

Another Porcelain duplicate exploded, the force throwing Emmett against the wall. His hands were still up, but he was barely on his feet.

Porcelain was still duplicating as fast as Clara destroyed them. And they were still going after Emmett.

Clara grit her teeth and made the decision to run.

THRUSTERS ENGAGED
BACKUP POWER ENGAGED

Clara rocketed forward, blasting and ramming her way to Emmett. She grabbed him tightly and flew down the hall—

Then through the outer wall of the building. Rubble rained down on the street as she flew away.

"Emmett, are you alright?"

He muttered something unintelligible.

"Don't worry. We're leaving. We'll get her next time."

He muttered something else, then, "...good."

Even though Clara knew there was no way Porcelain could follow them, she still looked back to be sure.

A single super stood in the middle of the hole in the building—her white body visible against the darkness of the warehouse district. Porcelain stared back at Clara as she flew away.

Then Clara sent a communication request to her dad.

"Did you get her?"

"No. We had to retreat. Emmett needs the med-bay... Again.""

When Clara got closer to the lab, she reluctantly stuffed Emmett inside a Fast-Response Drone. It would take him directly to the med-bay, both faster and safer than she could accomplish on her own trying to navigate the purposefully disorienting tunnels to the lab.

She rocketed through the passages toward the armory, fueled by her own intrinsic power which had already rekindled.

Despite having recovered, Clara's hands were still trembling when she climbed out of her exosuit and sprinted through the armory.

When Clara reached the main hallway, TINA's voice came through the intercom. *"You should keep your heart rate down."*

"I know!"

"Emmett is stable and being sedated until we can determine the severity of his injuries..."

Clara was already entering section 006 and quickly approaching the med-bay, leaving TINA's voice behind.

When she finally reached the med-bay, she was greeted with the familiar white, sterile room, and Emmett lying motionless in the hospital bed in the center. Her dad was hunched over him, wearing a mask, gloves, and smock. Two thin operating arms descended from the ceiling and hung beside him. Both he and the arms plucked pieces of bloody shrapnel out of Emmett...

Clara froze halfway across the room.

Emmett was bare from the waist up—the front of his shirt had been cut off and lay in a heap on the floor, presumably along with his mask. He was *covered* in blood. Pieces of shrapnel stuck out of him like tiny white islands in a red sea. There was a pile of shrapnel nearby that would soon cover an entire medical tray.

Clara had been there after the accident... but she hadn't *seen* Emmett—not really. Not when he was in the middle of surgery.

"He's fine," Venture said, standing up to look at something on a wall monitor that sat between empty glass tanks and bubbling tubes. The mechanical arms continued plucking pieces.

She wanted to believe her dad, but she knew that tone. It meant he was trying to stay calm, trying to reassure Clara as much as he was trying to reassure himself.

Clara forced herself to go over and look at Emmett.

She held her breath and leaned over the bed and looked over his injuries. Quick-set bandages were already wrapped around parts of Emmett's face and chest; they were red instead of pristine white.

Porcelain had been too dangerous. Emmett had been too weak. And Clara hadn't been able to protect him.

She muttered, "He never should've gone."

"He needed to," Venture said idly, his eyes not leaving the readouts.

"Is he okay?"

"He's stable and sedated—"

"I heard that part already."

She hadn't meant it to sound so harsh, but this was the second time that Emmett had been the centerpiece of this room. It wasn't a good track record, for him or for her.

Venture turned toward her. His face was stern but his voice was softer. "He'll be fine."

"Then why's he sedated again?"

Emmett groaned, and Clara jumped back. His arms and legs twitched and his head rolled side to side like he was distressed.

Venture walked over to the bed. "He's sedated because I wasn't sure how resilient his new body would be. Thankfully, they're not serious. But there's something else..." Emmett continued to struggle while Venture spoke. "The sedatives I've given him *should* prevent him from dreaming."

Clara's stomach twisted in an entirely new knot. "What did she do to him?"

"I don't know. He shouldn't be dreaming—shouldn't even be able to..." Realization dawned on her father's face, and Clara waited expectantly. "He's *not* dreaming."

Chapter 45

All That We See or Seem

In Emmett's mind, he'd never left the abandoned warehouse.

There was another flash of light as a duplicate of Porcelain detonated. Emmett managed to cover his face in time, but pain seared the front of his body—his arms and chest. Through the haze of light and dust, he saw circuitry between the cracks in his enemies' white skin.

...That wasn't right. Porcelain wasn't a cyborg. At least, there was no record of her being a cyborg.

But Emmett had been wrong before.

Maybe he was wrong again.

Either way, he didn't have time to ponder it. Porcelain's eyes were black and glossy, completely without recognition or pity. The Code wouldn't save Emmett. Porcelain was trying to kill him, and if he stayed to fight, she would probably succeed.

Emmett turned and ran, stumbling at first. It felt like he was running in slow motion. Stoney hands reached for him—tore at his hoodie and ripped it. The tatters of it billowed as he ran.

It wasn't until Emmett got to the end of the hall that his panic subsided enough to realize Clara was still in the room behind him. Flashes of light pulsed even faster than Emmett's racing heart.

It wasn't just him fighting for his life. Clara was fighting for hers, too.

"Run!" Emmett shouted, but his voice came out a muted whisper.

He didn't have time to shout again before a wall of duplicates tackled him. They crashed through the wall and out into the painfully cold night air of Belport.

They were so much higher up than Emmett remembered. Four stories up never looked so daunting. Now Emmett was falling—picking up speed until he was plummeting—and still the duplicates wouldn't let go of him. The ground raced up at them.

The duplicates' stone-white skin flaked away as they picked up speed. Soon their faces were nothing but blue cybernetics, metal, and wiring—

Then even the metal began to peel away, revealing skin and flesh beneath.

Clara's face peered back at him—Clara and Lock's three friends from the party. They stared at Emmett with unblinking eyes until they hit the ground.

Instead of concrete, Emmett splashed into dark water. The impact still knocked the air from his lungs, but now he was clawing his way to the surface, only vaguely aware of which direction was up.

Hands grabbed at his legs, trying to drag him back down.

When Emmett finally reached the surface, his lungs were burning and gasped for air. His mouth tasted like oil and copper. A bright, blinding light hung somewhere above, and all Emmett could see was the churning water—a swirling mix of deep red and utter black.

Emmett didn't know how long he swam or how long he fought off the hands grasping at his legs, but he made it to land. He lay face down on a shiny, metallic shore, with the dark waves lapping at his feet.

His feet...

Emmett looked back and found his skin sloughing off into the water. A mix of silver and flesh. Oil and blood.

Which of it was his? Which of it was *really* his?

Across the shore, Lachlan watched the scene through a keyhole in a door at the edge of the beach. Watched as his roommate struggled to stand.

Emmett had no idea what was going on, and there was no way that he should've been able to see the tiny sliver of Lock's eye through the keyhole, but somehow Emmett knew that his roommate was watching him.

Somehow, he knew.

As Emmett struggled to his feet, other figures rose up out of the sand: People and machines. They staggered toward one another, battering each other with fists. And as their fluids scattered across the shore, the swirling ocean rose up to drown them.

Emmett ran from the shore and through a barren forest. Branches scraped his arms and seemed to grab at him as he passed.

He didn't stop until he came to a sandy clearing in the woods, like he was standing on the beach again, unable to escape his fate.

In the center of the clearing, Lock stood over the lifeless corpse of Dr. Venture. Both men were completely still—Venture in death, and Lock staring down at him.

Emmett blinked in disbelief, and the two men switched. Now it was Venture looking down on the corpse of Emmett's friend.

"What are you doing?" Emmett shouted, but the words came out muffled and unintelligible. If Venture or Lock's lips moved, Emmett couldn't see them or hear their reply.

Tears welled up in Emmett's eyes. Each time he blinked, the two men swapped.

Clara's scream brought Emmett back to the moment—from somewhere deep in the forest. Before Emmett could run to her, someone lunged for him—

And knocked him to the ground.

Emmett struggled, but the attacker held him down. He wheezed as weight pressed down on his chest. No matter how he struggled, Emmett couldn't get out from under his enemy. Cold metal gripped Emmett's chin and forced his cheek against the sand.

Across the clearing, Clara's face was twisted into a silent scream. Far behind her, steel mountains rose up along the horizon and belched black snow into the air.

Emmett seized the cold hands that were around his face and neck. He squeezed and wrenched with all his strength, just managing to loosen them. Emmett struggled and turned his head upward to face his attacker.

It was like staring into a twisted mirror.

His own face stared down at him, a face cast in perfect, seamless metal.

Emmett felt himself losing the struggle, felt cold hands wrapping around his throat again. Felt his duplicate choking the life out of him.

Unblinking, unflinching metal.

It reminded him of that night on Champion street. Of how he felt as he saw that truck flying through the air right before it crushed him.

His strength was fading, not just from lack of oxygen, but from inevitability. Deep down, Emmett knew that there was no other way out of this. There was no other way the story ended.

His vision went white.

The white light didn't fade. If anything, it got brighter. Emmett squinted, but he couldn't see anything. He wanted to block the light, but his arms wouldn't move.

There wasn't any weight on him anymore, his arms just wouldn't move.

"It's okay. You're back in the lab," Dr. Venture said.

"You're safe," Clara added. She sounded relieved.

Emmett couldn't open his eyes wide enough to find them, but he knew they were close.

Was it over?

"What happened?"

"You were hallucinating," Venture replied, light glinting off his glasses. "Take a minute to wake up."

Footsteps sounded on the tile.

"Don't—don't go," Emmett muttered.

Venture replied, "We're not going anywhere."

Emmett breathed deep and nodded. He could finally see the outline of Dr. Venture as he looked at the wall monitors. And Clara's smiling face as she leaned over the hospital bed. Her eyes and her cheeks were red.

"You look relieved," Emmett said, trying to match her smile.

She laughed. "Yeah, well, you gave us a good scare."

"Like last time?"

Clara shook her head. "Not like last time. You must've been having some crazy dreams."

Emmett sunk down into the bed. His heart was still racing, and he could still vividly remember the feeling of being choked by his own twisted hands.

Finally, he said, "You have no idea."

CHAPTER 46

Makeup and Answers

E mmett had no desire to be confined to a hospital bed again. Despite the dull pain all across the front of his body, he sat up on the edge of the bed.

Meanwhile, Clara and Venture stared at him with tired, apprehensive eyes.

Emmett smirked through his bandages. "You know, being a super isn't as glamorous as people say." When neither of them laughed, he asked, "Was it worth it, at least?"

"Yes," Venture replied. "But first, tell us about what you saw while you were unconscious."

Emmett nodded, then recounted in as much detail as he could the dreams he had after the fight.

When he finished, Venture stuffed his hands in his pocket, like a professor about to deliver a lecture.

"With the sedatives administered, you shouldn't have been able to dream. Those were hallucinations brought on by a foreign substance—a poison. Poison contained in the shrapnel of Porcelain's duplicates.

"Now, there is very little chance of Porcelain developing a power like this, which leads me to think that she was poisoned by someone else. All this time Porcelain has been acting strange; First she was present at the Champion street attack, and Clara said Porcelain was incoherent when you found her.

"At some point, either directly preceding the Champion street attack or sometime during it, Porcelain was poisoned by an unknown super. The poison caused her to hallucinate and act irrationally, even violently.

"Most poisons break down over time or are broken down by the body, but due to Porcelain's unique powers and biology, the poison hasn't broken down. She's still suffering from the poison weeks later."

Clara stifled a yawn and shook her head. "Emmett, it's the middle of the night. You were only out for a little under an hour."

Emmett sighed. "Those dreams—hallucinations... They were *so* intense. I can't imagine being stuck like that for that long. Where is she now?"

"She's gone," Clara replied. "She got away."

"Is there anything we can do? Can we help her?"

Venture nodded. "We'll have to wait for her to pop on our scanners again, but yes. I'm already analyzing the traces of poison from the shrapnel. Unless it's something otherworldly, we'll be able to make an antidote. Getting her to take it, that's another story..."

Clara crossed her arms. "Then we can question her about what happened at Champion street."

"The League will want to question her," Venture corrected. "That's their prerogative."

Emmett listened, but couldn't stop his mind from wandering. Porcelain lost control of herself, just like Amarque...

"Are they related? Porcelain and Amarque?"

Dr. Venture and Clara shared a knowing glance.

Venture replied, "I'm still waiting on communication from the Summit of Heroes. Amarque still hasn't woken up yet but... Clara and I had the same thought."

Emmett sighed. It felt like the weight of several realizations all settling on him at once. "So a rogue super testing their powers, seeing just how powerful their poison is... Powerful enough to affect veteran members of the Summit... Didn't one of the mutagens result in something similar?"

Venture nodded solemnly, while Clara turned in surprise—apparently they hadn't gotten to talking about that possibility yet.

"When I tested the mutagen variants you brought in, one of them created cells that produced poisons. Some outright lethal, while others had a hallucinogenic effect similar to what Porcelain and you suffered," Venture said. "I just don't know for certain. The final effects of taking the mutagens aren't always the same, so there's not going to be a one hundred percent match... But if I had to bet, I'd go with your theory. Newly minted super testing the limits of their powers.

"Now the big question. Are they working alone?"

Emmett frowned and immediately regretted it—his face felt tender beneath his bandages. "Probably not. Athena said the knock-off mutagens were coming in ten plus shipments at a time—that's coordinated. And even if they're not tied directly to the shipments, there's no way some random newbie was able to get close enough to both Porcelain and Amarque to poison them."

Venture nodded, confirming his thoughts. "We're likely dealing with a coordinated team. Even if our suspect is a new super, the rest of the team is probably experienced."

Clara scoffed. "How experienced can they be? All they did was poison a member of the Summit of Heroes and possibly steal from one of the biggest corporations on the planet."

Venture smirked. "You both wanted to play hero. Welcome to the game."

Emmett sighed. "What time is it? I need to get back home."

Clara replied, "It's almost two in the morning."

Suddenly, the exhaustion that hung heavy over his allies found Emmett as well, and he covered up a yawn. "I need to get back."

Clara chuckled. "You need to do something about your face. You can't go back like that. Your roommate will freak."

Emmett gingerly touched the bandages on his face. He'd caught a chin and forehead full of shrapnel. Thankfully, he'd managed to shield his eyes from getting shredded. That would've sucked.

"The swelling is already going down," Venture said. "I'd lie low for the rest of the weekend. Stay in your room and fake sick. By the time Monday comes, you should be able to put makeup on to cover up the worst of it."

"Makeup?"

Venture rolled his eyes like Emmett was missing the obvious. "How do you think all those supers hide their scars and injuries so they can maintain a double life? They wear makeup. All of them."

Emmett waited, but Venture's expression didn't change.

Clara's eyes were locked on him. "You're not too *manly* for makeup, are you?"

Emmett scoffed. "No, it's not that... At least I don't think it is." He trailed off, not wanting to put his foot in his mouth.

"Good," Venture replied. "You better get used to it. Clara, why don't you get some of your extra makeup and show Emmett how to apply it."

Venture turned and left the med-bay, leaving the two of them alone. Emmett chuckled awkwardly while a devious smile spread across Clara's face.

All they had to do was wait.

Wait for Dr. Venture to make an antidote to the hallucinogen. Wait for Porcelain to show herself. Wait for news about Amarque...

Emmett hated waiting almost as much as he hated running away from a fight. He still wasn't sure how he felt about makeup.

Clara and Emmett were sitting on the edge of the bed in the med-bay. She'd pulled out a small bag of makeup and set it on a clean tray beside the hospital bed.

Alright, he felt apprehensive about it. But why? Why did he feel so clammy sitting next to Clara and staring down her supplies?

Emmett had turned it over enough in his head while waiting for Clara to return that he concluded it wasn't a *manliness* thing. Maybe in his parents' generation it would've been more common for women to wear makeup, but plenty of Emmett's peers—boys, girls, nonbinary alike—wore makeup.

Maybe it was because makeup was about hiding. He wasn't going to use it the way most people did. Emmett was going to use it to hide wounds... But was that so different from hiding an imperfection? Wasn't that what people used makeup for?

Emmett sighed.

"Oh, come on," Clara said as she looked through the tubes of makeup. "It's not that bad."

"It just feels weird. And I'm more weirded out that I'm not sure why it feels that way."

Clara chuckled. "Sometimes there's nothing to figure out. Feelings can be like that. Try to think of it like anything else—like a tool. That's all."

Emmett nodded and tried to tell himself that the rows of small squares and tubes were just mods—no different from mutagen vials or the smoke pellets that he put in his arm. Makeup was just another tool, just another way to hide—just another type of mask.

First, Clara helped him peel off the bandage on his cheek and another on his forehead, and applied a thin layer of liquid bandage to keep the cuts clean.

Next, Clara matched a foundation to his skin tone. She explained that it would make his skin appear more evenly colored and serve as a go-to solution if he wanted to cover up surface scratches or light bruises. It would also serve, literally, as a foundation for additional steps if he had particularly nasty bruises.

Though there were different ways to apply foundation, Clara primarily used gel-types that could be applied with her fingers—supers weren't going to carry brushes and sponges around. Emmett felt a little awkward as he tried it on his face, but it was easy enough to apply.

"Hopefully, foundation is all you'll need." Clara held up his bottle of deep tan foundation for emphasis, then she grabbed a different bottle. "If you need something more, you'll need concealer. Basically, you use the color opposite from the color of the bruise you're trying to hide. Peachy yellow cancels the blue from most bruises."

She put a bit on her finger, then dabbed a tender spot below his eye. "Don't rub. Just dab it in. If you're in a pinch, you can just use the concealer, but if you need it to last for a few hours, take a minute and put on foundation too."

Emmett grunted in affirmation instead of nodding. It seemed easy enough.

Clara smiled and held up a small mirror. "Your turn. You definitely need to put something over that other eye."

Emmett eyed his reflection. His face still felt tender, and so he'd been expecting the worst, but considering his recent beating at Porcelain's hands, he didn't look too bad. He looked... normal—

Except for the bruise under his right eye. Even with a layer of foundation, it was still a deep purple.

Emmett sighed and set to work while Clara held the mirror steady for him. In the end, he needed less concealer than he thought.

"A little bit goes a long way," Clara said, lowering the mirror. "You did good."

"Thanks," trying his best to return her smile. "Did your mom teach you?"

The question had slipped out, and for a moment, Emmett worried how Clara would react. She never spoke about her mother, and then Clara might see it as another comment about masculinity.

Clara burst into laughter, leaving Emmett to sit in worried silence.

When she finally stopped, Clara wiped a tear from her eye. "Dad taught me."

"Really?"

"Yeah. Dad's a super. He's had to cover up plenty of bruises and injuries. Mom... uh... didn't need makeup."

"That doesn't sound cryptic or anything," Emmett replied, attempting a joke.

Clara snorted a laugh. "I guess it does, doesn't it? Sorry. I just still don't know how to talk about her... God, that probably doesn't make sense either." Clara finally met his eyes and kept a straight face. "Tell you what, when Dad comes clean about his super identity, I'll tell you what I can about my mom, if you still want to know."

Emmett definitely didn't want to pry, but he had so many questions about Clara, Dr. Venture, and now about Clara's mom too. Even so, he understood the reason for discretion. If Venture wasn't ready to disclose his super identity, then talking about Clara's mom might inadvertently give it away.

In the end, Emmett would just have to trust them and be patient.

Emmett returned her smile. "Deal."

Chapter 47

Late Night Rendezvous

By the time they finished the makeup tutorial, it was 3 A.M. Saturday morning. Clara suggested he stay the night in the med-bay, but Emmett wanted nothing more than to get home and sleep in his own bed.

So Clara sent Emmett home with a small bottle of foundation and concealer, as well as makeup remover and cotton balls. Clara instructed him that if he ran out, he could just take the bottles to the nearest drugstore and get replacements. The last thing she gave him was a replacement folding knife and a small bluetooth earpiece.

"Keep that on you," Clara said. "If Porcelain comes up again this weekend, either dad or I will call you. The earpiece will tie into your burner phone, but it will also work without it—that way you have a direct line to us."

Emmett pocketed the earpiece and was about to say thanks when Clara interrupted him. "Don't forget. You're supposed to stay in and recover. So... maybe wait to test out the earpiece until *after the weekend*."

"Alright *Mom.*"

Clara punched him in the arm. He'd expected it to be playful, but Emmett actually winced in surprise.

"Alright, fine. I'll take it easy this weekend."

"That's more like it," Clara said, sounding pleased. Then she walked off down the main hall of the lab, waving before she entered the door to section 001.

Emmett rubbed his still tender shoulder. What was her power, anyway?

Since the buses weren't running anymore, Emmett jogged back to his apartment. The run was easy enough, but it was almost four in the morning by the time Emmett got back, and he felt exhausted in every other way.

Lock wasn't home, so Emmett penned a quick note and left it on the counter for him:

Sick and feel like shit. Sleeping.

Emmett slept well into Saturday afternoon and proceeded to do what Clara and Dr. Venture suggested: Spending the rest of the weekend inside.

It actually wasn't as hard as he thought it would be.

Lock came and left several times during Saturday and Sunday, and Emmett waited until he stepped out to make himself soup and to use the bathroom.

Twice, Emmett stepped out to use the bathroom while Lock was home, and a single nod was all that passed between them.

Aside from avoiding his roommate and questions about his injuries, it was just a matter of keeping busy. Between Emmett's classwork, his engineering project, superhero research, and media he wanted to catch up on, keeping busy wound up being the easiest part.

The hardest part was keeping his mind from wandering.

Emmett felt like he should be doing more—even when his eyes ached from staring at his phone trying to find more information about Porcelain, the mutagens, or recent superhero news.

Worse, when Emmett drifted off to sleep, his mind drifted back to the hallucinations he'd had under the poison. Dreams about washing up on blood and oil stained shore, of fighting a copy of himself. Twice he woke up in a cold sweat.

And Porcelain had been suffering from that poison for weeks.

They needed to help her.

Emmett laid back in his bed and groaned. First, they needed to find her.

He hated waiting.

If he was going to keep doing this superhero thing, then he had to find a better way of tracking targets. There was the radio locator, a project that, up until yesterday, Emmett had been proud of. Now it just seemed woefully inadequate.

Radio would help him keep up with certain communications, like police and emergency services, but it wouldn't help him find or track supers. Maybe cellphones would be a better way of doing that—it was common practice for supers to carry a burner phone, but that wasn't a reliable way of tracking someone. Burner phones were supposed to be kept *off* for that very reason.

But then, Dr. Venture was supposedly tracking Porcelain through her power signature. It wasn't foolproof—she needed to use her powers for Venture to track her—but it seemed infinitely more useful to Emmett.

Emmett turned over possibilities in his mind, realizing that Venture was already several steps ahead of him. Which made sense, given that he was an artificer.

Maybe Emmett didn't need to engineer it all himself. Maybe once Venture trusted him enough, Venture would share that tech with Emmett...

Emmett chuckled defeatedly and tried not to let himself think that all his work on the radio locator was for nothing. It was still a valuable experience, *and* he still needed to finish it to graduate. There was no getting around that last part.

Then there was Emmett's own development to worry about. Despite all the progress Emmett had made, it still wasn't enough. If not for Clara being with him last night, Porcelain might've killed him.

There wasn't anything he could do right now, but Emmett wasn't going to stay a Class 1 super forever. One day, he'd be able to take care of himself.

That meant getting stronger. `

So Emmett started brainstorming. It was all hypothetical and in super broad strokes, but it kept him occupied in between work for classes and episodes of *Full Throttle Heart*.

If he had a single option for a mutagen, what would he want to enhance? Maybe something to enhance his muscles that could make him stronger or faster in quick bursts. Maybe something to enhance his lungs to give him better endurance or one to give himself telekinesis. Emmett was sorely lacking a ranged option for dealing with enemies and still wasn't keen on using guns—nonlethal or otherwise.

Were there mutagens that could duplicate other powers? That would be something! There'd be nothing to stop him from taking the best powers of several supers for himself...

Maybe Gnosis had already done that. That wasn't a pleasant thought. But if that was the case, they wouldn't be able to hide a development like that—not from the public and not from the Summit of Heroes.

Emmett's mind kept wandering. What if he could make some other part of him mechanical? Would he want to replace another limb, or would it be possible to replace his skeleton with titanium? Or maybe he could make a neural interface so that he could seamlessly communicate with the lab or control a separate weapons platform. After all, in the last few years there'd been progress made with neural interfaces, and Emmett knew that as amazing as modern science and technology was, the stuff developed by the military, artificers, and the Summit of Heroes had to be even more futuristic.

His mind spun with the possibilities.

Emmett woke suddenly, his notebook splayed across his chest. It was the middle of Sunday night. His burner phone was going off. Emmett rolled over and grabbed it from the floor. When he saw the message, he nearly fell out of bed.

1:46 AM: *We found her. Drone inbound. Get to your roof for pickup.*

The message didn't have a tag, but Emmett knew it was from Clara or Venture.

Emmett got up, pulled on his bodysuit and clothes overtop of it. Then he pocketed his mask and burner phone.

Emmett left his room—

And ran straight into his roommate.

Lock stood in the kitchen, drinking a glass of water. He was still wearing his hoodie and shoes, like he'd just gotten in from a late night—

Well, semi-early night for Lock.

"Hey," Emmett said, trying to think of an excuse for leaving in the middle of the night... At least he still had makeup on.

Lock finished drinking the entire glass before he set it down on the counter and turned to Emmett.

"Hey man. You feeling better yet?"

Emmett nodded reluctantly. "Yeah, I guess so. I'm, uh, actually going up to the roof to clear my head."

"Want some company?"

Lock asked so flatly that it caught Emmett off guard. It sounded like Lock had a long night and just wanted to turn in.

"Thanks... but I just want to be alone." Emmett didn't know what else to say. Hopefully, being direct would be enough.

Lock nodded once, his eyes never leaving Emmett's. Silence dragged on until it was awkward and then intense.

Finally, Lock turned and went into his room. "I'm going to sleep. Catch you later, engineer."

Emmett waited until his roommate's door shut to go out onto the fire escape. He tried to push aside what had just happened, but Lock's eyes felt like they'd bored into him.

He could definitely see why Lock kept getting work as a bouncer. Emmett couldn't imagine anyone messing with his roommate.

Emmett just hoped Lock wouldn't worry and come up to the roof looking for him. Emmett had just pretended to be sick all weekend and now he was going to hang out on the roof in the cold night air, probably for several hours.

Hopefully Lock would just go to sleep.

CHAPTER 48

Venture / Lock

D r. Venture stared at the wall monitor, watching the view from Clara's exosuit camera and the view from the Fast-Response Drone intently. It was nearly to Emmett's apartment and would pick him up momentarily.

"Don't forget what we discussed," Venture said.

A moment later, Clara responded over the radio. *"I won't."*

"Maintain a one block perimeter, but wait to engage until Emmett and the other drones are in position. I'll brief him en route."

In an ideal world, Porcelain would've stayed in hiding for another few days, then Emmett and Clara could have practiced the plan in the Gray Room. It was more difficult this way, but ultimately better. They didn't have the luxury of time anymore.

Amarque was awake, and the Summit of Heroes would start their own investigation. Which was a problem because Venture hadn't exactly been upfront about the connection with Porcelain. Venture felt it was necessary, but the Summit wouldn't see it that way.

They'd think he was keeping secrets from them.

That was fine. Venture had given up trying to prove himself to the Summit.

While waiting for Clara to get in position and for the drone to pick up Emmett, Venture familiarized himself with the report on Amarque.

Amarque claimed they were drugged while they were in the Donjon club and reported similar hallucinations to what Emmett experienced. These hallucinations might've incapacitated someone like Emmett, who was both a low-powered super and without psychic powers, but Amarque was also a Class 4 psychic. Instead of losing consciousness, they experienced waking hallucinations vivid and disturbing enough to make them lash out.

Porcelain also maintained consciousness due to their different biology, but her version of *lashing out* wasn't nearly as devastating as Amarque.

...Or as devastating as it *could have been.*

After all, Paragon had stopped him before his warping became permanent and destroyed downtown Belport.

Dr. Venture pushed his glasses farther up his nose and sighed. The report ended with a description of the culprit—a female super who'd worn a purple dress and white gloves and had somehow charmed Amarque enough to get close to him. Venture shook his head in irritation.

There were dangerous implications: The culprit was clearly not working alone—someone had prepared her. There was no record of her attending the Donjon club before and the club's safeguards were not common knowledge. The only name she'd given was Juliet. Second, her powers were formidable and she clearly had refined control over them. She must've secreted the poison before entering and somehow shielded it from discovery. The third was Amarque, himself. His powers were perhaps the most formidable in the Summit of Heroes, yet he was a fool to be charmed so easily.

Venture breathed slowly and reminded himself that power alone didn't make someone worthy of being on the Summit. No matter the super, they were nothing special—people, demi-humans, occasionally aliens. Even those that fancied themselves immortal were just as fallible and flawed as their shorter-lived brethren.

The problem was that when Class 4 and Class 5 supers forgot their humility, lots of people tended to die.

Venture watched the screen with renewed interest. The drone was slowing down as it reached the roof of Emmett's apartment. It was almost time...

They would have answers soon.

Lock sat on the edge of his bed, listening intently as Emmett opened the outside window and climbed up the fire escape. He could follow Emmett's footsteps, even through the thick concrete of the roof.

Emmett claimed he'd been sick all weekend, then tried to cover up his bruises with makeup. It might've worked if Lock had been normal but he saw better than any normal person, heard better... And he could smell better than any normal person.

Lock recognized that smell as soon as he came home Saturday morning. He could smell it through Emmett's door as he slept. He knew it from Champion street, when those capes had fucked everything up and that super had gotten away from him.

It had been hard not to tear Emmett's door off the hinges that night. Hard not to question him about Porcelain.

Now his roommate was running off in the middle of the night—

Sorry, *going up to the roof to clear his head.*

Emmett needed to work on his excuses.

Once Emmett was up on the roof, Lock quickly got up, left his room and crossed the apartment in a blink. He paused at the fire escape, head hanging out the window to listen.

Emmett's footsteps came his direction again, and Lock pulled his head back in the apartment so he wouldn't be seen. Emmett wanted to make sure Lock didn't see what he was doing or, more likely, where he was going.

Lock waited just inside the window for Emmett to walk across the roof again, then he crept up the fire escape, stopping before he came over the top.

There was a faint whirring sound, quieter than the wind. Lock peered over the roof and saw Emmett standing on the other side. A moment later, something shimmered beside him. Doors appeared in midair, like a hidden closet opening up. Emmett stepped inside and the doors closed around him.

Lock would've been surprised if he hadn't already seen Venture's drones before. The last time, Lock had watched while the drone scooped up a lifeless body off of Champion street—

At the time Lock hadn't paid it enough attention. Hadn't realized that it was his roommate.

The drone shimmered as its cloaking reengaged fully, then the whirring grew fainter as it sped off across Belport.

Lock chased after it, hurling himself off the roof and sprinting down the streets of the West End, receiving a few honks of car horns and screams of startled pedestrians. Not many people were still out this early in the morning, and none of them were prepared for a super to pass by at highway speeds.

If the drone had bothered to change direction or vary its flight route, Lock might not have been fast enough to maintain line of sight. But once the buildings got taller and Lock leapt up to the growing skyline, he was able to keep sight of the drone even as it shrunk to a flickering pinprick in his vision.

Lock didn't hold back, running with the reckless speed across the skyline that he'd used on the street—easily leaping up three stories at a time and only avoiding the very tallest skyscrapers of Belport.

His lungs burned for the first time that he could remember and there was the slightest burn in his legs. The discomfort came and went as his body adapted. Even now, the Mutagen-X in his body was making him stronger, adapting his mind and body to new stresses and dangers.

He felt like a Class 3 super.

There was a good chance that Venture would discover Lock's involvement tonight, and if he did, Venture might change the cloaking device on his drones so that Lock could no longer follow them. But it was a chance that Lock had to risk.

He couldn't risk Venture and Emmett getting to Porcelain before he did.

The drone was heading toward the warehouse district, past Gnosis headquarters and the Eastside. Lock briefly considered calling in on his phone, then decided against it. They would want him to handle things on his own.

Soon the shimmer of the drone grew, and Lock knew he was getting close. He didn't even mind when he noticed five more shimmers in the sky—five more drones converging on Emmett's position.

It meant that he'd been right to follow.

And things with Porcelain would soon be over.

Chapter 49

Best Laid Plans

There was a slight lurch as the Fast-Response Drone stopped. The mesh inside loosened around Emmett, and a moment later, the doors opened. Cold night air rushed in, and Emmett grit his teeth.

It took Emmett a moment to get his bearings, but he stepped out onto a roof in the warehouse district. Nervously, he adjusted his mask and looked around for Clara.

She materialized beside him a second later, clad in her gray exosuit.

Dr. Venture had briefed him on the plan on the flight over. The drones would surround the warehouse while Clara and Emmett converged on it. Clara's exosuit had been outfitted with a sonic weapon that would prevent Porcelain from duplicating. Clara would shoot her with the sonic blast, then together they would destroy any duplicates until only a single copy of her was left. The drones were there to prevent her from fleeing if she figured out their plan. If an unaffected duplicate got away, it would all be for naught.

Clara handed Emmett two small sonic grenades about the size of grapes, which he stuffed into his upper arm compartment. Those were his backup in case Porcelain targeted him or in case she tried to get away.

Venture hadn't answered when Emmett asked how he'd come up with the sonic weakness. Emmett had just rolled his eyes and hoped Venture saw the gesture.

"Are you ready?" Clara asked, her voice slightly tinny from the intercom.

Emmett snapped back to the moment. He still felt sore from their last fight, but he adjusted his mask and nodded. "I'll follow your lead."

"She's in the basement this time. Drop to the street and we'll go in through the side entrance."

Clara descended, and Emmett swung down to the alley between warehouses. Then the pair snuck through side streets until they came to a creaky side entrance. They squeezed in sideways, careful not to push the door open anymore than needed.

She led the way into the gloom of the hallways. Neither she nor Emmett needed the lights to see, so they walked in near-complete darkness. The only sign to mark their passing was the occasional crunch of broken glass beneath their feet.

They pushed open a set of giant double doors and entered the warehouse's main floor. Rows of metal shelves littered the room. Most still stood upright, but several were toppled against the far wall, their criss-crossed braces giving the appearance of giant spiderwebs covering the room.

Emmett peered through the veil of metal and gloom, at first finding only the occasional box and wisps of trash—

Until he saw Porcelain.

She stood in one of the aisles, hands cupping her face in her hands like she was crying. Emmett pointed her out to Clara, and after watching Porcelain for several long seconds, Emmett realized she wasn't moving or making any sound at all.

If he hadn't already seen her before, Emmett would've thought she was a nude department store mannequin.

Slowly, Clara and Emmett stalked across the aisles. Emmett wasn't sure how close they would need to be for Clara to use the sonic blast, but he guessed that she couldn't use it across the room or through so many barriers.

There was a cut-through aisle in the center of the room, and the pair crept through it. When they came to Porcelain's aisle, they realized they weren't as alone as they thought.

There were two more copies of Porcelain, both of them unmoving: One had a hand on the crying duplicate's shoulder, as if reassuring her. The second stood in the next aisle over, peering through the bars at the first two with a mournful expression on her face.

"I'm sorry."

The voice came from behind them, and both Clara and Emmett whirled around, searching for it.

A duplicate sat perched at the top of a shelf beside them, peering down like a gargoyle, but it didn't move and it didn't speak again.

"I didn't know."

The voice came from the original group—from a new duplicate reassuring the crying one.

"I'm sorry."

"I'm sorry."

"I'm sorry..."

One by one, duplicates appeared around them, filling up the warehouse. Their voices overlapped until the room was deafening. But no matter how fast Emmett turned, he never actually saw them move—never saw them appear. It was almost like they'd already been in the warehouse, hidden from sight.

In seconds, Clara and Emmett were back-to-back and surrounded by hundreds of duplicates.

Emmett swallowed dryly. His hands were clenched, but he was afraid to reach into his arm compartment for a grenade.

Soon, he wouldn't have a choice.

Emmett searched the room, waiting for an attack to come from any angle. Every duplicate was completely still, frozen in a myriad of poses across the warehouse and atop the shelves.

Now they were silent—whether that meant Porcelain was at her limit and there were no more duplicates forming, or that she'd simply stopped apologizing, Emmett didn't know.

"What are you sorry for?" Emmett asked. The question came out as little more than a whisper.

Through the web of metal and dolls, one duplicate turned her head and looked directly at Emmett—

All of them looked at him.

Emmett flinched at the sight and pressed his back against Clara's armor.

Then the screaming started. Hundreds of white mouths opening, quickly turning from a discordant choir to an ear-splitting scream.

The duplicates descended on them, sprinting from the aisles and leaping from the shelves. Clara raised an armored hand and blasted—clearing entire aisles of copies.

Emmett lashed out with his whip, hoping to keep the first few enemies at bay. Surprisingly, his whip cracked two of them in half. He swung twice more quickly and cut down several more just as easily. He realized that Porcelain had divided her power as she made copies, and making so many had spread her thin.

Emmett wasn't going to complain.

He lashed out as quickly as he could while Clara let loose kinetic blasts behind him. Soon Porcelain's screams were drowned out by the thumps and cracks of impact.

Despite the sweat beading on Emmett's forehead, they were faring well. The only problem was he could already feel the duplicates growing stronger. For every one they destroyed, the next seemed even more durable. Soon, they were taking multiple strikes from Emmett's whip to destroy, and then his whip wasn't hurting them at all.

Emmett retracted his whip and waited for them to close in, meeting the first few duplicates with full power punches with his metal right hand. Thankfully, they fell and shattered.

Clara flew up and tackled the shelves, causing them to topple. Screeching metal filled the room as the shelves fell into each other like dominos, crushing dozens of duplicates beneath them.

"Here goes," Clara said, still hovering in the air behind Emmett.

The first blast of her sonic weapon echoed through the room. It sounded like the ringing of a glass, but even higher pitched. It felt like Emmett's teeth were ringing in his skull and the pain caused him to wince, mid-punch.

Unfortunately, the duplicates in front of him didn't flinch at all, and a Porcelain punched him in the face. The impact sent Emmett reeling and nearly tripping over the fallen shelves.

The punch left him dazed and Emmett could already feel blood pooling in his mouth. They'd destroyed enough duplicates that now Porcelain was probably back to full strength—far too strong for Emmett to trade punches with.

Emmett shook his head and managed to kick away the first duplicate that tried piling on top of him. He resisted the urge to use his own sonic grenades while more shots echoed from Clara's kinetic weapons.

Two more blasts rang out from the sonic weapon, and Emmett's eyes watered as he struggled to keep them open. A punch from his right hand bought him enough time to leap to his feet. Emmett had been about to scream from the pain in his ears when he saw the duplicates glowing in front of him—

Not glowing. Vibrating.

Each copy of Porcelain was surrounded by a thin haze as their bodies oscillated with latent energy. In the free moment he had, Emmett glanced quickly around to see the copies of Porcelain steadily dwindling.

"It's working!"

"Don't let up!" Clara replied.

Emmett leapt forward with renewed intensity. As the number of duplicates fell and Porcelain's durability increased, Emmett could no longer break her copies in two or even three punches. So he focused on pushing them away and keeping them from getting past him and attacking Clara from behind.

Even Clara was having trouble destroying enemies in one shot from her kinetic weapons.

Moment after perilous moment, the number of deadly white mannequins fell until there were little more than ten surrounding them.

Then each of the duplicates stopped and stared at them, completely frozen.

"I didn't know."

"I'm sorry."

Emmett didn't see any of them speak, but he heard them all the same.

No more copies appeared, and Emmett wondered if Porcelain had figured out their trick with the sonic weapon. From where Emmett stood, it looked like every copy had been tagged by the sonic weapon, so she wouldn't be able to duplicate anymore. Even if she was deep in a hallucination, she had to realize that her powers weren't working correctly... Maybe she was plotting her next move.

"Watch out," Venture said over the intercom. *"Third party inbound—fast! Brace for impact. Clara, sensors indicate Mutagen-X."*

Venture sounded like he was genuinely scared.

Outside, kinetic weapons sounded as the Fast-Response Drones engaged the new target. Emmett couldn't do anything but listen as a chorus of shots were punctuated by a hum of thrusters. Drone search lights flickered through the upper windows.

Emmett thought he heard footsteps—*heavy* footsteps. Not even a moment later, something like an explosion echoed through the warehouse. The floor trembled and the metal shelves squealed as they ground against one another.

Porcelain still didn't move.

Footsteps came from down the hall, coming closer.

Another crunch of steel like doors being torn open.

Emmett's heart was beating in his throat and he couldn't tear his eyes away from the hall across the room. Whatever super was coming their way, something inside Emmett was screaming at him to run.

Chapter 50

Third Party

The double doors burst off their hinges. The force sent the doors cartwheeling across the warehouse's giant room. They slammed into the opposite wall, half-embedded and sticking out.

Fast-Response Drones shone spotlights through the upper windows, highlighting the lone super. They stood in the entrance, clad only in black. It was an outfit much like Emmett wore—black mask, hoodie, and pants. Though the hoodie was torn, revealing rippling muscle beneath, the man wasn't bleeding from the injury. Normal enough, except that even from across the room, Emmett could feel that there was nothing normal about him.

Emmett hadn't felt a sense of overwhelming power and dread like this since seeing Paragon hanging ominously in the sky.

"Clara?" Emmett whispered.

"You have one chance to leave," Clara said, floating higher in the air. Her suit hummed with power, the air around her warped and flickered.

Despite Clara's show of force, it didn't make him feel the slightest bit better.

"I'm sorry—"

Emmett didn't see the new super move. One second he was standing in the searchlights. The next second, he was gone. The upper windows of the warehouse shattered as drones fired kinetic blasts at where the super *had been*.

To Emmett's right, the duplicate of Porcelain exploded as it spoke. Shards tumbled across the room. The super stood in her place.

He disappeared again, reappearing at another duplicate and simultaneously destroying her. This time, the fallen shelving screeched from where the super had stepped on top of it, and Emmett saw the super retracting a punch—

He wasn't teleporting or using psychic power. This guy was just that strong and that fast. Which meant Mutagen-X wasn't so different from Mutagen-A… That fact didn't make Emmett feel any better either, but he filed the mental note away for later.

Even the drones outside took a moment to register the target's movement—the *thunks* of impact from their kinetic blasts tracing across the room after him.

TINA's voice on the intercom brought Emmett back to the moment. *"Upgrading countermeasures."*

Suddenly, the *thunks* from the drone blasts converged on the new super. Emmett crouched low as the searchlights swept across him, but the drones' shots missed him completely. Even when the super ran across the room, taking out another duplicate of Porcelain, the drones' shots were right on top of him.

Whatever TINA had done to the drones had tuned up their shots so that each impact made the room shudder and missed shots tore chunks out of the concrete floor. But the super shrugged off everything.

Things had quickly gone from bad to worse: Not only did the drones' weapons not appear to be affecting their enemy at all, even Clara seemed caught off guard by his speed.

The super could've struck Clara or Emmett as he went past them. He wasn't going after them at all…

Clara screamed at Emmett, "Get Porcelain!"

Emmett turned to the nearest duplicate and sprinted for her. Since the new super had arrived, Porcelain hadn't moved at all. Every copy of her was frozen mid-pose.

Emmett reached her, grabbed Porcelain by the shoulders, and shook her. "We need to get out of here!"

Her skin was hard and cold as stone, and at first she didn't react, but then Porcelain looked Emmett in the eyes. "He's going to kill me."

Emmett had never seen Porcelain so clearly than he did in that moment. She didn't wear a mask—she didn't even appear to wear a bodysuit. Her skin was the texture of smooth ceramic, hairless and seamless. She had eyes that were unblinking and sterile white. Her powers had transformed her inside and out. But for a moment, Porcelain's dangerous, inhuman exterior fell away. She wasn't a super—she was scared.

His brother, Antony, had looked up at him like that when they were scared kids.

Behind them, dull impacts of metal on flesh echoed as quick as machine gun fire. Emmett glanced back just in time to see twin blurs as Clara fought the new super hand-to-hand. The broken shelves around them crackled with blue electricity like she'd deployed another countermeasure.

"Clara, disengage!"

"We need to run," Emmett said, grabbing Porcelain by the arm and sprinting for the closest door. She didn't resist, and if she replied, Emmett couldn't hear it over the maelstrom of battle.

By the time they made it to the door, Emmett heard something that sounded like the *thunk* of a heavy gear turning, but he didn't stop running. Clara had told him about her trump card—she'd overloaded her exosuit and was already using it.

She was already using her final attack.

Emmett and Porcelain had just managed to make it outside by the time the second explosion went off. All the matter around Clara's suit was condensing and solidifying.

Supposedly, Clara's attack would be confined within the building, but she'd explained the destructive potential it contained. Emmett wasn't chancing it. They didn't stop running.

A second later, an explosion tore through the warehouse. Steel screeched and the glass that was left was thrown across the streets. Emmett and Porcelain stumbled as a blastwave blew through the doors directly behind them.

Above them, the Fast-Response Drones dove into the warehouse to clean up.

Emmett and Porcelain hadn't even made it to the next warehouse when more explosions sounded from behind them. The wall of the warehouse crumpled as several things came flying out into the street—wrecked drones bounced across the pavement. A second later, Clara followed them. Her exosuit skidded down the street.

Emmett's heart dropped and he whispered through gritted teeth. "Clara..."

"My suit's down, but I'll make it," she replied through the intercom. Her voice was laced with pain.

Venture came through a moment later. *"Emmett, run. Porcelain isn't worth it."*

Emmett turned and ran through the warehouse, dragging Porcelain with him. After all this, Emmett couldn't just leave her to die.

They sprinted across another large open room of the second warehouse. Conveyor belts crisscrossed the floor and long plastic sheets draped down from the ceiling.

Something burst through the wall behind them, and Emmett didn't need to turn around to picture the super's ominous silhouette.

"Stop."

Emmett ignored the voice, tossing smoke pellets and noise makers behind them. Pops and shrill wails echoed through the building. Emmett and Porcelain sprinted down the hallway—

And made it precisely two more steps.

Porcelain turned around and grabbed him, quickly putting Emmett in a chokehold. Even with his training, he hadn't a chance of resisting Porcelain's strength when she was condensed. Emmett grabbed Porcelain's arms, as feeble as it felt.

Across the room, the unknown super strode out of the smoke. The noise makers were already done, presumably smashed.

Emmett struggled. "We're trying to help—"

"You were there the night I was poisoned," Porcelain said.

At first Emmett thought she was talking about him, but Porcelain didn't whisper. She was talking to the other super...

Even more startling was that the enemy super flinched in surprise. The expression was so quick that if Emmett blinked, he would've missed it.

Emmett moved to reach for a smoke grenade—

He barely registered the sound of rapid footsteps as the super crossed the room. Emmett was thrown sideways, slammed into the wall, and pinned there. The super had one hand on Emmett's chest, pressing so hard that he struggled to breathe.

Emmett pawed helplessly at his enemy's forearm, but it wouldn't move. Emmett squeezed the man's wrist with his metal arm and not even its inhuman strength phased him.

The super held Porcelain by the throat with his other hand. Despite both Emmett and Porcelain struggling, the super didn't even move.

He stood there, completely unfazed. His mask was still in one piece, but his hoodie was in tatters. Beneath it, his muscles rippled like they were alive, and his skin was completely unharmed.

The super glanced from Porcelain to Emmett, his white eyes the only part that peeked through the mask. "You couldn't stop me if you wanted to," he said in a low growl, like he was hiding his voice.

Emmett struggled to speak. "Please. She has answers I need."

"I'm sorry—"

Porcelain's voice was cut off as the super squeezed and her neck shattered. Her head and body fell to the floor, breaking and scattering shards across the warehouse.

Emmett's head hung, defeated, as he stared at the shattered remains of Porcelain. At his chance for answers.

Then he glared at the super that still held him by the chest. Emmett squeezed the man's wrist as hard as he could. The actuators in his arm whirred with effort, but the man didn't even flinch.

"I'm not your enemy."

Emmett looked up in disbelief. He didn't even scoff. "It doesn't feel that way."

The super shook his head. "It doesn't matter—I'm not your enemy... But don't cross Gnosis."

The next second, Emmett coughed at the sudden release of pressure around his chest. Emmett glanced around, but the man was already gone. As relieved as he was to be able to breathe normally, Emmett turned, ready to run and look for Clara.

But she was standing across the warehouse. She flew across the room and set down beside him. Her suit was mangled; plating was crumpled, or completely torn and missing, showing fibers and mesh beneath.

"Are you alright?" Emmett asked.

"My pride hurts worse than I do. What about you?" she asked.

Emmett nodded, then stared down at the broken shards littering the floor and winced. Pieces of Porcelain crunched beneath Clara's exosuit.

"I couldn't do anything," Emmett said. "I couldn't help her."

Clara put a metal hand on his shoulder. "He's gone, but we'll find him. I'm just glad you're okay."

"You too," Emmett said, nodding again. Even though he felt defeated, he breathed easier.

It was over... for now.

Chapter 51

Sleep Over

E mmett didn't go back to the apartment that night. More Fast-Response Drones arrived on scene to evacuate Clara and Emmett and take them back to the lab.

Apparently, their fight had attracted the attention of lower members of the Summit of Heroes. Clara and Emmett had just escaped before they arrived to cordon off the area.

Emmett was glad to be cocooned inside the drone. It was dark and quiet, and he was safe. No one saw him while quiet tears fell.

He couldn't get the image of Porcelain out of his head. One moment she'd been alive. The next, not. She was a pile of rubble on the floor.

Was that how easy it was? All that super had to do was squeeze. The Code made morbid sense.

As Emmett rode in the drone, he was grateful for the isolation. He needed... Emmett wasn't sure what he needed, but somehow, being alone felt right. Maybe it was penance for not being able to make a difference.

Emmett relished the numbness of his mechanical cocoon.

The drones deposited Clara and Emmett back in the armory unceremoniously. Emmett did his best to put on a neutral face. Physically, he felt fine. Tired, but fine. Far better physically than his other superhero outings. Mentally, though, he was drained.

Drained was being generous.

He'd come so close to getting answers, then Porcelain had been murdered in front of him. Thinking of her face made Emmett shudder.

Tonight could've been worse. Much, much worse.

Dr. Venture was there to greet them and barely waited for Clara to get out of her exosuit before hugging her.

"I'm alright, Dad. Honest!"

Despite the forced smile on her face, Clara walked with a limp and winced when Venture squeezed her.

"Easy, easy!"

Venture backed up, still holding her by the shoulders. "I'm just glad you're alright. Both of you." Venture met Emmett's eyes, relief apparent on his face.

But their relief was short-lived.

"Who was that?" Emmett asked.

Venture replied, "Most likely someone from Gnosis, given what they said to you."

"You heard?" Emmett asked. He was surprised, but also relieved. It saved him from having to recount the event. "...But that doesn't make sense. What does Gnosis have to do with all of this?"

Venture said, "If this rogue super or supers behind the attack on Amarque and Champion street were using mutagen derivatives, Gnosis might be trying to cover it up. They wouldn't want word getting out."

Clara added, "They're cleaning up their mess."

Emmett sighed. That meant Gnosis was probably tracking down the culprits, and that now it was a race between their group and Gnosis. The only other way to get answers about Champion street would be to question the Summit of Heroes and Emmett wasn't sure which organization he'd rather cross.

Emmett said, "That super... Porcelain thought he was there that night on Champion street."

"What was that guy?" Clara asked. "What does Mutagen-X do?"

"Over the last forty years, Gnosis has developed dozens of mutagen compounds. It's related to Mutagen-A in the sense that it affects almost every cell in the body. However, Mutagen-X is a late-stage capstone formula given only to the most qualified applicants. It turns a normal human into a Class 3 super. Most become assassins and super soldiers. It is Gnosis's most valuable formula and its most closely guarded secret."

Emmett's throat was dry. So that man could have killed them. *Easily.*

"How do you know all this?" Emmett asked. Venture had hinted at his ties to Gnosis, but never been honest about the extent.

Venture sighed. "I'll tell you. I promise. But that's enough for tonight. Come, the guest room is made up for you. You can get a few hours of sleep before classes."

Emmett stared, dumbfounded, at Dr. Venture. Slowly, he realized that it was almost 4 A.M.... Monday morning.

"Oh man," he muttered. "You don't have any special pills for sleeping, do you? Like sleep in a bottle?"

Venture smirked. "No. If I invented that, I would be rich enough that I wouldn't be doing *this* anymore. But your new body should help you manage better than most."

Emmett followed Clara and Dr. Venture out of the armory and down the main hall to the door marked section 001—the only wing of the lab that Emmett hadn't been in yet.

Their living quarters.

TINA greeted them at the door with one of the oldest looking lock and entry systems: A simple numerical keypad. Emmett made a point to look away while Venture entered the code, and Clara chuckled at him.

The doors hissed opened and Emmett followed them down a short hallway. It opened to a living quarters that wouldn't have been out of place in a nicely furnished apartment. The walls were white and a lush carpet covered most of the room. The only thing remotely odd was that the sofa and chairs were arranged to look at a wall without a TV.

Whether it was how out of place it felt down here or just his lack of sleep, Emmett snorted a laugh.

When Clara turned in offense, Emmett replied, "It just looks so... *normal.*"

She rolled her eyes. "As if. Tina, give us a view."

All around, the walls changed from drab white to a starry night sky, like they were in a high rise in the center of Belport. Even the door behind them had changed to give a 360 degree view of the city skyline and the harbor.

Emmett's mouth was hanging open as he followed the highway traffic and the boats out on the water.

"Is it in real time?"

"Approximated. And that's just one view," Dr. Venture said with a hint of pride. "It makes staying down here more manageable."

As awesome as it was and as many questions were swirling around Emmett's head, his eyes felt like they would collapse if he didn't get to sleep.

Clara must've noticed. "Come on. I'll show you to the guest wing."

Clara led him by the arm down the first hallway on the right. Emmett tried not to react—he could feel Dr. Venture staring at him as they walked away.

The hall was lined with about ten rooms in total. Clara stopped at the first door on the right and it opened immediately. Inside was a simple bedroom with two twin beds along the walls and end tables to match.

"You're not staying here, are you?"

Clara chuckled. "Mine and dad's rooms are on the other side. We just have extra guest rooms and beds in case people stay over... You know, for guests."

Emmett shook his head. "Right. Of course." The bed looked comfy enough.

Who was he kidding? It would do for a few hours—

Emmett didn't even want to think about how tired he would be in the morning.

"How do you do all this?" Emmett asked, exasperated. The question tumbled out of him. It definitely hadn't been what he'd meant to ask, but thankfully Clara read between the lines.

She put a hand on his shoulder to reassure him. "It gets a little easier. I know how that sounds—cliche and kind of horrible—but it does. But you know what else? It still hurts. I still cry. I still have nightmares.

"Every super deals with the bad days differently. You'll have to find your way of dealing with things, too."

Emmett nodded solemnly. He had no idea what *dealing with it* would look like for him, but Emmett knew that he would have to find a way. This was his life, and he wasn't about to walk away from it, or Dr. Venture or Clara.

"Thanks," Emmett said, and meant it.

Silence dragged on between them, and Emmett felt the weight of sleep pressing on him again.

Emmett rubbed the back of his neck. "This might be a weird question..."

As he spoke, Clara's eyes widened.

"...Do you have any notebooks I can borrow for class? Otherwise, I'll have to go all the way back home first."

Clara let out a long sigh. "Sure. Bathroom's at the end of the hall." Then she walked out and the door hissed shut behind her, leaving Emmett alone, and feeling like he'd missed something.

When the alarm went off in the morning, Emmett leapt up to check his phone. It felt like it was the middle of the night again, and he expected to see a text from Clara or Dr. Venture.

It was just his alarm.

For classes.

Emmett scrambled to get his bearings and found a stack of notebooks and pencils waiting on the nightstand for him. Emmett grabbed the stack and the rest of his things and stumbled out the bedroom door.

The smell of fresh coffee hit him and a moment later he saw Dr. Venture waiting for him in the living room. He was already pouring himself a cup.

"Want any?"

"*Yes,*" Emmett replied enthusiastically. "But can I get it to go?"

Venture grumbled. "Kids these days." He rummaged through the cabinet and handed Emmett a red thermos. "We've got milk, sugar, and, um, powdered creamer."

Emmett took milk and sugar and made his thermos. "I guess I'll see you guys after classes."

"Unless you'd prefer to take the day off."

As tempting as it was, Emmett had work to do. He had mods to make, mutagens to test...

Venture smiled somberly. "I can see that I'm not dissuading you. Come by after class. We need to talk about the next steps."

"Next steps?"

"Yes. We're going to track down that super, follow them, and find out who they're working for and what the end game is."

Emmett took a measured breath. He wasn't exactly keen on running into that guy again. Instead, Emmett asked, "You can track him? Because of the mutagen? ...How does that work?"

"Do you really have time for that answer?"

Emmett chuckled awkwardly. "No, I don't. But if you can do that... Does that mean someone could track me?

"How to do it isn't exactly common knowledge, and the tech to do it isn't something most people, even supers, would have access to, but theoretically, yes. Someone could track you if they wanted to. All the more reason to lay low while you're out on the rooftops."

Emmett nodded. It wasn't exactly a comforting thought, but hopefully he was a small enough fish that no one would bother tracking him like that.

"Emmett. You're doing well with all this, you know that, right? This life is hard, even when everything goes according to plan. You've just gotten a taste for when it doesn't." Venture's eyes were intense, but there was hope and pride in there as well. "I had high hopes for you, Emmett, but so far, you're exceeding them."

Emmett couldn't help but smile. As tired as he was, he felt renewed.

"Thanks, Dr. Venture. I won't let you down."

"I know."

CHAPTER 52

Normal-ish

M onday morning classes went alright enough, in that Emmett managed to stay awake for them. Dr. Venture's reassurance about success at being a super only lasted so long, and multiple times Emmett wished that someone had invented *sleep in a bottle.*

Lock texted while he was in his first class, and Emmett replied between classes.

Lock 10:04 AM: *Hey you good?*
Emmett 10:43 AM: *Yeah. Stayed at Marianne's place.*
Lock 10:46 AM: *Ha. Look at you*

Emmett pocketed his phone as he walked to class, knowing that Lock would probably grill him when he got back to the apartment.

It was a shame he couldn't just tell Lock. It would make things infinitely easier if he didn't need to keep half of his life secret from his roommate. And Lock wasn't just his roommate—he was one of Emmett's best friends.

Life had gotten in the way of that.

Emmett pulled his phone back out and texted Lock.

Emmett 10:52 AM: *We should watch a movie or something.*
Lock 10:58 AM: *No work tonight. I'm game*

Emmett winced at the thought of staying up. Hopefully, they could start the movie early or he could take a nap at some point today. He doubted he'd make it very late tonight.

By the time Emmett made it to the lab, he was doubting his choices. Physically, he felt great. Almost all his aches and cuts from Porcelain's shards were healed, but he was having trouble keeping his eyes open. He was so damn tired.

Training in the Gray Room helped a little.

Emmett and Clara's robot stood atop a five story building in faux Belport, trading punches. Clara's robot gradually increased its strength and speed as it fought. Emmett pushed himself, increasing his ferocity and testing his limits.

Even after all this time, he was still getting used to his new body. Every time Emmett felt like he found a limit or found something he couldn't quite do, he was able to push his abilities a little bit further.

He'd never felt so alive. Even down here, buried beneath Belport, looking at simulated skyline and fighting a robot, Emmett felt alive.

"What are you smiling at?" Clara said through the robot. She clearly thought Emmett was taunting her.

"Just having fun."

Emmett bid Clara and Venture goodbye and went home early on Monday. He resolved to take a nap, partly because of his plans with Lock, but also on the off chance he got called into *another* late night mission.

Lock was waiting for Emmett when he got back to the apartment. He was lounging on the couch and playing a game on his phone.

"There he is!" Lock said without looking up. His eyes were half-hidden by his hoodie. "Glad you could pull yourself away from Marianne."

Emmett made a point of laughing while he put his backpack in his room. "Well, you know, I watch a movie with her, then watch a movie with you."

"So long as you don't put the moves on me. I've seen your game."

At that, Emmett laughed in earnest, then came over and sat across from Lock on the couch. His roommate shifted his feet and sat up.

"I'd have better taste than you," Emmett countered.

"Once again, I've seen your game. Besides, you're already juggling two women as it is."

Emmett tossed a pillow, which bounced off of Lock's face.

Lock looked up and replied, "They hated him because he spoke the truth."

Emmett rolled his eyes and grabbed the remote.

"Have you told her?" Lock asked.

"Huh?"

"Man, have you told Clara about Marianne, or vice versa?"

"No," Emmett muttered, focusing on the TV.

"That's probably for the best."

Thankfully, Lock dropped it after that and didn't grill Emmett about spending the night at his fake girlfriend's place.

On the way home, Emmett had thought up a story about it in case Lock asked. Well, enough of a story that he would feel comfortable sharing anyway—it wasn't like Lock would ask for intimate details. The part that surprised Emmett was how easily he'd come up with a story and that he'd been prepared to share it.

Had lying really gotten so easy?

The important part was that Lock bought the story.

To take his mind off it, Emmett asked what Lock had gotten up to.

"The usual. Bounced at the club. Roughed up some punks that didn't know any better. Tossed them out. It was a pretty standard night for me."

Lock trailed off, and the pair looked through the newest movies for almost twenty minutes before finally settling on a road trip comedy they'd seen a hundred times—*Chasing Daisies, Losing Sheep 2*. It was one of the rare cases where the sequel was even better than the original. Both roommates agreed that it helped that the writers and director let the actors ad lib most of their lines for the sequel.

Emmett and Lock went back and forth quoting lines just before the characters said them, knowing almost the whole thing by heart.

For the first time since his accident, Emmett forgot about being a super. While the movie was playing, it was just Emmett and Lock going back-and-forth laughing at it. Just two college roommates killing an evening.

For an hour and forty-three minutes, it felt like nothing had changed.

The next few days were slow as far as heroics went. Emmett spent his time buried in school work and training in the lab. He spent his evenings patrolling the rooftops.

Twice he saw other supers running across the roofs and even another flying overhead, leaving a trail of icy mist in the air. None of them paid him any mind.

Now, it was Wednesday night, and Emmett was on the outskirts of downtown when a familiar face landed next to him on the roof.

"Been a while," Athena said, brushing a strand of long white hair out of her face. "I was worried you were taking a different route." The sunset shone red and orange in the glass embedded in her jacket.

"I've been keeping busy," Emmett replied.

"Good. There's only so many villains and henchmen to go around."

Emmett eyed her. "Is that what you're up to? Tracking another shipment?"

"Perhaps," she replied with a smirk. "I have a feeling it's going to be a good night."

"Mind if I tag along?"

"That depends. Did you think of a name yet?"

Emmett sighed. "Not yet." To be honest, he hadn't really thought anymore about it since the last time she asked.

"It will come to you," Athena replied, putting a hand on his shoulder. "So, what's with the arm... and the whip?"

Emmett felt the wrist of his right hand. "My arm's prosthetic. It's got compartments in it. It's where I keep the whip, *and* smoke bombs and caltrops. For now, anyway. The idea is that I'll be able to change mods out when I need to for different villains."

"Mods?"

"Modifications."

Athena raised an eyebrow. "So you're a nerd."

Emmett chuckled. "Pretty much."

Slowly, his jaw dropped as realization dawned on him.

"What?" Athena asked. "What's that face for?"

Emmett pulled out his phone to text Clara.

Emmett 9:02 PM: *I think I just figured it out...*

Clara 9:02 PM: *Figured what out?*

Athena scoffed. "You kids and your phones."

"Sorry," Emmett muttered. His face had widened into a cheesy grin as he met Athena's eyes. "I think I just found my name."

Epilogue

Venture

Dr. Venture leaned on the table of the hub in section 004. He'd given up on work for the day, and was reviewing drone footage from Clara and Emmett's run in with Porcelain and Lock.

There were several interesting moments, including Lock being affected by Emmett's noise makers and disadvantaged by the smoke—if only momentarily. But Venture had watched through the entirety of that night several times, but kept coming back to what Lock said to Emmett...

The camera view was from a half destroyed drone—one of the few that Lock hadn't completely destroyed. In the grainy footage, Emmett and Lock were small and far away. Their voices were taken from Emmett's earpiece and combined with the video.

Since there was little visible in the footage, Venture had overlayed the text.

Lock: *I'm not your enemy.*
Emmett: *It doesn't feel that way.*
Lock: *It doesn't matter. I'm not your enemy. But don't cross Gnosis.*

He replayed those ten seconds over and over.

Venture had only seen Lock once—the day he dropped Emmett off at his apartment after the Champion street attack. He'd been worried ever since.

And he'd been right to worry.

Not only was Emmett's roommate a formidable Class 3 super deeply involved with Gnosis's Mutagen-X program, he'd somehow figured out that Emmett was a super, also. It wasn't coincidence that Lock had intercepted their mission that night. He'd followed Emmett to the warehouse district that night.

Lock: *I'm not your enemy.*
...I'm not your enemy...
...I'm not your enemy....

"He knows..." Venture muttered. That complicated things significantly. How long had Lock known about Emmett? How long had Emmett been living on borrowed time?

The pit in Venture's stomach had gotten worse. Now he felt sick.

He had to tell Emmett about Lock.

Up until then, Venture had thought he was doing Emmett a favor by not telling him. Thought it would make Emmett's life simpler if he didn't have to worry about his roommate being a villain. But all the while, Lock already knew the truth.

But there was something else bothering him. Venture rewound the video, and TINA automatically cut the footage so it swapped to another drone. Now the camera showed the scene as Porcelain took Emmett hostage.

Porcelain: *You were there the night I was poisoned.*

She'd spoken loud enough that there was no doubt she was speaking to Lock, which was puzzling itself. But what Venture was focused on was Lock's reaction.

Lock flinched.

At first, Venture thought Lock had flinched at being remembered, but as he watched the video again, that theory didn't line up. The timing was off.

Lock flinched when Porcelain grabbed Emmett.

It wasn't out of fear—Lock was far too strong to be afraid *for himself*. He flinched out of concern for Emmett.

Venture rubbed the stubble on his chin.

That was a good sign.

Venture reclined on the couch in the living room of section 001. The night skyline of Belport wrapped around the wall displays. His eyes were heavy, and he contemplated whether he cared enough to get up to go to bed or just fall asleep on the couch.

TINA's voice came through the intercom. *"We have a visitor."*

Venture groaned. It was the first uneventful night they'd had in several days, or it had been. He couldn't imagine anyone he'd be happy to see.

His eyes narrowed as he looked at the screen. TINA had superimposed the front door camera feed over the skyline.

A ghost of a man stood at the door, waiting patiently to be let in.

Venture rubbed his chin in thought and apprehension. He'd been expecting a visit from the Summit of Heroes, but he hadn't known *who* to expect. Would they appeal to his sense of camaraderie and send Night Devil, a fellow retired super? Would they send Lucine of Palladia, his on again, off again ex? Would they send Paragon, and threaten him?

In the end, they went with the obvious choice and sent their spymaster.

Venture had been so preoccupied that he hadn't heard Clara come out of her room.

"Dad, is that..."

"Yes. You can go back to your room."

Clara grumbled, but walked away. She didn't need to be a part of this—not anymore than she already was.

Wight's voice came through the intercom. *"Open the door, Magnus. We need to talk."*

Venture cleared his throat, not realizing how dry it was. "TINA, open the door. Tell him I'm in the lounge. I trust he remembers the way."

The camera feed changed to follow Wight as he walked through the halls of the lab. Venture watched intently until his guest appeared at the door to section 001.

The door to the living room hissed opened and the spymaster of Summit of Heroes walked in.

Wight was an unassuming man as far as supers went—a tad under six feet tall, with a medium build. Non-threatening.

Most supers kept disguises and alter egos, or went to some lengths to hide themselves when they weren't working... Wight was always working. Always hiding. He just went about it differently.

Everything about the spymaster of the Summit was nondescript. Not just his build—with Wight's tan complexion and facial structure, he could pass for almost any nationality. He spoke over a dozen languages. Even his usual dress—gray slacks and earthen sweater—could pass for casual or business wear.

Everything about him was carefully honed neutrality. Easily forgotten or mis-remembered. He was an enigma, even to those on the Summit and DSA that knew him.

Between that and his powers, he settled on the nickname Wight—an old word for *ghost*.

Wight walked through the kitchen and took a seat on the second couch, so he sat perpendicular to Venture.

"Wight."

"Magnus."

Venture leaned back on the couch, mimicking his guest, and tried to relax. It didn't work.

The spymaster gestured around. "I like what you've done with the place."

"I haven't changed anything since you last came."

Wight smiled. "I know. It's one of the things I like about you, Magnus. Your whole angle as a super is being adaptable. Having a tool for any job. But you... You don't change. I knew what I would find as soon as I walked in."

"Why are you here?"

Wight's smile slipped away. "Right to the point... You're playing a dangerous game. You should have told us about the connection with Porcelain."

Venture forced himself to breathe slowly. "I did tell you. As soon as I was sure—"

"You should have told us *right away.*"

"It wouldn't have changed anything."

"Maybe... But tell that to Paragon or Amarque."

Venture scoffed. "Nothing will save Paragon's opinion of me, and I don't care what Amarque thinks. You should be scolding him, wherever he is, instead of here threatening me."

"I'm not threatening you," Wight said flatly. Venture didn't believe him for a second.

"Then what is this?"

"I'm checking up on an old friend. Contrary to what you think, not all of us hold it against you. Well, I don't, anyway."

"That's rich, coming from a man who lies for a living."

A flicker of irritation passed over Wight's face and was gone just as quickly. "I'm valued precisely for how little I lie to get the job done."

"Lies of omission are still lies."

Wight met his eyes. "Yes, Magnus. Yes, they are."

Venture rubbed his temple and sighed. Goddamn lies. "I don't want to do this."

"How's the kid?"

The question made Venture freeze, but he didn't look up. "She's doing well. Making progress. Slow progress."

"Slow is good. I'm sure she's following in her father's footsteps."

Venture bit his tongue. The implication was clear: Better his footsteps than her mother's.

"I hear you have a new protégé."

At that, Venture forced himself to look up. Wight was focused intently on Venture, trying to read his expression.

"I do."

"I hear you saved his life during the Champion street attack."

"I did."

"How?"

Venture quickly considered his options. Wight likely already knew how Venture had saved Emmett's life. He was really just gauging whether Venture would lie about it.

"I was able to make a prosthetic to replace his arm, but the rest of his body required Mutagen-A suffusion."

Wight nodded. "Uh, huh. And no one at Gnosis knows about this...?"

"Correct. And I would like to keep it that way."

"You can trust me."

"What's your point?" Venture asked, irritation bleeding into his voice.

Wight rolled his eyes. "You really don't see it? A retired member of the Summit of Heroes working on the side for Gnosis. Meanwhile, you stumble on an organized crime ring flooding the street with knock-off mutagens. Meanwhile, a rogue super using suspiciously related poison is involved in an attack on Belport and the Summit.

"There is a web of causality falling down around you, Magnus, and you're caught in the middle of it. Willfully blind to it! ...Just like before."

Venture's hands were balled into fists. "Don't."

Wight turned away and stared at the night skyline on the screen. Seconds dragged on while Venture tried to control himself.

"Sorry," Wight said. He looked like he meant it. "I'm still on your side, contrary to what you think."

"I know. That's why it hurts when *you* drag it up."

Wight stood up and walked over to the display of Belport, keeping his back to Venture. He gestured to the display. "I never understood this. You could change the view to anywhere in the world. Why keep it here?"

"Because I'm hiding from enemies, not from my responsibilities."

"Yeah, well, you're doing a shit job of it."

At that, both men laughed—short and under their breath. Then the moment was gone, forgotten as quickly and as easily as the ghost.

Wight said, "The Summit is reviewing the *cropped* video feed that implicates Gnosis. Of course, Gnosis denies any involvement and ultimately we have no proof."

Venture knew it was a long-shot, but he asked anyway. "What about the traces of blood at the scene?"

Wight shrugged. "Sure. They have residual mutagens at the scene, but half the world's soldiers and combatants are on *something* made by Gnosis. You don't want to know what the figures are for civilian zones."

Venture sighed. Gnosis was one of the untouchables. One of the pillars of the world, a horrific cross between a corporation and a group of villains. They wouldn't be taken down that easily.

Finally, Wight turned and looked like he was about to leave. "You're wrong."

"About what?"

"I'm not here to threaten you, Magnus. I came here to warn you. Don't sever the few alliances you have left. And keep your bloody kids on the rails."

A switch flipped in Venture. He stood and looked down slightly on his former colleague. He doubted it was very intimidating, but it lent weight to his words.

"Get out."

Wight nodded, face straight and unreadable. He walked to the door and paused.

"Be seeing you around, Magnus."

Then Wight walked *through* the door, phasing through it like he really was a ghost. Even after all these years, it was still eerie to witness. All the other skills and knowledge that Wight possessed were negligible compared to his superpower. So far as Venture and the Summit knew, no door or material could keep Wight out of a location. If he wanted inside a building, there was nothing to stop him.

The one thing that kept Wight from being seen as a boogeyman was his insistence on manners with his allies.

Venture stood and watched on the monitor as the spymaster of the Summit walked the long hall and then phased through his front door. Then he disappeared into Belport.

When he was sure Wight was gone, Venture looked to the small table beside the couch. Beneath the ornamental lamp sat one of the last photos of Clara, Narine, and him together. They'd been in New Venice on the rooftop of a little restaurant that didn't exist anymore.

Venture grabbed the frame and hurled it across the room. It hit the reinforced wall monitor and shattered. The broken frame fell to the floor, and Venture collapsed on the couch.

What irritated him the most, even more than the veiled threats, was that his former colleague was right. Venture *was* playing a dangerous game. He knew it, even if he didn't want to admit it.

Venture was working under the assumption that his old alliances were still unshakeable. Of course they weren't—half the Summit didn't trust him. Gnosis barely trusted him. His own daughter didn't trust him...

He was a fool. Narine would remind him of that. Things would never be the same, and he could never go back to the way things were.

Venture rubbed the wedding ring that was still on his finger.

He needed sleep.

SIMULATIONS

Mod V1 vs Zanté and Green Mask [One on One Rematch]

Mod fought against the villains known as Zanté and Green Mask twice in his first month as a mask. He was outnumbered in both engagements, having been forced to fight both villains at the same time.

Both times, Mod emerged victorious.

His first engagement was hard fought, and Mod owed much of his victory to Zanté's hubris. This allowed Mod to get the upper hand—quite literally—by using his prosthetic arm to overpower Zanté.

During their second engagement, Mod won handedly, despite his injuries. His training and newly enhanced sight gave him the advantage.

QUERY: How would Mod fair in one on one matches against his first enemies?

LOADING SIMULATIONS...

FIRST MATCH: Mod Vi vs Zanté

In Mod's very first iteration, he has few options at his disposal. His overall strength is enhanced by Mutagen-A, but it falls short of Zanté's strength. In nearly every physical measurement, Mod lags behind.

He has a slight advantage in stamina, which is hard to capitalize on. In 14 simulations, Mod is able to stay out of reach of Zanté and whittle him down, but in every other iteration, Zanté uses his superior speed to force Mod into close combat.

In close quarters, Mod's only option is utilizing his prosthetic arm to overpower Zanté. In almost every simulation, the best course of action is for Mod to attack ferociously and put his opponent down as quickly as possible—before Zanté realizes just how much of a danger the prosthetic arm is.

RESULTS:
Scores out of 1,000 simulations...
Mod Victory — 659
Zanté Victory — 334
Double Incapacitation — 7

CONCLUSION:
Even in the earliest iterations of his powers, Mod is a match for Zanté. In nearly every simulation, Mod wins if the fight lasts less than a minute. For every ten additional seconds of engagement, his chances of victory decrease.

SECOND MATCH: Mod VI vs Green Mask

Mod has even fewer options against his foe's darkness powers. He outclasses Green Mask in every physical aspect, but those things are of little help to him. Unfortunately for Mod, in their first engagement, he didn't have any vision or general sense enhancements to help him.

Green Mask's powers are adjacent to that of psychics, so there is potential to learn mental counters, but Mod had not yet had training to combat such threats.

Mod's one lucky break in such a fight is that Green Mask's powers have relatively low offensive capabilities. They are better suited for supporting a team.

RESULTS:
Scores out of 1,000 simulations...
Mod Victory — 297
Green Mask Victory — 703

CONCLUSION:
In every simulation, Green Mask is able to use darkness to blind Mod and to control the fight. From there, Green Mask is forced to close the distance and use melee weapons to finish off his opponent.

In every simulation, the fight is brutal and quick. In most instances, Green Mask uses a pipe to knock him out. When the first blow to the head either misses or doesn't incapacitate, Mod is almost always quick enough to grab his opponent—

Even in the early days of his superheroics, Mod recognizes the necessity for putting down an opponent quickly.

FOLLOW-UP MATCH: Mod V1.1 vs Green Mask

During his initial months leading up to his fight with Lock, Mod gained a variety of enhancements. All these have been grouped under the V1.1 iteration for further study.

Of these upgrades, the vision-enhancing mutagen obtained during a mission with Athena is the most helpful in this engagement. It alone completely negates Green Mask's powers, as evidenced in their second real engagement. In addition, Mod has learned several techniques with his whip to help against hidden attackers.

UPDATED RESULTS:
Scores out of 1,000 simulations...

Mod Victory — 995
Green Mask Victory — 5

CONCLUSION:

In every simulation, Mod achieves overwhelming victory. His upgraded vision completely negates Green Mask's powers and Mod's whip allows him to negate any melee weapon that Green Mask uses.

NOTE: Parameters necessitate that a Margin of Error be maintained for unforeseen circumstances, such as Green Mask procuring a firearm or having an unaccounted for power.

NOTE 2: Margin of Error will not always be accounted for. For example, in cases where two opponents are horribly mismatched and there is no conceivable way for victory to be achieved.

SIMULATIONS

Mod V1 vs Lock M-X

In Mod's earliest iteration (roughly the first month after his first accident), he never directly engaged Lock. Despite their living arrangements and opposition in the case of Porcelain, their only *official* meeting was during the night of Porcelain's death.

However, sufficient data exists to simulate combat between the two.

QUERY: How would Mod fare against Lock?

LOADING SIMULATIONS...

FIRST MATCH: Mod VI vs Lock M-X
　　In every measure, Mod is outclassed by his opponent.
　　Strength...
　　Speed...
　　Stamina...
　　Durability...
　　Healing factor...
　　Combat knowledge...

Even if Mod's entire body was composed of the same materials as his prosthetic arm, he would have no chance of victory. He cannot fight. He cannot run.

RESULTS:
Scores out of 1,000 simulations...
Mod Victory — 0
Lock Victory — 1,000

CONCLUSION:
There is no simulation where Mod defeats Lock with his earliest loadout.

Even in the few simulations that account for their friendship, Lock disables Mod so that he can no longer fight or run. In those simulations, Mod lives, but loses the fight.

NOTE: Margin of Error disabled in the face of overwhelming inferiority.

QUERY: Do Mod's additional upgrades alter his chances of victory?

LOADING SIMULATIONS...

FOLLOW-UP MATCH: Mod V1.1 vs Lock M-X

ERROR: ERROR: UNKNOWN VARIABLES
Mod V1.1 upgrades incomplete

Next Time...

END
Mod Superhero 1:
Initialization

CONTINUE Origin
Mod Superhero 2:
Execute

WAIT!

If you enjoyed this book, please consider leaving an honest review on your favorite store. Nowadays books live and die by the algorithm and even a simple star review can help it gain traction.

And of course, recommend this to anyone else in your life that's looking for a new superhero series!

Keep Reading

Mod Superhero is an ongoing series.
If you can't wait for the next book to drop, never fear!

Book 2 just finished
on Royal Road, ScribbleHub, and Wattpad.

And if that's not enough for you, we're
already on Book 3 on Patreon!

If you want to chat about Mod Superhero
or any other of Sam's stories,
stop by the Discord at
RealityLocked Worlds.

More Books

If you like the action and intrigue of Mod Superhero, check out these other stories:

A Battleaxe and a Metal Arm — Helesys is cunning, driven-and trapped. Her only ally is a towering barbarian who's as cold as his blade. They're trapped in a mad wizard's endless prison. Together, they'll have to survive impossible realms and find their memories in the process. As her powers come back, Helesys feels confident that the two of them will make it out or die trying... But even death might not be an escape.

Binge the complete series!

And there's more where that came from. Check out SamuelFlemingBooks.com for the full publication list.

THANKS

Thanks to all the early and constant readers online (in no particular order):

Cronofire, TofuuKnight, Eader, Cosy Curse, Gameknight2169, Bounce, Robort, Vadelent, The Bell Tolls For Thee, Newbage, Venn, Summer-ray17, KorenTiquar, Death Threat Collector, Morris Darkstar, Nomad1791 The Mimic Slayer, Weas97, 3SlicesOfBread, Dead Dragon, IDontKnowItTrueCipres, Arkhron, AI_March, namesare_hard, perfectgeneral, AmagiBestShip, Novitiate, sabbahillel, Khargol, Koooomakimi, georgylijf, Skoonting, Tormented Sage, Mister Bill, Solarus, Slayer_of_boxes, Andrexus Kasnia, Phan_Of_Wafflez, Ogoun, jpx, Jujubeanz, Laovi The Eldritch Banana, Katsurandom, , Usually Present, Barbarylion, 00x00123, Someonenoone7, Cassanunda, Accent, Linnoquake, Arad127, zorian22, Lionard, Aerodoth, EricTheMeek, Oroborozs, Doctor_C, Werotan, MurderHobo, Sir ReadsALot, Sazuroi, Apollobound, Omnivoyance, Cyeven, CentrisAce, Qwaz, playr543, Fatangry, Stevenblake, and more!

A big thanks to Cactus for helping me set up the Discord over at RealityLocked Worlds. Shout out to the rest of the Discord gang.

Thanks to all my early supporters on Patreon: BrainError, Oth, Felix Liebgott, Glennen Hopson, Quaternion, Nooooooooooool, Duco Van der Ploeg, jay, Steve McFarland, Ty Tuttle, Kyle, Josh Cothran, Jan L, backrest.puppy390, Charles johnson, Quadrivirus, Imspinnennetz, mafytoogamer, and Neorem.

ABOUT THE AUTHOR

Samuel Fleming, aka RealityLocked, is a Sci-fi, Dark Fantasy, and horror author.

He grew up in Maryland, spending most of his time swimming and writing. The thing about swimming is that it gives you a lot of time to daydream, so the two hobbies complemented each other well. Idle day dreams turned into stories, some of which stuck with him for years. These days he swims a little less and writes a lot more.

He loves a good story no matter the medium: Books, TV, video games, comics, tabletop RPG's, or podcasts–most of which he attempts to share with his wife and three kids, and occasionally on his blog.

Find him on social media at SamuelFlemingBooks.com

Made in the USA
Las Vegas, NV
17 January 2024

84439308R00218